IMMORTAL ROOTS

VELVET DAVIS

Cover design by Damonza.com
Book design by Damonza.com

First printing: 2018
ISBN: 978-1-7321042-0-4
E-ISBN: 978-1-7321042-1-1

For Kylan

PROLOGUE

THE AIR QUIVERED around the metallic cylinder, as if trying to erase it from the landscape. Imposing and machinelike, the cylinder seemed to mock the soft green and brown hues of the surrounding grassland. Sunlight reflected off the shiny surface, nearly blinding the three men who stood nearby. A foreboding presence had crept into their awareness once they'd set foot in the region. It was the reason the cylinder was not in its proper location, the reason the men were not on their way home.

They had already lifted it only to put it back down in the grass. It seemed heavier than the ones they'd built before, as if weighed down by consequence. The men shifted their eyes and cracked their knuckles, trying to convince each other without words there was nothing to worry about.

Jyan's gruff voice cut through the tension. "Let's get this over with."

The three men took their places around it, fit their hands at the bottom and shuffled their feet to secure their footing. Then they hoisted the cylinder up and over the hole they had dug and dropped it into the control pad. The ground shuddered as the energy beneath their feet flowed toward this new outlet.

The cylinder came to life, radiating light from its crevices and vibrating with urgency. The men backed away quickly, fell to the ground and shielded their faces. Deafening sounds erupted all around them. The cylinder rocked back and forth, as if unable to contain itself and ready to burst into a million pieces. The ground quaked so violently the men feared it would break apart and swallow them up.

The effects dwindled slowly. When the cylinder finally stilled, they stood and shook hands, relieved because now they could go home.

Something in the distance snagged Darmyn's attention. The smile faded from his lips. "Look there," he commanded, pointing between his companions.

Ravnor and Jyan turned and gaped.

"I don't remember that being there," Ravnor said. "Does this mean we put it in the wrong spot?" He looked the cylinder up and down. "It seems to be working alright."

"It wasn't on the map," Jyan blurted out. "It's not our fault if the cylinder isn't where it should be."

"Forget about the map," Darmyn said. "Where did it come from?"

"Since it wasn't on the map we overlooked it," Jyan said.

"How could anyone overlook that?" Darmyn threw his arm out toward the shadowy forest, gnarled and twisted like it had been there for ages. A wave of intensity flashed back, causing him to jump and stare at his hand with surprise.

Ravnor's face paled. "What's your point?"

"What I'm saying," Darmyn said, "is that forest, well, it wasn't there when we began…" His words left behind an eeriness that shrouded the trio. "That thing sprouted *while* we were in the middle of—"

"Stop," Jyan interrupted. "You've been in seclusion for too long. It's time to go back to Semadon. Good thing we're done."

Color flushed back into Ravnor's face, but Darmyn only shook his head. "Done? We're not done. We need to investigate and see what this is all about."

"No, bad idea," Jyan replied, but his coworker was already walking away.

"What good will it do for us to investigate?" Ravnor said.

"It's not for the good of us, but for the good of our people," Darmyn said over his shoulder.

"He forgets we're AT installers now," Jyan muttered. "He's living in the old days when we had to prove our worth."

"We haven't even notified High Service yet," Ravnor yelled.

"Go ahead," Darmyn shouted back.

"We can't leave him," Ravnor said in a low voice. "They'd say we deserted him."

"We'd go from heroes to criminals, just like that," Jyan agreed with a corresponding snap of his fingers.

Their annoyance at Darmyn overcame any lingering fear. So without further discussion and propelled by a sense of duty, Jyan and Ravnor followed him into the enigmatic woods.

CHAPTER ONE

IF DAYDREAMING WASN'T forbidden, then Ceera would have considered the distraction a bit fascinating. It wafted into the library with casual importance, affecting each patron to varying degrees as it swept past. She witnessed it in the glance up from a book, a sudden itch to the arm or neck, the wrinkling of a nose. Hands stopped midair in front of the arched bookcases or wavered back and forth between selections. The unsettling feeling clung to the walls and encircled the room. It even burrowed deep into her bones.

To her disappointment, her fellow library patrons ignored the odd sensation. They turned back to their reading material or settled for the book on the shelf closest to their outstretched fingers. Their stillness now rivaled the marble statues adorning the walls. These statues, ranging from miniature to life-size, were sculpted in various positions reading books. Strangely enough, the statues seemed more remarkable at present than her fellow library patrons. The elaborate design that connected them evoked mystery within its curling ornate pattern.

She glanced sideways at the row of empty desks beside her, relieved no other scribes were nearby to report her lapse in concentration. She had been on probation before for being idle at the PID, a piece of technology that, though useful, she tended to resent. This was due to her role as a scribe and the amount of time she spent before it. The Public Information Device stored all of society's happenings, recorded and uploaded by scribes, which made it a useful tool for research or catching up on current events.

She stared at the PID's glowing spherical screen which displayed her half-finished assignment. Her handheld recorder was plugged into the side of her keypad, having already transferred her notes from a recent event into the PID's memory.

Since she was undergoing transition, Ceera was required to send her recording into a secured file within the PID where it would await final approval by Drusilla Rune. If she had any other mentor, transition would last only six months beyond the age of twenty, but Drusilla insisted that age was secondary to skill level. Without the older woman's consent, she would remain in transition forever. The thought was as bristling as Drusilla herself.

When she glanced down at her keypad, the intrusive feeling grazed her once again. At the same time, a loud crash broke the silence. She looked over her shoulder. Several patrons were on their hands and knees picking up books. Clumsiness was frowned upon in the library, which meant no one was paying any attention to her.

She closed her eyes, gave her head a slight but firm shake, and attempted to proceed with her typing. Her fingers touching the keypad coincided with the wail of an alarm, and she snatched them back up in surprise. The disconcerting sound was like encountering an alien on your doorstep, or worse. Being in a library, the faint hearted who attempted to scream only opened their mouths wide in terror. Others raced to peer out the windows.

The librarian disappeared under her desk and Ceera slid beneath her own, her heart beating loudly in the tight space. She curled up in a fetal position and braced for disaster while footsteps thundered past. Moments later the alarm grew silent.

"Semions, please remain calm," a voice blared through Semadon's intercom system. "There's been an alarm malfunction in the Planetary Stability Laboratory."

Ceera found it difficult to accept the official's explanation. Precision was highly valued, order and correctness the codes they all lived by. How could there have been a malfunction? His words repeated several times before she crawled out and stood, smoothing the front of her skirt and straightening the sleeves on her blouse. She tidied her light brown hair and tucked it behind her ears. Then she spun her chair and sat down in a daze.

A boulder of a man hunched over nearby, picking up fallen books and slamming each atop the next into a pile near his feet. A woman scurried past, earning his glare when she barely missed stepping on his hand. The offending female joined a crowd that gathered around a much smaller man who had stumbled down a stairwell.

The librarian reappeared from under her desk and stared at herself in a small compact mirror, smoothing away stray hairs from her face. Some stood around with quizzical expressions, as if not sure where to turn or what to do next, while others tended to distressed children.

A lone woman, leaning against the far wall and reading from a book, distracted Ceera from the chaos. She squinted and leaned closer, then almost laughed out loud. Of course the woman wasn't real. Only a statue could be so unaffected by these surroundings. This one was a bit more realistic looking than the others. Ceera had never noticed her before, but the director of the library was prone to putting in new additions.

Ceera glanced over to where a larger crowd now gathered around the fallen man still slumped on the floor, but within seconds her attention went back to the statue. It was life-size, perhaps a few inches shorter than herself. The statue's billowing hair hid any facial expression, the only visible feature a perfectly curved nose. The sculptor had done an impressive job with the figure's dress. Although plainly decorated, it hung like real fabric. The bottom of the dress ended not far above the bare, delicate feet molded onto the floor.

The activity in the room increased. Someone pushed a book cart past, and she swiveled to avoid it running over her toes.

When she looked back at the statue, her gaze met empty space. Her breath caught in her throat. How could it be? She was certain a statue had been there. Daydreaming was a normal interference in her life, but this was beyond imaginary. It was unnerving.

She stood quickly, causing her chair to slam against the desk. Thankfully, the librarian did not notice, for she stood at the stairwell watching while the injured man attempted to stand.

Ceera scanned the room. The statue, no longer an inanimate object, was walking toward the door. As if that wasn't disturbing enough, the former statue still carried the book that had lain open in her hands just moments before. Despite a mental image of Drusilla's disapproving face, Ceera headed for the exit to follow the thief.

She barged through the main entryway and into the fresh air. The thief swung the book as she sauntered away. Ceera wove herself through the pathways in pursuit.

The roadways were circular. Just as the planets spun in orbits around the sun, the Semions had designed their village to mimic this phenomenon. The library was near the center of Semadon, as were all public buildings. Many of these cylindrical buildings had plant terraces winding up and around them. At ground level, these terraces linked up with smaller patches of trees and brush in the adjoining lawns.

Flashing lights and scattered chunks of metal preceded a larger heap around the bend. The travel pod collision blocked most of the roadway, and Ceera bit her lip in contemplation. Collisions were a rare occurrence, for the pods had tracking sensors that were designed to prevent accidents. If an accident couldn't be avoided on the roadway, then a pod would take to the sky. One of the sensors must have malfunctioned, a troubling coincidence considering what had happened earlier with the alarms. The travel pod owners argued loudly with Order Patrol nearby.

The elusive woman stepped through the wreckage and went unnoticed by Order Patrol as she slipped past. Ceera was not as successful at being invisible. She roused the attention of an officer, who looked up and gave her a disapproving glare.

"Excuse me," she apologized as she stepped over misshapen pieces of travel pod.

"Stay out of the way," the officer shouted after her.

Ceera followed the figure into the residential orbits, characterized by small dwellings made in the same circular clay brick shape. What set them apart were the color schemes of plants in the yards, or lack of them. A noise from inside a plain dwelling drew her attention. Through the open window, she caught a glimpse of Hegliod Avatus banging his head of unruly grey hair on the wall.

"It's gone. It's gone," he lamented.

She had no idea what that was about, but considered it evidence. If even the reclusive and most famed inventor in Semadon was out of sorts, clearly the cause of disorder was not a malfunction.

The woman crossed over into another orbit with Ceera close behind. She stepped around a Semion who was on his hands and knees picking up fruits and vegetables scattered across the stone walkway. Being on one's hands and knees was apparently the norm for the day. She breezed past.

Before long, they reached the outskirts of the village. The female moved down a path leading into a grove of trees, the book now clutched at her waist. The air became thick with the scent of vegetation, and the forest canopy dimmed the sun's rays.

Now shielded by trees, Ceera's curiosity intensified. Was the woman real or just a product of her imagination? No one else had seemed to notice her after all. Discomfort panged in her cramped feet, punctuating her desire to find out. She kicked off her shoes, preferring the wild freedom of bare feet to propriety, and burst into a run to catch up. She dashed around a tree and found the female facing her a short distance away. The woman's facial expression was obscured within the shadow of a tree that stretched above her.

Ceera stopped short, breathless from the exertion. "Who are you?" she sputtered.

The woman tilted her head in acknowledgement, her expression still unreadable, and held out the book. Ceera took a tentative step closer, which revealed to her that the book was bound in thick, worn leather and looked ancient. The cover displayed a glittering spiral design that seemingly defied the book's composition. Intrigued, she reached for it. As her hand neared, both the woman and ancient book disintegrated into tiny wisps of color that swirled and flew away like insects. Her fingers scraped against the bark of the tree.

Ceera backed away in disbelief. Bark from a fallen tree jabbed her calves and she sat on the trunk abruptly. Her breathing slowed as she stared at the trees and greenery all around her.

Her eyes transfixed as her surroundings overwhelmed her senses. The outline of plant life became hazy and pulsated, riveting with an energetic power so vibrant it reached a new dimension. Her ordinary life as a scribe slipped away, as the forest overtook her.

The trees rose taller as their trunks gained girth. The roots jutting from the ground grew more gnarled and interlocking. Moss crept onto every surface and tickled her toes. She did not feel inclined to stop it.

Suddenly, a gust of air blasted through the foliage. Branches bent to its whim, creaking and groaning as the wind coiled seductively around them. The air was hissing through the cracks in trees, saying something to her, repeating the same word with sleek precision.

Ceera shivered as the familiar sound penetrated her ears. Not knowing what else to do, she hugged her knees in wonderment as the forest took on a new life and the breeze spoke her name again and again.

❧

Only the humming of the communication orb could interrupt Hegliod from his despair. He had spent the latter hours contemplating whether he was truly meant to enlighten his fellow Semions. This had induced a compulsive smoothing of his mussed hair and wrinkled forehead with his fingers.

Earlier he had been the victim of a vanishing idea, an idea so audacious it had left before fully forming, before he could even capture it on the page. Hegliod took the abandonment quite personally, for what was an idea if not an extension of one's genius? If he could no longer master his own mind, how could he continue to master the world around him? His failure to do so would quickly reduce him to just another Semion participating in everyday life.

At first, he dismissed this travesty. The idea was merely playing hide and seek, as great ideas did from time to time. He searched for a trace of it within his brain but was left with a mere shadow of its existence. Since he was unable to retrieve his idea from the abyss it had escaped into, his blackboard had a small dent in it, his head ached, and items that had been on his desk now littered the floor.

When the humming began, he begrudgingly lifted the communication orb and wedged it between his ear and his mouth. "What?" he muttered into the mouthpiece.

"Hegliod," a voice replied firmly. "You must come at once. A malfunction has occurred with the AT system. We need your assistance."

The voice belonged to a High Service official named Leynin, one of his superiors in authority though not intellect.

"Why certainly," he said. "I will be there immediately."

On his way to the control room, Hegliod's spirits sank even further. The Atomic Transport system was his most prized invention, capable of eliminating the time it took to trek great distances. For once it was fully intact, one could transport to any spot where a cylinder had been placed, even the farthest reaches of the planet. Based on the day he had suffered, it was a terrible time for it to break.

The shiny white door leading into the control room was like a beacon of his recent failures. He opened it anyway. Two High Service officials, Leynin and Asfin, along with several white-smocked scientists in-training, huddled in the center of the room. Walls comprised of dials, buttons and accompanying oval screens surrounded them. Their conversation fell silent as he approached.

Hegliod ignored the wide eyes of the transitioning scientists and instead turned to the officials. "What happened?"

"Semions are not transporting where they are supposed to be. They are confused when they materialize. There was also a lady pair traveling together whose faces appear"—Leynin cleared his throat—"changed."

"The AT system switched the noses of the two women," Asfin said. "Understandably, Ms. Berda and Ms. Raveen are upset and hope to be back to normal as quickly as possible."

Hegliod frowned. Such news was appalling. He had designed his cylinders to atomically break apart, transfer, and reorganize the body of whoever climbed inside, not carelessly swap out body parts.

"Let me take a look." His fingers worked quickly with the buttons. He stared at the screens and the sequences of numbers they displayed, his frown deepening. He examined every one, mumbling to himself, but found nothing out of the ordinary. Turning to the officials who still hovered in the background, he said, "This is a complicated dilemma. Perhaps—"

"I got it," someone exclaimed. "I've figured it out!"

Hegliod turned to view the offender.

A transitioning scientist stared back with shining eyes.

"Look at this dial right here. It got jostled from its proper position. I noticed it did not fall into the same pattern the other dials were set at. Can you believe it was so simple?"

Hegliod was disgusted that such a trivial error had disrupted the functioning of his machine. And yet the young man looked so proud to have uncovered it. Arrogance was unbecoming on anyone, especially on those who had not yet earned a reputation like his own.

"Good observation, Cafold," Leynin praised.

The officials and scientists crowded around to look at the malfunction and left Hegliod to stand by himself in bitterness. It wasn't until later when he was back at his dwelling and staring at a blank piece of paper, that this bitterness dissipated into despondence.

∾

Once the system was back in working order, Leynin went to the correspondence center to check on the AT installers. Since no messages awaited him, he pressed a few buttons on the panel so he could analyze their progress. A tiny light flashed within the AT installers' region on the energy grid, signifying they had recently installed their last cylinder. The accompanying readout confirmed it was in proper working order.

Checking again that the message box was empty, his forehead creased. The AT installers were supposed to alert High Service upon completion to verify the cylinder had been installed correctly. Their failure to do so was perplexing, for surely the men would be eager to return home.

It was unusual for such negligence to occur, unusual unless the AT installers had encountered a problem. Worry trickled into his awareness. Had the issue with the AT system somehow affected them too?

Leynin forced himself to sit down. It was possible a message would be sent any time now. That is what his companion Asfin would say if she were here. He had come to rely upon her firm voice of reason during his moments of doubt. But where was she? Hadn't she told him she would be there shortly? He stared expectantly at the door and the screen and clasped his sweaty hands together.

As time continued to pass without any communication, Leynin sent a brief message he hoped would be acknowledged immediately. No reply came. His finger gravitated toward the emergency button on the panel, but he refrained from making contact. The men could be busy celebrating, and he would look the fool for overreacting. Perhaps he should go visit the cafeteria and give the men more time to respond.

He left the room and wandered absently around the hall, stopping short as he neared a group of his peers. Asfin and several other officials were talking in voices that matched the worry inside his own head.

"The region is unstable," an official said. "That's all I was told."

Asfin turned to Leynin. "A meeting will be called shortly," she said. "The Planetary Stability Monitor has destabilized."

"How so?"

"An area is emitting unusually high energy waves. There is no explanation..." Asfin's voice trailed away.

A peculiar feeling gripped him. "Do you happen to know what region?"

"Yes, this is why I didn't join you sooner. I got called

to the laboratory. Apparently, our superiors are so rattled by what's happened today that they didn't realize they had double assigned me—"

Leynin grabbed Asfin's arm and led her away from their peers, who resumed talking in earnest tones.

"Leynin, what are you doing?"

"I need you to show me what region."

"Why? The meeting will be held soon enough," she said as she stumbled behind him.

"Because our AT installers are unresponsive," he replied in a hushed tone. "I sent them a message over an hour ago, and they have yet to acknowledge it."

Their pace quickened. When they entered the correspondence center, he quickly pushed several buttons until the sphere displayed a map of their planet.

Asfin brushed the sphere lightly with her finger, causing the map to revolve until a large land mass was at the forefront. "It's here, I think." She pointed to a specific area on the land mass.

He pressed more buttons. The energy grid came into focus and overlapped the map. A tiny circle lit up in the spot where Asfin had pointed.

"Their most recent construction," was all he could think to say.

Asfin gripped onto the back of a chair to steady herself.

"We cannot wait another minute to have this meeting." His hand shaking, he pushed the button adjacent to all the others, the one he had never pushed before.

The recorded words resounded through the intercom system, "An emergency meeting will convene. All officials gather at once."

He and Asfin hurried to the conference room where the

other officials were assembling. After explaining the situation to an already troubled group of peers, the vote was in favor of intervention. The officials took action by engaging tracking devices.

The men were found many miles away from their intended destination, not even still together as a group, which meant something had gone terribly wrong.

❦

The two women stood before him with arms crossed. When they had first entered the room, Hegliod had stared shamelessly, too stunned to even apologize. He was acquainted with both women through village events and was astonished by how different they looked bearing each other's noses.

Ms. Berda's face had gone from being rounded with a soft prettiness to entirely unpleasant. With Ms. Raveen's large distracting nose, the rest of her face appeared much smaller and less significant.

Ms. Raveen's face had taken the other turn. Ms. Berda's smaller nose nicely complemented the shape of her eyes along with her cheekbones.

Hegliod stared and couldn't help continuing to stare until Ms. Berda loudly cleared her throat.

"Are you done gawking yet? Isn't it obvious the atrocity that's occurred?"

"Oh please, Ms. Berda," Ms. Raveen said. "Stop exaggerating. It's not that big of a deal."

"Maybe not for you," Ms. Berda snapped, "but to me it is a *huge* inconvenience."

Perhaps it was time to intervene before the debate got too ugly. Ms. Berda had grown quite ugly enough.

"Ladies, please relax. We will have your faces back to normal soon. The plan is to send you out together around Semadon using the newly secure AT system. Now that it's fixed, it will surely recognize its previous error and adjust this discrepancy. I have total faith in my machine!" Hegliod ushered them toward the door.

"I was hoping I would never have to ride in an AT cylinder with that woman ever again," Ms. Berda told Hegliod as Ms. Raveen exited the room. "Or for that matter, ride in an AT cylinder at all."

Her words struck him hard in the chest. "Dear Ms. Berda," he croaked out. "You are speaking under duress."

"Think whatever you want," she retorted. "But if this doesn't work I would suggest you find yourself a new profession. Try one where you can make things work properly." She stomped around the hall, trailing Ms. Raveen with her large nose held upward as if to warn of her displeasure.

Hegliod wrung his hands until they rounded the curve. Then he rushed to the control room to make sure the dials stayed in exact alignment during their travel. When it was time to return to the meeting room, he trudged back and sat with his head in his hands until the women's bickering traveled in from the doorway. He raised his head and was delighted to see that the noses had returned to their proper owners.

"It's ridiculous," Ms. Raveen said. "I can't believe it."

"Ms. Raveen, it appears you're back to normal. What's wrong?" he asked.

"She's jealous of what was once hers, although only briefly." Ms. Berda displayed her rightful nose between a pair of batting eyelashes.

"That's not the case at all," Ms. Raveen protested. "It

seems I have acquired Ms. Berda's foul attitude. When we first began our travels, I was happy. Now the AT system has swapped *her* rotten mood with my happy one. It isn't fair."

Hegliod was speechless as he stared at Ms. Raveen in disbelief.

"I was unhappy because I had your nose. Now that I have my own nose back, I am happy once again. So it's obvious to me the unhappiness comes with your nose."

Ms. Raveen turned an awkward shade of red and narrowed her eyes. She looked between both of them as if she were choosing who most deserved her wrath. Ms. Berda rolled her eyes and looked away. This only left Hegliod.

"I shall never venture by cylinder again," Ms. Raveen threatened. "Your Atomic Transport System is a joke." She shook her finger at him before storming with a fury out of the room.

"I will never travel by AT cylinder again either." Ms. Berda wrinkled her nose. "This was humiliating and embarrassing. I hope someday another means of transportation will be invented, a more reliable one that is." She gave him a deadly glare and stalked away too.

Dusk snapped Ceera out of her trance. The awareness that her surroundings were back to normal surfaced. The trees had shrunk back to size and their roots had regressed into the ground. The wind was calm. The only evidence anything unusual had happened was the leftover moss covering her exposed skin. She wiped her hands down her arms, but the moss clung stubbornly and she was only successful at smearing it. Perhaps it was a good thing it was getting dark.

She placed her toes on the cool forest floor and stood. Her head spun and she steadied herself against the fallen log. She pressed cold fingers to her forehead and waited for the dizziness to cease. Walking home would be a chore.

As she moved unsteadily between the trees, she remembered kicking off her shoes but knew that finding them in the dark would be next to impossible. Besides, what was more pressing than lost shoes was the realization that she had left her recorder on her desk, left the PID turned on with her notes typed on the screen. Drusilla would be furious.

At least she had an excuse. She would blame it on the aftermath of the alarm going off, say that it rattled her, which was partly true. Telling Drusilla the whole truth would give her mentor a reason to prolong her time in transition.

The outer orbits of Semadon were before her now, ringing the gleam of the larger buildings in the center. She trudged toward the lights, still making feeble attempts at wiping away the moss, and walked around until she came to a narrow opening between two dwellings. She tiptoed through, careful to duck her head when she passed by the windows.

The orbits were empty. Spherical glows from behind the dwellings' curtains confirmed many were tuned into the global update, most likely in hopes that High Service would explain why the alarm had sounded, malfunction or not.

She hurried up the walkway to her dwelling, hugging herself to keep warm, and hoped that everyone was too busy staring at their global update to notice her. She typed the code into the keypad on her door, and it swung open. She passed through her main room and entered her bathroom, where she removed her clothes and stepped into the shower. Moss dripped down her skin and formed clumps at her feet.

After showering, she slipped on her robe and headed to her global update. Drying her hair with a towel, she turned it on. Two High Service officials appeared on the screen.

"A meeting will be held in two days," the female official said, "to discuss the alarm malfunction. We request that everyone rally their energies toward conjuring up mystics to attend."

The words came as a surprise and she quickly sat down on her couch. "A meeting of the mystics," she mumbled aloud in disbelief.

Mystics were only called under the direst of circumstances. They were enchanted and possessed an innate wisdom that enabled them to give sage advice. Long ago they had devised the Semion's system of order and had even chosen the first High Service officials.

Their continued involvement in the Semion way of life had become quite controversial. The Council for Advancement, or CfA as they were called, denied the mystics' credibility and considered it insulting to rely on them for guidance. The CfA had officially declared them masters of deceit and refused to attend meetings with mystics.

Such a drastic measure implied that the officials did not have any answers to the problem they had attempted to conceal. She turned off the global update. Two days was a long time to wait.

CHAPTER TWO

CEERA HURRIED TOWARD the inner orbit of Semadon. The meeting of the mystics would begin soon and tardiness was unacceptable for a transitioning scribe. If only the PID at the library had worked properly, she would be strolling instead of half running. Her feet were trying hard to move as quickly as her mind.

The past two days had been a blur of curiosity and speculation. She had even fallen behind in her scribe work. Besides the controversy in Semadon, it was daunting to think that her daydreams were now mingling with reality. This is what she preferred to think, since upon asking the librarian a few discreet questions, she learned that all the old, rare books housed in the library were accounted for. There had been no theft, which meant the statue incident could only have been an extension of a daydream. Troubling as it was to her, an out of control daydream felt safer than admitting to an outright hallucination. Seeing visions was not part of her description.

Despite her efforts to downplay the incident, the forest now haunted her dreams. Leaves and bark engraved patterns in her mind whenever she fell asleep. The wind rustled through the trees and called her name. In these dreams, she was more than just a scribe. She would wake with a feeling of sly smugness, like some part of her had been waiting for this moment her whole life. Then reality would set in, followed by panic. Revealing this sentiment to anyone would set her back in transition.

Her mind was in such disarray that her attempts to conjure any mystics had failed. Since mystics existed between the planes of reality, conjuring them relied on intense mental focus. This focus projected outward, serving as an invitation to a mystic. Extracting them was a true art and required discipline. Hopefully, she had not turned any away with her muddled efforts.

She crossed onto the orbit leading to the Aurora, where all of Semadon's public meetings were held. Located at the highest point in the village, it was tall and carved immaculately with pictures of spatial entities. She was relieved that other Semions also hurried toward it.

Colorful rocks composed the walkway leading up to its entrance. Protesters swarmed this path. Ceera attempted to ignore the unruly crowd, who were mainly members of the Council for Advancement. Red rings, the CfA's insignia, glowed on their fingers.

"Stop this fallacy," shouted someone standing to her left.

"Believing in mystics is madness," a different voice protested from the opposite side.

Ceera gracefully squeezed through, careful to protect her recorder, and found herself at the entrance. An attendant opened the silver door and she stepped inside. The noise from the crowd became a faint buzzing in her ears. Small groups talking in hushed voices loitered in the hall. She walked around them and toward the meeting room.

She stepped through its arched doorway and stopped to gaze about.

The mystics drew her attention immediately, for an esoteric aura shrouded their large, circular table. She had never seen so many gathered all at once; there had to be nearly twenty of them, magnifying the effect. They wore long, hooded robes of muted colors. Some of their faces hid within the dark depths of their hoods. Incense smoke curled around them, but within the wisps wrinkled faces bore solemn expressions.

The only other item on their table was a large ornamental candle that had not yet been lit. Its intricate design covered the entire table. The main wick centered in a bulky pillar with wax appendages that snaked around itself before curling into various directions and joining with lesser wicks of smaller pillars.

She bowed her head quickly and looked away from the mystics. Staring would cause them to fade back to where they came. She did not want to be the culprit of a premature end to the meeting, an embarrassing misfortune which had been suffered by many transitioning scribes before her.

Smaller tables shaped like crescent moons encompassed the mystics' table. High Service officials sat at these, talking amongst themselves. They wore their signature attire colored in varying shades of silver. Some of the women wore silver gowns with embroidered designs on the bodices and fluttery sleeves, while others dressed like the men, who wore dark silver pants offsetting their lighter colored long sleeve shirts with collars.

More tables encircled the core of the room. On each were spherical screens similar to global updates which would portray the face of whoever spoke at the meeting.

Due to the structure of the room, there would be times when someone's face would not be visible to everyone. The spherical screens were also in place so the mystics could be viewed without dismantling their presence.

She headed to the scribe table.

"Barely on time," said Drusilla when she neared. Her mentor was dressed as posh as always with not a single hair escaping from her tight bun.

"The PID froze," Ceera said. "I'm so sorry." She smoothed her own attire self-consciously.

Drusilla responded with a stern look Ceera pretended not to see. She had narrowly escaped punishment for leaving her recorder on her desk. *I would expect nothing more from someone so prone to daydreaming*, Drusilla had said with disgust. Ceera attempted to look dignified as she walked past her mentor.

She approached her friend Litha, another transitioning scribe. Litha flipped her dark hair over her shoulder and smiled when Ceera slipped in beside her.

"The wait has been painful," Litha said, placing the back of her hand across her forehead in a dramatic gesture. "I hope we finally get some answers."

Ceera gave a short laugh at her friend's display. "Me too."

The Council for Natural Law, the CfNL, had claimed the tables closest to High Service. Each member wore a necklace bearing a round green emblem on which the silhouette of a tree was etched. Their leader, Marvus Crewn, stared into space with a serious expression. His hair had acquired a few more strands of gray since Ceera had last seen him. Desnia Marou, his companion, had adorned her hair in green ivy that seemed to be holding it up into a complicated bun, though Ceera suspected there were hidden pins involved too.

A young man dressed in black approached High Service, noticeable because he contrasted with all the shades of grey. A sleek, form-fitting jacket accentuated his broad shoulders. Dark hair framed his chiseled features and serious, deep set eyes. He took a seat and began speaking to the official beside him. He was surprisingly young looking for someone whose demeanor gave off a wealth of experience.

A spark of attraction flared up as she gazed upon him, but she immediately extinguished it.

"He's good-looking, don't you think?" Litha whispered in her ear.

Ceera frowned. "Who is he?" she whispered back.

"Don't know, but I think we'll soon find out."

Drusilla cleared her throat. The attendants stood to light the candles, and she was grateful for the diversion. She positioned her recorder on the table, her fingers poised on the keypad.

Officials leaned away as the attendants reached between them to ignite the wicks. By the time they reached the mystics' table and lit the ornamental candle, much of the conversation in the room had died down. The attendants drifted away and found seats at opposite ends of the room.

The official sitting closest to the mystics' table rose and looked around. Her hair was swept back with wispy tresses touching her rosy cheeks. "I am Risa of sphere five," she informed her audience.

There were seven spheres of authority in High Service, one being a novice and seven being of the highest order. Through experience and superior handling of situations, an official could increase their rank.

"We have called forth this meeting of the mystics," Risa said, "to help us understand this predicament we find ourselves in. Disorder surrounds us, disorder of a very peculiar nature. Chaos is rare, for we have all but mastered how to live peacefully on this planet. Yet perhaps our understanding is not as definitive as we had thought."

Murmurs rippled through the audience.

"The sudden turn of events has caused us concern. I will now turn the meeting over to my companion, Karnen, also of sphere five." Risa bowed and sat back down.

Karnen stood and cleared his throat. "I'm sure you're all aware of what Risa speaks about. We all felt the strange sensation that drifted through Semadon and the accompanying alarms, but there is even more to tell. It has to do with something which measures our planet's equilibrium."

The grave look on Karnen's face spoke volumes. A shiver worked its way up through Ceera's spine and wavered at the base of her skull.

"A few days ago, our Planetary Stability Monitor discovered that a region on this planet was radiating unusually high energy waves. Normally, its alarms would indicate a ground quake or volcanic eruption; however, after further analysis we determined the cause was unknown."

There were rustlings of indignation amongst the crowd. The words *malfunction* and *deceit* arose from somewhere within the room.

Sweat formed on Karnen's face, visible on the screen. Looking somewhat apologetic, he raised and lowered his hands to shush the crowd. "I understand how this could be perceived, but you must also consider the position of High Service. When it became apparent there was no immediate danger, we shut off the alarms and directed everyone to carry on with their daily operations. There was no point in worrying anyone further until we had time to evaluate."

The crowd noise settled down.

"Unfortunately, during the disturbance we had AT installers in this very location. Let me assure you, the high energy reading was not due to the cylinder's placement. Our monitors are programmed not to signal alarms for energy waves of this kind.

"Yet here is where things grow even more puzzling. After the men installed their last cylinder, they stopped responding to us. Using our tracking devices, we found them wandering around, in various locations away from the cylinder. They do not remember who they are, or what they were doing, and remain under the supervision of medical professionals."

A lump formed in Ceera's throat. She tried to force it away and swallowed loudly.

"Now what does all this mean?" Karnen continued. "Well, frankly, we don't know. We refrain from sending others to this area though we continue to monitor it. No council or scientist has any input. The only thing left to do is ask the mystics to see if they can bring insight to this perplexing matter." Karnen motioned toward the mystics and sat back down.

Several minutes dragged past in uncomfortable silence.

"The region where the AT installers were sent is imbalanced," a mystic's voice creaked out. "That is why they have returned to you so. The region is so imbalanced it forced this defect upon them."

Ceera squinted at the screen. The mystic's face was blurry due to his skin being as pale as the hovering smoke.

"The region contains an irregularity of nature," another

mystic said softly. "Being one with nature implies we are capable of addressing this issue. All we are a part of, we can determine."

"True," spoke another, "but this must be handled delicately and with the utmost attention to strategy. No one shall venture back without guidance from the Archaics. Only with their enlightenment, can you gain the assistance you need to conquer this anomaly."

The mention of the Archaics dragged at Ceera's memory, so elusive they were in present-day matters.

"The ancient practice of reading the elements is still carried out by the Archaics," continued another mystic in a feathery voice. "They know nature's secrets and can guide you toward understanding. For all that occurs is preserved within the elemental database."

"Only through knowledge of the past, can you gain rational sense of the present," the words of yet another sliced through the smoke.

The mystics bowed their heads, appearing to be on a different wavelength and oblivious to their surroundings. An undulating light formed around them and contracted slowly inward. Ceera's fingers remained poised on her recorder.

Risa stood to address the mystics. "Is it possible for you to tell us why this region is imbalanced?"

Her question did not break the mystics' trance. The glow around them shrunk even further, signifying that their time was drawing short.

"Do you have any idea," Risa asked more urgently this time, "of what we are up against?"

The silence this time was short but strangely ominous.

"What lies there is a forest permeated by days of old,"

a voice rasped from within the darkness of a hood. "It does not behave in ways an ordinary forest would behave. It has been corrupted."

It was as if the mystic had cast a spell. Ceera was too stunned to breathe or move. She sat helplessly while the mystic disappeared. His words lingered longer than his physical presence.

"Its growth spawned from the awakening of an ancient organism, a long forgotten root structure hidden within the layers of soil," another mystic said as he dimmed from view.

Ceera's body grew hot and she leaned forward in her chair. Her recorder dropped into her lap.

"It overtook the area with great speed…" the words of a different mystic trailed off as she, too, evaporated into the atmosphere.

Other mystics faded as well. Ceera fumbled for her recorder with a clumsiness her fingers had never before possessed.

"There is more to this forest than just the trees," the last mystic to disappear uttered. His warning was all that remained.

Once the mystics were gone and just a swirl of smoke billowed in their place, frantic chatter took over the room. Litha was saying something to her, but Ceera's focus was on High Service.

They crowded around the young man, talking privately with troubled expressions. Uncertainty bubbled around them, an uncertainty she did not share. For some reason, she needed to insert herself. Her vision had made the suggestion, and her dreams had verified this truth. She would ponder the reason why later. Her whole body was now brimming with an urgent energy she could not ignore.

An official asked the young man in black a question, and he responded with a swift nod. As if a matter were settled, Karnen then stood and waited for the crowd noise to die down.

"We had been hoping the mystics would endure longer and display a more vivid picture than what they have given us; however, we now know at least where to begin. I would like to introduce a man who, after much premeditated discussion, we believe can carry out the mystics' suggestion. This"—he paused—"is Dassius Rucien."

Dassius minimized the official when he stood, both in stature and in presence. Although he looked a fraction bewildered, his confidence did not waver and he flashed a charming smile around the room.

"Fellow Semions," he began, "I have spent my youth training for the Sci-Defense team. High Service implemented our program years ago, in preparation of our advancement to other planets, so that we'll have Semions capable of withstanding diverse environments."

Ceera recalled a few brief mentions of the Sci-Defense team during other meetings she had attended, but the particulars had always been glossed over. High Service tended to be that way with pilot programs until they were refined.

"The Sci-Def team," Dassius continued, "uses science to master adaptation and survival. Thus my learning plan exposed me to a number of unusual conditions. As a result, I can analyze my surroundings to the extent that I'm unfazed by the unexpected."

Ceera wondered how much of his surroundings he was analyzing at present. Was his easy tone an attempt to quiet the fear in the room, or a display of his own self-possession?

"My ability to react efficiently is a skill I've perfected over the course of many experiments. I've also trained in the use of weaponry and defense tactics. Due to the severity of our current situation, I will carry out these practices here on our very own planet." Dassius paused to make eye contact with some of the audience.

A twinge of annoyance brushed her when his eyes skipped carelessly over hers.

"Some of you may be wondering if my abilities can match the weight of the challenge. Let me assure you I won't disappoint, for I've trained for this moment my whole life."

His arrogance triggered Ceera's instincts and she stood. "It is my duty to venture with you, for I have dreamed about this forest and it calls me."

Drusilla's gasp drowned out the murmurs that took over the room.

The smile on Dassius's face disappeared. His dark blue eyes met hers. At first he seemed taken aback, but then he studied her intently. She sensed he was trying to intimidate and incite her to look away. Indignation fueled her confidence and she stood up straighter, hardening her gaze. He looked her up and down and frowned before turning to Karnen.

"Young woman," Karnen said sternly, "who are you and what is your description?"

"I am Ceera Kestlyn." Her face grew hot as all eyes in the room were now on her. "And I'm a transitioning scribe."

A puff of air escaped Dassius's lips, but she refused to acknowledge the insult and kept her gaze on the official.

"How is it you dreamed about this forest when it was only revealed to us tonight that it was a forest?"

"I had a daydream, perhaps even a vision, on the day the alarms sounded. I was unsure of the meaning until tonight. I even tried to ignore the incident, but the forest has since invaded my dreams. Now that I know why, it would be a crime to remain silent."

Drusilla's mouth was agape and her hand rested on her chest. It was inappropriate for a scribe to interfere with the flow of a meeting they had been assigned to record. Ceera would be reprimanded, set back in transition, if she didn't finish what she started.

Karnen eyed her thoughtfully. The other officials said nothing, but whispers resounded throughout the rest of the room. She glanced at Dassius, whose face now burned as bright as hers except with anger, and she couldn't help but take advantage of this.

"Dassius, you seem surprised," she said. "Yet you claim to be unfazed by the unexpected."

"I knew something like this would occur," he responded. "I just wasn't expecting it from such a young girl."

Ceera's chin stiffened and she turned back to the official. "All my life, I've been training to be a scribe. Thus, I'm good at capturing the moment. What's occurring needs to be recorded, whether for the sake of history, or even for the betterment of this new scientific field Dassius speaks about. I cannot shy away from this. The forest speaks my name so vibrantly I hear it when I sleep."

The tension in the room dissipated though Dassius still looked unconvinced.

"I am willing to hear a more detailed testimonial from you, Ceera." Karnen turned to the audience. "There will be a short recess as we hold a meeting in the adjoining room. Dassius and Ceera, please attend."

Risa and Karnen ventured to the door behind their table. Dassius joined them, but Semions surrounded her before she had a chance to do the same.

"What does the forest look like?" asked Litha, who was

now viewing Ceera with a cross between admiration and disbelief.

"Can you tell what's wrong with it?" someone behind her asked.

"Did you see any of the AT installers in your dream?" The question came at her from a different direction.

Ceera stole a glance at her mentor, who gave her a tight smile.

"Move along, dear." Drusilla's voice was firm yet gentle. "You only answer to High Service now."

Despite the implications, Ceera took her mentor's advice and ignored them all. She gave Litha an apologetic smile, bowed her head, and made her way through the crowd.

The commotion died down as soon as she shut the door behind her. Dassius stood facing the two officials, who sat at a table. The room was bare except for a skylight above. The moon illuminated the entirety of the enclosure.

"It's insulting. All the education I have only to be partnered with a mere scribe," Dassius said, indifferent to her presence. "And a transitioning one at that. I can write things down along the way if you'd like, but I'd prefer not to be bothered playing hero to this young girl who won't even be able to protect herself."

"Excuse me"—Ceera joined Dassius—"but first of all, I am not a girl, I am a young woman and probably near the same age as you. Secondly, it's disrespectful for you to refer to me as a mere scribe. Thirdly"—she was running out of breath—"you fail to realize what I bring to this trip. If you were more interested in success for our people, instead of your own conceit, you would accept my offer to help."

"Offer to help? Who will be helping who?" Dassius threw his hands up into the air.

"Now Dassius, will it really hinder you so much?" Risa placed her hand on Dassius's arm. "Remember, you are fresh out of transition yourself."

Dassius scowled and looked away.

"Ceera can at least accompany you to the Archaics," Risa said. "A few of them are friendlier to a feminine presence, so I'm sure she would be a benefit in that regard. If she can prove herself useful during these encounters, then perhaps she can also go with you to the forest. You are aware of the risk involved?"

"Of course," Ceera replied. "I'm a scribe. I listen well and remember details."

"How old are you, my dear?" she asked.

"Twenty."

"And in transition," Karnen declared. "What better time than now to prove yourself to your peers?"

His words left behind a residue Ceera couldn't immediately shake. She dropped her gaze, having the distinct impression that the ground had just shifted though she had not lost her footing.

"Dassius," Karnen said, "if you would like to conjure up a mystic in your defense then go ahead. But until one says that Ceera's involvement is unnecessary, we will allow her to go. Now Ceera tell me"—he turned to her—"what makes this forest different from the one outside Semadon?"

Ceera considered how to describe that day in the woods, but not before noticing that Dassius had turned his back on them. She was glad she could not see his face, for it shone brilliantly in the moonlight and he did not deserve such kindness.

Chapter Three

MARVUS SPENT A good deal of time in the room of the statues. The room was spherical and located inside the Council for Natural Law's building. It was very unorthodox, yet fitting, and also greatly inefficient, as he was told. The architect had insisted that spherical rooms eliminated a vast amount of space. Regardless, the effect the room was meant to have on its occupants weighed heavier than the amount of space ideal to walk within. So the room had been built as initially conceived.

The painted walls depicted the sky above and the planet below. The purpose was to evoke an enclosed rendition of the real world so as to intrigue the senses. In its center, statues of the Archaics stood in a circle, each holding an arm upward. A model of the planet, encompassed with swirling colors of blue and green, balanced precariously on their fingertips.

Marvus stood on the flat ledge that wound around the room, stroking the green emblem hanging from his necklace. Although he wished he could view the splendor for time on end, he had actually just paused to gain his bearings before attending to his business in the gardens.

He planned to speak about his council's position regarding the abnormal energy reading. It was, quite obviously, the CfA's fault. In a matter of two sentences, the head of the CfA had put their whole culture in jeopardy, and of course, Semions were likely not up-to-date in their PID viewing. And if they were, they wouldn't recognize the severity of what was spoken, the vulgarity for what it truly was.

Marvus savored his last moment staring at the statues, before descending the steps leading to the backyard gardens and opening the door. The sky was green in the gardens, or at least there was enough foliage hanging above that gave this impression. The artist who had designed the gardens that year had created a horticultural masterpiece.

Long ago, a member of the CfNL had discovered the art of influencing plant growth. This gentle manipulation tactic had been passed down over the years, but only to those worthy of knowing it. The CfNL guarded the secret to prevent its abuse, for if the public had access to it, they would frivolously take advantage of nature to no end.

The Council for Advancement tried but failed to duplicate the practice. This only convinced the CfNL of their own superiority, which they relayed to anyone who would listen. In retaliation, the CfA declared the practice was in direct dispute of the principles the CfNL strived to uphold, and that nature was being exploited by its supporters.

The dispute ensued until High Service put an end to it, proclaiming that nature could continue to decide for itself what was appropriate. The CfNL continued to practice what they considered to be their divine right, and the CfA continued to refute these actions in the privacy of their own meeting room.

Nevertheless, the greenery surrounding Marvus was not brimming with indignation; it was alive with health and vigor. Large bushes arched over his head and offered berries from thick stems. Flowers lined the stone pathway in colorful patterns. Tree roots made intricate designs along the ground. These, of course, were permanent and did not change from year to year.

Marvus approached his audience, who sat on large decorative rocks arranged around the speaking area. Desnia stood nearby the podium, wearing a lilac corsage that matched the tiny purple flowers hanging at her ears. A global update sphere had been placed at the edge of the gathering. Marvus bowed to Desnia, who returned the gesture of respect, and took his place before the podium.

"Good afternoon," he said. "I am pleased to see so many of you in attendance. I also thank those who are watching on the global update. I trust my words will end your confusion about our mounting problems.

"As head of the Council for Natural Law, I am committed to preserving the truth that nature is the driving force of all life. In compliance with this principle, we analyze the course of cultural progress and determine whether or not it abides with nature's guidelines. It is our duty," he continued emphatically, "to ensure all actions follow the laws of nature, are justifiable, have no detrimental effect on our environment and are carried out with the utmost of integrity."

Cheers rose from the crowd.

"While we cannot control the actions of every Semion, it is within our power to expose those who do not follow this principle and, yes, such an action has occurred. It put our culture on the brink of instability. This action is why we have AT installers, loved ones, in medical beds. It serves as a catalyst for all the troubles we now face."

Roars of indignation erupted from the crowd.

"This catastrophic action was committed"—he paused—"in the form of words. That's right. These careless words were spoken with the ease of arrogance and spite. We all know that words hold power. They are a measure of our intelligence. They control our relationships and success. The words we speak can either promote or degrade us.

"Let me tell you something else about words. Once spoken, they cannot return to where they came. It's true. Once words are uttered into existence, they cannot be erased. They come alive and stay in our memories, but this is not the only place where words have permanence. Words become wedged in nature's grand design and can alter the standing we have with nature.

"This is why nature presents this state of disorder to us. The words of one man have affected life on this planet for all." Marvus stopped talking to give his accusation time to sink in.

⌁

Falken Grihne stared at his global update sphere, watching Marvus with sardonic amusement. He tuned in not only due to curiosity, but also because of what had happened to him when the alarms sounded. The memory was quite painful.

It began with him admiring his solar system model at his desk: a reproduction encased within an energy field that drove the tiny planets in perfect revolutions. Amidst his thoughts spinning peacefully with the planets, an odd feeling struck him, like he was being watched. Falken whipped his head around to view the entirety of the room. Shelves overloaded with equipment and jars lined the walls. His pet bird and rat looked bleakly back at him from within their cages. The door was still shut. There was no one.

Still troubled, Falken had spun back around. Then he witnessed the impossible. His planets still revolved around the sun but in the opposite direction. He leaned closer to examine the bizarre behavior until his nose was centimeters away from the surrounding field. That was when the alarm sounded, causing Falken to lose his balance and fall head-first into the model.

His head was now heavily bandaged from his forehead coming in contact with the sun replica. The pain had been excruciating and he had suffered severe burns. It could have been fatal had he not rebounded backwards when his arms hit the table. He had lain sprawled on the floor for hours until regaining consciousness. Though his head still throbbed, he had decided against seeing a doctor and instead told no one of his misfortune.

"Now, who would be so bold as to corrupt the good life we live with his words?" Marvus's voice resumed from the global update sphere. "Let me tell you who. His name is Nimren Sebious! Yes, the head of the Council for Advancement has taken it upon himself, to mar the reputation we have with the divine workings of nature! He is the cause of this confusion. His words spoken at the past meeting ruined—"

Falken pressed a button on his remote. Marvus and his surroundings disappeared into nothingness, a sorry triumph for such infuriating implications, but Falken had heard enough. Marvus's slanderous speech was bound to sway the opinion of those vulnerable to the CfNL's lies. No doubt the Council for Advancement would be left defending itself. This was a true shame, for the words spoken by Nimren had been deserved, well spoken.

Falken tossed a small sphere he'd been toying with

up into the air. It modeled the Semion's planet and had revolved in his now broken solar model. He caught it and repeated this action, letting the repetition tame his flashes of aggression.

Stifling his internal fire had become routine practice for him over the years, and he expertly brought his mind back to a quiet state. He should have known Marvus would somehow find a way to blame the CfA. While his actions were maddening, hating the man didn't solve anything, unless of course, Falken chose to convert this hatred into a valuable resource.

This he had experience with, for hatred raged quite frequently within him. Hatred he could use to fuel a solution. His surroundings blurred as he paused with the sphere clutched in his hand. He liked how it felt there, compressed within his palm. If his fingers applied just a bit more force, he could crush it into a thousand pieces. The thought was tempting but seemed untimely. Instead, he loosened his grip and continued to toss the sphere in the air with control as he plotted what could be done.

⤚

Hanging vines possessing verdant leaves interlaced the arched trellis serving as the entryway to the garden. Their fresh scent tickled Ceera's senses as she passed through. The scenery before her created the same ripple of delight she experienced whenever she came to gather food.

Brightly colored flowers adorned the landscape in small clusters. Trees and shrubbery were spaced evenly to give each a good space for growth, and a large area to the side had been cultivated to produce vegetables and herbs.

It was the prime time of year for plant life to flourish. The fruit was ripe and the vegetables were mature. It would be easy picking pieces that looked suitable for consumption.

She hadn't planned to collect anything from the gardens since she would soon be leaving Semadon, but had eaten the last of her food earlier in the day. Although High Service had said they would be contacting her, this had yet to occur. She refrained from calling them since she didn't want to be perceived as unprofessional. Besides, she knew what was holding them up.

It had to be Dassius Rucien. He had probably been attempting to thwart her involvement this entire time. She had no idea how they would coexist during their travels. Despite his skepticism, the forest continued to creep in on her during her sleep. It was always the same, inviting her into its montage of wood and greenery, before the wind would intone the sound of her name with its billowing breath.

She approached a young tree, found a plump apple unmarred by insects and dropped it into her satchel. She picked another that looked ripe and juicy. She was just about ready to pick a third when someone spoke behind her.

"You'd better pick more than that. Who knows how long we'll be away."

Ceera turned and was surprised to find Dassius standing there. He smiled in his confident way and she almost dropped her satchel. "Dassius, why are you here? Is your orbit's garden closed for rejuvenation?"

"It is but that doesn't matter. I'm here to see you."

"Oh." A mild pang of satisfaction struck her. "How did you know I was here?"

"Let's just say I'm good at making assumptions."

"I should have known," she responded dryly and turned back to the tree. "And by the way, I'm picking fruit for myself."

"I came to call a truce and put a halt to the bitterness between us."

Ceera pretended to stare at the apples. "That sounds awfully noble of you, but perhaps what would exalt you even higher is a simple apology."

Her words were met with silence, so she wandered over to a plum tree and began plucking them absent-mindedly. His feet crunched the grass behind her.

"You shouldn't resent me for how I acted the other day," Dassius said. "It was hard to take you seriously."

"So what changed your mind? Guilt? Or are you just following orders by High Service?" She shoved the plums roughly into her satchel.

Again he had no immediate response.

"Well, which is it?" She whirled around.

"Of course our travels will be easier if we're on good terms." His eyes flickered away before returning her stare. "I don't need anyone from High Service to tell me that."

"What about how you treated me? You called me a mere scribe."

He looked down at the ground between them. "Look, I do regret that. It was just hard for me to accept your help. But I'll try harder. In fact, I'm trying right now."

Dassius glanced back up. His eyes rested carefully on hers, and she allowed their gazes to lock together. An understanding was forming, and perhaps something more, but she had enough on her mind. Some of her anger drifted away.

"So what changed your mind?" she asked.

"Do I have to tell you?"

"Yes, if you want me to forgive you," she said tentatively.

"I did as Karnen suggested and conjured a mystic. I conjured a second when I didn't like what the first one had to say."

"You got a second opinion from a mystic?" Ceera was incredulous.

"I know," Dassius said quickly. "It was wrong of me. The second refused to even acknowledge my question."

"What did the first say about me?" She turned back around to hide her smile.

"I'd rather not tell you."

She watched him stuff his hands in his pockets out of the corner of her eye. "Perhaps you could redeem yourself by telling me."

She strolled to a blackberry bush. He followed. She picked some berries and watched them turn her fingers purple. "Dassius, what did the mystic say?"

"The second one suggested we meet with the Caretaker of Ancient Affairs. He said the Caretaker could give us advice about the Archaics."

"Advice, what sort of advice?" Ceera allowed her selfish reveling to come to an end. She stopped picking berries and let their juice drip off her fingers.

"Advice about dealing with them. Do you know anything?"

She paused to think since her frustrations with Dassius had consumed most of her speculation for the past few days. "They never came up in my scribe work. Not that I haven't been curious."

"Me too. I remember hearing stories when I was young, but I didn't pay much attention."

"Well, being trained in such a special field you must have some sort of instinctual opinion." She was careful to keep her tone businesslike.

Dassius smiled rather nicely at her. "I have a feeling dealing with them will be tricky."

She nodded and walked over to a row of vegetables, scanning the area until she spotted some potatoes. She knelt and pulled one out of the ground. Dassius stooped beside her, half crouched on one knee. He wiped the dirt off the potatoes she accumulated in a pile.

"Hopefully, the Caretaker will clear things up. Are you available first thing tomorrow? I made an early appointment since we're leaving the next morning."

"We are?" She looked down at her satchel and the pile of potatoes beside it. She removed her fingers from the dirt and brushed them off.

"Hey, what's on your thumb?" Dassius asked.

It took her a moment to register what he was talking about, since she was preoccupied with the reality that High Service had not notified her. "Oh this?" she said, holding her thumb out so he could see it better. "It's my birthmark." The reddened lines squiggled on her thumb rarely surfaced in her thoughts anymore.

Dassius stared at it until she grew self-conscious and lowered her hand. "Several females in my lineage have had the same marking."

"Really?" He continued to stare, but his interest only irritated her.

"So we're leaving in two days? Less than two days even?" she asked impatiently.

"Yes, we're leaving at dawn. The global update will

break the news tonight. All Semions are invited. Apparently, it will be quite the event." He grinned.

"How flattering," Ceera responded, annoyed she would have learned the news from the global update if Dassius had not found her in the garden.

After they discussed where they would meet in the morning, she let him walk her home.

"What do you think about the problem between the two councils?" she asked as they strolled around an orbit. She had viewed a troubling segment by the CfNL on the global update earlier that day.

"You mean the Council for Advancement and the Council for Natural Law?"

"Yes, did you watch the segment too?" she asked.

"I never watch the global update."

"How do you keep up on current events? Through the PID?"

"It's part of my training to try and sense what's occurring. The global update and the PID are off limits to me."

"Oh." Ceera stared down at the sidewalk and watched their feet. "So, on your own you figured out there was a conflict between the two councils?"

"Isn't there always a conflict between the two councils?"

Ceera laughed. "Yes, but this new one has to do with the alarm sounding. Or did you already know that too?"

"I assumed so. Are you a member of either one?"

"I'm not allowed to join a council. It's considered a conflict of interest since I'm a scribe. I just record their meetings for the PID's. How about you?"

"No," Dassius said. "The Sci-Def team is a professional and private entity. The arguing between the two councils is tiresome anyway."

"I agree. There was a heated debate the other day during a meeting I recorded. Nimren Sebious gave a speech that offended the other council. I haven't been paying much attention since then, but apparently his words had quite an impact."

"Not been paying attention?" Dassius teased her.

"Yes, it feels strange, but you do know I've been relieved of my daily operations, right? High Service told me to discontinue since I would be leaving Semadon soon."

"I heard. I was just joking."

"It does bother me not to know what's going on."

"Well Ceera, I guarantee the councils' argument has nothing to do with our travels."

Ceera's dwelling was now around the curve. It was then she realized that Dassius had been leading the way. "How do you know where I live?" She stopped walking and glared at him. High Service was not allowed to give out her private information without her permission.

His eyes gleamed with amusement, and the corners of his mouth wavered in an apparent attempt to keep a neutral expression.

"Did High Service tell you?"

"No, you heard me explain my abilities at the meeting, right?"

"Well yes, but"—she faltered—"maybe I don't fully understand."

"Don't worry," Dassius told her with a wink, "you will." He grabbed her arm to escort her up the stone walkway.

His manners distracted her from asking more questions.

"How long have you lived alone?" Dassius asked as they stood by the door.

"Since I turned eighteen. How old are you anyway?" She was growing weary of all the focus on her age.

"Twenty-one," Dassius said. "Be sure you bring your recorder tomorrow."

"I will."

"See you in the morning." He gave her a half smile and waved before turning to walk back down the orbit.

She sighed. Dassius had eluded from revealing what the mystic had said about her. She glanced once more at him and stepped inside.

The correspondence orb hummed as she entered. Its frequency reading indicated a message from High Service. She pressed the button to listen.

The message confirmed everything Dassius had told her. The official stated that although everyone was invited to watch their departure, the emphasis would be placed on the event itself, not the two of them. They were also expected to attend a minor briefing before they left, which would take place tomorrow evening. The official insisted she contact High Service if she had any questions.

Ceera walked into her kitchen and began emptying the fruit and vegetables from her satchel.

"I'm only a scribe," she murmured to herself, "but somehow, in the past few days I've become so much more. Strange, but I always knew I was more."

Now that the words had broken free, she could never revert back to her old way of thinking. She was different now, forever.

Chapter Four

THE COUNCIL FOR Advancement's elaborate head-quarters was in an orbit exactly opposite of where the Council for Natural Law's building stood. The public debated whether this was on purpose or coincidental, since there was no evidence the two being on opposite ends was intentional. Some speculated it was a mischievous detail executed by the builders, yet others argued whether the builders would have bothered with such an idea. Whatever the case, the fact they stood at opposite ends of the village center was very appropriate since the two councils forever opposed each other.

Even now this truth was on Nimren Sebious's mind, as he sat inside his office and polished the bright red sun adorning the ring on his pudgy finger.

"So who will be meeting with us today?" Casma Blyte, his companion, asked in a haughty tone. She sat stiffly at the edge of her chair, an aura of self-importance cloaking her figure.

"I have invited Falken Grihne." He tossed the polishing cloth aside and watched her.

"Mr. Grihne?" Her look of discontent exaggerated

every wrinkle on her aging skin. "What made you think he would be a good candidate?"

"To be honest, it was a difficult decision. We have so many fine minds working for the council. I spent an entire evening pondering the decision, thinking about credentials and such. But I always ended up back at Falken."

"Why? He is the scourge of the council." Casma twisted her ring in agitation.

"Yes, that is precisely why," he said, pleased by her comment. "Falken Grihne already has a poor reputation. If matters do not turn out as we hope, then we have someone to blame."

Casma raised an eyebrow.

"And he'll have no chance of ever clearing his name. Better his demise than the council's." He folded his hands behind his head and sat back in his chair.

"It's deceitful but I like it," Casma said. "You're right; we cannot risk the reputation of the council."

The correspondence orb hummed. Nimren pressed a button. "Yes?"

"Mr. Sebious, Falken Grihne is here to see you."

"Thank you. Please send him to my office."

Nimren gave Casma a knowing smile which she returned. The knock came seconds later, and he rose to answer the door. "Falken, it is good to see you," Nimren said as he opened it. Then he frowned and stepped aside.

Falken's face had undergone a massive transformation. A swollen eye bulged; the other had shrunk into a sickly crease. Small bumps covered his face. Most distracting was the red circular scar centered on his forehead.

"It's good to see you too Nimren, Casma." Falken entered with his head bowed self-consciously.

Casma leaned away in disgust.

"What happened to you, young man? Were you one of the Semions aboard the AT cylinders when the alarm sounded?" Nimren asked.

"Nah, I was studying my solar model. The alarm tripped me up and I fell into it headfirst."

"How horrid." Casma shuddered. "That event managed to affect us all, hasn't it?"

"It seems to have affected me more severely than everyone else." Falken said flatly as he sat down across from Casma.

"Well, there were the two women whose noses switched on them but—"

"But they are back to normal," Falken interrupted. "I remain disfigured."

"There are the AT installers too, but they will probably regain consciousness and return to normal any day now." Nimren sat back down. "Sadly, I doubt the same can be said for your recovery. And we are sorry this is the case."

"I'm more than sorry, perfectly enraged to be exact." Falken glared down at his hands.

"Then our meeting with you has more meaning than I had previously concluded," Nimren said. "I would consider the irony to be unfortunate, but the coincidence itself is stirring. The alarm's effect on the village is the reason we have asked you to come."

Falken looked up suddenly, causing Casma to gasp and look away.

"How would you, Falken, like the opportunity to discredit what happened and expose it for what it really is? You are aware of the accusation the Council for Natural Law made?"

"Absolutely. I saw it on the global update. They think it was a sign by nature that the CfA is misusing its knowledge. That it's due to the words you spoke in regards to our proposal."

"So ridiculous," Casma said. "There is no way to prove such a thing."

"But that is what their council is conspiring to do," Nimren said. "Not only have they manipulated the goodwill of High Service, they have also enlisted the help of those bothersome mystics. Now we have two Semions who have been given the task of uncovering some hidden meaning behind what is just a naturally occurring forest: Ceera, the young woman who has tired of her description as a scribe before she even began it; and Dassius, the human science experiment."

"And it is clear High Service's motivation complies with the convictions of the average Semion." Casma shook her head in exasperation. "Presently, the average Semion is in a state of panic and will believe whatever nonsense the CfNL says. Just imagine the slanted conclusions that will come of this."

"I was at the meeting when you spoke, Nimren. I saw the effect your speech had on members of the CfNL. It's obvious to me their actions are a sign of desperation."

"You're right, Falken. My words drove fear into their hearts. They're in denial that our culture is advancing so quickly, they'll soon have to find themselves a new description altogether. Their council is on the brink of oblivion."

"What was it you said, Nimren?" Casma asked coyly.

"Ah yes"—he puffed out his already large chest and cleared his throat—"I said the Semion culture is on the verge of rewriting the laws of nature, that soon our council will be commanding nature to abide by the laws of the Semions."

"Quite just." Casma smirked.

"Yes." He looked slyly down his nose at his two fellow council members. "It was time to unleash reality on our foes. They have hindered us long enough."

"So what's your plan? Why have you called me here today?"

"Because we feel you are a capable young man. We have seen your ideas come into fruition and recognize your superior intellect." Nimren paused to watch the effect of his words.

Falken acknowledged them with a nod of his head. A faint glimmer of satisfaction radiated from his dark eyes before they again went dim. "How can that be true when the council has disregarded all my achievements thus far?"

Nimren frowned while Casma shifted in her seat.

"I can understand why you would believe this," Nimren said. "But you have to think of it from the council's perspective. Would it have been fair of us to recognize you for something one of your peers developed first?"

"He was a day ahead of me. It would have been fair to recognize us both," Falken retorted.

"We regret we were unable to give you the credit you deserve for your solar model, but now is not the time to dwell on the past. Today we are setting before you an opportunity of unequaled importance. It has the potential to elevate you higher than you've ever imagined."

"Don't underestimate me," Falken stated with a flicker of menace, "or what you think I've imagined."

"We would never do such a thing," Nimren replied quickly.

Falken shifted his eyes between them. His glare faded in the silence that followed.

"The council is at risk, Falken. We must retaliate. How do you feel about taking on the classified assignment of preserving what we have worked so hard to create?"

"What would you like me to do?"

"Keep an eye on Ceera and Dassius. Figure out a way to bring us any information they discover before the CfNL learns of it from High Service. That way we have time to prepare a defense before they attack us again on the global update."

Falken nodded his head slowly.

"What do you say?" Nimren asked. "Do you think you are up for it?"

"That depends."

"On what?"

"I would like a chair on the council. I would deserve it after this."

"You certainly would, young man," Nimren said, careful to keep his face expressionless.

Falken stood and extended his hand to both of them in turn. "I will be back," he said, "when I have uncovered something of importance." He closed the door and his footsteps faded down the hall.

"Why did you agree to give him a chair on the council?" Casma's tone was accusatory.

"I agreed to nothing," Nimren said. "And there is nothing he can do about it. When this ends, there will be no one he can tell without incriminating himself."

"True," Casma replied, but her demeanor was no longer so self-assured.

It had to be Falken's hideous transformation that was causing her alarm. His plan, after all, was genius.

&

Ceera finished putting away her supper dishes and was just about to settle down in front of the global update, when someone knocked on her door. She went to answer, expecting an official or even Dassius to be standing on her stoop. Instead, when she opened the door she found her father. Her heart skipped a beat, and she took a step back.

He was shorter than she remembered. Or perhaps she had grown. He stood like a man whose body had been weakened by the grueling physical labor typical of a farmer's life. Tiny lines creased his face. As she stared, his mouth curved into a tentative smile.

"Ceera honey," he said, stepping inside and closing the door behind him. "You look great."

Her body tensed when he kissed her cheek. His skin smelled like sweat and damp soil. She couldn't believe it was really him.

"Look, it's been awhile," he said with a sigh, "but I'm here and I'd like to talk."

Ceera nodded stiffly. She hadn't seen her father since she was fourteen years old, when he had come to her graduation from secondary school. They had barely spoken since. It was difficult to maintain a relationship with a man who never answered his communication orb.

He gently grabbed her hand and led her over to her couch. "Nice place," he said as he took a seat. "Semadon treats its devoted citizens well."

As if she'd had a say in that. She blinked and looked away.

"Will you sit down? You're making me uncomfortable."

She perched at the edge of her couch.

"Relax," he said. "You know I'd visit more if I could."

She cringed. "Why are you here?" Her words came out in a half whisper.

"Because Drusilla called me. She said you're going on an adventure with some young guy, into a forest. You think I could just hear that and let it go?"

Well, why not? He had let a lot go, mainly her. Yet here he was: solid flesh and bone before her. The look on his face seemed genuine. Perhaps he did care after all.

A tear ran down her cheek and she lunged forward, throwing her arms around him. "I miss you," she said, her voice strained though she refused to succumb to her tears.

"I miss you too." He kissed the top of her head. "You're almost done with transition soon, about to be a scribe?"

"Yes, or I was anyway. Hopefully, I haven't messed that up."

"I hope so too, though I wouldn't worry about Drusilla. I got to know her a little when I arranged for your schooling. She's fierce but has the heart of a kitten."

Ceera rolled her eyes. "I don't know about that."

"Well, I do. Now back to these dreams you've been having, when did they start?"

"Just recently, on the day the alarm sounded. And when I found out what was going on at the meeting, I couldn't just pretend like they weren't happening."

"I see. So now you're ready to find out what these dreams are all about." The lightness in her father's eyes had faded.

"I suppose, but it's not just that. I'm being summoned I think. I may be able to help figure out what's wrong with the AT installers."

Her father's mouth twisted as if he were thinking. Then he spoke. "Your mother had dreams like that too, you know, before she died."

Ceera's heart stopped for the second time since he'd arrived. "No," she stammered, "I didn't know."

Memories of her mother were sparse. She had been quiet and kind, the type of woman who coddled her young daughter to the extreme. This had frustrated a young Ceera, desperate to have free reign around the farm. Of course, this had ended when her mother became bedridden.

"Well, you were pretty young when she passed."

His matter-of-fact tone was like a slap in the face. She stared past him. "Yes, I was young"—she fought to keep her voice level—"and you couldn't raise a daughter by yourself. So you gave me up to the authorities."

"I gave you up to give you a chance, a life better than the one on the farm."

"That would indicate you cared," she snapped as reality closed in around her. "So why haven't you visited me?"

"I do care," he said in a gruff voice that matched his appearance. "But you were too much like your mother. I had to send you away."

Ceera's vision blurred with tears. "Coward," she whispered.

"Cowards don't give up their only daughter to protect her."

"Protect me from what? A loving home? Oh wait, you couldn't provide that. So you're back telling me this why?"

"Look, no matter what you think, I thought sending

you to Semadon would keep your mind away from the woods. I didn't want you to end up like her."

"Like her, what is that supposed to mean?"

"It means on the verge of being committed to an insane asylum." Her father's cold voice tamed her flaring temper. "Like her."

"An insane asylum?" she asked in shock. The fenced in property on the far side of Semadon had always caused her to shiver on the few occasions she had reason to walk past.

"I hid her condition as best I could," he added more quietly, "to prevent it from happening. But word always gets out eventually."

Ceera swallowed loudly. "What did the dreams have to do with it?"

"Maybe nothing," he replied. "They were deep inside her, not as vivid as yours. She couldn't reach them. It bothered her. If you ask me, they're the reason she went crazy."

Ceera closed her eyes and remembered the feel of her mother's soft caresses down the back of her head. The memory was replaced by a reassuring pat on the shoulder. She opened her eyes. Her father's dirt-stained hand now gently gripped her arm.

"Just be careful. Don't let these dreams get the better of you like they did her."

Chapter Five

CEERA BARELY KEPT pace with Dassius on the way to the library the next morning. Her thoughts had turned chaotic since her father's visit, and she had no choice but to reanalyze everything she had ever known. He had sent her away to protect her. So he said. Could she begin to forgive him for that? More importantly, did he care if she did?

His visit had been brief. He had left before she could ask more questions, said he had to get back to the fields. She wasn't sure if she believed his promise that he would tune into the global update to see how she was faring. After all, according to him she had followed in her mother's footsteps. If he couldn't handle it when she was younger, he couldn't be expected to deal with it now. Although she had reassured him that the dreams were not adversely affecting her as they had her mother.

Even so, it was safer to consider the whole encounter a fluke and not the beginning of an actual father daughter relationship. And if not a fluke then a warning, one even a man as apathetic as him felt compelled to relay.

The news about her more affectionate parent was even more troubling. Her mother had been plagued by similar dreams. They may have even contributed to her mental downfall, which meant their meaning went deeper than village affairs. It was also personal, in a potentially negative way. How it all connected was a mystery that needed to be unraveled very carefully.

When they entered the library, Dassius strode over to the front desk and stood in front of the librarian, who was inserting cards from a disorganized pile into a file.

She looked up and gave him a thin smile. "How can I help you?"

"We have an appointment with the Caretaker of Ancient Affairs," Dassius said.

"An appointment?" The woman glanced at the screen on her correspondence system and pressed a few buttons. "Yes, of course. The Caretaker's office is near the very back of the library. He will be awaiting your arrival."

They turned and walked past the row of PID's and several large curving bookcases. Countless statues of all sizes reading books protruded from the walls, but the spot where she had seen the female statue remained empty.

They passed though the planetary orb room, which contained a replication of the solar system to scale including the eight planets, their many moons and a giant luminescent reproduction of the sun. Each orb spun and moved at the rate of real time, which of course was remarkably slow. A gate encompassed it to discourage any Semions from sabotaging the flow of the orbits.

Someone had trespassed into the display area once and caused a few planets to misalign. The gate was erected to avoid such a mishap from ever happening again. The true shame was each orb pictured the planet it represented with beautiful accuracy, but from behind the gate it was impossible to view these details.

They continued around a dim hallway until they reached its lone wooden door. *The Caretaker of Ancient Affairs* was carved with a flourish at eye level. A metal orb hung under the words, and Dassius knocked it hard against the door.

Moments later, the door opened. A fragile-looking older gentleman, several inches shorter than Dassius, peered out at them. A long gray beard hung to the middle of his chest. Wrinkles etched his skin, and he wore spectacles a bit too large for his face. His eyes were lively though, and he opened the door wide. "Mr. Rucien and Ms. Kestlyn, please come in and sit down."

He motioned them toward two wooden chairs facing his desk. Atop it, a globe leaned against a tower of books that threatened to topple over the edge. Ceera and Dassius sat down carefully.

Overfilled bookshelves covered the walls, each reaching to the height of the ceiling which stretched far above. A portable stairwell wedged against one of the shelves: a contraption on wheels with steps spiraling upward alongside a corresponding railing.

The room had a musty smell. She muffled a sneeze within the crook of her arm.

"Can you imagine the time it would take for me to dust each and every book inside this room?" the Caretaker asked her.

"No, I can't," she replied. "There has to be thousands of them."

"Even opening a window would surely help," Dassius said.

"I could if I had one." The Caretaker sat down behind his desk.

"I assume you already know why we're here," Dassius began, but the look on the Caretaker's face stopped him.

"Quite actually young man, I'm clueless. Do tell."

"Didn't you attend the meeting at the Aurora the other day, the meeting with the mystics?" Ceera asked.

"The meeting with the mystics," the Caretaker repeated as he looked up at the ceiling. "I haven't been to a meeting at the Aurora with mystics in attendance for quite some time."

"Then didn't you view the meeting on the PID?" She thought everyone tuned into them on a regular basis, except for Dassius as she had recently learned.

"I'm behind in my PID viewing. It's difficult for me to keep up with current events when I am expected to be the expert of antiquity."

Ceera glanced at Dassius, who hardly appeared stunned. A light smile grazed his lips, and he held his hands in the air with his fingertips touching.

"I suppose you were in no way rattled by what occurred last week?" Dassius asked.

The Caretaker gave him a blank look.

"An alarm went off!" Ceera said with a tinge of exasperation. "You had to have heard it."

"Why yes," the Caretaker exclaimed in a jovial tone. "It certainly was odd. I'd been standing on my stairwell looking for this book about a particular ground quake, you know, the one that caused that crack in the artist's orbit, when it sounded. So loud it almost knocked me down the stairs. After I regained my composure, I thought maybe someone had entered without knocking, that I was being spied on. When there was no one in sight, I just attributed it to my growing senility. I am nearing ninety-two years old you know."

The Caretaker winked, hopped to his feet and began

climbing his stairwell. "I never did finish finding that book," he called over his shoulder.

"Do you think we should fill him in?" Ceera whispered.

"No point in cutting short his life expectancy," Dassius whispered back. He cleared his throat. "Well, to make a long story short," he continued loudly since the Caretaker was gaining distance, "Ceera and I will soon be traveling to unexplored areas."

The old man jerked his head away from the book he'd been thumbing through and looked down at them. "You are planning to equip yourselves with weaponry to protect you from predatory beasts, I presume?"

"We've taken care to think of everything. What we need from you is some information about the Archaics. Our travels begin with them. We're told they can bring forth knowledge contained within the elements."

"Ah! Visiting the Archaics? That will be quite an experience indeed." The Caretaker nodded excitedly. The motion rocked the stairwell, and Ceera stuck her hand out to prevent it from rolling.

"Yes, and we're looking for some advice. We only have vague recollections about them from stories told to us in our youth."

"Well, don't expect an easy time of it," the Caretaker said.

"I know what to expect," Dassius replied defensively, then went on to add more calmly, "at least I'm aware it will not be a leisurely venture. Do you know anything else about them?"

"Of course, there are books and books." The Caretaker swung his arm out and almost fell down the stairwell.

"We don't have time to read books and books. What we need from you is an abbreviated account of—"

"Will you please sit down here with us again?" Ceera interrupted. "I don't wish to see you fall."

"Why, certainly madam." The old man stepped lightly down and perched on his chair. "I didn't mean to scare you."

"Thank you."

"Now, the Archaics," the Caretaker said. "Their personalities can be a trifle multifarious at times."

"What do you mean?" Ceera positioned her hand on her recorder.

"Well, you see, they embody contradictions. Good and evil all wrapped up together."

The comment left her feeling unsettled. Her fingers moved stiffly as she typed.

"The mystics said nothing about good or evil." Dassius drummed his fingers on the arm of his chair. "They just said their advice will be helpful."

"It will be helpful," the Caretaker agreed, "but you may also find yourselves receiving more than just advice."

Ceera's fingers froze. "Like what?"

"You just never know," he said. "Life can be precarious when dealing with them, although some of the Archaics are more good natured than others."

"You make it sound as if we'd better watch our backs," Dassius said.

"Better you hear it from me than learn it from them," the Caretaker said with a shrug.

"Are you implying they are dangerous or just powerful?" Ceera forced herself to continue typing.

"Why both, of course. Anywhere there is power there is

danger and vice versa. They have their good days and their bad days; just don't be the cause of either one."

"Can you tell us more about their personalities?" Dassius wore a look of intense contemplation.

"Certainly, now if I were you I would begin with Oc~ea of the water. She is the one who mothers children, and this compassion may carry over to the way she treats you."

"She mothers?" Ceera exclaimed. "How did she find a breeding partner compatible with her genetic design? I thought the Archaics were enigmas without any Semion instincts in the slightest."

"Oc~ea is one who creates her own paths, my dear. She is so strong with the ways of the water that she conjured up an ancient sea god to impregnate her. Very intuitive, that one."

Ceera fumbled in her typing and almost dropped her recorder. Dassius only smirked. The old man looked back and forth at them as he waited for the next question.

"How will we find her?" Dassius said. "Near what body of water does she reside?"

"Where she or any of them reside is not common knowledge, nor can it be found in any of my books." The Caretaker smiled sadly. "In fact, figuring out where they dwell can be tricky enough by itself."

"I didn't know they kept where they lived a secret," Ceera said. This venture was becoming a lot more complicated than she had foreseen.

"Secrecy is part of their nature. You don't think they are just sitting around waiting for guests, do you?"

"I suppose not," she replied.

"What would you suggest we do to overcome this riddle of finding them?" Dassius asked.

"The answer to your riddle can be found within the legend. What does each signify? They live in areas most compatible with what they stand for."

"That makes sense, but how do we incorporate what you just said into a way of finding them? This planet is by no means small."

"Getting started is quite simple. Input the name of each one, along with the element they represent, into the Atomic Transport System. It will scan the planet for the strongest reading and draw up coordinates approximating their whereabouts. The system will place you in the cylinder nearest to their dwellings. From there, you must use your instincts to pinpoint the exact location."

"I was not aware the AT system contained this feature, and I thought you were not knowledgeable about current events and thus recent inventions." Dassius raised an eyebrow.

The old man chuckled. "Normally I'm not, but while he was in the process of inventing it, Hegliod came my way for information. He wanted to ensure his idea was original, so he discussed with me all the intricacies of his system. He said it could communicate with the energy grid and thus could transport between cylinders based on all types of input data. This being the case, I expect the system would be able to detect the locations of the Archaics, especially since they have such an impact on this planet."

"So you are certain the AT system has this feature built into it?"

"Quite positive," the Caretaker replied. "Hegliod visited me again upon completion. He presented me with a book that outlined the specifics of his machine, claiming it was important the future have a detailed account of his process of invention. He had been rather disgusted with my collection of books about inventors from the past."

"Why?" Ceera asked.

"Most of them were not firsthand accounts and were written by Semions who did not fully understand the manner in which a particular invention worked."

"So we will have to use the AT system for travel." Dassius nodded slowly before turning to Ceera. "I will inform High Service."

Ceera remembered the recent system failure and tried to ignore her discomfort.

"Is it possible we can borrow this book?" Dassius asked. "It may come in handy."

"No question I would let you borrow it, except—" the old man paused as he shifted his eyes around the room.

"Except what?"

"Except it is missing," the Caretaker said in a hushed tone. "Don't tell Hegliod. It will surface again eventually."

"That's okay; we'll do fine without it."

"Most of the book is just technical information anyway." The Caretaker waved his hand dismissively.

"I hope there are cylinders near where they live," Dassius said. "I hear they are spread out quite evenly on the grid."

"For your sake, I hope so too."

"What about the other three?" Dassius asked.

"Atmos is a lively fellow. His personality can be a little up in the air. He bounces from facetious to serious and back again in mere seconds. He will make you think and tell you a good story, that's for sure."

"And the other two?"

"Beware of Luma and her fire. She has a short fuse.

Her temper flares up quicker than a fire in a brush. Tiptoe delicately in her presence. She is not afraid to lash out when she feels the need."

"Lash out?" Ceera frowned. "At us?"

"Sure, and she'll take pleasure in it. So be on guard."

"Okay, so who's left?" Dassius gripped the armrest of his chair, as if ready to stand.

"Baric is the most omniscient of them all. He lies in the shadows and is prone to focus on the root of an issue."

"He sounds like someone I can relate to," Dassius said.

"Just remember that Baric is very loyal to what he represents. He will take from you as easily as he gives."

There was silence as Ceera and Dassius pondered the statement.

"Anything else you think we should know?" Ceera asked.

"Don't forget to be courteous. If you fail to show even the slightest bit of respect, you will be turned away." The Caretaker squinted at them as though he were sizing them up himself.

"Why wouldn't we show respect?" Dassius said.

Ceera looked purposely up at the ceiling.

"You never know how you will appear to an Archaic. Watch what you say and be careful," the Caretaker warned.

The old man was now winded. Most of his vigor had dissipated. A slight whistle intermingled with his breath.

"I suppose we will let you get back to what you were doing." Dassius stood.

"Thanks for all your advice," Ceera said as she turned off her recorder.

"If you need anything else just let me know," the Caretaker told them. "And if you have any problems with the Archaics, just mention names of the ones you visited prior.

Although they may clash from time to time, they're still very dependent upon one another."

Ceera stood and smiled while Dassius headed toward the door.

"And one more thing," the Caretaker continued, causing both of them to hesitate yet again. "Can you remind me which book I'd been looking for when you asked me to come down from my stairwell?"

"You were looking for a book about a ground quake." Ceera said. "Let me fetch it for you." She ascended up the stairwell to retrieve the book the Caretaker had set sideways on the shelf.

Dassius waited with his hand on the doorknob.

"That's right." The old man gave her a weak smile. "What a good memory you possess, my dear."

"I'm a scribe," she responded as she handed him the book. "I remember everything."

Hegliod had not been particularly thrilled when he was called to the Aurora for another conference with High Service. All the distractions were making it impossible for his idea to return. Granted certain matters required his immediate attention, such as fixing AT controls and the two women's noses, but what now? His machines remained in working order. What could possibly be left?

He knocked heavily on the door to the Aurora. An attendant answered and escorted him to a small conference room. Leynin and Asfin stood when he entered.

"Hello Hegliod," Leynin greeted him. "Good to see you again."

"Same to you, my pleasure," he replied.

"We're glad you were able to come on such short notice," Asfin said.

Hegliod responded with a quick nod, not a fan of what was rightfully called small talk. They all sat down. Hegliod's hands fumbled nervously under the table.

"We would like to discuss the safety of your AT system," Leynin said. "Two Semions will be using the system to travel the planet, and we need to make sure you are confident it will continue to work properly."

Hegliod swallowed loudly. "Of course I am."

"Tell us," Asfin said, "your thoughts about what happened to the AT installers. You are aware of their misfortune?"

"Yes, I've heard. Terrible circumstance."

"Do you feel what happened to them had anything to do with your system or more to do with the Planetary Stability reading?"

"The reading of course. Why else would so many other cylinders been built without consequence?"

"Very true, and we have considered that point as well. However, it appears your AT system has been put in question ever since the nose swapping incident. Let's just say the two women involved share a common feature. Do you understand what I mean?"

"Yes," Hegliod replied wearily. Both the women were well-known gossips.

"Their gossip has aroused suspicion," Asfin said. "Several Semions have voiced their concerns. We have no choice but to address them."

"Before we elaborate, let's make one thing clear," Leynin said. "High Service does not doubt the integrity of your system; however, we cannot ignore the concerns of our people, no matter how insensible they are."

"I understand your position," Hegliod grumbled. "Now what do you need from me?"

"We would like you to issue a statement in defense of your AT system so we can put all these worries to rest. Do you think you can have one ready by tonight? We know it's short notice, but our two travelers will be leaving tomorrow morning."

Hegliod nodded though disdain consumed him.

"Great," Asfin said. "We would like it read over the global update during the evening program. We will stand by to show our support."

Hegliod hung his head as he walked home after the meeting. The two women who had suffered the bodily misfortune had a right to be skeptical. What was difficult to endure was that everyone else now held this opinion as well. Why all the scrutiny?

Several years back when he had presented his invention to the public, they had reveled at his intellectual genius. AT cylinders had been installed all over Semadon. He had even been the first Semion to travel by AT cylinder to prove their safety. So they didn't work as fast as his original claim, most everyone forgave him of this oversight and let the flawless performance of the machines measure his accomplishment.

Then, while in the process of expanding the scope of his system, the Planetary Stability Monitor senses an irregularity and his machines are immediately blamed. He knew his machines had nothing to do with it, but everyone's senses were running amok. If the reason for disorder was unclear just blame innovation. What better excuse than something most Semions were not able to understand anyway?

Now, to top it all off, he had the mundane task of writing a speech he would have to relay in a few hours. After concentrating on this chore for the rest of the afternoon, not to mention devoting time to its revision and the actual reading of it, his former idea would surely slip away forever.

Hegliod kicked a pebble and watched it roll across the orbit. This action roused an enormous amount of dust. It mingled with the air before settling back down around his feet. He wrinkled his nose and continued walking.

It occurred to him that he had never seen anyone sweeping the orbits. They were covered in dust and littered with rubbish. Most of it was small enough to go unnoticed by the casual passerby, but to someone staring as attentively as he was, the visual was disgusting.

Hegliod allowed his frustrations to subside as he continued to stare at the filth surrounding his feet.

✀

Upon Risa's insistence, High Service assigned both her and Karnen the task of checking on the AT installers every day. The men were housed at the Recuperation Clinic: a tall building on the far side of town. The officials exited their travel pod and walked toward it. The grand revolving door opened automatically when its sensor registered their approach.

The pair walked through the doorway and waited while the platform rotated, before stepping into the plainly decorated foyer. The receptionist glanced up from behind her desk and motioned for them to pass. She had grown accustomed to their visits and did not require them to sign in since they were High Service officials. She pressed buttons on the correspondence system.

Risa and Karnen continued through the bare, white hallway to the elevator. Risa chose level three. The button lit up and rang when they reached their desired floor. A medical attendant waited outside and ushered them to the AT installers' room.

Doctors holding clipboards huddled around the three beds. They looked up when the officials entered and moved to the side.

The men were cocooned in white blankets. Machines monitoring heart rate and breathing patterns hooked into each man. Although they were awake, their pupils were unmoving. Incoherent words spilled sporadically from their lips.

Risa found the sight upsetting. She and Karnen observed the AT installers for a few moments before joining the doctors to discuss whether there were any new developments. The doctors confirmed their status remained unchanged. Risa pulled Karnen away from the group for privacy.

"I hope we are making the right decision," she said quietly.

"Our backing of Hegliod's system is crucial to the well-being of all Semions," Karnen replied. "How could we be making the wrong decision?"

"Hegliod's agreement to issue a statement may calm the nerves of the people, but what will it do for them?" She motioned to the three men.

Their chests heaved up and down beneath the bed sheets. An unsettling vibe rose and fell with each breath.

Chapter Six

SEMIONS MILLED ABOUT the inner orbits in anticipation of the departure. The farewell ceremony was about to start at the main AT cylinder. Spectators clustered around the newly-erected stage on which a group of officials stood alongside Ceera and Dassius.

Dassius chatted with the officials, but Ceera was preoccupied with her own thoughts. She had watched a speech the previous night on the Global Update. Hegliod's words had been reassuring; they had succeeded in terminating most of her trepidation about relying on the system for travel.

Dreams from the previous night overshadowed her leftover apprehension. Amidst her tossing and turning, the forest still lurked vividly in her subconscious as did fleeting thoughts about her mother. Though she had not slept well, fatigue dared not hinder her. A sense of purpose fueled her energy unlike ever before.

At the briefing, High Service had supplied them with clothes designed for ease of motion. Ceera wore light grey pants with long pockets on the front of her thighs and ankle-high boots made for climbing and running. Her shirt was a soft black with short sleeves and a hood. She had stuffed her jacket in her pack.

Dassius's attire was similar to hers except colored in darker gray and black. He wore sturdy black boots and a belt replete with a knife holster. His shirt had both a collar and detachable hood.

Though comfortable in her new clothes, being the center of attention had the opposite effect. She scanned the crowd for a familiar face. Drusilla and Litha stood with a group of scribes she knew as acquaintances. Litha waved excitedly while Drusilla held her hand up and wiggled her fingers in acknowledgment.

Ceera hesitated before waving back, trying to ignore the guilt that surfaced. She had not had time to return Litha's call the previous day, though her friend hardly seemed bothered by the slight. As for Drusilla, she was a difficult woman to like, but she had been the only adult figure in Ceera's life since childhood. That had to count for something, and she hadn't bothered to consider how the turn of events had affected her mentor until now. Perhaps Drusilla was the reason for High Service's delay in contacting her and not the man she stood beside.

She glanced over at Dassius, who was thriving on all the attention. His posture reminded her of a picture of a warrior in a book she had read during her youth. She hoped her amused look resembled a noble smile.

A giant hush swept over the audience as Karnen approached the microphone and began speaking. Other scribes in the audience would record the event, so she allowed her mind to wander. Besides, there was nothing he could say that would inspire her more than the summoning inside her own head.

৯

Falken slunk up the walkway to the Aurora. Normally an official or attendant oversaw the area, but the post was vacant. He commended himself for acting on his assumption that everyone in Semadon, even High Service officials, would be watching the much anticipated departure of Ceera and Dassius and not be in their proper positions. Any officials remaining inside the building were most likely of a lower sphere and thus not the most experienced. He had a better chance of pulling one over on a sphere one than a sphere three.

He reached the door and lightly knocked to make sure no officials stood near the entryway. When no one answered, he took this as his chance to enter unseen. Instead of inputting a code into the keypad, he manually opened the door and stooped down to pick up a tiny sphere wedged alongside the door frame. It had prevented the door from latching in place and thus requiring the use of the code.

"Well placed," he mumbled.

Falken had hid in the bushes all morning waiting for the opportune moment to place it there. It was a simpler solution than picking the lock or guessing the code. Plus, its small size caused the door to appear shut to the casual observer. There had been much in and out earlier, what with the carrying of equipment to the departure site. The door had been carelessly propped open, enabling him to take advantage.

He crept inside and around the hallway, passing several closed doors, and stopped when he came to one partway open. He peeked inside. Several officials slouched in chairs around a global update sphere which displayed an official giving a speech with Ceera and Dassius standing nearby.

Falken swung back around and pressed his back against the wall by the doorway. He took a slow, deep breath to strengthen his nerve and tiptoed past, pausing when an official in the room cleared his throat. He turned and backed away, waiting for someone to appear. Only the faint talking coming from the global update sphere met his ears. His breathing returned to normal as he continued down the hall.

When he entered the control room, the vast array of buttons, dials and monitors overpowered him. How would it feel to be the inventor of this technological masterpiece? Not that he wished this to be the case, for he was too proud for envy. Still, he reveled at the array of control mechanisms, some of them linked to screens showing swirls of colors and patterns that aligned with specific areas on the planet.

He ran his fingers over the controls, wistful of the impact he could cause by tampering with any one of them. The power to prematurely end the travels of Ceera and Dassius was his, but he shrugged the temptation away. He had already learned his lesson. Mischief by itself brought only trouble. His meddling in the Planetary Orb room years ago had earned him the punishment of a few added years of transition. Mischief coupled with strategy, on the other hand, now that combination could spawn profit.

He studied the entire arrangement until he found the screen representing Hegliod's energy grid. He pressed a button to overlay it with the map. Red dots designated the location of each AT cylinder. One currently flashed, the one Ceera and Dassius would soon be using. He didn't have much time.

He scanned the controls for the correspondence dials and examined them. It appeared all the AT cylinders corresponded with one place, and of course it was inside the Aurora. He pressed more buttons. Images of different rooms flashed onscreen. He stopped when it displayed where communication between the AT system and High Service was set up. Memorizing the location, he set out to find room 5R.

Falken exited the room and snuck around the hall. He turned into a different hallway and counted the doors he passed. When he reached room 5R, he tried the handle and was pleased to find it unlocked.

Upon entering, he neared the correspondence area where a few chairs faced a large spherical screen and a set of controls. He pried open the panel beneath the controls to expose a silver orb that shone brilliantly though it was encased in darkness. He removed a tiny black oval from his pocket. It resonated between his fingers. He attached it securely behind the much larger orb and winced when they touched. A sharp high-pitched sound echoed before dying down to silence.

Falken quickly attached the panel back to the compartment. Fearing he had drawn the attention of the officials, he looked for a place to hide. He hid behind the door, his only option, and waited for oncoming footsteps. There were none. The officials were so engrossed, so complacent even, that if they had heard the sound they had disregarded it as nothing.

He edged his way out of the room and into the hallway. He walked in the opposite direction to avoid passing by the room where the officials sat around the global update.

When the door to the Aurora shut behind him, Falken breathed a sigh of relief. His vantage point was entirely empty of anyone. All that was left for him to do now was go back to his dwelling and wait.

∽

While the official spoke, Ceera's mind wandered to the briefing she had attended with Dassius the previous evening.

The two of them sat facing a group of officials of varying sphere levels.

"We would like your travel to be uninterrupted," Risa said. "Please do not come back to Semadon until after you have spoken with each Archaic. This would only prolong matters and could cause feeble-minded Semions to stalk the main AT cylinder. We do not want to encourage idolization or disrupt daily operations, which will indeed happen if this area is clogged with admirers.

"This doesn't mean you won't be allowed to return to Semadon at all," she continued. "Just keep in mind it will only be acceptable due to an emergency."

"What kind of emergency?" Ceera asked.

"I will elaborate in yet a moment," Risa responded.

"You will be required to check in with us through the correspondence system after conversing with each Archaic," Karnen said. "This is important so that we can keep the public informed through the global update, and also so we can keep each other informed. If the health of the AT installers improve, and they are able to remember anything about their venture, well, let's just say it could be very beneficial for our endeavor.

"Ceera," he continued, "you will record what the Archaics say so that Dassius can transmit their words back to us. You must also keep track of the consumables. If you are unable to find anything edible along the way once you run out of your food supply, do return to Semadon. But again, we stress you only do so in case of an emergency."

Ceera gave a quick, attentive nod.

"Now"—Karnen's voice dropped and he studied her closely— "we are very interested in this ancient manuscript you've mentioned, or relic as we'll call it. Any new information about it needs to be relayed to us immediately, whether it be from the Archaics or these dreams you've been having."

All eyes rested on her during the ensuing silence. She suddenly felt like she was under a microscope, except for what reason she did not know. She dug her fingernails into her palms, forcing herself to remain calm. "Of course," she responded softly.

Karnen glanced at Risa, and she took the cue to continue with the lecture.

"Dassius will carry the weaponry, and it will be his responsibility to keep you both safe. His training will ensure he will be ready to act if danger arises. If an injury occurs, please return to Semadon."

Having to rely on Dassius for her safety was too aggravating to dwell on. Yet this was the repercussions of living in a peaceful society with no reason to teach combat to a scribe. Welfare over warfare had been drummed into her head at an early age. For that matter, she should be thankful they were even allowing weapons.

"Dassius, you will also chart the course of travel. We are expecting your foresight abilities to be at full capacity. Also, we are providing a tent for you to take along."

Ceera hadn't slept in a tent since the environment training she had undergone in school. This class had taught her what nature produced that was edible and a rash of other things she assumed would be useful during their travels. The tent she shared with Litha had been very small. There had barely been enough room for the both of them.

"How large will the tent be?" The words spilled out before she had a chance to think about how they might sound.

Everyone in the room turned to stare at her.

"Don't worry, close quarters may prove themselves to be more of a comfort to you than a burden," a sphere seven spoke slyly to her with a wink.

Though he sat on the outskirts of the conference area, his words were quite audible to everyone in attendance and her cheeks grew hot.

"Harnol!" Risa cast a glare at him. "Ceera asks a legitimate question." She turned back to Ceera. "Don't worry. It's large enough for four Semions."

"Good," Ceera said, refusing to look Dassius's way. "I toss and turn a lot."

"Can we get back to the important stuff?" Dassius broke the amused silence with a wave of indifference.

"Only if Ceera hasn't any more questions," Risa replied.

"Ceera?" Karnen asked.

His inquiring tone played in her head as her name was spoken in real time as well. The memory of the briefing left her thoughts, and she returned to the present. She eyed the same official who was scrutinizing her once again. "Yes?"

"Yes, you do have something to contribute?" Confusion creased Karnen's brow.

"Of course I do, thank you." Ceera whisked the microphone out of the official's hand and held it near her lips. "I would like to say that Dassius and I are fully committed to the task before us." She handed the microphone to Dassius's already outstretched hand.

"Rest assured," he said. "We will return with answers."

She was surprised when he promptly handed the microphone back to the official.

"Now without any further ado, we shall see the both of you off. Good luck and please be careful." Karnen motioned them toward the cylinder.

Loud cheers from the crowd filled Ceera's ears as she descended down the stage. An official opened the door to the cylinder and she entered. Dassius lingered in the doorway for a moment, apparently savoring his last moments of glory, and waved before shutting the door.

She allowed her pack to slide down her back and drop onto the floor. Dassius also dropped his pack and together they faced the destination panel.

His fingers worked the controls; corresponding beeps responded at each press of a button. When he finally pushed the transport button, a series of symbols popped up on the screen. The sequence coiled inward as it lengthened. Then the entire design disappeared and a set of coordinates flashed in its place.

A familiar feeling washed over her, one she experienced whenever she traveled via AT system. Her body went numb while her surroundings disintegrated before her eyes. The concept of time became ambiguous. Her physicality melted away, reducing her to a phantom of tangibility. Her oscillating essence traversed space, existing only as a stream with infinite possible directions. But the AT system was a well-built machine and did not patronize potentials. The journey was ending just as abruptly as it had begun.

Ceera's body reformed while the blurry images encompassing her molded back into reality. She again stood in an AT cylinder with Dassius at her side. They took a moment to gather their senses.

"Always a little unnerving, wouldn't you say?" Dassius

turned to her, his face regaining the color it had lost during their travel.

"I can never get used to it," she replied.

"Don't worry, our children and theirs will become so used to traveling in these things that over time our discomfort will fade from Semion consciousness."

She couldn't help but give him a funny look, which seemed to startle him.

"I mean the children of our generation of course."

"I know what you meant," Ceera said.

There was a moment of awkward silence. She took it as a cue to pick up her pack.

"Ready?" His hand clutched the lever on the door.

"I think so."

He turned the handle and opened the door.

A field of tall grass stretched into the distance. The grass was not so high that it hid the patches of water up ahead. Ceera took a deep breath and stifled a look of dismay. There had been nothing in her dreams insinuating she would be traveling within the unpredictable terrain of a wetland.

CHAPTER SEVEN

"YOU REALLY HAVE to have an appreciation for these AT installers." Dassius stepped out of the cylinder and held his hand out for Ceera to follow.

She ignored his hand and stepped beside him, her feet squishing onto the ground. At least her shoes were waterproof.

"Although as you can see," he continued, "we are right on the outskirts." He shielded his eyes from the sun and pointed behind the cylinder.

Trees towered in the distance. Clusters of large leaves fanned out atop long, jagged trunks.

"Are we going that way?" she asked.

Dassius laughed and started walking away from the trees. "You think Oc~ea can be found on dry land? Did you think this was going to be easy?"

"No, of course not," she said quickly.

"Just follow close. We'll get through it."

A clump of grass swallowed Dassius up to his chest before he splashed into some water. She stepped delicately behind. It was clear Dassius was unaffected by the water. He trekked through it with the same sure-footedness as he did the dry grassy patches.

Ceera made every effort to keep dry. She paused on a

mound of dirt and contemplated her next move while he surged ahead. She leaped to the next dry spot, but her back foot splashed behind her.

Dassius turned and gave her an annoyed look. "What are you doing back there?"

"Trying to stay dry."

"You're wasting time. This is nothing compared to what's ahead."

She couldn't argue when she knew he was right. Heaving a huge sigh, she stepped into the cool water. It splashed up to her knees.

Dassius waited with his arms crossed in front of his chest. "It's not the water you should be afraid of," he told her. "It's the creatures swimming around in it you need to watch out for."

"What creatures?"

"The snapping turtles are more of a bother than a threat. The larger reptiles are more dangerous. They can swim as fast as they can run."

She whipped her head around to critique her surroundings.

"We may have to venture deeper before we encounter one of those. Still, you better stay close. Wild animals don't always do what is considered to be most likely."

If his intention was to frighten her so she would move faster, it worked. She did not allow him to be more than a few feet ahead. Remembering how he had offered his hand outside the cylinder, she regretted not accepting it. Grabbing onto him now would reveal that she was scared. She didn't want to make this truth so obvious.

White birds with long necks swooped overhead, dropping down occasionally to perch on mounds of dirt. They stood on skinny legs, their beaks darting sporadically into the grass. Raising their wings majestically, they flew away when Ceera and Dassius neared.

The surroundings switched back and forth between solid dirt and muddy water, as if the area itself was indecisive and didn't want to commit to either one. She followed him into some waist-high water and stood still momentarily to steady herself. The water forced her to walk in slow motion as unknown things moved past her legs.

The sun shone down vibrantly. It warmed her though her pants were soaked and water had trickled into her boots. Her feet slid around inside them.

After what seemed like hours, Dassius stopped atop a grassy mound. "It's going to be a lot rougher now."

She peered around him. A swamp edged the land up ahead. Trees with large buttresses protruded from the murky water.

"Unless…" Dassius cupped his chin in contemplation.

"Unless what?"

"See that tree?" He pointed to one on the edge of dry land. Its trunk leaned precariously over the water. "Sit as far up on it as you can. I'm going to gather some wood to make a raft."

Only a few branches poked out of the grass. Most had fallen into the water. "Don't you want my help?"

"No, stay on the trunk. I'll have to do some scavenging along with some climbing and hacking. Reptiles are sneaky animals, especially the ones we're concerned about, but as far as I know, they have a hard time climbing trees."

Ceera willfully obeyed. She climbed halfway up the trunk and sat, observing Dassius's movements with keen attention. He made a pile near the base of her tree, parting the long blades of grass to see what hid below. The water was still, yet she knew its calm demeanor could be deceptive.

The pile of branches grew steadily once Dassius gave up searching the ground. He climbed a tree and cut off several large branches, tossing them into his pile. He then focused on acquiring the smaller, more flexible ones and dangled these over his shoulder until he had a thick bundle. He swung down with one hand keeping his bundle intact while the other braced for when he hit the ground.

She was impressed by his work ethic, for he didn't let himself get distracted and his energy never seemed to wane. She, on the other hand, appreciated being able to rest. Her legs stretched along the trunk so the sun could dry her. She was just starting to entertain the idea of taking off her shoes to dry them out too, when a loud splashing sound burst from the swampy edge.

A large alligator darted out of the previously tranquil water and lunged at Dassius as he again swung down to dry ground. Ceera screamed and almost fell off the trunk.

He flung his bundle of ropelike sticks toward the pile and jumped backwards. Several of them fell short, but she didn't dare attempt to retrieve them. She watched in panic as the reptile ran toward him on bent stubby legs that boasted an unbelievable swiftness. Its large flat jaw opened up to a mouthful of sharply curved teeth. The alligator stood half the size of Dassius's height, its length so immense she could not yet see the end of its tail.

Dassius clenched the handle of his knife between his teeth. He catapulted himself off a nearby tree and onto the reptile's back. The creature tried to bite him, its entire body twisting to such extremes they both rolled into the water.

"Dassius," she screamed again, leaning dangerously over the side.

The wild thrashing beneath the water was almost too much for her to bear. When it stopped, tears sprang into her eyes. The alligator floated peacefully on top, apparently the victor.

When Dassius poked his head out from the water moments later, she felt like laughing and crying at the same time.

"I cut its throat," he told her, climbing back onto dry ground. "I didn't want to, but I didn't have much choice." A streak of blood ran down his arm.

"Are you okay? You're bleeding."

"It's not mine." He bent over and splashed water up and down his arms.

"It came for you when you jumped from the tree, like it was timing its attack." Her heart was still beating rapidly.

"I knew it would happen," Dassius said with a shrug. He walked over to his pile of branches and scooped up the ones that had fallen short.

"You did? You didn't seem worried."

"Worried? About what?"

"About the alligator!"

He crouched down and began separating the smaller and larger branches into piles. "I've been trained for circumstances to change suddenly. In fact, I was expecting it. How could I not be prepared for what I knew would happen?"

She said nothing as a newfound respect for him formed.

"Did you think my training was a joke?"

Ceera shook her head quickly. She didn't want to admit that she hadn't thought about it much at all until now.

⌁

After the send-off, Leynin and Asfin visited the Planetary Stability Laboratory to check on the status of the device that had triggered the alarm. An attendant escorted them to the room containing the Planetary Stability Monitor. The large sphere levitated in an atmospheric bubble that was held in place by a treelike stand with legs branching onto the floor.

A technician named Griven waited for them. He led them to where the control panel jutted from the front of the stand. "As you can see," he told them, "nothing has changed. The forested region is still lit up." He gestured to a thumb sized area on the sphere that glowed bright red.

"Why has the annunciator stopped beeping?" Asfin asked.

"Ah." Griven grinned ruefully. "It hasn't. As you can imagine, it was quite distracting to have it continuing to make sound. We had to adjust the volume to save our sanity, quite frankly."

"Although I understand the reasoning, isn't this a potential hazard?" asked Leynin. "Doesn't the beeping correspond with the intensity of the energy waves it measures?"

"Yes, however, the light remains red. Plus, we've programmed the device to override our volume setting in the event the reading intensifies. An energy wave increase would trigger the onset of the beeping yet again."

"Now that's a clever feature," Asfin murmured.

"We thought so," Griven agreed.

The trio stared at the globe. The glowing area continued to throb rhythmically.

"What you see is what we have observed since the onset

of the initial beeping. As ironic as it sounds, the abnormal reading has, for now, stabilized."

The two officials raised their eyebrows at the comment, yet continued to stare at the lit up area. Its propensity to remain lit was, for the moment, out of their hands.

ᔎ

Dassius arranged the larger branches into the shape of a raft. Ceera mustered the courage to join him, and she sat on her knees, attentive to their surroundings. Her hands rested on her lap in tight fists.

Dassius glanced at her and chuckled. He grabbed a handful of the ropelike twigs and used them to tie the larger branches together.

"What's so funny?"

"You. So eager to come, yet you've been completely on edge this entire time."

"What do you expect," she snapped and then added in a quieter tone, "when I am not in the position to predict what is going to happen as you seem to be?"

"As I seem to be," he repeated. He tied another ropelike twig around the limbs to tighten them.

She waited for him to elaborate.

"It really is a shame," he said, nodding his head at the alligator's dead body floating nearby, "to just let the poor thing rot."

Of course he would change the subject and only focus on the part of her statement involving him. Was it too much to ask for him to acknowledge why she may be less at ease than he?

"Well, I can't say I have a need for anything made of

reptile skin at the moment," she said crossly. "Plus, it did attack you."

"True," Dassius said as he focused on what was looking increasingly closer to a usable raft. "It just seems a little wasteful."

"I'm sure something will make use of it."

"You're right; it will probably be gone by the time we make our way back through these parts."

Ceera watched him secure the bond between the thick branches on the raft. As he yanked the ropelike twigs into firm knots, so too did she tighten her resolve. Bravery had never been a job description for a scribe, but strength in character had aided her in growing up without a family. Or perhaps growing up alone had made her into who she was. Either way, she had never fallen prey to weakness. She wasn't about to let it overcome her now. She just hoped her emotions would comply with this conviction.

Until recently, the most controversial event in Semadon was when the Council for Natural Law and the Council for Advancement met at the Aurora to debate their agendas. Despite the typical drama that ensued at these meetings, Semions were not usually gathered outside bantering back and forth across the lawn.

The thick garble only spoke commotion. It grew louder as the council members marched up the stone pathway. Order patrolman checked the identity of each member as they passed through the entrance. Attendants led the members by small groups into the meeting room. The tables formed a wide circle around a larger table at the forefront, which was designated for High Service since they would be conducting the meeting.

Marvus and Desnia sat on one side of the table. Nimren and Casma sat directly opposite. Both pairs acted quite busy and avoided each other's eyes expertly, though they snuck glimpses of each other, careful to do so when the others were not looking.

The rest of the council members filed in. The remaining seats filled with Semions who had been waiting outside. A scribe sat near High Service.

The female official stood. "My name is Hetia and I am of sphere two. If there are no objections, we will begin."

She glanced around the room before continuing. "During our last meeting, the Council for Advancement proposed they begin formation of a weather enhancement project. Due to the Council for Natural Law's concern, High Service placed the project on hold until further analysis. Now, I would like to direct everyone's attention to the head of the Council for Natural Law so he can relay his findings." Hetia bowed at Marvus and sat back down.

"Fellow council members," Marvus said as he stood. "Several of our members spent time in the CfA laboratories during the past few weeks, testing the equipment and analyzing the plans of this ambitious scheme.

"Our members also conducted briefings with the scientists involved. What these fair-minded souls determined is that the CfA lacks the degree of expertise to successfully actualize what they have proposed. Thus, their plan has not been adequately formulated."

Marvus paused to glance over at the CfA. Several members had narrowed eyes while others shook their heads in disagreement. Nimren stood out from the rest, for he appeared even larger than his usual rounded self. He added to his girth with every incoming breath.

"We recommend," Marvus continued, indifferent to the reactions he had just witnessed, "they withdraw these plans. It would only result in disaster.

"We also feel this endeavor is ill-timed. Not only is this weather controlling proposal disrespectful to nature, we ponder whether both the suggestion of this idea and the show of arrogance that came with it, serve as underlying reasons for our current misfortune." Marvus bowed and sat down. A tremendous amount of tension emanated from the opposite end of the room, but he held a solemn gaze and blinked his eyes with humility.

Hetia stood and gestured to Nimren. "It's time for a rebuttal from the CfA. Let's turn our attention to Nimren, the head of the opposing council."

Nimren bolted upright and glared around the room. "This evaluation is insulting. The CfNL members who visited our laboratories perhaps did not comprehend the scope of our plans. As a result, they are minimizing our abilities.

"Secondly, it's obvious that the CfNL is fearful of how this development could affect the stability of their council. They are placing unnecessary caution over the progress of Semion culture. They refuse to accept we are evolving to new heights, and as this occurs, their own purpose becomes meaningless."

"I have a mind to suggest"—Nimren paused with a devilish look in his eyes—"that perhaps this misfortune Marvus speaks of is not caused by our suggestion to enhance the weather, or even by my so-called offensive slip of words. I think the Council for Natural Law plotted for the alarms to sound, in order to defame my council and put an end to our success for their gain."

Desnia gasped loudly, placing her hand across her mouth. Marvus had his own hands clasped together in an effort to stop them from shaking. Murmurs echoed throughout the room.

"Perhaps the CfNL even enlisted Hegliod Avatus. Isn't it ironic that the region responsible for the monitor's abnormal reading is in the exact spot an AT cylinder was installed? I think Semions need to wise up to what is really going on here."

Hetia stood and turned to Marvus. "Have you a response to this accusation?" she asked, attempting to shadow her surprise with a neutral tone.

"It's apparent," Marvus replied nervously, "the CfA is trying to cover up their actions. The alarms sounded just days after the CfA proposed their idea. This could only mean there is a direct correlation between it and the words spoken by Mr. Sebious at our last meeting."

"Or"— Nimren leaned over the table to stare straight into the eyes of Marvus, who gaped at such an audacious gesture —"the abnormal reading could have been created by your council as a direct tactic to thwart our progress."

"Your accusation is baseless," Desnia spat out, standing as well. "Even if we had fallen to such dishonorable motives, we had no time to enact such a plot."

"It's not as if you had your greatest minds visiting our laboratory. What, in fact, were they doing?" Casma retorted, her red cheeks rivaling the ball of fire on her ring.

The audience replicated their actions prior to the meeting, engulfing the room with noisy banter. Council members glared defiantly across the table at each other. Both officials waved their hands in attempt to quiet the audience.

"Silence, I am Fresdin of sphere two. Silence I repeat." His words were barely audible over the noise.

"Cease your squabbling." Hetia's voice resounded loudly above all the rest. "High Service commands your attention immediately."

This tone of voice coming from a sphere two caused all noise to come to a standstill.

"This display is disgraceful," Hetia continued. "It is our turn to speak, and only ours. Fresdin, please resume."

Fresdin also seemed surprised by Hetia's assertiveness. "Firstly," he began, "High Service does not condone the accusations made by the CfA. Secondly, Hetia and I have decided all communication between the two councils be temporarily cut off. We are prohibiting the CfA from furthering their project until a cooperative decision can be reached. It is evident this will not occur anytime soon. So, we are adjourning this meeting and all debate until further notice."

He nodded to the attendants in the back of the room, who began rounding Semions up and shooing them out the door.

Hetia strode over to the CfA table and observed as they readied themselves to leave. Fresdin did the same to the CfNL. Both councils gathered their belongings in a huff while speaking in agitated tones. They made plans to gather at their own headquarters to discuss these new developments. The debate had publicly ended, but would continue behind the closed doors of each council for well into the night.

Ceera and Dassius drifted through the swamp on the newly constructed raft. She sat as close to the middle as she could, hugging her knees to her chest, as he maneuvered them through the maze of tall trees protruding from the water. He used a long, hefty branch to propel them forward.

"What will you do if we see more reptiles?" she asked.

"You already asked me that question."

"But you didn't respond."

"What do you want me to say? I'm analyzing our situation on a moment-to-moment basis. At present, you have nothing to worry about." He steered them again with the branch.

"I didn't say I was worried."

"Good," he said with a smile, "because you were the one who wanted to come."

Why must he continue to remind her of that? "Of course I wanted to come. Who argues with their destiny?"

He stared at her, but she wouldn't return his gaze.

A fish flopped in and out of the water near the raft. Birds cackled repetitively overhead.

"How much longer until we find her?" she wondered.

Dassius steered them into a channel of water that branched away from the swamp. "This river should be our final stretch. I have a feeling it will run into the ocean, and we can look for Oc~ea there."

Ceera let the calm waves of the water pacify her as they continued to float slowly down the channel.

Chapter Eight

CEERA COULDN'T BELIEVE it was only midday when Dassius maneuvered their raft to the bank. The current had brought them near the ocean as he had predicted; it was visible up ahead. When the raft touched dry ground, they stepped out and he dragged it away from the water. They stretched their legs before following the remainder of the river on foot toward the onset of the ocean.

They approached a sandbar. The ocean spread out in the foreground. Ceera's boots sank into the sand, and the smell of salt grew thick as they walked alongside the coast. The damp air emitted an aura of freshness.

The ocean roared relentlessly, spitting bits of moisture at them and washing waves upon the shore. Colorful rocks and broken shells intermingled with the sand.

They neared a rocky cliff with streams of water rushing down. The waterfall sparkled with brilliant streaks of green and blue. Splashing sounds and laughter came from behind the glistening curtain. A bare arm poked out, along with a fleeting glimpse of hair. Then the noise dwindled into silence.

"Oc~ea?" Ceera's whisper floated into the stillness.

A young girl peered out from behind the water spraying

down the rocks. She disappeared. There was low discussion and sounds of discontent. A huge splash erupted that sent droplets over them like rain. Another smaller splash came after, barely impacting the ocean's surface. The perpetrator of the larger splash went straight down. The smaller one brought a trail of bubbles to the water's edge. The young girl's head emerged, along with the rest of her, as she walked onto the shore.

Her bare feet stepped lightly across the sand before coming to a stop in front of them. She stood shyly and stared, though she was clearly unafraid.

"Hello," Ceera said. "What's your name?"

"I am Anemona. I heard you call for my mother." The girl's startling blue eyes asked questions. Her pale skin emitted a bluish glow. Orange starfish clipped her light colored hair up at the sides. She wore short pants and a loose-fitting shirt woven with seaweed. A necklace with a single green shell hung around her neck.

"I'm Ceera and this is Dassius." Ceera gestured.

"My brother went to get Serpa. He will take us where we need to go." She burrowed her toes into the sand and smiled.

"What do you mean where we need to go?" Dassius's voice was stern, but Anemona did not waver in the slightest.

"Mother told us you would be coming. She is in deep waters. She said to take you to our observatory, and she will meet us there. Why have you come?"

"We are here to ask your mother questions," Ceera said. Since an Archaic had birthed her, she wondered if Anemona was more mentally advanced than a Semion child would be. She looked about ten years old.

"My mother is good at answering questions," Anemona said. "Look! Here comes Waive with Serpa now."

Anemona pointed to where a serpentine creature undulated toward them. A boy sat atop. He was older, in his teens, perhaps even close to Ceera's own age. Instead of greeting them, he splashed yet again into the water and disappeared.

"Waive is unsociable," Anemona explained as she gestured them to the serpent. "Lucky for you, Serpa is not." She giggled and took her position in front. She stroked the long neck of the serpent affectionately.

"I'm not sure I trust these children," Dassius muttered as they approached the water's edge.

"The girl seems innocent enough," she whispered back.

"Yes, I'm going to keep an eye on the boy though."

She wondered how Dassius planned on doing this when Waive was nowhere in sight.

"Come on," Anemona said. "Serpa is ready for you."

The serpent's body was wet though warm and covered with thick scales. When they were situated, the creature moved into the open water.

The ride was soothing. Ceera clutched onto the serpent as it swam smoothly through the current. Water dispersed from the waves, creating a refreshing mist.

As they rode, she was more skeptical of Dassius's suspicions than she was of the children, for the girl's age matched her behavior and the boy would not resurface. Winds blasted them, the intensity heightening the further they traveled. Anemona's hair whipped around her face, causing her to squeal with laughter. Ceera was glad she had pulled her own hair back.

Unlike Dassius who was silent, Anemona's mouth would not stop moving. "Riding Serpa is one of my favorite things to do. I was so glad when mother told Waive he had to bring him from the depths."

"He doesn't normally do this for you?" Ceera asked.

"Waive is mean to me." Anemona frowned prettily. "He only lets me ride Serpa when mother tells him to."

"Is your brother protective of this serpent?" She glanced at Dassius, who stared into the water with a look of concentration.

"Yes, Serpa is his pet. Pretty soon I will be old enough to choose an animal to master. Waive looks for animals from the deep to control, but I may choose a dolphin or a manatee. They are so fun to play with."

"Your brother," Dassius spoke up, "where did he go?"

"Who knows." Anemona sniffed. "He goes off on his own a lot. We used to play together all the time, but now he thinks he is all grown up. Mother told him to stay with me until you came."

"How did your mother know we were coming?"

"Mother knows all kinds of things. She just stares at the water and it tells her everything. Someday I will be just like her. There is our observatory over there. Slow down Serpa! At this rate you will wind up inside, not at the doorstep!"

The serpent slowed and drifted to the edge of an opening carved into a stone cliff. Anemona stepped off first then flattened herself by the edge of the doorway, while Ceera and Dassius hoisted themselves up from the serpent and squeezed through the entrance. Anemona led them the rest of the way inside.

The entire room was composed within the hollow of an enormous rock. Its thick walls muffled the outside noises coming from the wind and ocean.

A repetitive dripping sound gave the room an eerie sense of calmness, like time was moving slowly. Ceera noticed a circular aperture in the ceiling that revealed the sky, which was as clear as it had been when they left Semadon. Exotic plants sprouted from crevices throughout. Colorful shells were arranged like figurines. In the center of the enclosure was a hole about six feet wide, revealing the ocean below. Fish and sea creatures swam within, indifferent to their presence.

"Please sit." Anemona motioned to a pair of coral structures shaped like chairs.

Ceera and Dassius sat down on them carefully. The seats were thick and rough to the touch.

"While we're waiting, please tell me why you've come," Anemona pleaded. She bounced ever so slightly as if she couldn't contain her own energy.

"We already told you," Dassius said. "We're here to talk to your mother."

"Yes, but why?" Anemona asked. She batted her eyelashes at him in an attempt to charm him.

Dassius didn't look amused.

Ceera smiled at the display. "We came to ask your mother about a forest," she said, ignoring Dassius's jab to her side. "We don't know why, but this forest is causing an abnormal planetary reading. The mystics insist the answers can be found within the elements, and we are here to ask your mother to ask the waters."

Anemona's eyes lit up. "I can ask!" She skipped over to the large opening in the middle of the room, dropped down to her hands and knees in such a careless manner she almost fell headfirst into the opening, and paddled one of her hands in the water. She then switched to a circular motion.

Dassius shook his head at Ceera and folded his arms over his chest. "I will not be held liable for this," he said quietly, but she could tell he was angry.

"Perhaps we should wait for your mother," Ceera said to Anemona.

The girl pretended like she didn't hear. Her hand did not falter and remained inside the water. "Let me see," she said, emphasizing each word as she peered down farther into the reservoir.

"How does it work?" Dassius asked stiffly.

"I stir the water and ask it what I want to know," Anemona said over her shoulder.

"I hope your mother doesn't get angry with what you're doing and blame it on us," he said.

"Mother doesn't bother herself with pettiness." She squirmed this way and that, brought her face away and peered again. Like most children her age, the girl seemed incapable of sitting still. Suddenly, her movement came to an abrupt halt. Anemona jerked her head away. She scrunched up her face and her lip began twitching. Her change in demeanor coincided with the odd mood the observatory emitted.

"What is it?" Ceera leaned forward in worried anticipation.

Dassius, on the contrary, pressed himself onto his chair, looking ready to spring into action if need be. A concerned expression crept onto his face.

"As I was searching for answers, I came across something so dreadful I can't bear to repeat it." Anemona stared upward at the opening in the ceiling and sighed.

"Go ahead and tell us what you saw," Ceera coaxed. "I'm sure it's not as bad as you think."

Anemona shook her head, her shoulders trembling.

"Go ahead and tell us," Ceera repeated gently.

"I'll try but I don't understand."

"Perhaps you are too young to understand."

"I can see," Anemona told her sadly, "what the water is telling me, just not why it is so." She placed her hands over her eyes.

"Why what is so? Are you sure you are reading it correctly?"

"The water would never lie to me."

"Go on, you'll feel better once you tell us what's upsetting you."

The child uncovered her eyes and stared listlessly at the opening. The fish swam rigorously about. Her breathing became slow and steady, like the mild washing of waves on the coastline.

"There was a time," she said in a small voice, "when life in the oceans had mostly vanished. The water was not pure like it is now, but contained"—she paused dramatically—"poison."

A tear formed in the corner of Anemona's eye. It seeped out and ran slowly down her cheek, dangling at the bottom of her chin. After a brief moment it fell, and as it spattered to the ground there was a great rushing sound in the distance. She whirled to face them. "Poison!" she wailed.

Anemona's green-blue eyes contained tiny oceans that swirled viciously around her pupils. As more tears welled and gushed onto her face, an ominous sound erupted overhead.

Dassius jumped to his feet. "Anemona!" he shouted. "Stop crying!"

Stunned, Ceera stood and clutched onto Dassius's arm.

The sky opened up with a terrible rumbling sound. Rain poured down on them through the opening. Anemona curled up into a little ball and rocked back and forth. Her hands covered her face. She murmured to herself, oblivious to them.

The water pounded down harder, drenching Ceera's clothes and blinding her. The pressure of the water bearing down restricted her from crying out. She gasped for air, but water forced its way inside her mouth. Clutching her throat, she staggered backwards and sank down to the floor.

Without warning, the tides turned. A huge wave washed over them.

"Anemona!" called an angry voice in the distance.

Ceera sputtered but did not move.

"Stop your insolent crying at once! It's impolite for you to inflict your distress upon our guests!"

The command was effective. The sky ceased its pouring and water now drizzled down weakly. Ceera took large gasps of air and heard Dassius do the same. He was on the ground nearby, already attempting to stand.

"Just look what you've done to them! What's wrong?"

"I saw poison in the sea," Anemona whimpered.

The sky rumbled again and Ceera covered her face, but the noise died down quickly. When she finally had the courage to look up, a woman was embracing the girl.

"Poison? In the sea?" the woman repeated. Her eyes traveled to the opening on the floor, which was now overflowing, and she sighed. "But Anemona, what's so frightening about something that's not current? This was ages and ages ago. The sea mended itself; it no longer contains this poison." She stroked the child's wet head.

Anemona looked up into the face of her mother and smiled brightly. The sun's shine on the water reflected at Ceera and began to dry her. Dassius held out his hand

and this time she grabbed it, allowing him to help her to her feet.

"It's time for you to go back to the waterfall and play. Be glad water triumphed." The woman patted her head.

Anemona stood up and skipped to the entryway. She turned to smile mischievously at Ceera, who suddenly felt tricked. Then the girl dove out of the observatory with a powerful jump and vanished out of sight. Ceera turned to view Oc~ea in full scope.

The Archaic wore a turquoise gown that clung at her torso and flowed down to her ankles. Her glistening eyes matched the dress. Wavy blond hair adorned with tiny shells fell to her waist. A plant wound around her wrist and entwined between her fingers. A pouch made from scales dangled at the other side of her hip.

"I am Oc~ea, but I assume you have already figured that out."

It took a moment for them to adjust to the authority of her presence.

"I'm Dassius and this is Ceera. We did not ask your daughter to explain things to us."

"I believe it," Oc~ea said. "The child has strong will but is young and therefore still sensitive. You mustn't blame her for your trouble. She is quite powerful but has yet to master the ways of the water."

There was a brief silence.

Dassius cleared his throat. "The mystics told us to ask for your help, that you could search the waters for answers about a mysterious forest."

"Of course," Oc~ea replied with a firm nod, "but before I begin I must ask why you need my help."

"We don't have any records of the region. Plus, we don't study the elements anymore; we mainly study space."

"Only looking forward is unwise. It leads to the loss of fundamental knowledge."

"True," Ceera spoke up, "but your help is essential. Semions are suffering as a result of this oversight."

"I will not tell you all the answers, for you must figure them out yourselves. I will help though, for your culture with its obsession of pushing forward is still young, and need not be punished but redirected. May this serve as a lesson to you, for those who forget the past cannot adequately analyze the present."

Dassius looked like he wanted to object, but Ceera interrupted him. "We strive to be wiser," she said, pulling her recorder from her drenched pack, "which is why I brought this. If you don't mind, I plan to record your words so we never have to come begging for the knowledge of the elements again."

"We shall see. Do what you must. I understand your culture studies many things. I only study the water. But the water by itself also covers many things. And here is where I will begin."

Oc~ea shifted her attention to the opening, which had since pushed its own excess away. A trail of water had followed Anemona to the entrance and was in the process of leaving the observatory.

She did not kneel like her daughter, but loomed over and stared solemnly down. She extended her hand toward the water, which rose in a wide circular motion and filled the room.

Ceera and Dassius flinched as it surrounded them.

"What I present to you is an image nothing more,"

Oc~ea said calmly. "My daughter is correct in saying there was a time when the cleansing water you see around you was drowning in contamination. Damaging substances flourished in what now is pure enough to consume. Life in the ocean had all but vanished. All creatures living in its depths were tainted. Creatures near the surface had poisons flowing through their blood. Here, I will show you."

Oc~ea continued to remotely stir the water. Something began to take form in the middle of the swirling vortex. Ceera squinted in concentration.

"You must accept the image naturally to view it," Oc~ea said.

Ceera relaxed her senses. The image came into focus and she gasped, stepping backward.

Gruesome looking creatures swam out of the hole and into the current rippling around the room. Extra fins stuck out of their bodies. Eyes bulged from sickly raw flesh. One of the fish turned to face her.

"Is this what your daughter saw when she tried to read the water?" she whispered, her eyes locked with the fish.

"On the contrary," Oc~ea said. "My daughter is not as adept as I am. I am saving you from the mortifying visual someone with her skill level would have concocted. She would have seen the horror in all of its totality."

The fish gave Ceera a reproachful look before swimming back into the vortex. The other creatures followed.

"I want to see what she saw," Dassius said.

"We've seen enough." Ceera frowned at him.

"If you would like," Oc~ea said gravely, "for other creatures also suffered." She directed her next comment to Ceera. "Look away if you must."

Ceera closed her eyes. There was movement all around

her. Strange sounds plagued her ears. She heard a breath of air escape Dassius's lips, but she stifled her curiosity and kept her eyes shut.

"That was appalling," he said in a troubled tone.

"Living death is never perceived favorably," Oc~ea replied.

The sounds withered away.

"Are they gone?" Ceera asked.

"They have been swallowed back up, don't worry," Oc~ea said.

Ceera opened her eyes to see the water was now vacant of inhabitants.

"No creature was strong enough to survive without sinking to the innermost depths to escape the peril above. Channels streamed through the planet in which the wiser creatures hid, saving themselves."

Oc~ea's eyelids fluttered. She turned her face to one side and let out a huge sigh. "The currents ceased to flow their normal course. The water became salty where before the salt had sunk and drifted elsewhere. The temperatures became erratic and ice melted, causing the oceans to engulf whatever lived on its banks. Water became a deadly entity feared by all."

"I cannot believe the Semions would let this happen," Ceera said.

"I never said they did." Oc~ea's response drifted their way almost too casually. "What I tell you is water's version of the story. You are asking about the past, when your forest became what it is, correct?"

"Yes," Dassius said. "And what you are saying does coincide with what little information the mystics told us. They said the forest was corrupted. I have a mind to suggest the two went hand in hand."

"The forest was handed the same fate water suffered, but only the forest remains as tainted now as it was then."

"It's strange," Dassius said, "that the forest was unable to rejuvenate itself when water did so."

"Let me explain. The forest did purify itself from the poisons of the past. Something of an entirely different nature now taints the wood, a presence the forest was unable to shake during this time of climatic turmoil. You could say it remains out of necessity or perhaps even convenience; however, this presence shields the truth you are looking for."

"Now I am truly confused," Ceera said.

"It's quite simple. You must withstand the forest's mischief to solve the riddle."

"How do we do that?" She glanced sideways at Dassius, who looked deep in thought.

"By using the powers of the elements of course."

"But we do not have any special powers like you do," Dassius said.

"Nor do I plan to accompany you. I suppose I can offer you something though, a bit of my essence: a substance specially designed to contain my powers. I will tell my brothers and sister to do the same. You must use each when the time is appropriate."

"How will we know when to use them," Ceera said, "when we don't even understand what we are up against?"

"Use them when you need protection, and do not fall prey to temptations of using them sooner. Keep in mind the forest will not allow you to travel through it easily; however, if you find water, it will lead the way." She extended her arm and opened her hand. A vial shaped like a water droplet glistened in her palm. Fluid swirled around inside.

Dassius stepped forward to take it.

"It looks like ordinary liquid, but it is so much more. Open the vial when you feel a need for the power of water."

Dassius held the vial up toward the opening in the ceiling. The sun's rays reflected off the glass and shot out in various directions. Then the watery image around them dissipated, and they stood once again within the hollow of an enormous rock.

Chapter Nine

OC-EA UNHOOKED A large, pink shell hanging near the entrance and placed it against her lips. She blew into it, causing a low-pitched noise to echo over the sounds of the roaring sea. Moments later, water lapped into the observatory from the ocean. The serpent floated at the entrance.

"Is it safe to ride the serpent without an escort?" Dassius asked, his mind reverting to what Anemona had told them about Waive.

Oc-ea bent over and whispered into the serpent's ear. She patted its head. "Don't worry," she replied. "Serpa will take you back to shore safely."

Dassius climbed onto the serpent and held his hand out for Ceera to follow. She accepted it, her fingers sliding into his palm. He steadied her as she swung one leg over Serpa's body and gingerly sat down behind him. When he turned to face forward, Serpa was already moving. He glanced back over his shoulder, but Oc-ea had vanished from sight.

"This hardly seems capable of protecting us," Ceera said, reminding him that he needed to reclaim the vial.

"Here, I'll take it. We need to put it somewhere for safekeeping." He held out his hand, but his gaze flickered downward at the waves.

"I'm not done looking at it," she said.

Dassius glanced back at her. She held the vial upward, staring intently. The liquid rolled around and splashed onto the sides, projecting an array of flashing colors. When the serpent rocked to one side, she steadied herself with her free hand.

"Let me have it before you drop it," he said, his attention split between her and the depths of the sea.

"It's so pretty and colorful," she marveled.

"We need to put it away before…" Dassius stopped talking to focus. A premonition formed in his mind, signaling the present was about to drastically change and not for the better.

"Before what?"

The wind blew harder. His hair was just long enough to scratch at his eyes.

"Look, something's up. I can feel it."

"Something bad?"

"Yes." He continued searching the surrounding water, swatting his hair away from his face.

"Anemona was sent back to the waterfall. I don't think she would disobey her mother."

"Not her. I think it's the boy. He's down below us and watching our every move."

The sudden sound of flapping wings caused Dassius to jerk his head up in surprise. A very large bird hovered over Ceera's head. Its skinny feet clasped onto her pack, and an oblong beak pecked at the vial in her hands. Ceera's face turned white and she froze. Her fist tightened around the glass.

"Don't let go of the vial," he shouted as he swung his pack around. "I'll get a weapon." Wrestling the bird with his bare hands would be difficult balanced on the back of the serpent. If he fell into the water, then Ceera would be at the bird's mercy.

"Hurry!" she cried out as its beak jabbed her skin.

"It wants the vial. Don't give in!" He dug frantically in his pack.

As if she weighed nothing, the bird lifted Ceera up and began carrying her away. She screamed and wriggled fiercely in its clutches.

Dassius set his eyes firmly on the two of them as he pulled a large slingshot out of his pack, along with a dense, round object. He took a moment to position and aim. The object whizzed at the bird and collided with a wing. It contorted inward, jostling the bird out of flight. Ceera fell out of its clutches and into the ocean with a huge splash. Her abductor flew crookedly away.

Dassius stood on the back of the still-moving serpent and dove toward where she had fallen. He had only moments to rescue her. The impact from hitting the water could have knocked her unconscious, and with the pack on her back, she would sink straight to the bottom.

He swam downward. Something thick wrapped around his leg. He tried to break free but instead the hold tightened. He turned to see what restrained him and encountered a pale bloated face. It sent shivers through the core of his body. Large oval eyes protruded out of its cone shaped head and peered at him in a way that caused him to feel like prey. Its head floated backward. A long tentacle kept him rooted to the spot.

Taken aback by the eeriness of its features, he twisted his body in an effort to slip away from its grip. Though he had never seen one up close before, he suspected he was entangled within the clutches of a giant squid.

Continuing to hold his breath, he tried grabbing onto the knife attached to his belt. His fingers grazed it. The creature was already wrapping its remaining feeder tentacle around his waist, restricting him so effectively his struggles were in vain. For the first time since his training, a fit of worry gripped him, tighter than the tentacles winding their way around him, and he wondered what the probability was of getting himself out of this one.

❧

Ceera hit the water with a thud and sank. Though she had the wherewithal to take a large breath prior, the impact weakened her so she made no attempt to thwart her descent into the depths.

Hands caught her and a body braced alongside her own. The force of falling caused both her and her rescuer to continue downward. He drew his head back, and she made out a wide face with soft features. He was decidedly not Dassius. She struggled. His light blue eyes urged her to remain calm. There was a moment of uncertainty, and they spun cartwheels as he tried to break the fall.

They landed on a bed of soft corals. Her sense of gravity shaken, she had no desire to move. He shook her ever so gently. His blurry image pointed upward and motioned for her to follow.

A loud vibration came from somewhere down below. How far had they sunk? He motioned more urgently now, and she decided to trust him. He was going to rescue her from the depths and escort her back to the surface before all breath escaped her. He would take her to Dassius, who would lead her back to the AT cylinder and normality.

She swam behind him obediently, and he paused when she needed to catch up. His hair streamed behind as he wove in and around plant life, up and over schools of swimming fish. He turned and winked, his hand beckoning again.

As they swam farther, her oxygen levels wore thin. She had been trained to hold her breath up to three minutes, and it had to be close. She grew more uncomfortable by the stroke.

He kept turning and waving her forward. They passed a coral reef, a beautiful assortment of colors and aquatic plant life, but the way it was positioned caused an unsettling feeling in her gut.

Ceera's zealousness faded away. As if on cue, the pressure of the water bore down on her. Her lungs felt ready to burst.

She tried to catch up so she could tell him he was taking her the wrong way; she needed to be taken to the surface. He looked back at her and smiled, as though oblivious to her plight. He turned around again and kept going. Although she still followed him, she was now lost.

Cries for help bounced inside her head. They could not reach him, would not, and she placed her hands on her chest. Her desperate pleas would not project outward to him no matter how much she willed them to, and she watched helplessly as he ventured deeper into the unknown.

Fear ran rampant within her. A fish swam past unperturbed, signaling her unimportance. She tried to speak but her words came out in a gargled choke. She clutched her neck and began sinking, drifting up which was now down.

He turned to view her progress. His eyes widened and his arms flailed at her to stop, but it was too late.

When the darkness overcame her, Ceera found herself floating wildly in the torrents of her own perception. She let go of her remaining sense of reality and drifted even deeper into a place that did not continue moving, yet resonated within its own dominion.

&

The tentacles pulled Dassius toward an opening containing a large curved beak. It would slice him apart, before he would be further ground up by the teeth inside the beak he could not yet see. He scrambled to figure out what went wrong as he aggressively jerked his arms and legs to prevent the squid's ingestion. Its suckers held on, but his movements did slow their progress.

A familiar surge of confidence flowed through him. Perhaps there was nothing wrong, for he was not dead yet. He reached for his knife and touched the handle with his finger. Every second was an opportunity. As long as he was alive, he would continue to fight. He jerked his elbow back and managed to jostle the knife loose with the side of his hand. The beak was a few feet away now. Determination overpowered him as he made one last attempt to grab onto his weapon.

Whether he would have succeeded in freeing himself, Dassius will never know. When his hand clutched the handle, something slammed into the squid. The resulting quake caused both of their bodies to catapult through the water. The tentacles released him, and he swam to the surface to catch his breath.

He gasped for air and it flooded into his lungs. The rhythm of the water told him he was still in harm's path. Water slapped his side, and he turned to view an oncoming entanglement of scales and tentacles.

He braced himself as he was forced under and through the water once again. Since he had nothing to hold onto, he went with the thrust of the flow. He used its force to maneuver away from the turbulence and back up to the surface.

The serpent he'd been riding had challenged the squid to a duel. Their bodies intertwined beneath the water, the commotion making waves in every direction as they struggled to overtake each other.

He watched with interest for a moment, before the realization that Ceera was still down below somewhere struck him. He took a huge breath and plunged downward in hopes of finding her still alive.

⚘

During what should have been a peaceful afternoon spent in solitude, Hegliod was bothered by an unlikely knocking that he could not immediately place within his grasp of reality. The sound was so unfamiliar, yet stirring, he considered whether it was his past idea preparing him for its return. He perked up and waited for it to enter his brain. Instead, he heard the knocking again, and it dawned on him it was a real sound coming from the door of his dwelling.

Huffing with disgust, he walked over to answer it. Two High Service officials, Leynin and Asfin, stood on his doorstep. His disgust turned into dismay. It was the same two he had conversed with regarding his AT system's fall from favor. Could it get any worse? He reluctantly let them inside.

"Hegliod, we apologize for our unexpected visit. Normally, we would summon you to the Aurora," Asfin said as she sat down on Hegliod's couch.

Leynin sat beside her while Hegliod lowered himself on a chair across from them. In any other dwelling, a global update sphere would be positioned in the center of the curved furniture, but Hegliod's was stuffed in a closet.

"Yes, I believe this is a first."

"We had to breach protocol due to the severity of what recently happened. Have you been at your dwelling all day?" Leynin inquired.

"I have," Hegliod replied, troubled by their invasion. Sweat formed on his forehead.

"I suppose we should get straight to the point. Are you aware of the position the Council for Advancement has taken?"

"What do you mean, in general?"

"Well," Asfin said, "you're aware they have a habit of acting as if all matters of consequence revolve around them, correct?"

Hegliod rolled his eyes. He was so tired of hearing about those disgraceful councils. They had both lobbied for his membership and support some time back, after he had established himself as a respected inventor, but he had refused. How would he ever have accomplished anything with their constant bickering clogging his brain?

"I am aware, yes," he grumbled.

"Then this shouldn't come as a surprise. They are making a personal attack against you. They are at odds with the CfNL, have accused them of somehow causing the abnormal planetary reading and have declared your involvement through the use of your AT system."

"What? That's preposterous! I have no involvement with either one! I am dedicated to my own pursuit of invention. I have nothing to gain by collaborating with them."

"Yes." Asfin lowered her eyes. "We agree the CfA is resorting to disingenuous behavior. They're using you."

"Me? But why?"

"Unfortunately, your system's recent failures make you vulnerable to controversy," Leynin said.

"Recent failures?" Hegliod was dumbfounded. "But my speech…"

"The speech you gave was very convincing," Asfin said. "I believe it would have ended any doubts about your system."

"It's true," Leynin agreed. "This is why the remarks of the CfA were particularly ill-timed. They have managed to destroy your honor before it was fully restored."

"Well, what should I do?"

"It's not your safety we are concerned about," Asfin said. "Everyone knows High Service does not support the accusations of either council. It's more your reputation that's at stake."

"My reputation," Hegliod repeated. His surroundings became fuzzy.

"Yes, due to the nature of the argument, Semions are falling prey to a mood of distrust." Asfin shook her head regrettably.

"We hate to say it," Leynin said, "but don't expect to be treated with the same respect you are accustomed to."

The officials gave him their condolences before leaving, but Hegliod was at a loss for words. Within a matter of a few weeks he had gone from well respected to derelict. And it was all due to that meddlesome council no less! The very one that had petitioned for his support some time back! If he refused to be involved in their business, they insisted on being involved in his. They were obviously retaliating against the insult of being rejected.

If it weren't true that even his own ideas were renouncing him, he may have overlooked the entire fiasco.

&

The incessant roaring nudged Ceera awake and she opened her eyes. The ocean rippled into what seemed like eternity nearby. She was stretched out on a giant rock that hung over its edge. Dassius sat next to her, expressionless, as he stared into the distance. She breathed a pathetic gasp of air, and he looked down at her.

"You're awake." Though relief was evident on his flushed face, he did not smile.

"Barely." She tried to sit up but the ache in her body caused her to fall back limply onto the rock. "How did I end up here?" She strained her brain to remember.

"Not sure," he said. "I couldn't find you. I dove down deeper and deeper, but you were nowhere. I almost went back to Oc~ea to beg her to search the waters for you, but instead I kept looking." He stared into the horizon. "I went farther, thinking maybe you drifted to shore or even got caught in something. I was so panicked my senses escaped me. Finally I found you here. This was on your chest."

He held up a fossilized shell. It swirled into a perfect spiral. A thin rope dangled from a hole that was perhaps the result of an imperfection.

She took the ammonite fossil from him and studied it. "Where did it come from?"

"You don't know?"

"I have no idea," she admitted. Her most recent past was not available for recall. "Where's the vial?" she asked, while she hung the rope around her neck and stuffed the ammonite behind her shirt.

"I thought you lost it, but then I found it in your pack."

Ceera managed a faint smile. She attempted to nestle her head into the rock. The harsh reminder of where she was put a halt to the comfort she had anticipated. "I don't remember putting it there, but I'm glad I did."

"What happened to you down there?" Dassius asked. "Why couldn't I find you?"

"I was with Waive. You were right; he was watching us. He caught me when I fell and led me down even further."

"You were down there a long time. I had to keep returning to the top for air. I'm still in shock you didn't drown."

"I almost did," she quickly stated then lowered her eyes.

"So why didn't you? Are you gifted at holding your breath?"

"I don't know what happened. I blacked out." She shifted so he couldn't see her face.

"You blacked out and magically ended up on this rock?"

"You expect me to know what happened while I was unconscious? Look, he must have brought me here. I couldn't have done it myself."

"So he rescued you, led you to die, and then rescued you again?" Dassius picked up a rock and threw it forcefully into the water. "I told you he wasn't to be trusted."

"He kept me alive in his own weird way."

"It should have been me keeping you alive, without the

weirdness. If it weren't for that giant bird…" Dassius threw another stone into the water. "I'm going to have to tell my trainers about this. We need battle simulations with different opponents attacking us at once. Right now, it's one enemy type per battle."

Dassius seemed to be missing the point. While he rattled on bitterly, she forced herself upright and rubbed her face. Her head throbbed in pain.

"If only you could see yourself," he said. "Your face is so pale it reminds me of the giant squid I encountered when I was trying to find you."

Ceera leaned over the side of the cliff to see her reflection. She cringed at the hideous face staring back and patted down her hair. Deep circles hung under her eyes. Catching a glimpse of something swimming underneath her image, she thought of Waive and spun around. "Let's get out of here," she said, heaving both herself and her pack from the rock. She tried to ignore the mounting pain in her forehead.

"What's the rush?" Dassius jumped to his feet. He grabbed her shoulders and gently turned her around. "Look over there. You drifted back to where we started."

Ceera was surprised to see the same waterfall Anemona had played at earlier about a half mile down the coast. The beauty of its flow was evident even from a distance.

On the way back to the raft, dusk gave way to complete darkness. She listened to the sounds of Dassius walking in front of her.

"You came into contact with a giant squid?" she asked.

"Yes."

"Did it attack you?"

"It tried to eat me."

"What happened?"

"Waive's serpent attacked it. I have a feeling the serpent won, although I didn't stick around to find out."

"We are both lucky," she said.

"Luck is only a misconception," Dassius said. "At least, this is what I'm taught in my line of work."

She was too tired to think about what he meant, and he did not offer anything more. The sand became more and more difficult to trudge through.

"There's the raft. I'm going to set up the tent here."

Ceera sat in the cold sand while he assembled the tent. Tiny bugs nipped at her ankles, something that would have bothered her earlier in the day. When Dassius tossed their packs inside and held open the door flap for her, she gratefully complied.

She positioned her blanket and lay down, trying to adjust to the bumpy ground beneath her. He was no more than a few feet away, already situated. She couldn't see his face. "Dassius," she whispered.

"Huh?" He responded in a tired voice.

"Have you figured out what Oc~ea was trying to tell us?"

"Not really," he responded with a yawn. "Now that you're safe, I may take time to mull it over."

"Mull it over while you sleep?"

"Yeah, why not?"

"You're right," she told him sleepily. "Maybe we will find some answers in our dreams."

⁓

Marvus was staring at the planet centered in the room of the statues when someone approached.

"Perhaps you should take a break from all your worrying," Desnia said.

He did not even turn to look at her. "It's not worrying. I am contemplating a plan of action." He continued to hunch over the railing, his necklace dangling over the side.

"That's not your responsibility. We came to this conclusion with the rest of the council members, remember? High Service is handling it. Plus, we know for the time being the CfA is unauthorized to continue with their idea. You should be happy by that development at least."

"I know. I just feel it is my duty to come up with something."

Desnia placed her hand on his shoulder. He glanced at it. The daisy on her ring was wilting.

"But you have. You relayed our suspicions regarding the CfA. Everyone is paying close attention to what is going on."

"Don't forget we are under scrutiny as well. There are some who believe the CfA's lies."

"Yes, but our council will be redeemed in the end."

"What about poor Hegliod?" Marvus spun around.

"We denied his involvement." She shrugged.

"Still, what a hassle for him. You and I, we are accustomed to the viciousness of the CfA. He must feel horrible."

"Only the CfA can remedy that wound."

He repositioned himself on the ledge. "Going back to the issue, don't you think nature is trying to tell us something?"

"We've done all we can," Desnia insisted.

"I'm not too sure. My gut tells me much is going on beyond our control. Things are happening we should be aware of but aren't. I cannot rest knowing this."

"When is the last time you've slept?" She asked the question sternly.

"I will not incriminate myself by answering that question."

Desnia breathed a huge sigh. "Have you no faith in what we stand for?"

"I do, but I am forever weighing the signs. They speak to us. If we do not figure out what they are saying, well"— Marvus paused for effect— "who knows what will become of us."

She shook her head vigorously. He chuckled at her display.

"I don't know what to do about you sometimes," she said. "I suppose you'll only sleep when you see a sign telling you to do so."

"You know me well. Good night to you."

"Try to get some sleep Marvus." She turned and left the room.

He continued to stare at the planet balanced before him. It was true; his brain was inactive, but he could not resign himself to sleeping just yet.

Something out of the corner of his eye drew his attention away from the planet. He leaned closer and rubbed his eyes. His body stiffened against the railing. Strangely enough, there had been a change in the décor.

A young girl peeked around the pillar near the feet of the Oc~ea figure. Her long hair fell in waves, and her eyes shone even though they were sculpted from stone. Marvus started and took a step back. He fixated on another figure leaning against the pillar on the other side of Oc~ea. This statue depicted a young male with defiance brewing on his stony face.

Not one who liked to patronize absurdity, he shook his

head in disbelief. Had anyone been assigned the task of creating these two new stone figures? How long had they been there? He had been standing there most of the day and had not noticed them before now. The thought made him uneasy, which he found did not complement fatigue well at all.

Perhaps this was the sign he had been looking for. It was time for him to go to sleep. Marvus winked at the stone girl and was sure when she winked back it was just his mind playing tricks on him. He then exited the room in a hurry he could not explain and headed for his dwelling.

Ceera was back in the forest outside of Semadon. She knew this instinctually, although from where she sat, she would not have been able to see the village anyway.

As before, moss crept onto her toes. It felt soothing. She allowed it to proceed up her calves and thighs. It traveled from the log onto her fingertips. Soon it covered her arms and blanketed her chest. Plants grew toward her, reaching out as if she were the sun. Even tree branches pointed her way.

Grass and vine wound between her toes and up her legs. Branches enclosed her in their web. The forest was binding her to the spot she sat in, willing her to stay, forbidding her to venture. At least, this is what she thought at first. Only when the moss neared her neck, did she realize what was truly happening. The forest was taking over her body, attempting to convert her into nature like itself.

Opposite from her was the outline of someone sitting on a log exactly as she was. Although she assumed it was a reflection of herself, her own shadow, it did not occur to her that the figure did not resemble her own.

Chapter Ten

AN UNFAMILIAR BRIGHTNESS coupled with the hard ground beneath her made for an unpleasant awakening. Ceera's eyes shot open. The sun was shining through the thin walls of the tent, illuminating the outlines of strange looking insects crawling on the outside. She flung her blanket off and looked around. Dassius was no longer in the tent. The food compartment in her pack was hanging open.

She tucked her hair behind her ears and crawled over to the door flap. She moved it aside. Dassius sat in the sand nearby munching on his breakfast.

"I had another dream last night," she said as she neared.

He looked up and offered her a vegetable bar. "Was it like the others?"

"No." She kneeled down next to him. "It wasn't." She accepted the bar, glad it was her favorite green vegetable kind. She pried open the wrapper and took a bite.

"Are you going to tell me about it?"

"I was sitting in the forest outside the village again." She took another bite. "Then all the plants began growing toward me."

"They grew toward you? What do you mean?"

"The plants and trees closed in on me. I couldn't move. It was like we were joining together."

Dassius laughed. "That can't be good."

"Why?" She was taken aback by his mocking appraisal.

"Becoming one with the forest? Do you know what that means?"

"I know how it sounds"—she put her vegetable bar down on its wrapper—"but you are jumping to conclusions. At no time was I afraid."

"Anything else? Did you get completely overtaken and then sink into the dirt or something?"

"No, I woke up."

"We should tell High Service about this one. They are taking your dreams quite seriously after all."

Ceera stood up and looked down at him scornfully. "You will tell them nothing. They asked for information about the relic and nothing more."

"Surely they'd want to know about this," Dassius said.

"Dreams are always open to interpretation. They rarely mean what seems most obvious. I think it was just a reiteration that the forest is summoning me."

"Relax." He wadded up his wrapper. "We're trying to keep you safe, remember?"

"Sometimes I feel like you're dying to get rid of me."

"If that were the case"—Dassius stood and brushed the sand off his pants—"I would take you to the forest first thing." He tossed his wrapper next to his pack and walked to the tent. "I may have even left you half dead on that rock."

She glared at him. "What are you doing?"

"I'm going to take this thing down so we can head back."

She chewed the bar and watched him suspiciously. He opened the flap and crawled inside. One folded blanket appeared through the doorway, then another. Her pack flew out moments later; it landed heavily and sprayed sand in her direction. He crawled out and began undoing the knots at the top of the tent.

"You don't have to worry about me telling High Service about your dreams," he said, "at least for now."

"Why not?" She wondered how much she could trust him. They weren't exactly friends, but they had stopped being enemies.

"Because," he said, "I'm glad you came."

"You are?" She was touched he would openly say it, that he enjoyed her company.

"Yes." He paused. "It's good for my training."

Her cheeks grew hot and she frowned, but Dassius was oblivious to her dissatisfaction. He continued taking down the tent, not even giving her a backward glance.

"Thanks a lot," she muttered to the back of his head, although she sensed there may still have been a compliment tangled within his words.

The silence taunted him. Falken had never been a patient man. He paced his dwelling, his mind overcast with clouded thoughts. The fact his progress depended on the doings of others nagged him to the bone.

He had not left his dwelling since Ceera and Dassius had departed from Semadon, had even skipped the recent meeting between the councils to await their correspondence. Still there was nothing. He could have done a better job out there himself.

He did watch the meeting between the councils on the

global update. Marvus insulting the CfA was maddening, but when Nimren spoke in defense of the CfA once again, Falken reveled in the vindication. When Hegliod Avatus's name was brought into it, Falken could feel his blood raging through his veins. Finally, the arrogant old man would be thwarted from his pedestal. Who cared whether Hegliod deserved it or not.

The weather enhancement project had been in the works for close to a decade. Falken had been fresh out of transition the day Nimren introduced the idea to the council.

"The weather," Nimren spat out contemptuously, "a force guided by the whims of the planet. Who has not been inconvenienced by it? How many times have our gardens dried up from lack of rain or died from inopportune cold and frost? How often is our prediction of when lightning strikes mistimed, and thus we fail to capture its energy?

"What if," Nimren continued, "the weather was controllable and conformed to what was convenient for the Semions? What if we decided when the sun shone, when lightning strikes, when rain beats down upon us?"

Nimren's words created a riveting energy among the audience that was evidenced by Semions sitting up straighter and the thoughtful hardening of gazes. When Nimren concluded with a challenge to enact this feat, Falken's goal was to be the leading scientist. His involvement would outshine all others, and thus his focus for the past ten years had been the study of the sun.

His agenda was further motivated by the undermining of all his achievements so far. How could his council deny glory to the one who discovered a way to harness the energy of the most powerful entity in the sky?

While it was true the sun did not directly affect weather

patterns, its energy could be used as a tool in controlling atmospheric events. The sun, the gravitational ruler of all planets in the solar system, was the center of life itself, and he had figured out a way to not only collect but project its heat.

The use of solar energy had been mastered by the Semions decades ago. Heat-cores stored the energy garnered from the sun and were the source of power for most everything in the village and beyond, from warming homes to powering correspondence orbs and global updates.

He had figured out how to increase the storage capacity of the heat-core and fit it into a handheld device, that could also project the energy back out in a flash of intense heat capable of igniting fire. The amount of heat and range of impact were both controllable based on what he programmed into the device. Its existence would impact society just as heavily as the AT system.

Falken would be known as the mastermind of the weather enhancement project. It would be he, standing with a prideful expression, when the sun's energy flowed from the palm of his hand and lit up the area of his choice as convincingly as the enormous ball of light in the sky itself.

These workings had been in his mind for some time; he was just waiting to unleash them on his superiors. He needed to ensure he wasn't going to be overlooked yet again, that no one would beat him to his rightful reward. For if he were to create something of this caliber, there was not a single Semion who would make a mockery of him ever again.

❧

Their trek back to the AT cylinder had been quick, though Ceera's body was stiff from sleeping in a tent and sore from the day before. She lagged a few paces behind Dassius, ignoring the pain as best she could. In her mind lingered the leftover impression from the encounter with Oc~ea and her dream from the previous evening. Whenever she attempted to speak about either one with Dassius, her feet dragged and their speed declined.

So she continued on with him in silence, partly because she wanted to get back to the cylinder quickly, avoid any messy encounters with large reptiles, and partly because she wasn't sure what to say about either topic anyway. She certainly wasn't fool enough to tell him what she had learned about her mother going mad. Was it even true? Perhaps her father was just a liar, and her mother had been weakened by the sickness. With a hopeless sigh, she blocked the thought out of her mind.

Soon they were splashing through knee deep water again, and the AT cylinder was within view.

"Did your recorder get wet?" Dassius asked.

They now stood next to the cylinder on dry ground.

"It's fine; I have it in a waterproof compartment." She dug through her pack and pulled it out.

"I'll need to update High Service right away," he said.

"Do you stand by what you said earlier?" she asked him, not quite offering the recorder to his outstretched hand.

"Of course, you can trust me."

Ceera eyed him shrewdly. He looked back at her without a flicker of deceit in his eyes. If he was acting, he played the part of trusting companion well. She allowed him to take it, and he did so casually. He went inside the cylinder and left the door cracked behind him, signaling to her he had nothing to hide.

She sat in the grass to ponder the recent developments.

Poisonous water? A vial for protection to use in the tainted forest? Why would she need protection if the forest was summoning her? And what did her recent dream mean? Tying it all together seemed impossible, and she had no idea where to start. As she brushed her hands atop the grass, her only certainty was their journey had just begun.

∾

The correspondence orb began humming at 9:45 that morning. Leynin clicked on the screen, and Asfin turned the dial until the image was clear.

They scanned the words with focused attention. Upon finishing, they looked at each other with puzzled expressions; then they read the message again. Leynin transmitted a message back stating that they had already surpassed the expectations of High Service and to keep up the good work. He also told them the officials would be having a meeting to analyze their encounter with Oc~ea.

After a few more words of encouragement, he ended his transmit and Asfin pushed more buttons. Wordlessly they stood up, exited the room, and walked around the hallway to another room where officials were already beginning to assemble. Taking their place at the head of the table, they waited for everyone to arrive.

When every official was seated, Leynin summarized the information relayed over the AT system by Dassius. His speech was concise. As he concluded, he looked to Asfin for the final words.

"I will inform everyone on the global update about these new developments," she declared.

"Let's not be too hasty," Zivan said slyly. "We had better think this through."

It was unusual for a sphere seven to speak. Their role was mostly that of quiet observer, to ensure the spheres below them were making good decisions. A sphere seven interrupting the flow of events meant a grave error was about to occur.

"Excuse me." Asfin was visibly startled. "Please redress." She gave Zivan a quizzical look.

"Do not be shamed, Asfin," Zivan continued. "Sometimes even we in High Service must alter our normal course to accommodate remarkable circumstances."

Asfin bowed her head and sat back down.

"The question we must ask ourselves is this." Zivan stood carefully using a wooden cane. "What exactly will we gain by revealing all we know to the public? Nothing, I say. This information will only create an overwhelming sense of doubt. Our citizens are already troubled. It would be better to hold back, at least for the time being."

"What Zivan says is true," Sadra, his companion, said. "Alluding to a time in the past when our water was contaminated will enhance their insecurity. In this state of mind, the public's actions can become quite unpredictable."

"Unpredictable in the sense our own safety could be in jeopardy," Zivan said. "If we have the masses losing faith in us, which they will do once our history is put in question, who knows how they will react. There would be no controlling them. This could lead to the dismantling of our entire culture and even ourselves."

"Well, what should we say?" Karnen said. "We have to tell them something."

"Yes," Zivan agreed. "We will be sure to tell them about the protection offered by the Archaics. We will also reiterate the forest is tainted. We will keep our dialogue brief and to the point. And we will leave it at that."

&

Once Nimren and Casma received Falken's message that the first transmit had come through, they requested his presence immediately. He came, but not quickly, a blatant insubordination that Nimren chose to overlook for the time being.

When he finally arrived, Nimren noted Falken's much improved appearance. The reddened spot on his forehead from the miniature sun was the only mark that remained from his injury.

"It's good to see your face is almost back to normal," Nimren said as he ushered Falken inside.

"Yes, I am left with only a scar." Falken seemed to be moving in slow motion as he took a seat.

"Most scars fade in time," Nimren said. "Though as it is, it's not too noticeable."

Falken did not respond but looked back at him smugly, obviously enjoying his position as informant. Nimren resisted the urge to slap the expression from his face. They were the ones using him after all.

"So what have you found out Falken?" Casma asked.

"Ceera and Dassius began by visiting Oc~ea. She told them about a time when the planet was inhospitable, when water itself was poisonous."

"What information was this based on?" Nimren questioned.

"Oc~ea's interpretation of what she sees when viewing the water."

"And how is this interpretation relevant to what's going on?"

"Oc~ea told them our confusion now is a direct result of this past."

"So what does she suggest they do about it?" Nimren tapped his foot.

"They must venture into the forest. She said it shields the truth they are looking for." Falken's lack of enthusiasm showed on his face.

Nimren opened his mouth but no sound came out. Then a roar of laughter escaped his lips. "What is this nonsense?" he demanded.

Casma, too, looked alighted by the comment. Her smile deepened all the wrinkles on her face. "How silly," she said.

"There's more," Falken continued, visibly pleased by their reactions. "They were given what she called a bit of her essence contained inside a vial. It's to be used as protection in the forest. The other three Archaics will give Ceera and Dassius the same when they go see them."

"What do you mean?" Nimren narrowed his eyes.

"I'm not sure. From what Dassius stated on the transmit, it sounds like it's some sort of water sample. How it's to be used remains unclear."

"If only I could get my hands on it," Nimren spoke wistfully. "I would have it under a magnifying glass in no time to discredit its potency."

"No doubt just ordinary water," Casma added.

Falken nodded his head, a glint of amusement in his eyes. "I wonder what these meetings with the Archaics will prove."

"You are asking a very important question," Nimren

said, "considering the Archaics, their present-day status, are products of the Council for Natural Law."

"Is this true? High Service seems to believe in them."

"High Service gives credence to the mystics as well, but that doesn't have much to do with reality, now does it?" Nimren said.

"Enlighten me," Falken said, "for I am not very current on my knowledge of the Archaics."

"That's not hard to believe since we've had no recent interactions with them until now," Nimren said. "The Council for Natural Law cannot accept they have long perished. I am speaking of the original Archaics. Long ago, members of our council studied them, taking into account all recorded encounters along with the myths. They determined the Archaics were based on real figures in history.

"The present-day belief in their existence, however, is pure naivety and ignorance," Nimren continued. "It's a scheme contrived by the CfNL, one they have been careful to present as fact. Apparently, they're so fearful their precious council will disappear that they maintained the existence of these four figures of divine importance to keep Semions believing in their doctrines."

"But they spoke with someone," Falken said. "Dassius and Ceera wouldn't lie."

"Whoever Ceera and Dassius visited must be working for the CfNL, and therefore is spewing information that fits into their agenda."

"How could they get away with such a thing?"

"Don't forget, there are settlements scattered all over the planet. Some who reside there are members of the CfNL. It would be very easy for one of them to disguise themselves as an Archaic."

"I'm embarrassed I didn't think of this," Falken said.

"Don't bother being embarrassed," Nimren said. "The topic never came up before now. Besides, High Service frowns upon discussing the validity of the Archaics."

"We are forever scorned for our rational outlook," Casma said in a dismayed voice.

"What do you make of all this? Yesterday on the global update I watched the meeting where you accused the CfNL of setting us up."

"I think the council has more up their sleeves than I originally gave them credit for," Nimren said ruefully, rubbing his chin.

"They must have been planning this for quite some time," Casma added.

"The information you have brought us will be useful in our defense," Nimren said.

"What's next?" Falken asked. "For me?"

"Just keep doing what you're doing," Nimren said. "At this point we need to see how this trash is portrayed on the global update before we make any moves. Thanks to you, we will be ready."

"I will continue to inform you about any and all transmits." Falken stood and bowed his head before leaving the room.

"He never did say how he intercepted this information, did he?" Nimren said.

"Perhaps we can call for him. He probably hasn't left the building yet."

"Nah," Nimren shook his head. "All the better for us if we don't know."

Chapter Eleven

WHEN THE DOOR to the AT cylinder swung open and they stepped out, Ceera was momentarily awed. An aesthetic view dominated by an imposing mountain range soared high into the sky. Fluffy clouds encircled its peak. The cylinder sat in a grassy area near the mountain's base. Behind them was a strip of forest. The cool breeze swept past her face.

"Looks like we lost a few hours of daylight," Dassius said as he squinted up at the sun.

The prospect of traveling between time zones had not occurred to her until then. She wasn't sure she liked the idea.

"That's where we're headed." He pointed to a cliff jutting from the mountainside that was cloaked in mist.

"How can you be sure?" she wondered aloud, but Dassius was already ascending the gradual slope. Was he ignoring her? Certain he'd never reveal his secrets anyway, she decided to switch topics. "We never did discuss what Oc~ea told us," she said as she rushed to catch up.

"Shouldn't High Service be doing that?"

"Yes, but we have the firsthand account which should give us the advantage."

"To be honest, I'm trying to figure out the connection between your dreams and the forest."

Ceera's mind reverted back to her recent dream. "Isn't it obvious?"

"If you want me to say your dreams are implying that you are the one who can withstand the forest's mischief as Oc~ea mentioned, I suppose it's possible. The real question then, is why."

"Why the forest is tainted or why it is calling me?"

"Both. But there's some sort of a discrepancy. I can't quite place my finger on it."

"What is it? Try."

"The forest closing in on you, or you becoming one with it, does not seem like a promising scenario."

A loud clatter reverberated from farther up the mountain, distracting her from the sliver of doubt that his words provoked.

"What was that?" she hissed.

"Let's find out."

They proceeded cautiously up the rocky terrain. Sounds of a scuffle converted into a heavy pounding.

"Wait here," Dassius said. He scrambled up the slope and peered over the side. Then he turned and motioned for her to follow.

She looked at him doubtfully.

"Come on. You have nothing to worry about."

Ceera reluctantly bent over to scale the incline. He reached for her hand and pulled her up to a standing position. She grabbed onto his arm to steady herself.

Two bighorn rams tussled together in the foreground, using their large curled horns for combat. They galloped away from each other, only to turn suddenly for another face-off. Heads bowed, they ran back to collide again with their horns. She covered her ears.

"Let's see which one comes out on top," Dassius said.

Ceera was annoyed that this display of male aggression was enough to stunt their progress. "I thought you said we need to keep moving," she reminded him.

"We do." Dassius smiled at her. "But it doesn't hurt to take a moment to enjoy the finer points in life."

The animals loudly butted heads again. This time their horns stayed locked together as they attempted to push each other backward. One ram maneuvered the other toward the edge of the cliff. With one ruthless surge of power, he shoved his opponent over the side.

"That was a convincing display of dominance." Dassius winked at her.

Ceera was mildly disturbed. The winner raised its horned head in victory. He pawed the dirt for a moment and looked around. Seeing the two of them, the ram paused before proceeding up the mountain.

"Let's follow him."

"Why?"

"Didn't you see how easily he defeated the other ram?"

"Yes but—"

"He's very skilled and experienced. There are no females around, so I'm betting this was a battle over territory." Dassius began to follow the ram up the slope.

Ceera followed, still confused.

"I would assume he knows the area quite well, even the more secluded parts."

She fell into step behind Dassius, who had his eyes locked on the ascending figure of the ram.

⌘

When Falken heard the humming, he was disappointed it came from his correspondence orb, though he hadn't expected another transmit until much later in the day. He turned it on. Nimren and Casma appeared on the screen.

"Falken," Nimren said. "We would like a few words with you."

"Sure Nimren, Casma. Go ahead," Falken replied coolly.

"Did you happen to view the segment on the global update earlier today? The one where High Service informed of the first transmit?"

"Yes, I did." He knew what was coming next.

"Didn't you find it a bit"—Casma faltered momentarily—"sparse, in comparison to the version you told us?"

Falken knew her suspicion was more about him than High Service. "Yeah, I find myself asking what High Service has to gain by hiding information."

"You're sure you interpreted the transmit correctly?" Nimren asked.

"It came through clear enough."

"This is getting even more complicated," Nimren said. "High Service excluding what Oc~ea said implies they are giving credence to it."

"Or perhaps the Council for Natural Law is more transparent than we thought," Falken said. "It could be High Service didn't repeat it because they don't accept the council's obvious ploys."

"Or perhaps they value them too greatly," Nimren said. "Don't forget High Service does not dispute the credibility of the Archaics. The fact they are keeping information to themselves is worrisome."

"Yes," Casma said. "High Service not mentioning it means they are protecting it."

"If they believe such nonsense then it can only mean one thing for us," Nimren said. "Resistance. When it comes time for them to make a final decision about whether we will be allowed to further our plans, the answer will be no."

"Do you think the CfNL had this in mind when they planned everything?" asked Falken.

"Oh sure," Nimren replied. "You can't gain an advantage like that through luck."

"Well, I'm still waiting for the second transmit."

"Very good," Nimren said. "Keep us informed."

"Of course." Falken shut off the sphere. The image of Nimren and Casma disappeared. They would learn not to question him. He would see to that.

❧

"You think it's leading us somewhere," Ceera said. "Yet perhaps it's just trying to get away from you."

The day had transitioned from late morning to early afternoon. Every time Ceera suggested they stop to eat or rest, Dassius rejected her plea. She resented the ram's powerful hold on his motivations. She even started to question his sanity.

"Trying to get away? You think our victor is a coward?"

Fatigue hindered her desire to argue. The farther they proceeded up the side of the mountain, the thinner the air quality became. Talking intensified the effect.

To her dismay, the ram traveled in the same manner as Dassius. It did not take into consideration it was leading others. Its hooves traveled swiftly up steep cliffs, and they could not match its speed or agility. At times, she thought they would lose the animal. Once they reached the top of an incline, however, it would be waiting in the distance, taking a moment to bend down and consume a tuft of grass.

Ceera struggled with a double bout of frustration. First of all, the ram always managed to get a few quick bites in, whereas she kept getting turned down whenever she mentioned her hunger. Secondly, when the terrain became difficult, Dassius would help her along rather roughly so as to not lose sight of the ram.

Once, the ram turned to stare at them when it paused for a bite to eat. Ceera thought she saw a human element in its face, like it was no longer a ram but a wrinkled old man with a cunning wisdom radiating from his eyes.

"Did you see that?" she gasped as she straggled behind Dassius up the mountain.

"See what?"

"The ram's face!"

By then the ram's face had returned to normal, and Dassius just turned to look at her with raised eyebrows.

"It had the face of a man," she insisted.

"You really are hungry aren't you? Can you just deal with it a little bit longer?"

Ceera glared at the back of his head.

The next span of level ground led them to a cliff. The ram stopped at the edge and bent its knees to rest in the dirt. Ceera did not bother caring whether their entire pursuit had been in vain. She wrestled out of Dassius's clutches and sat on the ground with stubborn resolve. She pulled a vegetable bar out of her pack and began chewing it defiantly.

Dassius glanced down at her before shifting his gaze to the ram.

"See," she said between bites, "it just came up here for the view. It had no intention of leading us anywhere."

Ascending was no longer possible. Although the ledge was wide, it ended where the ram sat. The rock wall beside it was too steep to climb.

"That can't be."

Ceera took a long, cool drink of water. She held the bottle out to him, but he motioned it away. "Aren't you thirsty?"

"No, I'm thinking." Dassius walked up behind the ram. When it was clear the animal was not going to get skittish, he edged closer to the cliff. "Aha," he said with a grin.

"What?" She stood, having recovered a portion of her energy back.

"Our path is here." He pointed to the rock wall.

"You expect me to climb that?"

"Look again." Dassius smirked "There's a narrow footpath leading up."

Ceera leaned closer to view the protrusion on the wall. It could be considered a path. "It still looks dangerous," she said. "How can you be sure it's where we need to go?"

"Because this is the same cliff I noticed by the AT cylinder. See where it leads?"

She tilted her head back. The cliff protruded from the mountainside and stretched into the clouds. "I'm not so sure about this," she said and sank back to the ground.

The ram turned its head to look at her. Then it got up and moved a few feet away only to rest in a seated position again.

Dassius laughed. "He doesn't like you."

Ceera thought that the feeling was mutual. "There has to be another way."

The ram stood and began climbing up the pathway.

"Look how easy it is."

"Right."

"You can either go first"—Dassius motioned for her to follow the ram—"or last. If you are in front of me and end up falling, I may be able to catch you."

The ram's hoof loosened a small stone from the cliff, and it tumbled down the side.

"If you are behind me and fall, there's no chance I can prevent you from suffering the same fate as that rock."

Annoyed by the amused look on his face, Ceera hoisted herself up onto the platform. She clung to the rock wall as he ascended behind her. His body aligned with hers. He gently grabbed onto her waist and inched her away from the wall to make room, his strong grip the only thing keeping her from plummeting over the cliff. His breath brushed past the side of her face, calm and steady, unlike hers.

"I guess this is a bit wider than I thought," she said, ignoring the flutter inside her stomach.

"Just walk slowly and carefully," Dassius whispered in her ear, "and keep your attention directly in front of you."

With great reluctance, Ceera forced herself to take a step. She stared intently at the steep wall and refused to look over the edge.

"There you go. See, it's not so bad."

As she continued upward, her confidence remained on the level ground below. Though she wouldn't admit it, Dassius's presence behind her felt more secure than her bond with the rock wall that she climbed.

⁂

For the first time in ages, Hegliod had dragged his global update from the closet and turned it on. Not that he was watching it. Although he stared vacantly at its screen, his mind was somewhere else entirely.

He couldn't stop thinking about how cluttered his life had become. No longer was his mind free to roam complex ideas or the relationships between numbers through equations. Instead, he was forced to ponder the narrow-minded motivations of other Semions.

Not only was this a fruitless endeavor, for it lacked inventive prospects, but it also entailed an unanswerable question. How could one find reason in something lacking rationality? How was his AT system to blame for something it had no involvement in? How could he be entangled in this insidious plot to cause chaos, when he never interacted with anyone on more than just a superficial level outside of High Service? Was there any evidence whatsoever to tie him to this crime?

No, of course not, but realizing this was expecting too much of the general public, for logic was something the average Semion did not have. Logic required one to use his or her own brain, and most were too simple-minded to go beyond the basic senses of ears and mouth, taste and touch. Some Semions had a direct link from their ears to their mouth, skipping the brain entirely.

He had never understood it, this lack of thinking that infected so many. It had to be a product of laziness, either that or a deterioration of thought process due to lack of use. Society had become so advanced the adequate thinking skills of an individual were no longer necessary for mass survival, which was the primal motivation after all.

He could handle the nonsense if he was able to focus on his own pursuits. The problem was he was unable to focus on anything of importance, anything at all. It wasn't just the finger pointing that bothered him whenever he walked the orbits; it was his own finger he pointed at himself.

His talent was eluding him. Grand ideas no longer found sanctuary in his mind. He no longer even deserved the reputation he once had. Perhaps the condemnation of his peers was justified, but for reasons the perpetrators themselves were not aware.

His mind had been jumbled for days. Reason and despair had dueled inside it for too long. It was time to act, do something, so his mind could rest.

Looking desperately around his dwelling, Hegliod's eyes rested on the official who talked on the global update. The words *Special Report* were displayed on the bottom of the screen though the segment had been playing all morning.

The words triggered a solution in his mind. He, too, had a special report to give. He would go to the Aurora at once. This time it would be he making an unexpected visit to Asfin and Leynin, and there would be nothing they could do to change his mind.

Chapter Twelve

CEERA HAD NEVER moved her body with such discipline in her life. Placing her foot just a few inches to the left, where there was nothing but empty space, would cause her to topple over the side. Brushing her shoulder against the cliff on her right could have a rebound effect, and cause her to do the same. Dassius was close behind, but it would be better for both of them if she maintained her footing. This meant their progress was slow and methodical. Even uttering words seemed unnecessary and therefore dangerous.

As they ascended, the air around them turned into a cool mist. The ram vanished somewhere above, cloaked in the enveloping fog. She could no longer see the distant ground out of the corner of her eye. Her only view was of the rocky incline in front of her. She moved as if she were wading in slow motion through a dream world.

Her trance was disturbed when a realization unveiled a startling truth. She stretched her hand ever so slightly to the right to confirm the wall of the cliff was gone. "Dassius," she said, trying to hide the panic in her voice.

"Yes?"

"We're not walking alongside the cliff anymore." She

pressed her arms down to her sides in an attempt to compress her body inward.

"I know."

"Why didn't you say something?"

"I thought you knew too."

She could not bring herself to move.

"Just keep your feet on the path." Dassius lightly touched her back. "We have been walking like this for awhile."

She visualized him standing behind her, waiting for her to continue, and forced one foot forward. "Can it get any worse?' she asked. Her question got caught in the mist. It lingered close by and followed them down the path. After several more steps, she realized she could no longer see her own feet. The mist now blanketed the ground as if she walked on a cloud.

This time when she stopped, she said nothing. Just like in a dream when words are meaningless to speak, they stayed inside her. Dassius placed a hand on her shoulder. She grabbed it and turned, hoping her attempt to look calm masked her fear.

"I think it's time we changed positions," he said nonchalantly. "Don't move." He squeezed past.

"Careful," she whispered, feeling if she spoke too urgently that it would force him over the edge.

Only fog remained where Dassius had stood.

Ceera turned back around ever so slowly. His outline was now the only thing in her line of sight. "There's no way of knowing which way to go. We could walk straight off the cliff."

"How do you know we are still near the cliff?" Dassius said. "We are now on level ground."

Ceera did find comfort knowing they were no longer

climbing upward. She stayed close behind, clinging to him just as stubbornly as the fog hovered within their surroundings. She focused intently on the vague outline of his back, feeling as if she pursued a ghost.

In some areas, the thick fog was suffocating. Deep breaths seized her lungs. Determined to not let it bother her, she slowed her breathing to calm herself.

Dassius continued to edge cautiously through the fog, pausing now and then to look around, as if the mist was not obstructing his line of sight. She wondered how he kept going in the right direction, whether he was apprehensive about his position in front.

Then, without warning, he stopped and held his arm out to keep her from moving forward.

"What is it?"

"We are here."

The scenery had not changed in the slightest. "Where? We seem to be nowhere."

The breeze picked up. The haze swirled around them, faster and faster, until she was on the verge of dizziness. She grabbed onto Dassius's arm.

Finally it blew past, revealing the expanse of the sky as their surroundings, and whirled before them as a great pillar of mist which settled into the image of an old man. Wispy hair floated past his shoulders. His pale face was covered in wrinkles, though his whimsical expression made him look a bit younger than the wrinkles suggested. The rest of him stayed immersed in fog, as if it did not want to reveal too much of him at once.

"Look what the wind blew in," he said in a jovial voice. He winked playfully at their stunned expressions.

Was he talking about them, or himself? For a brief

second, she considered there was something vaguely familiar about his face, but the recognition faded quickly, not
wanting to stabilize in her thoughts.

"You must be Atmos," Dassius said.

"I must be, and who are you?"

They were no longer confined to a narrow pathway, but
it was difficult to grasp the totality of their surroundings,
for the mist condensed around them once again.

"I'm Dassius and this is Ceera."

"Nice to meet you," she said. "I thought the air would
be thinner up here."

"Well, I'm not as scant as I used to be," Atmos said with
a grin.

"That's not what I meant," she said, taken aback.

"But it's what you said."

"No, what I meant to say—"

"Save your explanation for why you've come," Atmos
told her with a twinkle in his eye.

"The mystics suggested we come," Dassius said. "Semadon is in a state of disorder, and we have questions we hope
you can answer."

"I would be willing to clear some up for you."

"Should we talk here?" Dassius asked.

One moment, a glimpse of the sky was visible, only
to be obstructed by the whitish haze moments later. Even
Atmos faded into the mist from time to time, before forming back into the hazy image of a man.

"How silly of me. Let's have a seat," Atmos said.

Some of the mist gathered between them and formed
the shape of a large mushroom before flattening into a table.

"Ahem," Atmos said, prompting three stools to form

out of the mist at equal distances around. He gestured at the stools with a flourish.

The stools did not appear strong enough to hold weight. Ceera watched as Atmos sat down. He hovered on his stool of mist, oblivious to the absurdity his position inflicted on them. She stuck her hand through the cloud of air he called a stool and looked up at him with disbelief. Dassius eyed the chair suspiciously, his hand cupping his chin.

"I don't mean to be rude," she said, "but I can't sit on that; it's practically nothing."

"Ah yes, nothing: a word that bears great misunderstanding," Atmos responded with mock seriousness.

"But I can tell just by looking at it, I'll fall right through."

"Don't be so fooled by your eyes, young woman. You'll be easily deceived if you only trust what you can see."

Ceera stared at the stool, not quite sure what to make of the situation.

"Better take a seat before it disperses," Atmos warned.

Dassius sat down slowly. To her surprise, the mist held him. She followed his lead and lowered herself down onto the mist until it held her up too.

"There. Comfortable?"

Ceera nodded though the stool's composition still bothered her.

"So tell me about this disorder in Semadon."

Ceera pulled her recorder out of her pack and began to record while Dassius summarized the events.

"Oc~ea advised us about a time in the past when the sea contained poison," he continued. "She implied this strange event was somehow related to our forest. She also gave us a bit of her essence to use as protection in the forest. We're hoping you can offer the same."

"Poison? If I am to reminisce that far back in time, I will have to call forth a powerful enough wind to accommodate us."

"Wait," Ceera said. "How powerful?" She struggled to grab onto the table, but it refused to allow her any security. Her fingers raked through the mist several times before she gave up.

"We are uneasy about the prospect because we had an unpleasant experience with Oc~ea's daughter, Anemona," Dassius said. "We almost drowned in her sorrow."

"To be polite, I will of course contain my apparition. I am very skilled, don't worry," Atmos said with a chuckle.

A look of concentration consumed him. His chest expanded until his whole body swelled. When it looked as if he would burst, he instead exhaled slowly and a great gust released itself from his lips. It blew in a cylindrical shape between them with such turbulence that it attracted some of the air around them.

Atmos's breath separated from and became replaced by the air it amassed. Ceera was not sure how she knew this but decided not to overanalyze. It rested on the table before them, a tiny whirlwind producing only a subtle draft. It traveled around the tabletop, weaving in between three stone cups that suddenly appeared.

She leaned forward to move them, but Atmos shooed her away.

"No need. Everything I own is windproof of course."

"Of course," she echoed.

Atmos stared at the whirlwind intensely; his eyes followed it around the table. As it careened around the cups, a serious expression came over his face and he cleared his throat. "Stirring up the past is not always a pleasure," he said regretfully. "First, let me backtrack and elaborate on what Oc~ea revealed to you about the water. Yes, it contained poison. It's also true the air mirrored the water; they both reeked of poisons."

"Why?" Ceera asked.

"They are very closely related," he replied.

"But we have no record of any of this."

"Well, I do. Do you need history written down for it to be real?" Atmos looked at her sternly.

"Of course not," she replied. "I was just hoping you would give some sort of explanation."

"To be quite honest, it was due to the transgression the planet endured."

The weight of Atmos's words caused his spiraling whirlwind to twirl most aggressively. It ricocheted between the three cups until it finally broke free and reeled sideways. It continued to spin, picking itself back up with momentum and resuming the orderly course it had ventured previously.

"Transgression?" Dassius looked up from the tabletop. "When?"

"Hmmm. Yes." Atmos paused, considering. "You ask a multitude of questions before I have even had a chance to graze the initial inquiry." He motioned to the cups on the table. "Have some tea."

Ceera leaned over and examined the contents. A white substance intermingled with itself within the walls of the cup. It smelled sweet and fresh.

"Drink it," Atmos said. "It will elevate you to new understandings."

She took a sip. The creamy froth tasted delicious. She took another sip and licked her lips. Dassius drank his slowly. A cloud formed in his eyes, and he gave her a half smile. He tilted his head back, allowing the rest of it to drift down his throat.

"Quite tasty, eh?" Atmos winked at them.

"It's good." Dassius set his cup back down on the table.

"I've never tasted anything like it," she said.

"Now that you both are ready, we shall proceed. Get comfortable."

Ceera realized she was slumped over to the side and repositioned herself. Dassius shifted his weight before settling back onto his stool.

"First, let us postulate this truism; the existence of air is rampant with irony. Although it's a fundamental component of life, it's also a discreet entity. Its presence lingers inside what appears to be empty space. As you can relate"—Atmos looked directly at her—"it's possible to underestimate what is not visible to the eye."

Ceera sank in her stool. Disgraced by Atmos's words, she was rescued from her shame when the stool strengthened once again beneath her.

"Air functions automatically," Atmos continued, "which can downplay its worth. You take in a breath; you let it out, simple right? It's so simple you do it all day long without even noticing. Breathe in; breathe out. No big deal. It's so much not a big deal you can understand how such a thing could be taken for granted."

"Taken for granted by whom? There are codes within our culture that maintain such obvious necessities," Dassius said.

"And these codes, have they always existed?"

"We have no reason to believe otherwise. I'm quite confident they have always been there."

"So what does this imply?"

"No Semion could be responsible for such negligence."

"If it wasn't one of you…" Atmos's words trailed away.

"It wasn't one of us," Dassius said.

Uncertainty eased its way into Ceera's awareness.

"That does pose a problem," Atmos said. "What we have is an effect without a cause. I assume it would be difficult to consider this consequence without a source of origination."

"Yes, it's quite bemusing," she agreed.

"Ah!" Atmos's eyes brightened. "I've got it. Since a reason has not presented itself, we shall play a game and create one! We will concoct an opposition to fit our scenario. To make this process of enlightenment easier, mind you. Hmm, what shall we call them?" Atmos looked upward in thought.

"Them?" she asked.

"Yes them, the 'whom' Dassius was referring to earlier."

Dassius opened his mouth as if to protest but no words came out.

"We have to pick the right word for them. It will add to the fun if we complement it with appropriate verbiage. Any suggestions?"

"Well, it takes a certain mindset to disregard the importance of breath," Ceera said. "The word we are looking for would have to indicate a reckless mentality, which is derived from an illogical way of thinking."

"Precisely! So based on your input, we could call them derelicts or better yet, how about imbeciles?"

"The word must also imply irresponsibility. Or a sense of incompetence," she continued though her speech was sluggish.

"Cretins! Fools!" Atmos spoke each word with vigor.

"I'm not following why you've placed an emphasis on

what to call these imaginary vagrants." Dassius's words tumbled weakly out of his mouth.

"Nice contribution Dassius, but I don't think the word vagrant is one hundred percent applicable."

"How about halfwit?" she suggested.

"Ha! I have it!" Atmos raised a pointed finger into the air. "We shall call them degenerates!"

"Degenerates?" Ceera was more surprised by the word itself than the fact she and Dassius spoke it in unison. "I've never heard that word before. I don't even know what it means. Can we choose another?"

"Nonsense, we just discussed what it means and believe me, it is quite accurate enough. Besides, we are playing a game, and this word heightens the entertainment value."

Atmos gave them a moment to adjust to his decision before continuing. "As I was saying, we all know taking something for granted can backfire. If you take something like air for granted, you are not devoting proper attention to it because you assume it will continue to do what it has always done. This careless attitude equates to being careless with your link to life itself.

"Let's go one step further by saying air quality doesn't naturally deteriorate. Now this is where the degenerates come into the picture, for these poisons devastating the planet were put here by them. In fact, these poisons were their most effective invention by far! They flung it into the air without a care in the world. Soon they ended up having massive amounts of it everywhere, capable of spoiling every breath in; imagine the same breath out. A huge blunder on their part, don't you agree?"

Ceera nodded though her brain was expanding into a state of disarray.

"These degenerates weren't entirely ignorant, well not all of them anyway. How do you suppose they reacted once they finally realized what was going on?"

"They held a meeting to discuss ways to amend their destructive habits?" she said.

"Wrong. Dassius?"

"The meeting instead focused on repairing the damage?"

"Nope, instead of figuring out ways to eliminate it, they argued about it. They bantered back and forth about whether or not poison in the air was a bad thing, even if it was really there. Some thought they would destroy this planet. Can you imagine such folly?"

"No," Dassius said.

"Now this planet, she just laughed while all this went on. She laughed so hard her water rose up and splashed ferociously on the shore, wreaking havoc on entire villages alongside the coast. And she laughed so hard again that a mighty wind lashed up out of nowhere and destroyed other villages. And she laughed so hard, she caused other things to happen as well, but I'm not going to talk about those things, for they are meant for others to explain, not I."

Atmos talked with such an animated demeanor that it was difficult for Ceera to accept the gravity of the situation. Even Dassius's face was held captive by an amused expression.

"The degenerates caused all this muck to occur and even allowed it to continue. And while they argued over whether or not the planet would be destroyed by their misdoings, she plotted their demise. And do you know how she plotted their demise?"

Ceera was too entranced to attempt a reply.

"This planet has been around a while, and no doubt

will continue to thrive for longer than either of you can comprehend. She is omnipotent, wise beyond her hundreds of billions of years," Atmos said matter-of-factly.

"Well, what did she do?" Dassius asked.

"Nothing." Atmos tossed his arms up with glee.

"Nothing?" she repeated.

"Correct," Atmos said. "Can you imagine? So powerful she did nothing, and it destroyed every last one of them!" He shook his head fondly, a huge smile brimming on his face.

"But wait, you said her waters splashed upon the shores and her winds wreaked damage. How is that nothing?"

"My dear Ceera"—Atmos's tone caused her to deflate—"didn't we already discuss the almighty nothing? Must we reiterate?"

"No, what I'm saying—"

"To be fair, let's view it from an alternate perspective. Doing nothing is leaving things how they are, which means leaving things in their natural state. So is it not true the planet was behaving in natural ways, to all these unnatural offenses?"

"I suppose so—"

"What else would you expect? These shortcomings the degenerates suffered were the planet's natural reactions, not acts of conscious motivation. What happened was as effortless to her as a leaf dropping off a tree. Do you catch my drift?"

"It all makes perfect sense!" Dassius blurted out loudly, startling even himself.

"The leaf of a tree?"

"Why, of course," Atmos said. "A leaf dropping from a tree is as natural as it comes. Not allowing the leaf to drop from the tree is comparable to not allowing the degenerates to breathe deadly air. It's that simple."

"I do see what you mean," she said. "If the planet had fixed the degenerates environment, that would have been doing something. In doing nothing, she allowed them to suffer the consequences of their own actions."

Atmos gave her a nod of approval.

Dassius looked deep in thought. "So what does the parable about the degenerates have to do with us?"

"No, you've got it wrong. The degenerates were pawns in our game of make believe, to accommodate for the missing link in your chain of thought."

"Well, how does all this relate to our forest?" she asked.

"You don't know how air affects a forest?" Atmos sounded offended.

"No, I mean yes. Of course I know." Ceera was also having difficulty reasoning in her defense.

"I am just here to clear up a little fog, not whip up answers to your every inquisition." The lightness in his tone had faded. He now looked at them very seriously. With a flick of his wrist, he whisked the whirling formation off the table. It floated into the distance and dissipated.

It became apparent there were no more details Atmos was willing to part with. A somber mood invaded him, and he shrunk into the configuration of a tired old man.

"We are off to visit Luma next," Dassius said.

"Ah yes, Luma." Atmos perked up. "We have a love hate relationship, her and I. She is still annoyed the sun sets in my turf."

"We hear she is difficult," Ceera said.

"Yes, but just mention my name and Oc~ea's, and her demeanor will change quickly."

Ceera and Dassius gave each other a look that spoke departure. They both stood.

"I suppose we should be on our way," Dassius said.

"It has been a very interesting visit," she said. "I had fun playing your game."

"Don't leave so sullen looking." Atmos flashed to the lively old man again. "Aren't you forgetting something? Oc~ea mentioned your need for this."

He held out his hand. An oblong vial shaped like a cyclone nestled in his palm. "My essence. It may come in handy when you are in need of a steady wind to ground your forest."

Dassius took it and held it between them. A whitish haze whirled about in what little room it had for freedom.

"Follow the force of the wind and let it guide you," Atmos said in a voice that sounded far away. "And keep a close eye, for the wind is ever changing."

As he spoke, the mist consumed him. A gust of air blew past. Atmos's mist and the leftover haze surrounding them got caught up with it. They watched it float away, swirling into the atmosphere with mysterious intention.

Chapter Thirteen

DASSIUS ATTEMPTED TO lead Ceera back to the cliff, but his movements were slow and hesitant. For the third time he paused to stare up at the sky, then lowered his eyes to scan the ground around them.

"Let's set the tent up over there." He pointed to a level spot containing a few patches of grass. "I don't want to climb down that cliff in the dark."

Ceera nodded. The mist had been bad enough, but wandering around cliffs at dusk was more dangerous than she could fathom. Besides, her body hurt all over and the tea had stolen the clarity from her thoughts.

Together, they gathered bits of grass from the nearby vicinity and added it to the patchy spot for extra cushion. The temperature dropped while Dassius erected the tent. She paced and rubbed her arms to keep warm. Darkness tinted the sky when they crawled inside.

She wrapped her blanket around herself, but it was no match for the cool air swirling outside the tent. Her feet were like icicles and she couldn't stop shaking.

"Dassius," she said, watching her breath mingle with the air.

"Let me guess," he responded. "You're cold."

"More like freezing. Aren't you?"

"Yeah, but if you think warm thoughts it's not so bad."

"I want to believe you"—she shivered—"but I'm too cold to try."

"We'll have to lie together then," Dassius responded.

Ceera sat up so eagerly she wondered whether she was delirious from the cold. "You don't mind?"

A short laugh escaped Dassius's throat.

"What?"

"I'm just remembering back to the briefing when you were so concerned about how big our tent would be."

Anger swelled up inside her, surely enough to warm her for the rest of the night. "Forget it," she snapped, flopping back down and turning her back on him.

"Oh, be quiet and come here." Dassius slung his arm around her waist and pulled her beside him.

His spot was less cold, but the gradual warming she felt came from the inside out. She basked in the comfort while he sat up to reposition the blankets. He placed hers on top of his and tucked the fabric around them. When he lay back down, he pressed against her. The heat from his touch spread all the way down to her toes. She buried her face into the blanket. He wrapped both his arms around her.

"Better?" he asked, tucking her head under his chin.

"Yes, thank you," she responded, glad the blanket muffled the pitch of her voice. She closed her eyes quickly, as if it would excuse her from having to answer any more questions.

The wind blew wild outside the tent, but the rhythmic beating of his heart led her into a deep sleep.

⟨⟩

Marvus stared soulfully at the planet in his room of the statues. Desnia's hand rested on his shoulder. She was trying to calm him, but tension radiated from her fingers.

"I just don't see the point in addressing the public again," she said. "We have nothing to gain by it."

"You're right, of course. Based on the content of the first transmit, we have nothing to gain by addressing the public."

"You agree with me?"

"Oh yes. We have nothing to gain." Marvus turned to look at her. "But we have much to lose."

Desnia threw her hands up in the air before resting them on her hips. "And just what would that be?"

"We could lose the respect of the public."

"Who says?" Desnia countered.

"If we do not speak, our opinions become nonexistent; this is the same as admitting defeat."

"The Council for Advancement has not voiced any opinions lately either."

"And why would they? They are trying to hide their involvement."

"Marvus, your logic enrages me sometimes," Desnia said in a voice as prickly as the thorny roses in her hair.

"You shouldn't be enraged. You should feel enlightened."

"Enlightened by logic that hasn't seen a decent day of rest for two weeks now? Don't flatter yourself."

Marvus chuckled. "Sounds like you are the one who could use some rest."

"You're right. I should have gone to bed hours ago. Everything else you've said tonight is nonsense, but since you don't sleep anymore, I suppose that's all I can expect." She walked brusquely to the door and slammed it behind her.

Marvus didn't know what she was talking about. Sleep had always been an inconsistent activity for him.

He slouched over the railing. His vision became bleary. One of the Archaics, Atmos to be exact, melded into the haziness his drooping eyelids now produced.

Marvus watched him drop in and out of his line of sight, not bothering to notice or care that the other three Archaics did not pander to the same ambiguity.

✥

Ceera wandered through a maze of trees, stumbling across thick roots. Mist whispered between the trunks. A woman's image sharpened up ahead, her tan dress swaying. Ceera was following her, the same female who had lured her into the forest outside of Semadon. Unaware of her pursuit, the woman wove between the trees with purpose, pausing periodically to peer around the trunks. Her long dark hair blew lightly with the wind. A bulky bag decorated with beads hung at her waist.

Ceera tried to catch up, but her pace refused to match her ambition. The brush wrapped around her ankles and slowed her progress. She struggled with every step.

The woman walked into a clearing and toward a large tree at the far edge. Its thick roots were parted, creating an opening near its base. She pulled the relic out of her bag. Then she knelt down and crawled inside.

When she emerged empty-handed, Ceera caught a view of her face for the first time. The woman looked strangely familiar, as if she resembled someone Ceera had once known. The pained expression on her face overrode its beauty.

She looked around quickly, searching for someone, though still oblivious to Ceera's presence. Closing her eyes, she placed her palm to her lips and kissed it gently. Then she held her hand outward momentarily, before letting it fall back to her side. Tears glistened down her cheeks.

Ceera wanted to approach but found herself unable to move. The woman turned and vanished into the scenery.

Darkness seized the woods, obscuring Ceera's vision. Dread chilled her skin. Something came up behind her, its raspy breath slithered across her neck and coiled around her ear before venturing inside.

She awoke with a start and bolted upright. Dassius stirred beside her. Reality sank in and the beating of her heart slowed. She burrowed back into the blankets. The dark night air surrounding her was not calming, though for the time being, she preferred it to the thought of falling back asleep.

Chapter Fourteen

WHEN CEERA AWOKE the next morning, she was glad to find herself alone. It would have made an awkward start to the day if she were still curled up beside Dassius. She smiled and stretched but her peace was short-lived. Something was nagging at her. Her recent dream slowly etched into her mind. She shivered despite the warm temperature. Was this the type of dream her mother had endured?

She crawled out of the blankets and exited the tent to find Dassius. He was perched nearby in the grass, staring up into the sky.

"I had another dream last night. If I tell you, do you promise to keep it between us?"

"Good morning." He looked up at her, squinting from the sun. "Didn't I agree to the same thing yesterday?"

"Yes, but I need to make sure it carries through today."

"It carries through forever, how's that?"

"Does it?"

"High Service doesn't need to know everything." Dassius winked and leaned back on his elbows.

Suddenly feeling as if she were on a stage, she sank down to her knees. "You're in good spirits this morning."

"I got enough sleep," he said. "Unlike you."

"Maybe you're having a tea relapse," she replied, smoothing her hair behind her ears.

"Maybe I'm trying to help you relax."

"Do I seem uptight?"

"Just tell me what happened."

She told him everything about the dream.

"That sounds more like a nightmare," he offered.

His suggestion was unwelcome and the weight of it scattered her thoughts.

"How did you get any sleep after that?" he continued.

"Once I realized where I was and you were there—" Ceera stopped talking abruptly.

"You felt safe?"

She plucked a few blades of grass from the dirt. "Sort of." Was he patronizing her?

"So you're finally starting to see it," he said with a grin.

"See what?" she demanded. "It was arctic in that tent, you know."

"How useful my training is."

Ceera released a breath she hadn't realized she'd been holding. "Oh I guess, but back to my dream. Do you think it means anything?"

"Do you?" he countered.

"Yes. Something doesn't want me to find the relic."

"Yet the woman does. And the forest sometimes does too."

"It's so confusing," she said, "and while we're on the subject, why me?"

"Who knows? Just remember, no one is forcing you to do anything."

He was right. She was the one who decided. High Service had just agreed. She could have sat silent at the meeting of the mystics though it would have tormented her to do so. But it wasn't that simple, not since she had spoken with her father. Something else drove her now too, something she could tell no one about. Not to mention that a sense of misgiving now pervaded everything.

Dassius tapped her knee. "We need to get going. You got more sleep than you realize. It's almost noon."

Ceera found the idea of walking down the cliff more frightening than going up it. At least when she ascended her focus was above and away from the threat of falling. Descending meant she had to keep her attention on the distance to the ground.

Dassius offered to go first, telling her she could grab onto him if she fell forward. He also offered to go last. She couldn't bring herself to agree to either arrangement.

Finally he tied their waists together with a stretchy rope. "If you fall, then we either fall together," he told her as he pulled on the knot, "or I grab onto the rope, and you swing into the wall but survive."

She couldn't quite grasp his logic, tried to envision it unsuccessfully, but for some reason him tying them together eased her fear. She had the sneaking suspicion this was why he suggested it, instead of thinking he could save them, but it was good enough for her.

Their painfully slow descent wracked her nerves. When they finally made it down, she laughed with delight and, without thinking, gave him a brief hug.

A smile played on his lips while he untied the knot

between them. "Or would you rather I left it?" He paused and she caught a teasing glimmer in his eye.

"Nope, set us free," she replied.

He finished untying the rope and stuffed it into his pack. Then they began their trek down the mountainside and back toward the cylinder.

✺

Falken waited impatiently for the second transmit to come through. The sooner he received more information, the sooner he could formulate his plan. Eventually he would be taking more rigorous action. Being the middleman was not as satisfying as the grander role he imagined for himself.

He had fiddled with his intervention equipment all day, attempting to strengthen its connection. If by chance the officials in the correspondence center made adjustments on their end, this could cut him off from the next transmit. All his fiddling could create this problem for them as well, and in fact he hoped so. Their inadequacy secured his gain.

Falken drummed his fingers and stared at the intervention device. He had no choice but to wait, which was a dangerous activity for him. For it was when nothing occupied him that his mind lost all restraint. When this happened, all the structure ingrained within him during his youth scattered, and what lurked in the dark corners of his brain surfaced. These tiny evils were clever; they came forth with prankish innocence, yet had the wickedness to corrupt their host when allowed to linger too long.

✺

It was early evening by the time Ceera and Dassius reached

the AT cylinder. Their route was less direct without the ram leading them, though Dassius managed to keep them headed in the right direction. They sank down in front of the cylinder and heaved sighs of exhaustion.

Dassius rested a few minutes before jumping to his feet to send the transmit. "Are we telling High Service about your dream?"

Anxiety rippled through her, and she looked at him in alarm.

"It's up to you," he told her. "We can just say the relic was hidden beneath a tree."

"That's not noteworthy," she replied. "There are thousands of trees in a forest."

"True. I'll say nothing about it then," he assured her before entering the cylinder.

Ceera arranged a meal to distract herself. When he returned, they devoured the food eagerly, having eaten nothing since they had woken up.

"Let's call it a day," Dassius suggested. "No more traveling."

"Sounds good to me," Ceera replied. "I'll take all the rest I can get."

While Dassius erected the tent, she settled back in the grass and stared up at the blue sky, thankful it was clear and devoid of any of the poisons that ravaged it so long ago, though the question of how it could be so remained.

✧

The quality of the second transmit was disconcerting. Leynin squinted as he tried to make out the words. Beside him, Asfin peered closer and frowned. The message was on the verge of unreadable. He struggled to keep his expression calm.

Asfin told Dassius his initial transmit was defective and asked him to resubmit. Leynin sighed deeply and sat back in his chair. He interlaced his fingers and placed them on his head. This faulty transmit intensified what had happened the day before. A renowned inventor, the man who designed the AT system, had declared he was calling it quits.

Hegliod's visit to the Aurora was unexpected, though his heavy knocking foretold the weight of his intentions. He informed the attendant who opened the door that he had pressing business to discuss. They ushered him into a conference room, where he droned about his recent failures to several officials. Apparently, a few weeks ago a concept of momentous importance had aborted itself from his brain. He was stricken it would not return. His AT system breaking down only added to the upset.

He spent the last few weeks trying to recover but to no avail. Matters managed to get even worse. He was informed that not only had his peers lost trust in his machines, but they also thought him the collaborator of a crime. These insults in conjunction with his previous failings further deteriorated his ambition to resume his scientific duties. He was no longer motivated to do much of anything.

It was time, he had stated, to end his stint as an inventor, before the stress took too much of a toll. After taking an afternoon off to mourn the loss of his description, he insisted he would pursue a role in daily operations as an orbit sweeper. According to Hegliod, the orbits were covered in filth and needed someone's immediate attention.

High Service made attempts to change Hegliod's mind,

but he would not be dissuaded. He left them with a promise to begin his new duties the following day.

The officials, including Leynin, were stunned. Never before had any Semion demanded to change descriptions once established.

The situation also read potential disaster. The AT system was still a new mode of transportation. Hegliod's expertise would be needed for maintenance and potential updates. Equally troubling was that two Semions on assignment relied on it as a means of travel. The faulty transmit only enhanced the dilemma.

If Hegliod was unwilling to fix the AT system, and not just unwilling but outright incapable due to his mental collapse, what would happen if the system broke again?

Chapter Fifteen

FALKEN DIDN'T BOTHER telling the lady at the front desk his purpose for being in the library. He walked right past her and through several rooms filled with books. He even stifled his usual bitterness as he passed through the planetary orb room. When he found the Caretaker's door, he rapped forcefully on it.

A faint voice from inside called out, "Just one moment." He waited impatiently until the Caretaker swung the door open and eyed him curiously.

"I am Falken Grihne. May I have a word with you?"

"Falken Grihne?" The Caretaker tapped the side of his chin with his pointer finger. "Do you have an appointment?"

"I don't have an appointment, but I do have a question. I'm a member of the Council for Advancement and need to resolve an important matter."

The Caretaker looked taken aback. "Your Council for Advancement never inquires about anything. Are you sure you have the right man, or are even dealing with the right council?"

"Believe me," Falken said in a strained voice. "I know what I'm doing. Can I please come in?"

"I suppose you can, but you will have to pardon the dust."

Upon entering, Falken was nearly overcome and sneezed three times in a row.

"I might have dusted had I known you were coming." The Caretaker motioned to an empty chair.

"I hardly notice it." Falken cleared his throat several times.

"So tell me what information your council sent you for."

"Well, some classified information has been exposed. Highly classified," Falken stressed. "And I must learn everything I can about this issue."

"Information about the past I presume?"

"I'm told you are the expert."

"I am the Caretaker of Ancient Affairs and all that entails; however, I must admit this is the extent of my knowledge. As time moves forward, I find it difficult to keep up. As a result, I am practically clueless about anything recent."

"Very good." Falken restrained a smile. "What I need is information about the period before the Semion's. Do you know about this time?"

"Yes, I do," the Caretaker said. "And there is quite a selection of books about it. Let me recommend a certain few." He turned to one of his shelves, grabbed a book, and started flipping through its pages.

"Actually, I would prefer a verbal telling—" Clouds of dust traveled toward him, and he found himself in the middle of a coughing fit.

"If you could survive it, I would suggest you start here." The Caretaker waved the book at him.

Falken's eyes watered profusely. He shook his head and covered his mouth to stifle his loud coughs.

"Too much for you, eh?" The Caretaker clapped the book shut causing another cloud of dust to appear. He grabbed a different book off the shelf and held it out. "You could try this one, but it is a trifle drab at times. Thorough but dull."

"No thanks. No." Falken cleared his throat again. "I just have a single question. If you answer as I suspect you will, then my inquiry ends."

"I'm not surprised. Members of the Council for Advancement are never that interested in the ancients. Keep pushing forward as you do, and you may find yourself right back at the beginning."

Suppressing the urge to roll his eyes, Falken decided to get straight to the point. "Has any culture ever lived before the Semions, anywhere on this planet?"

The Caretaker's expression grew serious. "Not that I'm aware."

"And you are the one who would know."

"I know what can be found in these books. There is nothing of that nature suggested in any of them. They speak of the beginning, when the Semions came forth from the planet, called into existence by the will of nature itself—"

"I am well aware of the parable," Falken interrupted. "It's quite the intriguing tale; however, we from the Council for Advancement consider that story a fabrication of reality."

The Caretaker eyed Falken skeptically. "If you know so much, then why are you coming to me?"

"To verify the facts. So you are telling me nothing

in those books even briefly mentions anyone besides us, correct?"

"Correct, not a single book implies it. Why do you ask?"

"I am here to ask the questions," Falken replied.

"Then do you have any more?"

"No sir." Falken stood. "Your response is all I needed."

"Good." The Caretaker smiled slyly. "Perhaps I shall spend the day pondering why a member of the Council for Advancement, being as progressive as you are, would resort to looking for answers in places that do not always house information up to your standard."

"Where else would I look?"

"Doesn't your laboratory contain all the answers?"

"Not yet."

The Caretaker returned Falken's gaze with a dubious expression.

"I must be going." Falken backed away. "Don't bother pondering anything. It was a trivial assignment."

"If you say so. I'm not one to argue."

As Falken turned to go, he noticed something poking out from behind one of the bookshelves. "Thanks for seeing me on such short notice," he said over his shoulder. His eyes focused once again on the object on the floor, which was a book of course.

"Goodbye, I hope you find all the answers you are seeking."

Falken could not bring himself to move due to what he had read on the book. The entire cover was not visible, but on the top portion were the letters *AT*.

"Is something wrong Mr. Grihne?" the Caretaker asked with a hint of irritation in his voice.

"No, well maybe." Falken went over to the bookshelf and started fumbling with the bottom of his pant leg. Knowing his cloak would conceal his next move, he scooped up the book and stuck it inside one of the inner pockets.

"Sorry, there was just a problem with my attire." He straightened and adjusted his collar.

"Well, it looks fine to me. Have a nice day, Mr. Grihne." The Caretaker's politeness was quite obviously forced.

"You do the same, sir." Falken shut the door behind him and walked swiftly around the hall, through the planetary orb room, past the shelves of books and into the main lobby. His objective was to get back to his dwelling as quickly as possible so he could examine what hid inside his cloak.

The suspense was overwhelming. He made eye contact with no one as he wound his way around the orbits. Finally, he reached his own small dwelling located on the outskirts.

He burst through the door and shut it before reaching inside his cloak. Sure enough, what he read inside the Caretaker's office still graced the front cover, along with the most satisfying continuation. The entire cover read: *AT System: A Technical Guide, by Hegliod Avatus.*

He flipped through the pages. All the particulars of the system, along with diagrams of the controls and lengthy formulas taking up entire pages, were now literally at his fingertips.

His luck had finally caught up with him. He had not even been aware such a book existed, but here it was: the complete workings of the AT system explained within one hundred and twenty pages of technical jargon. This book would enable him to control the entire system and clinch his victory against the other council.

Now, how to keep old Hegliod out of the picture? After

all, what good would it do to have control of the AT system with Hegliod around to counter all his progress? There had to be a way, and a tiny voice inside his head answered that there was.

⁊

Falken placed the book on his desk. He leaned back in his chair and closed his eyes. It was time to formulate a plan. Outsmarting High Service to intercept the transmits was one thing. Outsmarting Hegliod by altering the course of travel was another. It would require his planning to stretch into more devious territory.

Too bad the old man couldn't be induced to the same state the AT installers suffered, although no one knew how long they would be confined to their condition. He could snap out of it at the least opportune time, say when Falken traveled via AT cylinder to meet up with Ceera and Dassius. No, Hegliod had to remain out of commission indefinitely.

He could accuse Hegliod of committing a crime, one requiring jail time, but his council had already tried that. High Service was obviously incapable of believing Hegliod had any sort of ill intentions.

He wondered how Hegliod felt about the CfA's accusation. Was he upset? Did he even care? A tiny thought stirred inside his head. Yes, it was true. Hegliod was a very private man, did not interact much with anyone. If he didn't know how Hegliod felt about the matter, there was a good chance neither did anyone else. Opportunity always lies in the unknown.

A rustling sound came from within one of the cages nearby. The rat stared at him from between the closely laid metal bars. With the sudden turn of events in his life, he had neglected his two pets. He rose and wandered over to a small refrigerator and pulled out a clear bag stuffed with ground up plant parts.

He walked back to the cages, pulled a plastic glove onto his hand, and sprinkled some of the plant into the rat's cage. It began feeding with quick, greedy movements. He also sprinkled some within the bird's cage although that creature tended to be less receptive. It had far surpassed both the dog and the cat, but he wondered how much longer it would live. He fed it real food in proportion to how much of the oleander it consumed, and the bird only took a few nibbles each time he offered. The rat had taken to the poison much more so than all the creatures he studied thus far.

His mind shifted back to Hegliod, and a sliver of thought broke free from his brain. He paused to admire its potential. It had worked its way into his scheming with skillful ease. But it was not alone. With it came an idea that at first revolted him, but quickly stroked his thoughts into submitting to its cleverness.

The answer to his dilemma revolved around the theme of both the transmits he had intercepted. The Archaics thought the planet had been rampant with poison in the distant past. True or not, he could only guess, but here in his own dwelling Falken was experimenting with how much poison certain types of animals could ingest without dying. He was ready to put this knowledge to use in a way he never considered before.

Suicide was rare within Semion culture, but occasionally someone resorted to it when life's problems grew too harsh to bear. Hegliod's fall from grace set him up for this end quite nicely. Falken just had to settle on which type of

poison to use, for most Semions had a difficult time keeping oleander in their system. He would have to make a visit
to the lab to acquire one easier to retain. He glanced over at
his clock. He had one hour to make it to the lab before it
closed down for the evening.

The quicker its effects the better as well, he decided as
he slipped on his shoes, for both the old scientist and his
own warped agenda.

❧

When Falken entered the laboratory housing the supplies,
he was pleased to see only a handful of men and women
doing research. A pair discussed a DNA molecule displayed
on a large screen that corresponded with the slide beneath
their microscope. A few others hovered around test tubes
and metal pots. In another area, someone studied a circular
glass cage containing genetically engineered plants.

The scientists glanced up at the sound of the door but
quickly looked away when they saw him. Falken was not
bothered by the snub, for he knew their disregard for him
would bode well for what he planned.

He walked across the room until he came to the doorway marked Chemicals, entered the code to unlock the
door and went inside. Small jars, arranged alphabetically,
lined the walls. He scanned the labels for the *C*s while listening for the sound of the door opening behind him. He
was fairly certain no one else would join him due to the
welcome he had received upon entering the lab; however,
there was such a thing as an impatient scientist.

Finding a small jar containing cyanide, he stuffed it in
his pocket and guided the jars behind it to the front of the

shelf so they appeared undisturbed. He grabbed a dummy jar, which contained a harmless substance, and left the room with it.

The checkout area was nearby. He placed his jar on the table in front of the man behind the desk. It teetered, and he held out his hand to steady it but inadvertently knocked it over. It rolled toward the annoyed man, who caught it and set it before Falken on the table.

"Good thing it didn't break," he grumbled. "Hope you're not this clumsy with it when you put it to use." He took out his ledger and wrote the name of the substance on it. Placing the clipboard in front of Falken, he pointed at the signature line.

"Don't worry," Falken replied as he swirled his name onto the page. "I've been out of transition for almost a decade now."

"I couldn't tell by the way you placed it on my desk. Keep in mind there is not an endless supply. There would be a waiting period if you waste it."

"I'm aware." Falken snatched the jar up, gave the man a dirty look, and strode out of the room.

Eyes averted him as he departed, but Falken paid no attention. He was already planning how to get Hegliod to invite him into his dwelling the next morning.

↊

While most Semions were tucking themselves into their beds for the evening, tired but perhaps still tuned in to the global update, High Service was holding a meeting nowhere near adjournment. The recent transmit sent by Dassius, coupled with Hegliod's resignation, created a furor within the Aurora that needed to be addressed before any officials could even consider sleep. Some were still in shock about Hegliod. Others were concerned about Atmos's advice. Thus, the conversation went between the two quite liberally.

"I cannot fathom what Atmos intended to convey when he proposed the idea of a culture preceding ours," Karnen declared from his position near the front of the meeting room.

"He said he used the idea as a way to answer their question," Fresdin replied.

"That's what he said but you have to wonder," Karnen said.

"I am most concerned with Hegliod's turn from science. What if the AT system breaks? The man seems incapable of fixing it at the moment," Risa said.

"The transmit did come through faulty the first time," Leynin reiterated for the third time. "But it could have been a bad connection."

"It's futile," Asfin interjected. "He is completely changed. I wouldn't trust him to fixing anything at the moment."

"He wouldn't comply anyway," Leynin said. "He says he is done."

"How do we tell such a thing to the public?" Risa said.

"You mean how do we tell them about Hegliod? Won't they see for themselves?"

And so the conversation went. The sphere sevens sat back and watched the lower spheres converse back and forth, not one of them offering any real solutions, their comments only feeding each other's worries.

Zivan leaned over to talk quietly to Sadra. "How long are we going to let this go on?" he croaked out. He was old and not accustomed to staying up so late.

"It's good for them," Sadra insisted. "They've never had any real controversy during their reign."

Zivan leaned back in his chair. It was true. Most of the lower spheres only had experience with trivial matters. He, Sadra, and all other sphere sevens, had come into their positions during tumultuous times. If it weren't for Draevik, their cunning leader, perhaps things would have turned out quite differently. Unfortunately, the sphere seven was severely ill and could not advise at present.

"Too bad Draevik isn't here," Zivan muttered. "He has a way of inspiring solutions."

Sadra raised her eyebrows at him. "Jesra was also quite adequate, before she passed."

"His companion? Yes, of course," Zivan responded as he scanned the lower spheres.

"Perhaps Ceera and Dassius should be brought back to Semadon," a sphere two said.

The suggestion made Zivan cringe.

"We can't do that," Hetia said firmly. "The Planetary Stability Monitor still reads abnormal and our AT installers remain incompetent. We cannot surrender our cause just because difficulties arise. We have an obligation to our people."

Sadra winked at Zivan. "I like her. She has a good head for a sphere two."

Zivan grunted in reply. If she could put an end to the meeting, now that would impress him.

"I say we turn in for the evening," Hetia proclaimed. "The solution to these problems will clarify itself with time."

Zivan perked up. It was as if she had heard him. Or maybe she did have a good head on her shoulders, or as he liked to put it, a way with the spheres.

Chapter Sixteen

THE SUN WAS still a few hours shy of presenting itself when Falken left his dwelling to pay a visit to Hegliod Avatus. He hadn't planned on waiting until it was almost daylight, but it had taken him awhile to decide his course of action. He had to make his deed look deliberate, intended by Hegliod of course.

He wasn't proud of what he was about to do, but it was necessary and would free the path to his success. Soon he would be the lone Semion versed with the intricacies of the system. With Hegliod out of the picture, he would be the one in control of its doings, the mission, and the two Semions traveling around in the cylinders.

Nimren and Casma would be impressed once they knew he possessed the book. Unless, Falken paused as he made his way through the orbits, did he even have to tell them? Or should he? Perhaps it was best not to reveal all his secrets; the coincidence of Hegliod's misfortune coupled with the book's discovery could cause Nimren and Casma to question him even more. Incriminating himself would take him out of the game. Dominance was not about exposing information, but about deciding when to reveal your advantage. Timing was key.

Something out of the corner of his eye made him jump. A figure trudged toward him, unaware of Falken's desire to remain unseen. He narrowed his eyes at this newfound enemy and did a double take upon closer inspection.

It was Hegliod, the very man he planned on paying a visit, but in the secrecy of the man's dwelling not out in the orbits! He gaped as Hegliod neared, in shock for two reasons. One being that Hegliod was not at home like he assumed he would be at this early time of day, the other centering on the fact the old inventor was pushing a broom.

Instead of walking past, Hegliod stopped to drag his broom around the outline of Falken's feet. Then he continued on, never once making eye contact or even acknowledging Falken as a living Semion.

The encounter stripped him of all motivation, for his plan was now impossible. Struck by the oddity of the circumstance, he fled back in the direction of his dwelling.

Ceera awoke the next morning with a strange feeling of contentment. Blankets nestled around her, their soft warmth lulling her to stay put. Her softly blinking eyes then fixated on her own bedding, empty and ruffled nearby. Panic seeped into her bliss. She shifted slightly to confirm her suspicions, her shoulder bumping into Dassius's hard chest. What was she doing beside him?

She rolled away quickly, causing his eyes to flutter open.

"You're up early today," he said with a faint smile.

Did he know she had been next to him? She ignored the tempting urge to lie back down. "I'd like to get an early start."

Dassius didn't need much persuading. He sat up and began folding his bedding. "Just because it's early right now doesn't mean it will be wherever the cylinder takes us."

"Right, I keep forgetting." Ceera busied herself with her own unused bedding, preferring to pretend that the sleeping situation had been the end of an unwanted dream.

They packed up and ate a quick breakfast. Before long, they were traveling between cylinders.

When they reached their destination, a barren landscape strewn with various sized boulders surrounded them. Rock columns nearly a hundred feet high dominated the terrain. In the far distance and enclosed within a wide expanse of greenery was a gray mountainous protrusion.

"That must be where we can find her," Dassius said.

"I have never been to a volcano before," Ceera replied. "I'm not sure I'm comfortable with the idea."

"Just be glad it's inactive. My instincts tell me it's been a few hundred years since its last eruption." Dassius headed toward the massive plateau.

She followed. "For some reason, that does not console me."

"You're right. We're stepping foot on volatile territory so let's be careful."

"Are you having second thoughts?"

"Just because there may be danger ahead, doesn't mean we should give up."

Stone structures arched above them, and they sidestepped mounds of rock obstructing their path.

"Do you think it will be worth it?" Her stomach churned restlessly.

"Yes, we need her vial. I bet it will be especially helpful."

"Why?"

"Because the greater the risk, the greater the profit," he said.

"Aren't you frightened?"

"I don't acknowledge fear." He said the statement as if it were a perfectly normal thing to say. "My training focused on eliminating it."

Struck by the concept, she reached around to her pack and unzipped a side pocket. "Tell me about it."

"I will if you promise to keep your fingers off your recorder."

Her hand fell back to her side. "How can I resist?"

"It's your choice. What I tell you has to stay between us."

"Ok," she said. "I promise."

"Normally I wouldn't even talk about my training, but I think hearing about it could help you. You see, in order to maximize my capabilities, I needed to be able to regulate my mind. My logic suffered whenever my feelings had control over me. To avoid this, my superiors analyzed and ranked all the basic emotions." Dassius paused for a moment and looked around. He shifted direction to the left and began walking again.

"And the findings?"

"It was unanimous. My superiors determined fear was the least helpful emotion. It carries no advantage whatsoever. Usually it just obstructs intelligence or holds one back from doing something useful. Granted, it may also keep one from doing harmful things, but one's intelligence can do that much more efficiently. Being in my line of work, it was important to reduce my fears, which is not as difficult as you may think."

"Well how is it done?"

"The researchers designed a special program. The purpose was to strengthen my ability to ignore outside distractions. My mentors exposed me to all sorts of unpleasant situations to help me with this."

"What sort of unpleasant situations?"

"One day I was placed in a glass cage with hundreds of fire ants. They crawled all over my body and bit me."

"You did this for an entire day?"

"Yes, I was terribly itchy afterward."

"How horrible," she said. "It sounds like your training is in conflict with the Semion code of ethics."

"I could have denied the test. I accepted it though because I knew it would make me stronger and besides, fire ants can't kill you. I can deny any test whenever I want."

"You're making me glad I'm a scribe."

"Do you still want to hear more?"

"Yes," she replied.

"After the fire ants and a bunch of other tests, my emotions had been thoroughly numbed. I was now able to control their intensity. With fear, as I stated, the goal was to eliminate it entirely. I was taught visualization techniques and association games that affiliated fear with a multitude of repugnancies. I spent hours differentiating it as its own worthless entity."

"It sounds almost silly, but I suppose it makes sense."

"Now that fear was both minimized and essentially demonized," Dassius went on, "the last step involved redirecting my thoughts."

"Visualization again?"

"No." Dassius shook his head. "I was hooked up to a machine."

"Oh," Ceera said softly. "What sort of machine?"

"A mind reading machine. It monitored my brain waves and alerted me when it sensed the onset of fear. My motivation was to outsmart the machine, and the only way to do so was to avoid it."

"I don't understand. What made you fearful while you were hooked up to the machine?"

"The specifics don't matter," Dassius stated dismissively. "Let's just say after being subjected to that, fear is something I have no time for. I have practically abolished it from my life."

"I wish I could say the same thing. Although I'm not too sure about what you went through to achieve it."

"What I went through worked. You should figure out a way to manage your own fears. And in the meantime"—Dassius gently grabbed onto her arm and whirled her to face him—"don't be so hard on yourself."

He could see right through her, apparently, but his expression was kind.

"I don't like relying on others," she admitted.

"Don't look at it that way." He rested his hands on her shoulders and stared at her intently. "We've both been trained in different fields. Let me do what I'm good at and don't feel ashamed if you need my help."

Ceera smiled tentatively. "I won't."

"Good." His dark blue eyes glimmered with satisfaction.

They drew back from each other at the same time, almost too quickly, and she fell into step beside him. He was turning out to be different than she expected, but she wasn't willing to dwell on that.

Instead, her mind shifted to his scientific approach of controlling emotions. Her own feelings were well kept when it came to her work as a scribe, but succeeded in influencing her when outside of this capacity. If only she could break away from this pattern and keep her emotions in check all the time.

Stone formations towered above her head. They inspired wonder and gave her a sense of adventure. This fresh point of view made her feel courageous. Visiting Luma was just part of her job. She would remain as professional as if she were recording a meeting at the Aurora.

Soon the stubble beneath their feet transformed into lush grass. Elk grazed in the distance.

"If the elk can exist so peacefully within Luma's domain, I suppose I can survive for part of a day," she said.

"There you go, think rationally."

The volcano was approximately a few miles ahead. She moved toward it with confidence, though she kept close to Dassius as they neared.

❧

Hegliod didn't appear to notice the attention he drew when he began his role of orbit sweeper. Many heads turned his way during the first few hours; whispers trailed behind him after that. The fact that Hegliod Avatus, once celebrated inventor of the AT system, trudged around the orbits pushing a sweeper was a heavily discussed topic when he wasn't within hearing range. Although truth be told, Hegliod wasn't listening anyway. Only one subject littered his mind, and it wasn't what his fellow Semions may or may not be thinking.

Garbage. Yes, filth now consumed his thoughts, cluttering his every waking notion. He must rid Semadon of the rot immersed within the cracks of everyone's path. This task elated him, filled him with a sense of purpose he had not felt for some time. Since he was unable to partake in a gratifying endeavor within the realm of science, had lost his newfound idea weeks ago now, he satisfied himself with this new task.

So the sight of Hegliod wandering around the orbits like clockwork, taking a break only when necessity plagued him, came to be accepted. Soon all Semions viewed him as part of the normal scenery.

"Poor Hegliod," some would say after he brushed past. "What happened messed him up more than it did the rest of us."

Followers of the CfA spoke a more vicious language. "Look at Hegliod," they would scoff. "See how he suffers for his underhandedness."

Although High Service defended the integrity of his AT system, some still accepted the viewpoint of the Council for Advancement and thought Hegliod was in cahoots with the Council for Natural Law.

When Hegliod came around, they would say things a little too loudly and throw litter after his passing figure. Sometimes it would fall behind him; other times it would flutter within his line of sight. Hegliod would keep walking and sweeping, indifferent to the why or the how in the arrival of this garbage, sweeping it up with the vigor he had only previously felt upon the realization of a grand idea.

❧

Forced to forfeit his insidious plan, Falken focused on the remainder of his agenda. First, he needed to inform Nimren and Casma of the second transmit before news of it came on the global update. Secondly, he would be indulging in the book.

"What nonsense has this next Archaic revealed?" Nimren asked once Falken entered the meeting room.

Their eyes searched him greedily as he took a seat, and he reveled in the satisfaction of having information they wanted.

"He elaborated on what the previous one stated, and he gave them another vial. He also hinted at the existence of a culture living before our own."

"Before us?" Nimren was astounded.

"It was presented by way of a game. The Archaic made the suggestion, insisting he had done so for the sake of fun."

"This didn't strike them as strange?"

"It did and they weren't alone. I took it upon myself to go visit the Caretaker and inquire. Only because I wanted to confirm what I already knew. He verified there was no record of any such culture."

Falken hoped they wouldn't ask him when the transmit came, for he would have to explain why he waited so long to tell them. He wanted to leave out the reason behind his delay, knew they wouldn't take kindly to his plan to dispose of Hegliod that morning.

"I wonder what the CfNL hopes to gain by creating this idea," Casma said.

"Frankly, I think the Archaic was duping them, playing with their heads."

"You must be right. He was attempting to create a sense of disorder in their minds, for when this occurs, one will believe anything," Nimren said.

"Yes, although the intent of it backfired."

"What do you mean?"

"While I was at the Caretakers I came upon something useful."

"What is it Falken?" Casma said.

"This." Falken whipped his secret out into the open for the first time.

Nimren was the first to get his hands on it. Casma leaned over to inspect the cover with him. Looks of amusement swept over their faces as he flipped through the pages.

"So Hegliod the inventor wrote a book about his marvelous AT system," Nimren said as he swung his arm up toward the ceiling. "Perhaps he should write a book about maintaining one's sense of self as well."

Casma chuckled.

"I'm confident it will enable me to manipulate the AT cylinders to do whatever I want."

"What do you have in mind?" Nimren asked.

"I'll make it so High Service can't respond to any transmits sent by Ceera and Dassius. Then, I'll manipulate the controls so they can't receive them either. Only we will be aware of what is happening to them."

Nimren nodded his head slowly. Casma's eyes glistened with excitement.

"After High Service is completely cut off, I'll join Ceera and Dassius without them knowing. You said you would love to get your hands on those vials. I could intercept them when Ceera and Dassius first arrive at the forest. This would destroy the CfNL's plan."

"What happens if they come back to Semadon before they go to the forest?" Casma asked. "If they realize their correspondence has been cut off?"

"I've skimmed the contents of the book. Very soon, I'll be able to alter their course by the press of a few buttons. They will be where I program them to be."

Nimren looked deep in thought. "Not only could this

cause a greater rift between us and the CfNL, but it could be the downfall of our council if you are found out. How do you propose to do this without setting us up for blame?"

"Taking over the AT system is foolproof. There's no one besides the inventor capable of finding me out. I'm convinced he will remain out of the picture. You've seen how disconnected he's become."

"His slip from his duties is rather appalling," Casma agreed.

"My plan to meet up with Ceera and Dassius is foolproof as well. I'll disguise myself so I can't be incriminated."

"Have you thought about how you will fend off Dassius?" Casma said. "He is supposedly quite skilled."

"Not yet, but I promise you, I will think of something and it will work."

"Ah," Nimren said, "it seems your plan is well on its way."

"We knew we could count on you Falken," Casma said. "Justice to our council is impending, this much is evident."

Falken sensed her appreciation was artificial. He picked up the book. "I must go. I have lots of studying to do."

"Keep us informed," Nimren said.

Falken responded with a swift nod before exiting the room.

When she was sure Falken had distanced himself from the office, Casma turned to Nimren.

"I didn't realize it would come to this," she hissed at him. "He's taking it upon himself to concoct his own plans, without our consent."

"He takes his job very seriously," Nimren responded.

"Yes, but it could backfire. I'm not comfortable with his underhanded scheming."

"And just what do you consider enlisting a spy to be?"

"That's different and you know it. This, well, he could destroy our council."

"You forget," Nimren said, "we have a plan too. Remember, involving Falken gives us a scapegoat in the event we are found out. His coming up with his own plans goes along with ours."

"I suppose," Casma said tentatively. "But I'm not convinced. I'm not sure I want to be involved in this any longer."

"It's too late now," Nimren said. "You cannot excuse yourself from all this without resigning your chair. Doing so would alert Falken to your lack of confidence. Is that really what you want?"

Casma shuddered. No, she did not want to subject herself to that.

Chapter Seventeen

DUSK APPROACHED AS the sun set on the horizon. Dassius veered away from the pinnacle of the volcano just as their feet grazed the onset of its slope.

"She is not near the mouth or at its incline. Let's wind through this narrow passage here." Dassius walked over to a rocky decline partially hidden by the flank of the mountain. He edged his way down using flat stones jutting from the dirt.

Ceera followed using the adjacent rocks to steady herself.

Once they reached the stubble below, a small open area connected to another stone pathway snaking upward. The walls enclosing it were steep and layered. Colorful igneous intrusions streamed across and made thin grooves adequate for clenching onto. They scaled their way back up using the grooves for support.

Upon reaching the top, Ceera found herself facing a breathtaking spectacle. Still miles away they had a good view of the volcano and the spectacular sunset hovering over it. A broad strip of orange melted fluidly into a majestic purple that was presently ruler of the sky.

A figure perched at the edge of the cliff, accentuated by the vibrant colored beams radiating from the horizon. Red tresses whirled in the breeze. They stepped closer to this apparition until they were only a few feet behind. Then the figure turned ever so slowly, and Ceera was momentarily spellbound.

The woman before them emanated an overpowering sense of self. Fiery-red iridescent hair tumbled halfway down her back and offset her pale luminous skin. Amber colored eyes gripped them profoundly and bound them within her gaze. Her facial features were sharp and angled, matching the gems adorning the necklace wrapped around her ivory neck.

The gown she wore was two-toned. The bodice and most of the skirt gleamed a coal black tinted grayish purple. The ends of the gown and its bell shaped sleeves looked as if they had been dipped in red dye the color of molten lava. The material of the dress clung to her body and had a swirling rubbery texture unlike any ordinary cloth.

"I have been waiting," the words slipped passionately out of her shimmering lips. She gestured toward the distance and returned to viewing its splendor. Her body swayed as if she were in a trance.

Minutes went by before Dassius spoke. "We are honored to meet you, Luma."

She stiffened; her gaze dropped.

"Charmed even," he continued.

She turned again from the natural spectacle and observed them head on. Her face was unreadable.

"My name is Dassius."

"I'm Ceera."

Luma narrowed her eyes. Her lips formed into a smile devoid of pleasure. "Come this way."

They followed her slow, even steps to an area encircled

with large blocks of pumice. Ash covered the ground. Luma motioned at the pumice for them to sit and they obeyed.

"How can I assist you?" she asked, her voice dripping with contempt.

An aura of hostility now hung thickly in the air. Ceera's body shrank inward.

"We're sorry to bother you, but we were told your knowledge could help us," said Dassius

"By the mystics," Ceera said. "They advised us to come."

Luma glowered at her. Contention radiated from her eyes. "I see."

"We visited your sister Oc~ea," Dassius said. "She was kind enough to help us."

Luma sniffed. "Oc~ea keeps watch on my worms. They thrive near my vents at the bottom of her ocean floor. A very strange arrangement indeed, but we make it work. Although we are forever in opposition you can say we are close, antithetical, but very much compatible all the same. Odd, don't you think?"

"Atmos helped us as well," Ceera said hesitantly as she pulled her recorder out of her pack.

Luma cringed as her cheeks turned a rare hue of crimson. "Atmos," she repeated. "Why the thought of him materializes whenever I view the sunset." There was a moment of silence in which Luma appeared to be brooding about something.

"We need your take on a certain matter," Dassius said. "Atmos and Oc~ea revealed there was a time when the planet was rampant with poison."

"You see, a forest caused our Planetary Stability Monitor to read abnormal," Ceera said. "This mystery spurs our inquiry."

"And we need to know if you would be willing to part with any knowledge you have of this era." Dassius ignored Luma's deliberate frown. "Most importantly, Oc~ea mentioned you would be willing to give us a bit of your essence to use for protection in the forest."

"I am quite aware of your reason for being here. Spare me any more details," Luma said, a look of boredom inherent on her face.

Ceera was taken aback. She glanced sideways at Dassius, who frowned slightly.

"I apologize," he said. "But both Atmos and Oc~ea asked for explanations which is why we filled you in."

"They asked so they could determine whether or not you were worthy of their time. I, however, am a much harsher critic than my contingents. It is better for you if I do not analyze your situation. What matters is you are here, and I am obligated to serve you." The bitterness in her tone overshadowed her assent.

"So you will help us?" Dassius asked.

"If I must, but first"—she scanned the piles of ash—"I shall make fire."

As she stepped into the center of the circle, the ground rumbled. It rose and widened, forming a small caldera that fit perfectly within the encircling pumice. Red lines zigzagged like streaks of lightning across the elliptical crater beneath Luma's bare feet. A strange smile grazed her face, and she stepped down onto a block of pumice opposite of Ceera and Dassius. She then turned to face her creation.

Stretching out the fingers on her right hand, she stared in admiration at her rings. Fine-grained swirling stones decorated her middle and pinky fingers. Each projected their own significance with blunt precision. Adorning her ring finger was a stone speckled white and light purple. The stone encircling her pointer finger was smooth, black and impeccably glossy.

"I used my andesite just the other day." She lowered her middle finger. "My dacite isn't too engaging at the moment." Her ring finger dropped too. "Aha!" Her eyes lingered on her pointer finger. "My obsidian will do the honor." She flicked the ring open and blew.

Her breath skimmed the top of the opening. Specks of red dust emerged and settled in the mouth of the caldera. Upon contact, a fire flared up with a fierce crackle, illuminating Luma atop the pumice, before settling back down to a modest blaze. It flashed shadowy images all around them.

Luma stepped off the pumice and sat down. She locked eyes with the blaze. Her pupils grew large and small, flickering with the flame. "Very interesting," she said.

Ceera positioned her fingers on her recorder.

"What do you see?" asked Dassius.

She lifted her gaze from the fire. "I will tell you, but I must admit it does not disturb me."

"Was fire affected by the poisons too?" Ceera asked, wishing her voice didn't sound so small.

"Poisons? Fire?" Luma laughed derisively, throwing her head back. "You must be joking right?"

Ceera did not know how to respond.

"Please. You can fight fire with fire, but it only strengthens the blaze. You can't beat"—Luma paused dramatically—"heat." She tossed the word off her lips with such force the flame blazed spasmodically, casting a wicked glow which closed in around them.

Ceera's neck grew hot and she touched her cheeks with her hands. It was definitely getting warm.

"Heat and fire are unstoppable," Luma continued. "Even when extinguished, if Oc~ea feels the need to assert herself, they always rise again. There is no such thing as plundering such a powerful union."

"What are you talking about?" Dassius eyed her shrewdly. His reddened face had taken on an oily appearance.

"Oc~ea thinks because she mothers children that she has rule over the play of my two specialties as well. She can certainly ruin my fun."

"No." Dassius shook his head. "That's not what I meant. How does all this relate to us?"

"I forgot we were talking about you, how silly of me." Luma's voice was thick with sarcasm. "It relates to you because the time you are inquiring about began with an increase in heat. Not an excessive amount all at once, but a few degrees here and a few degrees there."

As Luma spoke the temperature increased further. Ceera felt dampness where her hair met her face.

"Now even just a few degrees can have an impact. Let's just say it is enough to stir things up."

"What caused this increase in heat?" Dassius asked as sweat trickled down his forehead.

"The cause?" Luma feigned confusion. "Perhaps you mean to ask what ignited this advance in temperature. It was sparked by fire, of course, in preparation for an extraordinary battle."

"Battle? We've heard nothing about a battle," Dassius objected.

"Seriously? No one made mention? Well a magnificent battle flared up, one depicting a fusion of cataclysm and beauty."

"Cataclysm and beauty?" Ceera lifted her hair off her neck, wishing she had something to tie it up with.

"Oh, they mingle from time to time, when inspired by the elements of course. I suppose you are unfamiliar with what is called nature's paradox?"

"I studied it in school when I was younger."

"You should think about studying it again. It may deter you from asking such redundant questions now that you are older."

"Pardon me," Ceera responded in a withered tone. Beads of sweat formed on her forehead, and she fanned herself with her free hand.

"Blazes Ceera," Dassius snapped. "When will you learn to think before you speak?"

Ceera's face grew even hotter. So much for the benevolence he had shown earlier. She glared at him bitterly and responded with an indignant spout of breath.

Luma chuckled. "Feeling a little testy, Dassius?"

"I know about the paradox." Dassius tugged at his collar, which was now discolored, and fumbled with loosening the top few buttons of his shirt. "Nature's positive equals its negative. What's bad for one is good for another."

"At least one of you is clever." Luma's eyes rested on his open collar, flitted back up to his face and then flashed about the rest of his body. "Perhaps you are even more than clever."

Dassius used his sleeve to wipe the sweat from his forehead.

Taking a deep breath that accentuated her ample chest, Luma hugged her ribcage and arched her back slightly. Then she leaned toward him, causing her breasts to bulge out over the top of her gown. "It's getting rather hot around here, don't you think?"

Dassius looked back at her coolly. "No."

"But you're sweating," she teased, lifting her hand to her forehead and tracing her fingers along the side of her face and down her neck. Her fingers dropped to the hollow between her breasts and lingered there, stroking a pool of sweat that had formed.

Dassius watched her momentarily before his expression hardened. His gaze traveled back up to her face.

Ceera tucked her hair roughly behind her ears as she stared between the two of them. The fear owning her upon arrival transformed into anger. It was all she could do to contain it.

"I'm fine," Dassius said in a low voice, but his lack of composure showed in the way he fidgeted with the bottom of his shirt.

"Sure you are," Luma said with a smirk. "Now back to nature's paradox, as you know, the elements are chained to it and, of course, were involved in the conflict."

"Neither Oc~ea nor Atmos indicated the elements were involved in a battle," Ceera said with a newly found authority.

"Our perceptions are as varied as our specialties. But no matter, if you weld our opinions together, the result will indeed portray a very accurate representation of what happened."

"But you said war," Dassius interjected. "Why?"

"Why you ask? You Semions are always asking the question why. Your culture is supposed to be so advanced, yet the both of you have been cavorting around the planet throwing the question around like children confined in a schoolroom."

Dassius stood up so quickly his block of pumice tipped over.

Ceera rolled her eyes at him. "Supposedly you're in such control of yourself. I guess we're dealing with more than fire ants though aren't we?" She threw the words in his direction with a viciousness she had never felt toward anyone before.

"Fire ants?" Luma sounded mildly aroused. "So small yet so pestilent."

Dassius ignored them and paced the area so sporadically that Ceera could not keep up on his whereabouts. Her own mental state became spotty all of a sudden.

"Just tell me why you think you're justified in classifying what happened as war," Dassius said.

Luma's cheeks flared. "The elements were fighting a war; it must be so, for never during the course of history have they ruled this planet with such cruelty. Heat waves stifled entire regions. Storms ripped mayhem across the land. Fire raged across the planet and soared over oceans to destroy everything in its path. I wish I could have witnessed such feats, or better yet, have been the culprit of them."

Ceera was undeterred by Luma's latter comment. "Oc~ea did mention that glaciers melted, and water deviated from its normal routes," she said.

"Of course," Luma replied. "Extreme temperature can bear quite an impact on what is subject to influence."

"Plus, Atmos revealed to us the weather became erratic," she added.

"What you call weather is at the mercy of the elements."

"So our forest existed during all this, during your supposed war," Dassius said.

"Yes, and how peculiar your forest resurfaced after everything it went through," Luma said in a patronizing tone.

"But there is something I still can't grasp. You say this war was incited over a few degrees?" Dassius did not bother to hide his skepticism. He now looked entirely disheveled.

"All over a few degrees that came again and again." Luma sounded perturbed. Her entire face glowed red. "What happens gradually can be difficult to detect, but that doesn't imply it is ineffectual. It still amounts to an increase in temperature which, when continual, will reach the telling moment when instability reigns. Over time, what's unstable becomes unpredictable. Soon the state of disorder is prevalent; before you know it chaos rules. This is true from the tiniest molecule all the way up to the weather patterns of the very planet you inhabit, the universe, and of course everything in between."

"Really Dassius," Ceera said. "Don't you have better sense than to ask a question like that?"

Dassius stared past Ceera with a serious expression on his face. "We need to leave right now," he told her.

"Why? Is the temperature making you uncomfortable? How selfish! You think only of yourself." Ceera deliberately turned away from him. "Were the elements fighting each other?" she asked the Archaic.

"The elements may clash from time to time"—Luma leaned toward Ceera, catching her off guard—"but as much of a pity as it is, we do not fight amongst ourselves. We coexist in equilibrium. Nature never allows one of us to prevail indefinitely."

"Why do you think it's a pity?" Ceera whispered. Only the flame separated her from Luma's face.

"Intense heat is glorifying. Perhaps you would like to try a touch of it yourself." Luma examined her rings.

"No thank you." Ceera shrank away.

"Tell me," Luma continued, "what you Semions have been doing with yourselves. What distracts you? How did you lose sight of what's really been going on?"

"Ceera, we must go now." Dassius grabbed onto her shoulder. She shrugged it away.

"Most of our studies are on spatial entities," Ceera explained. "We're focused on figuring out ways to travel to other planets."

"Whatever for?" The patronizing tone was back. She drummed her bright red nails on the edge of the caldera. Her eyes glowed like burning embers.

"In the future, our planet will be obliterated by the sun. We're trying to avoid being destroyed with it."

"Oh." Luma narrowed her eyes. "You're referring to the day the planet reunites with the sun! How could you plan on missing it?" Her fingers trembled. A red glow streaked out from her rings and provoked a strange energy throughout her entire body. Her fiery eyes matched the glow, and the ends of her hair danced like flames.

Ceera was too shocked to respond.

"You act as if this planet wasn't formed by the sun. What's so wrong about it deciding to revisit its origin?" Luma pouted as the effects overtaking her died down. She sighed, sensing her words had fallen on deaf ears.

"We haven't merged with fire as you have. We are chained to our own mortality." Dassius's hand returned to Ceera's shoulder.

"Some are bound by their own devices." Luma's words

flickered in the space between them and frolicked playfully around the circle of pumice.

A slow shiver crept up Ceera's spine. She tucked her recorder into her pack.

"Let's go," Dassius said again to Ceera. He grabbed her hand and began pulling her away.

"So Oc~ea volunteered my help. I suppose I shall adhere to her request." Luma tossed something quickly in their direction.

Dassius's other hand flew up and caught it. He slipped it into his pocket.

"What expert reflexes. Good thing you caught it. Who knows, had it fallen it may have cracked open and engulfed both of you in flames."

"It's been a pleasure," Dassius told her insincerely as he backed away, dragging Ceera along with him.

She was too frightened to resist.

"You may have caught the vial, but the peril is not over. Fire is unpredictable and an outburst is brewing. When I told you earlier I was waiting, you wrongly assumed it was for you. Let's hope you escape as well as you catch."

Dassius spun them around quickly. Together, they ran wildly down the slope. The sound erupting behind them was so deafening that Ceera was sure it could be heard even as far away as Semadon.

"It's the volcano," Dassius shouted. "It must be active after all."

They jumped a good four feet down into the grassy area they had passed earlier in the day. Ceera fell to her knees upon impact; Dassius landed in a crouch. He lifted her to her feet. The area was no longer peaceful. Pandemonium had taken over, and they had emerged in the middle of it. They were now running amidst the elk.

The clomping of feet filled her ears. Dassius broke free and ran ahead, his pack bouncing within the jumble of fleeing animals. He removed a bundle of rope from his pack and unraveled it. The large creatures raced past him with immense speed. He made a loop and fumbled with knotting it.

Did he think he would come close to roping one of these fast-moving animals? She was surprised when he threw the rope not ahead of himself but behind.

It hung in the air at the perfect position to rope an elk's neck, although it looked more as if the animal ran into the ring on purpose. The elk kept running and in seconds surpassed Dassius. The rope tensed, causing the elk to rear up on its hind legs and throw its antlered head backward. It began running again with such force that Dassius, who still held onto the end of the rope, went crashing down and skidded along the ground behind the animal.

"Dassius!" Ceera cried out, sprinting to catch up.

The extra weight slowed the elk. A group running in a pack veered in front and cut the animal off course. Dassius scrambled to his feet and climbed onto the back of the beast. It reared up again, but this time Dassius yanked the rope so hard the animal's front end fell back to the ground and didn't move. When Ceera reached them, Dassius grabbed her outstretched hand and pulled her up behind him. He slapped the elk's side and it galloped away.

The air became noxious. Ash and debris marred her vision.

"Cover your face," Dassius commanded. He yanked on the hood of his jacket so it fell over his head.

Ceera did the same, rested her chin on his shoulder and held on. The elk continued to carry them farther away, but soon her throat hurt and nostrils stung. Dassius finished a bout of coughing before reaching around to grab onto her. They tumbled off the back of the elk and hit the dirt with a thud. Though she landed on top of him, she struggled to breathe. Dassius rolled them away from the galloping hooves and came to a stop overtop her. He lifted his body just inches from hers. Heat swirled as a barrier between them.

"That hurt," she sputtered.

"The AT cylinder," he said between breaths. "It's right over there. Come on."

Coughing, she allowed herself to be led the short distance to the cylinder. Dassius jerked the door open, yanked her inside, and quickly followed. Ceera fell limply onto the floor. Dassius leaned against the wall of the cylinder as he caught his breath. She held her hand up to him.

"Not yet. We're still in danger." He peered out the doorway.

Ceera caught a whiff of stinging air.

"We have to transfer immediately." He slammed the door and hit buttons on the control panel. Before she could brace herself, they faded into the atmosphere.

Chapter Eighteen

FALKEN WASTED NO time. After his meeting with Nimren and Casma, he went straight home to read Hegliod's book. He studied each page, soaking in the knowledge with rapt attention.

After several hours, he clapped the book shut with satisfaction. If he followed the blueprints laid out in Hegliod's technical manual, he could inject a certain code into his intervention equipment and have access to the AT controls inside the Aurora. He would not even have to leave the comfort of his own dwelling.

He loved moments like this, when the facets of modern technology worked harmoniously together. This was why he was such a strong proponent of his council. Long ago, they had introduced this open network allowing technology to interact with all components of the past. This was working out very well for him. Soon he would be in control of the entire AT system and all those relying on it for communication and travel.

Falken began making the adjustments. Using the manual as a guide, he entered codes and added pieces of equipment stored on his shelves. He spent most of the day refurbishing the device and even went to the Technology

Center to grab more pieces. His excitement grew as he neared completion. His reveling came to an abrupt end when he input the code and his intervention equipment did not react.

He skimmed the manual to find the section referring to the codes. After rereading it word for word, disgust swelled in his gut. The code he needed was not one of the standard codes that worked for most machines. No, Hegliod had taken it upon himself to create his own code and it was not mentioned within the book, which could only mean one thing. The only place it could be found was inside Hegliod's head.

Falken threw the book across the room. Its spine cracked when it hit the wall, the noise causing his bird to take flight momentarily within the confines of its cage. The rat didn't budge. He stood up and dusted himself off. For the second time, he was off to meet the crazed old man, and this time he knew exactly where to find him.

⌘

Hegliod slowly wound his way around the orbit. Falken stopped directly behind him, careful to stay out of his line of sight. He was relying on the fact Hegliod had become as indifferent as everyone said. He had seen this for himself already, but did not know how the old man would react once spoken to.

"How's it going Hegliod?" Falken said in a low voice.

Hegliod kept walking and sweeping, his eyes glued to the ground. "Humph," he uttered absently.

"Good, good," Falken responded. He stayed neatly

behind him, out of sight with quiet steps. "I was wondering if you could do me a slight favor."

"Perhaps."

"I was thinking about a recent invention. The Atomic Transport System to be exact. Are you familiar with it?"

"Of course." Hegliod paused to maneuver his sweeper around the bend.

"Quite a spectacular invention, wouldn't you say?"

"It has its flaws," Hegliod replied matter-of-factly.

"You don't say? Is it possible then for the system to work only on a partial basis?"

"What do you mean? Aren't you aware of its latest transport error?"

"Yes, but I'm not speaking of what happens during the transfer. I'm asking whether the system can pick and choose between where its correspondence travels, and which cylinders are capable of transport."

"No, not possible for the machine to pick and choose."

Falken grew agitated. Did Hegliod not remember what he wrote inside his own book? Or was he playing dumb?

"It runs on a complex energy grid. All points are equally connected. The system would have to be manipulated by a Semion to be altered."

Falken perked up. "And no Semion knows how to do that. Except the inventor, correct?"

"Yes," Hegliod replied. "Only the inventor knows the password to do such things."

Falken waited for Hegliod to continue, but was disappointed when he did not offer anything more. "What dedication you bring to such a menial task," Falken told him, resorting to flattery.

Hegliod wedged the sweeper in a dirt-filled crack. "Disposing of filth is a necessity. It paves an unobstructed path."

"Very true," Falken said. "And disposing of secrets can be just as helpful for the mind."

Hegliod huffed. "My mind is quite clear young man."

"There is nothing interfering with this task you pursue, nothing hindering your progress?"

"Nothing besides you."

"I can vanish quickly, my friend," Falken said. Then a thought crossed his mind. "Actually, High Service sent me to reclaim this password you mentioned. They wish to record it in the event it's needed sometime in the future, before it slips your mind. You do understand, don't you?"

Hegliod muttered something under his breath.

Falken hovered closer until he could smell the sweat on Hegliod's neck. "Pardon?"

Hegliod muttered it a little louder, sighed disdainfully, and again wedged his sweeper between the cracks near their feet.

Satisfied, Falken continued to stand beside Hegliod. In case there was anything left in Hegliod's upstairs, he wanted to properly distract him before venturing away.

"How long does it take you to sweep the inner orbits of the village?" he asked with mock curiosity.

"Over half the day," Hegliod replied.

"What do you do for the rest of the day?"

"I get a head start on the next."

"How remarkable." Falken slowly backed away. "Who would have thought that you, Hegliod Avatus, could have such a fabulous stint as an orbit sweeper, and without any special training?"

The words did not impact Hegliod in the slightest.

He was busy freeing a particular clump of dirt from the walkway. Convinced he would remain anonymous, Falken headed home.

❦

Risa and Karnen entered the Recuperation Clinic with low expectations. The status of the AT installers had remained the same for weeks, making it difficult for the officials to carry any hope inside the building with them. Even the staff acted despondent. They didn't greet the officials with the same enthusiasm they had at the onset. The unconscious men still tossed and turned in their beds, with strange sounds spilling from their lips.

Karnen had just confirmed with a doctor that nothing had changed, when a hoarse gasping sound filled the room. Everyone turned their heads toward the unfamiliar noise.

Darmyn was sitting upright with open and unblinking eyes. Fear ravaged his face. He raised his hand and pointed into the distance, past the doctors and officials. Then he spoke intelligibly for the first time in weeks. "The forest," he sputtered, "it lures you close, invites you in."

The onlookers stood frozen with uncertainty, disturbed yet fascinated.

"Once you're in," he continued ominously, "it lets itself inside of you." His eyes grew vacant, and his body rocked back and forth before falling back down with a thud.

The staff sprang to life. One of the doctors shouted out commands as the others attempted to revive him back to consciousness. The officials stood helplessly in the midst of the chaos.

"What was that all about?" Risa whispered to Karnen.

"And to think only minutes ago, I was disappointed their condition remained unchanged."

"You're right," Karnen agreed. "Surely no development would be better than this."

They watched in uncomfortable silence as the doctors worked on Darmyn, who now lay stiff as a statue. His brain was dormant once again.

❧

Marvus stood in the gardens, facing a small group of Semions and the global update sphere. The green emblem on his necklace protruded from his chest. Desnia stood at his side. He gave her a quick nod which she acknowledged with obvious resentment. She wore the roses in her hair again, their thorny nature complementing her own.

"Semions," Marvus began, "some of you may be wondering what I stand to gain by addressing the public yet again. You can rest assured; it is with the noblest of intentions, for I have an important request." Marvus clasped his hands together firmly. "As Ceera and Dassius continue their pledge to restore order, we must revere their progress. On the same token, it is not just their responsibility to solve our problems. Although it would be easy to leave everything up to them, we must not fall prey to laziness. For you see, we too, have a duty to uphold."

The audience was silent, hanging onto every word,

"This involves paying attention to the signs around us," he continued. "Don't forget, nature speaks to us not with words but with signals. She alerted us to the impending disorder. She made every indication our lives would soon change. I have no doubt she continues to talk to us, but it will take a cunning mind"— Marvus tapped the side of his head—"to interpret her signs."

"Now, there are some who have made every effort to muddle our perceptions with slanderous accusations. They wish to divert this crisis away from themselves. I cannot elaborate on who the guilty ones are, but you must see through their deceit. For if you let their lies cloud your mind, then nature's signs will remain unseen.

"Semions, what I ask is for you to heighten your awareness and look for these signals." Marvus stared meaningfully at his audience. "Hear my words and follow, so together we can see what nature intends for us to see."

❧

Nimren stabbed the off button on his global update sphere with his ringed pointer finger. He turned toward Casma with a look of disgust.

"He always finds a way to blame us," she said. "It's revolting."

"Someday he and his council will get what they deserve." Nimren glared at the blank global update sphere.

"Although it's probably not worth stewing over, I couldn't help but be offended by the look on Desnia's face. Did you happen to notice?"

Nimren grunted in reply.

"They act like they consider themselves to be of the same importance as their precious Archaics," she added.

"Yes, perhaps they'll remove the statues from their spherical room and put their own likenesses there instead."

They chuckled and some of the tension died down.

"At least we are one step ahead of them. I wonder what

Falken is up to, whether he has received any more trans-mits." Nimren gazed over at his correspondence orb which was dull and thereby empty of messages.

Casma stiffened at the mention of Falken Grihne. She should be pleased with the work he was doing for the council, but she could not allow herself to trust him just yet.

Chapter Nineteen

DASSIUS WASN'T SURE how long it took to gain consciousness after they materialized again. He was drained and had completely lost his sense of reality.

He did know that he had set their destination to a familiar spot where they could relax. It would be a safe place to gather both their senses. Unlike his, Ceera's had severely decayed. In obvious need of rejuvenation, she sat motionless and stared blankly, not yet aware the AT ride had ended.

He crouched down to look at her closely, saw she was still breathing, and stood back up. It was considered taboo to revive someone who had not transported well. In moments like this, it was best to leave her alone until she snapped out of it by herself. Serious damage could be inflicted by arousing her prematurely.

He opened the door quietly and stepped outside. They had traveled across time zones again. The sun was out, and a field peppered with wildflowers surrounded the cylinder. He took a hefty breath of fresh air as his body eased away all the tension that had built up over the past hours. It had served its purpose: the extremity of their situation enabled his physical abilities to stretch beyond their usual limits. There was no use for it now though; his need for physical exertion had come to an end. Letting it linger would only hinder his mental state.

He stretched his arms overhead and leaned back to catch a full view of the sky. Clouds drifted in the blue tranquility above.

"Where are we?" The words came softly from behind him. "And why are we here?"

He turned. Ceera stood in front of the AT cylinder looking dazed. Her hair was mussed. He refrained from reaching out to her.

"This is one of my favorite places. It's peaceful and I thought it would help us recuperate, although I was beginning to wonder if I'd have to take you back to Semadon." He grinned.

"Never. At least not until we're done." She wandered over and sat down. Hugging her knees to her chest, she stared somewhat vacantly toward the horizon.

"You're in this with me till the end, aren't you?" He sat beside her.

"With or without you. I need answers."

"There is no without. We're both equally in this."

"True, but I'm the one the forest summoned. You, on the other hand, are following orders by High Service to see if your training is as advanced as you say it is. I think I believe you, although there are times I don't want to."

"Why?"

Ceera shrugged. They stared in different directions.

"For some reason, I'm not even angry with you anymore." Resentment tinged her words.

Dassius recalled how they had lost their tempers earlier. "We reacted in the heat of the moment. Luma was toying with us."

"So you insulted me because it was hot? Or was it really how you felt?"

Dassius winced. "I suppose it was really how I felt, that you asked a redundant question. If it weren't for the scorching heat, I wouldn't have considered it a big deal. When we get back to Semadon, I'm going to suggest to my trainers I undergo more extreme temperature exposure."

Ceera looked unimpressed with that answer, which Dassius took to mean she needed a bit of consoling.

"Come on, you were rude to me also. You ridiculed my training by bringing up the fire ants and patronized me when I suggested it was time to leave. I had a good reason; I sensed our surroundings were going to change rapidly, and I was right."

"But how did you know?"

He watched her annoyance with him dissipate. She was now overwhelmed by what had to be pure curiosity. Her hands fidgeted, probably wishing to type on her recorder which was nowhere in sight.

"I could get in trouble for talking about it. You know we're supposed to keep the technicalities of our descriptions private."

"That didn't stop you before. Besides, do you really foresee that happening?"

"Foresee what happening?"

"That you'll get in trouble for telling me?"

Dassius chuckled at the thought of being reprimanded. "Not really."

"Remember, High Service doesn't have to know everything." She gave him a sideways look.

"I suppose I can tell you a few things," Dassius said, satisfied when her eyes lit up. "Now this will be difficult for you to understand, so I'll explain it the best way I know how."

She leaned forward attentively.

"First," he began, "I have to lose my sense of self."

Ceera was quick in turning her face away so Dassius could not see her expression, but not so adept at holding back the laughter that escaped shamelessly from her lips.

"What's so funny?" He could not help but feel betrayed.

"I find the irony amusing."

Dassius narrowed his eyes. "What irony?"

"Well, not to be blunt, but you have an aura about you that rings"—she paused—"anything but selfless."

"Did you ever consider it a matter of overcompensation?" Dassius countered.

"Huh?" She gave him a blank look.

"I'm self-centered because I rarely get to be myself?"

"I guess it didn't occur to me." She lowered her eyes.

"That's the heart of the practice. Losing yourself gains a broader perception."

"So then how is it done?"

"My mind pulls away from my body, until my physical self is just an object I'm looking at. Believe me, it feels weird. Then I go even further, mingling with my surroundings. Are you still with me?"

Ceera nodded, probing him with her eyes.

"The intent is to become one with my environment so that I can determine what it will do. Anything factoring into the here and now, I view as components of probability. What the future holds will depend on these components' interactions. I can sometimes sense what someone will say before they say it, or if and when, the present situation will change."

"Did you know Luma was going to flirt with you?" She blurted out.

"I knew she was going to try to upset you." He smiled slowly. "Did it work?"

"Upset me? You were the one she victimized. It was so creepy watching her stare you up and down." She frowned at his expression, bit her lip and looked away. "I think your field is dabbling with what the mystics practice."

"Yes, but the difference lies in proximity," Dassius continued. "Mystics have no boundaries and are good at giving advice. I can only read my immediate surroundings or the nearby vicinity. I serve as a reactionary, guided by instinct."

"Perhaps there will come a time when we don't need the mystics anymore."

"Very possible. But I'm not sure how probable. It would take eons before Semions would be ready to accept their own kind as carriers of such powers."

"What do you mean?"

"Semions are focused on progress, but they aren't ready to leave behind all their long held beliefs. You can't just tell them the mystics' powers are accessible traits they, themselves, can utilize. It will jumble their grasp on reality."

"It's wrong to keep such vital information from the public."

"And that is why you are not in High Service. You cannot tell the masses something that can dismantle your entire civilization."

"It's the duty of High Service to tell us everything."

"No, it's their duty to uphold stability. Honesty rarely does that."

"I don't know what you mean. That's the entire purpose of my job as a scribe."

"What happened when the alarms sounded? How long did it take High Service to admit there was a problem?"

"Well"—Ceera hesitated—"I'm sure they had every intention of revealing what was going on as soon as possible."

"Let me tell you, what's possible has nothing to do with what's probable."

"I don't like what I am hearing," she admitted, shaking her head.

"I don't believe you'd be expected to."

"So moving on, how is your training considered scientific?"

"The natural world follows laws. By studying these laws, we can determine the effect of almost any situation. We do experiments to refine this mastery of outcome. Based on these experiments, results are placed on a computerized grid that maps the possibility and probability of occurrence."

"What kind of experiments?"

"All sorts." He sat up a little straighter. "One example is me."

"You?"

"Yes, my experiences will be analyzed and charted upon return."

Ceera stared into space for a moment. "Am I being studied as well?"

"No," he was quick to respond.

"Perhaps my involvement will also be factored in."

"I doubt it."

"Just imagine"—Ceera rolled onto her knees and leaned toward him—"the amount of depth I add to this study."

Dassius tensed up. While attempting to thwart his aggravation, he also searched his brain for an adequate response. Before one surfaced, he noticed the tiny sliver of light shining in her eyes. The look on her face gave it away. She was teasing him.

"I guess sometimes I'm just a normal Semion reacting to the whims of my peers," he told her ruefully.

"Don't look so glum." She smiled. "Maybe I'm just skilled at riling you."

"Now who's the smug one?"

Ceera laughed. She glanced down at herself, and a look of distaste crossed her face. "I feel squalid and I smell like ash. Where can I clean up?"

"There's a creek over past those trees."

"That sounds heavenly. I'll be back after while."

She disappeared into the cylinder and reemerged with her pack slung over her shoulder. She dropped her recorder on the grass beside him. "For the transmit," she said as she sauntered away.

Dassius watched her until she was out of sight behind the trees. Ignoring his urge to visualize what she would be doing next, he changed positions to distract himself. Closing his eyes, he eased his mind of any lingering thoughts about her. Then he shifted his brain to a neutral phase that would allow him to recharge.

&s;

Much to the dismay of High Service, the AT system was performing strangely. They were unable to respond to the third transmit sent by Ceera and Dassius. They received it well enough, were quite thankful the pair evaded the unexpected volcanic eruption, but a failed message signal resulted whenever they attempted to respond.

This led them to shut down the system within Semadon. They sent warnings through the global update to the settlements alerting of potential travel failures. The officials did not want any more Berda and Raveen situations. But this also put them in a very difficult position. They had no way to relay to Dassius and Ceera the danger of using the system.

The words of the momentarily awakened AT installer hung over the whole situation like a dark cloud, ready to burst at any second, for now there was a heated debate amongst officials over whether Ceera and Dassius should be brought back to Semadon. Unfortunately, they were thousands of miles away, and it would take days to reach them by travel pod. Plus, there was no guarantee the two of them would stay put or which direction they would head next.

To make matters worse, the entire problem was at a standstill since the inventor of the AT system now spent his time cleaning orbits. Of course, efforts had been made to restore Hegliod's mental state. Begrudgingly, the crazed inventor allowed Order Patrol to escort him from the orbit he was sweeping to the Aurora, on the condition he could bring his broom. He, along with his broom, met with a neurotechnician whose job was to evaluate and fix Hegliod's mind.

After analysis and testing, the neurotech met with officials.

"We did some brain imaging and it's conclusive. His mind is stuck in a loop. His thoughts are incapable of diverging from it. Has he ever flaked out like this before?"

"Never," Asfin responded.

"Is there anything you can do?" Leynin asked.

The neurotech sighed. "We did try. We made him listen to brain wave frequencies, but his brain would not reorganize to the sound patterns we prescribed. He refuses to heal."

"Do you have any other suggestions?"

"I suppose you could force him to work on the controls, but in my opinion this could have fatal repercussions. You have to ask yourself whether you really want someone in this condition meddling with the system."

Hegliod was released from custody and went back to sweeping. The neurotechnician returned to his office, and High Service returned to worrying.

In another attempt to remedy the situation, High Service called in the young novice who figured out the problem with the AT system on the day the alarms sounded. He spent hours inspecting the control panel with focused attention.

"It's almost as if the system lost a connection," Cafold said with a confused look on his face.

"Why would this happen?" Risa asked.

"I don't know," he replied. "All I can say is the system should be in working order. Yet there's a break in the current."

"Why would there be a break in the current?"

"Again, I don't really know. Perhaps something invaded its course of operation."

"I still don't understand," Risa said.

"Neither do I," he admitted.

⁓

Ceera felt refreshed. She had taken a leisurely bath, changed clothes, and now smelled like lavender soap. The air was just beginning to chill for the evening, and the sun was setting yet again, which meant they were reliving the day on more comfortable terms.

She arranged some veggie sandwiches and fresh fruit on a blanket. When she finally saw Dassius in the distance making his way through the trees, her eagerness overrode her desire for food.

He came toward her casually, his hair wet but no longer sweaty, with his shirt unbuttoned halfway down. She scooted over on the blanket to make room for him.

"Good, I'm hungry," he said, but instead of joining her he took off his shirt.

His chest was still damp as evidenced by the leftover bits of sunlight. Her eyes followed the curve of his muscles as he tossed the shirt and bent down to unzip his pack.

"I forgot a clean shirt," he said, pulling one out and shaking the wrinkles out of it.

Ceera's stomach burned with an intensity that had nothing to do with food. Her cheeks grew hot. In an attempt to shield their redness from him, she lifted her hands to the sides of her face.

"Are you cold?" Dassius pulled the shirt over his head and sat down next to her on the blanket.

She wondered what would happen if she said yes, but instead shook her head.

He was now staring at her closely. "What's the matter?"

"Nothing," she said, averting his gaze

"No seriously, your face." He lightly touched the bottom of her chin.

"What about it?" She dropped her hands and let him draw her face up to his.

"It's glowing."

The space between them wavered in her thoughts as she reflected on how his midnight blue eyes delved into her own. She placed her palm on his chest. His fingers brushed the side of her face.

"What's going to happen next?" she asked softly.

"Sometimes you can't predict it," he said as he drew closer.

Ceera closed her eyes and fell willingly into his lips. His hand pressed into the small of her back, guiding her toward him. She traced the muscles in his back and down his arm, feeling the bulk of his bicep. He kissed her again and she relented to her physical craving, allowing her soft curves to melt into his broad frame. Before the pleasure could consume her, he pushed her gently away. She stared at him breathlessly.

"Too many possibilities," he said with a certain gleam in his eye. He took a long, deep breath as if trying to tame something inside him.

No longer looking at her, he picked up a sandwich and took a bite. Ceera's relief combined with disappointment as she chose a peach and lifted it to her lips.

∿

Dassius finished eating but gained no satisfaction from it. Ceera left a half-eaten sandwich in the grass a short distance away from the cylinder. He erected the tent while she cleaned her recorder with a special cloth. When the tent was ready, she went in to lie down.

He stared at the moonlight and swatted mosquitoes off his skin. He was tired but also restless which meant he shouldn't go into the tent just yet.

His mind kept reverting back to Ceera and their kiss. He had been aware that his feelings for her were growing. Of course she was pretty, with her light blue eyes and delicate features, but that wasn't what he found most appealing about her. An aura of mystery surrounded her, something he was unaccustomed to dealing with in his interactions with people. So it seemed, most had their motivations written across their foreheads. Ceera was protective of her feelings. And she was genuine. He had been skeptical at the onset, but their time together had proven him wrong.

Their kiss was unexpected. Something in her face had stirred him, and her lips had drawn him closer. They were soft and pressed against his with an eagerness he returned. Along with the moment came feelings he never had much time for and an overwhelming aching in his gut. His thoughts strayed to a million places at once, places to where the kiss could lead. He wanted to merge with her as he did his surroundings, in a way that differed from his training. Backing off seemed most appropriate, at least until he had a handle on these new sensations. They still had days together. Maybe more.

Dassius checked the cylinder to see if High Service had sent a reply to his transmit yet. The blank screen annoyed him. With a shake of his head, he decided he was far too tired to worry about it at the moment.

He crept into the tent, took his shoes off, and crawled into his bedding. Ceera did not stir from where she lay a short distance away. Would they end up curled together again like the previous night? He wouldn't mind. By her slow and steady breathing, he guessed she was already in a deep sleep. It did not take him long to join her.

❦

Ceera stood in a dimly lit wood. Gnarled trees cast shadows

in her path. Their limbs pointed her in a certain direction and she obeyed.

Darkness crept behind though it did not threaten to overtake her. The brush once again entangled her feet. Every step she took broke ties with the plants trying to keep her still.

A clearing up ahead drew her. The large tree stood at its center, its monumental shape growing atop a complicated root structure. There was more to it than just its stature, more than just the obvious antiquity of its life span. She sensed a vibration coming from it internally, almost as if the tree possessed a heart that beat life into its bark. She knew the relic hid within its trunk.

She dropped down to her knees. As she peered into the dark interior of the tree, on the verge of learning its secrets, a sinister presence approached her from behind. When she turned toward the danger, all she saw was darkness. Her fear alighted as the dimness enclosed her, suffocated her, and she could not bring herself to scream.

Chapter Twenty

CEERA'S REALITY WAS left tainted by the nightmare. Shadows moved odd shapes outside the tent. She almost woke Dassius but decided it would be best to lie still. He didn't need to know how much she relied on him for comfort. She could barely admit it to herself. It bothered her that she had allowed him to kiss her. She hated herself for liking it.

Despite Litha's best efforts to set her up on dates, Ceera had always refused. Dating would make her vulnerable. She could do nothing about how her father had deserted her. She did, however, have control over how other men treated her and had lost some of that control to Dassius when he kissed her. Then he had pulled away from her as if she were nothing. She had spent her lifetime trying to feel as if she were more than nothing. And now, an unwanted possibility about herself burgeoned within her nightmares. Was fate so cruel that she'd end up crazy instead? The thought added an extra layer to an already disturbing night.

Once she calmed down long enough to close her eyes, she found herself in the midst of a fitful slumber, weaving in and out of the dream state every time she heard a sound.

Finally, the sun woke her for good. She sat up and

rubbed her eyes. Dassius, too, had just woken up. He gazed over at her with half slit eyes. She debated whether she should tell him about her dream. Before she could decide, he sat up quickly and rolled onto his knees, crawling over to the door of the tent.

"I need to check the cylinder. High Service never sent a transmit last night." He unzipped the tent and crawled out.

Ceera grabbed enough vegetable bars and juice for both of them, and followed Dassius outside.

The door to the cylinder was ajar, and he was inside staring at the controls. "They still haven't sent us anything."

She handed him half of the breakfast when he stepped out of the cylinder. "Are you sure you even sent one to them?"

"I'm sure."

"We had a long day yesterday," she said. "Maybe you forgot to press send."

"Yeah maybe." He didn't sound convinced. "I'll send it again before we look for Baric. If we haven't received it by the time we get back, then we can worry."

Ceera decided for the time being she would keep her latest dream to herself. Dassius had enough on his mind, and she was sure none of it had anything to do with her.

⚘

Falken visited Nimren and Casma to update them about the third transmit. They were amused by Luma's antics yet surprised she attempted to kill Ceera and Dassius.

Casma's alarm showed when she said it was curious the CfNL would set themselves up for such a risk. Nimren waved her worries away, saying the CfNL loved indulging in drama and that it just showed they had confidence.

Luma stating the elements had waged war further proved the CfNL's involvement, Nimren pointed out. It was obviously a direct tactic to elevate the elements of nature as powerful entities, or at the very least, he stated, it was a good story, if not a little over the top.

Nimren and Casma also voiced concern that High Service had shut down the AT system during the night. Falken admitted this was a result of his meddling with the transmits, and his plans were just beginning. He managed to slip away before they interrogated him about the details. He now sat comfortably inside his dwelling.

The story told by Luma inspired him to create a weapon that would ensure his victory against Dassius when he accosted them in the forest. His only obstacle was that any weapon created had to be sponsored by a council or a scientific entity, and face the ultimate approval of High Service. This weapon, therefore, would have to be created in secret, for its intended potency would not warrant an approval.

It was quite against the doctrines of Semion culture what he conspired to do, but high stakes and the need to succeed overruled his obligation to obey. Besides, if High Service was doing their job properly, he would not have to intervene in the first place.

The weapon would need to induce fear and allegiance at the sight of it. Falken looked around the room, hoping something would spur his inventiveness. His eyes grazed his solar system, still broken, with planets spinning in strangely shaped orbits. Some planets hadn't revolved fully around the sun since he had fallen face first into the model.

The sun grabbed his attention away from this grievance. Unharmed, it throbbed and shone illustriously from its space at the center of the model. A miniature heat-core powered it. When his forehead made contact without any protective headgear, he had suffered, just like Ceera and Dassius soon would if they did not comply with his demands. At the thought, he almost fell out of his chair, but righted himself with a crooked grin.

This was the first time it ever occurred to him to use the sun's heat as a weapon. His contribution to the weather enhancement project would be put to use sooner than he expected. Direct contact with the heat rays would cause severe burns and even be fire-inducing. Dassius would not be immune to its powers. If he worked fast and according to the steps he had already configured, he would not only hold the sun's power in the palm of his hand, but also the entire village of Semadon.

He was marked by the sun in his model; its round outline still burned red on his forehead, and now he knew why.

⟋

After Dassius resent the transmit, he directed the AT system to draw up coordinates for Baric. He confirmed Ceera's readiness before pressing the transfer button and crouched down beside her. She drifted in and out, much like her sleep the previous night; except once reality surfaced, it was there to stay.

When they exited, they found themselves in the midst of a forest similar to the one outside Semadon. Oak and pine stretched high above them. The understory brimmed with plant life and nature's scents filled the air.

"Baric's domain," Dassius said.

Ceera surveyed the area carefully. She spied several different types of flowers and tree species within her immediate viewing range. Such variety was indicative of a healthy ecosystem. Of course, Baric would reside in such an environment. "I couldn't have imagined it better," she said.

A trio of colorful butterflies flew in front of her. When she reached out to them, they circled her hand before fluttering away.

"This way." Dassius tilted his head to the right.

"So what do you think about the Archaics?" she asked as she fell in step beside him.

"I think they're leaving things out. They know the answers to our questions but are unwilling to part with them. The truth is immersed within the realities they wish to convey."

"I'm curious what will happen when we use the vials, and whether we'll know when it's time to use them."

"I think we'll know," Dassius said.

A throaty moan erupted from somewhere in the distance, before transforming into an off-key howl.

"Was that what I think it was?" she asked uneasily.

"It was a wolf," Dassius replied.

"At this time of day?"

"Are wolves only allowed to make noise at certain times of day?"

"I thought they did their howling in the evening," she said.

"Wolves can howl whenever they want."

Ceera's heart beat quickly, and she made an effort to stay close.

"Wolves in the forest equate to an ecologically sound

predator prey relationship," Dassius said. "You can tell they keep the hoofed animals in check."

"Yes, the understory is full," she replied.

"Who knows, maybe there are bears too."

Ceera kept her eyes trained ahead, in silent trepidation they would come face-to-face with the shaggy creature. The howl had sounded far away, but they were moving steadily forward, and thus, too, the wolf could be moving toward them just as steadily. Lost in thought, she hadn't noticed Dassius no longer led the way.

"Hold on," he said irritably. His pants were caught in a patch of weeds, and he freed himself with an aggressive jerk. "Better be more observant," he grumbled, taking the lead position again, though his pace had slowed.

☙

The area around the main AT cylinder had been vacant ever since High Service shut down the system. Now several officials encircled it, along with someone else who stood tall and attentive. All eyes were upon him.

"Are you ready for this, Sidorn?" Risa asked.

Sidorn solemnly nodded. Determination radiated from his face. He had trained for moments like this. He and Dassius, along with a few others, were students of the same discipline. If anyone were to try and bring his friend back, Sidorn wanted it to be him.

"Let me reiterate the risk involved. The AT system is unreliable. We cannot guarantee it will function properly."

Sidorn's expression did not change.

"Thus, we are cutting short the mission of Ceera and Dassius. You have taken on the courageous task of going to retrieve them." Risa paused, her composure wavering. She looked over at the other officials.

Karnen stepped out of the group and continued for her. "Since it would take weeks to reach them by travel pod, you must use the AT system to do so. Your attempt will endanger your life, for the sake of rescuing theirs. Do you agree to this task?"

"Yes," Sidorn said. "I do."

"We thank you. If our worst nightmares come true and you are unable to return to us, your bravery will live on." Risa's words were thick with emotion.

The severity of the situation bore down on Sidorn for his expression hardened, but he did not falter in his stance. His broad chest was unyielding and his fists clenched. "I'm grateful for this opportunity to help out," he said. "I'm ready when you are."

Risa clasped onto the handle of the cylinder, pulled the door open and motioned him inside. When Sidorn entered, she closed the door and shut her eyes for just a moment before going back to join the other officials.

They stood nervously together and waited. The machine began vibrating but not with the usual urgency. It jolted and went still. Minutes went by. They viewed each other with troubled expressions.

"Should we go to the control room?" Karnen said. "See if they can tell what's going on?"

The door burst open in reply and Sidorn emerged. "The rescue failed."

Risa rushed forward to grab his arm.

"The cylinder wouldn't accept the destination code."

"All for the better," she said to him.

"She's right," Karnen said. "Better it breaks now than during the course of travel."

"But what about Dassius and Ceera?" Sidorn said.

He and the officials stared forlornly at the AT cylinder. Its open door invited, yet no answers lay within.

A bout of uncertainty hit Dassius. Though the woods still seemed calm, something was different. He stopped and held his arm out sideways to stop Ceera.

"What's wrong?" she asked him.

"I need to figure out if we're going the right way." He looked around, considering, before his eyes traveled back to the path. He blinked and waited. A large figure stepped within their line of sight.

It was the largest wolf Dassius had ever seen. Its slanted eyes viewed them with such interest that he reached for the knife attached to his hip. He felt nothing but a broken strap and recalled the weed he struggled to loosen himself from earlier.

"Not to worry," he said, reaching for his pack and rummaging inside. "It's not likely to attack." Dassius glanced back up at the wolf. Its bared teeth exposed an impressive set of sharp canines. "Be still and don't look him in the eye."

A low throaty growl was the only audible response, accompanied by a corresponding draft of air beside him. Dassius's head jerked up. He now stood alone. Twigs snapped and leaves rustled in the near distance: the sound of Ceera running through the trees. The wolf started trotting in her direction. Dassius dropped his pack and sprinted after her. The wolf picked up its pace behind them.

"You were supposed to stand still," he hissed as he overtook her. "Now it thinks we're prey." He grabbed her by the shoulder and spun her around.

Ceera looked close to tears. "Don't touch me!"

"What?" He threw his arms up in exasperation before turning to face the wolf. It stood a few feet away with a look of concentrated intensity. He had nothing but his bare hands to defend them. He lowered his eyes from its menacing gaze.

"Bend over slowly," he said, "and see if there are any thick branches on the ground."

The wolf circled them with its head sunk low, keeping its distance. Dassius stood close to Ceera as she stooped down, not wanting the wolf to take advantage.

She dug through the weeds. "There's nothing," she whispered as she stood back up.

The wolf lunged at them and Dassius shoved Ceera forward. She began running wildly and he faced the wolf. It lunged again and growled. Another wolf, a bit smaller, burst out of the trees. The first wolf turned toward the newcomer, and Dassius took the opportunity to catch up with Ceera.

He could practically feel the wolves nipping at his heels as they raced behind him. "Back the other way," he shouted to her.

She was trying to climb a tree. "I can't reach the branches!"

"Run back the way we came," he commanded again, throwing his arm out in the direction he wished her to go. "I left my pack; it has all my weapons!"

Ceera made an effort to run where he motioned. One of the wolves leapt several feet through the air and landed in her path. A low rumble came from its throat. She let out a shriek and started running in the opposite direction.

Dassius found himself once again in a face-off with the wolves. He backed away. "Try climbing another tree!" he yelled over his shoulder.

When she screamed, he turned his back on the skulking creatures and broke into a run. She stood next to a tree with low branches, her arms unmoving yet extended, her climb halted by another snarling wolf. Dassius heard paws hitting the ground behind him.

Ceera whipped her head toward him as he neared. Her eyes widened. She ignored the nearby wolf and began climbing. The wolf knocked her onto her back with its paws. She curled up into a ball, and the wolf brought its muzzle to the back of her neck.

Dassius bellowed a loud noise that came directly from his gut. The animal jerked its head his way and lowered its ears. It focused on the two wolves tailing him and trotted toward them.

Dassius ran to Ceera and pulled her to her feet. "Climb now," he said, looking desperately for something on the ground to use for defense. The understory hid all potential weapons well. His search ended when one of the wolves leapt over his head. Its paws hit the tree and it rebounded to the ground, landing on its feet with a low-pitched growl.

Ceera inched away. Within moments, she was running again. Dassius tore off behind her. One of the wolves jumped onto his back and knocked him down.

"Ceera," he called out as he hit the dirt. He rolled over to defend himself, but the three wolves had already run past. He scrambled to his feet.

Ceera's running came to an end when a wolf stepped in

her path. She turned and stopped abruptly when she found herself facing yet another. A third wolf blocked her escape from another direction. Her eyes met his. They edged toward each other slowly.

He grabbed her hand when it was within reach. The three wolves now stood together, their tails wagging in a jerky fashion.

"They are toying with us," Dassius decided. "Wolves can run faster than Semions."

The largest wolf howled that same familiar sound from earlier. The other wolves joined in the ragged melody.

Dassius backed away, pulling her with him. "Now," he commanded.

They turned to run, almost missing the cave opening in a small hill just a short distance away. Dassius halted before it and yanked Ceera to his side. A massive wolf stood atop the hill over the entryway. It growled down at them and bared its teeth. If they ran up the slope, they would surely have to contend with this unfriendly creature.

A few yards behind them, wolves sat on their haunches and watched. Encouraged by their sudden docility, he tried to lead Ceera around the hill, but a trio of wolves emerged from behind some trees in the distance. The docile wolves now stood and stared menacingly at the two of them once again.

Trying to evade an entire pack of wolves was a game he no longer wished to play. He peered into the cave. A tunnel wound out of sight and probably into pure darkness, but he sensed it was more than just an escape route. Plus, Ceera had a flashlight in her pack.

"Follow me," he told her, motioning toward the mouth of the cave.

"In there? What if the wolves follow?"

"They won't."

"But if they do?"

"You can trust my instinct and come with me, or stay here with the wolves; you decide."

The wolves stood about restlessly. One of them tilted its head back and let out a long howl.

Without saying another word, he dropped her hand and walked through the entrance. The tunnel snaked up ahead. When he was enclosed in darkness, he paused and waited. "Come on," he called out to her.

She approached soon after and he grabbed her hand again. She shook it away.

"Why did you run?" Dassius asked.

Ceera was silent for a moment. "Something in the wolf's eyes told me I should," she finally said.

"You're not supposed to stare a wolf in the eye."

"I know," she replied, "but I couldn't stop myself." She shook her head in frustration and bit her lip.

Dassius gave her a long, hard look. "Find your flashlight," he said. "We're going to need it."

❦

When Ceera and Dassius reached the first curve, the tunnel narrowed and they walked single file. Then the ceiling gradually dropped, forcing them to crawl. Dassius positioned the flashlight through the knife strap on his hip so it lit the path before them.

The tunnel sloped upward then downward. It took sharp rights and lefts. Dirt fell from above and blurred their vision. Dassius even felt the dull taste of it on his tongue.

They crawled in silence. After hours of twisting and

turning in near darkness, Dassius noticed the ceiling sloped upward again. He stood and tried to help Ceera to her feet, but she pretended like she didn't see his hand. He huffed in annoyance and turned away from her.

They brushed the dirt off themselves before continuing around the curve. When the tunnel widened, doubt surfaced in his thoughts. It was as if they were experiencing the exact inverse of the path they had already traveled. A passageway opened up ahead, and he half expected it to lead them back outside, but it did nothing of the sort.

Upon entering, he waved the flashlight around the room. "Amazing," he said while Ceera breathed in slowly.

Large chunks of brightly colored minerals wedged sporadically within the dirt walls and protruded from the ground. The elaborate display gave the room a mystical aura that was disarming and pleasurable at the same time.

After taking a moment to admire the splendor, it occurred to him that the room was a dead end. His mouth dropped open in disappointment, and he narrowed his eyes. He moved to the center of the room, shone his light in all directions, hoping for a clue or a sign proving he had not guided them in the wrong direction.

All he received in return was his own bewildered expression reflecting from the crystals. The taunt was effective, but Dassius also knew there was more to the room than met the eye, and he would need to be as sharp as the multifaceted gems jutting from the walls to figure it out.

⁋

It didn't take long for Falken to transform his sun model into a weapon. He changed some settings to broaden its intensity and range of impact. Rays now poked out from around its perimeter. Though the visual made the piece look all the more impressive, the addition was not cosmetic. The rays were made from nonconductors. Holding onto these, instead of the sun's body, would lessen the heat on his hand. Heat protective gloves were useful but not foolproof, especially for the amount of heat he would be releasing from the weapon.

He decided against trying it in the forest outlying the village. Forest fires could be a hassle to stop, and it was possible the fire would be overlooked for quite some time. At least long enough to cause some long-range damage. Thus, he would test it in the garden outside the CfNL's headquarters.

Lighting the garden within the village could be damaging as well, but it would be noticed quickly, and the resulting irony was well worth the danger of being caught. How amusing it would be for the CfNL's garden to burn down. It was no ordinary garden, but their most valued prize, devised using techniques that manipulated plant life.

What a message this would send to other Semions, High Service, and even the council itself. Perhaps it would signify, or at least everyone would think it signified, the Council for Natural Law falling out of favor with nature. Hadn't the council been quick to blame the CfA for the developing problems? Hadn't Marvus asked every Semion to look for a sign to help explain what was going on? The fire would suggest the CfNL did not have the grasp on nature's will like they thought they did. If so, why would their garden go to the trouble of burning itself down?

Falken could hear the talk making its rounds in the village. It would spread faster than the flames in the garden ever could.

As for keeping out of trouble, he learned his lesson with the planetary orb room years ago. Only meddle with the forbidden when you know no one is watching. Late at night would be best. Not much happened when the stars came out, especially in that side of town. Any star gazers spent their time where there was equipment to view spatial entities in detail, which did not include the garden where towering trees blocked the sky.

He also factored in another safety guise. That same evening, he would relieve High Service of any more AT system monitoring. The ensuing panic inside the Aurora would distract from his meddling in the garden. Not only that, but the simultaneous burning of the garden and the AT system failure would be a great coincidence. If there were any Semions not suspicious of how things were being handled in Semadon, they would be after he enacted his plans.

He would make his move that evening, and he would tell no one, not even his collaborators in the CfA.

Chapter Twenty-One

"AS MUCH AS I like it here," Ceera said, "I guess we'll have to turn back." The jewel-like surroundings glistened around her, enhancing the blue in her eyes and the contours of her face.

Dassius turned away from her, refusing to be distracted. "No," he said. "Give me some time." He placed the flashlight on a rock to illuminate the cavern. The answer to his puzzlement stared him in the face, but where? He surveyed the room inch by inch.

A massive chunk of clear crystal, with a height rivaling his own, gave him reason to pause. Was it due to the size and beauty of the mineral, or his blurred image staring back?

A movement flickered beyond his reflection. He squinted and leaned closer. The faint glimmer pulsed again. He glanced over at Ceera, who was running her fingers over a purple gem atop the floor.

"Come stand beside me."

She rose and wandered over, her eyes gleaming as she neared the crystal. The movement flickered between their reflections.

"Look," he urged.

"It's beautiful."

"No, look here," Dassius replied as he touched the fluttering movement in the crystal.

Their surroundings twisted into geometric shapes that shrank away to nothingness. A multi-faceted world of crystalline brilliance remained, illuminating the image of a man who managed to be everywhere at once. Patterns of his figure stretched in all directions, growing incrementally smaller. His fingers beckoned, and the gesture mimicked a thousand times all around them.

It seemed natural to obey. They followed the man toward a speck of darkness that grew into an opening as they neared. When they stepped through, the brightness faded as did the effects, enclosing them within a dimly lit room. Slivers of light shone through cracks in the ceiling.

The man's now solitary figure evoked a sense of wholeness. Rounded muscles and light brown skin accentuated his body. He wore long pants made from animal hide. Brownish grey hair curled over his ears.

The depth of his piercing eyes, the color of nickel, caused Dassius to reconsider his own self. He felt paper thin, transparent even, as if the Archaic compressed his entire life into a meager existence, and his lack of density allowed the nickel-colored eyes to see right through. He questioned his own integrity and even his motives for being there. This, he soon realized, was a reaction to the all-empowering quality of the man's demeanor. It was well grounded, poised. The expression on his face was humble yet aloof.

"You must be Baric," Dassius said.

"I am." Baric's voice resounded from the depths of his being. His words were like an offering to Dassius, who began to feel more comfortable.

"I'm Dassius," he said, "and this is Ceera. We consider ourselves fortunate to meet you."

"My wolves led you to me," Baric said solemnly. "It is fortunate you followed them."

Dassius glanced over at Ceera.

"It felt more like we were chased," she said.

"They did their duty. Did they not?"

"Perhaps in the only way they knew how," Dassius said quickly.

"I am aware you come to me with questions." Baric studied them.

"Yes," Ceera said, "but first, how did your wolves know we were here to see you?"

"I told them. I heard your footsteps. I know of your travels. First you visited Oc~ea, who left you flooded with even more questions than you had when you began. Next, Atmos whipped up a sense of confusion in you. Luma infused you with panic and sent you running from her ideals. I am always next. For some reason it always comes down to me in the end."

"You are by no means the end of our travels," Dassius carefully stated.

"I am privy to such matters. I know where your foot-steps will go after our encounter. Nature shares her knowl-edge with me which is infinite and infinity reaches in both directions, don't forget."

"So you already know why we're here," Dassius said.

"Of course I do. The doings on this planet are embed-ded within me. I know everything about your situation. I will even go so far as to say I know more about it than you do."

Dassius shifted his stance and looked away, bothered by the suggestion.

"Come," Baric said, holding an arm out and motioning them further inside. "Let us talk and see if we can mold some meaning out of your conundrum."

Clay shelving lined the walls and displayed various rocks and insect specimens. Dassius paused to pick up an unusually large beetle with thick mandibles protruding from its head. The insect came to life at his touch; its thin legs wiggled frantically and mandibles twitched. He dropped the beetle, and it scurried across his jacket and onto the dirt wall, taking its rightful place back on the shelf.

"They don't like to be handled." Baric's tone was stern.

"Sorry. I was impressed by its size."

"I'm sure it felt the same about you."

An area to the side tunneled downward. Jars containing varieties of dirt and clay filled more shelving, categorized by dates etched along the shelves.

"Have a seat." Baric pointed to a large curved structure held up by many legs.

"It's made of rock?" Ceera asked politely, but Dassius could read the disgust on her face.

"Yes, it's the largest fossilized invertebrate species in existence."

Dassius grinned at her and took a seat.

"What a unique piece of furniture." Ceera slowly sank to a seated position.

"Don't worry, it's solid. It's already survived thousands of years intact." Baric sat across from them, using its head as an arm rest. "How was the tunnel my ants dug for you?"

"Adequate," Dassius said.

"They must have been very large," Ceera added with a deadpan expression.

"Their size is a tribute to their success in these parts. The closer they get to me, the more they thrive. All types of insects are drawn to me for that reason. Once they get here they realize there is not much for them to do and head back to the surface."

"Do you ever walk the surface?" Ceera asked.

"I go everywhere. I tread the entire planet on certain occasions. I even graze the edges of Semadon, though I haven't been to your ancient forest in ages." He spoke the words like he was aware of their heaviness.

"Why not?" Dassius asked.

"The area suffered an unnatural circumstance. It's not a territory I like to visit."

"Is it dangerous?" Ceera whispered.

"It depends on who you are and why you have come."

A troubled look crossed Ceera's face. "How dangerous?"

"There is something unresolved there. Conflict always begets danger."

"Its appearance was sudden. For some reason, I even dream about it. I don't know why."

"What happens in these dreams?"

"I'm searching for a certain tree. There is an ancient manuscript hidden at its base. I know this because I followed a woman and watched her place it there. I have yet to view this relic up close."

"Why don't you go look at it?"

"I try but an evil presence restricts me…then I wake up."

"Then finding the relic must be important."

"Yes," she agreed, "but I don't know why."

"Perhaps you know," Dassius interjected.

"It's not my place to tell her. You must search for the answer within your dreams."

"I don't know how. They always end abruptly."

"Perhaps you can ask the forest for help when you get there."

Ceera gave him a blank look.

"You think I am fooling you, don't you?" Baric said. "Let me tell you, I am not that type."

"How is that possible?" Dassius asked.

"Now wait one moment, the forest called upon you, correct?"

"Yes," Ceera said softly.

"Then don't underestimate it."

"I don't understand," she admitted, "but I believe what you mean will reveal itself in time."

"Yes," Baric said. "Many truths will become apparent before all is said and done."

"What more can you tell us about the forest?" Dassius asked.

"You are looking for answers about its origins, correct? Well, if you want to know why this is happening, you have to start at the beginning, the roots. It's all about roots."

Baric winked at them and stood. He walked a few steps into the tunnel and scanned the shelving. "Let me find the correct time period. Here we go." He whisked a jar off the shelf and smudged the date beneath it, before walking back to sit down.

"Having infinite knowledge makes it difficult to talk about single moments in time. This soil grazed the surface during the time your forest became tainted. It will help me form the right words."

Baric emptied the jar into his hand so that the soil

covered his palm. Tiny white lines became apparent from within the dirt, snaking this way and that, creating an intricate design that extended up his forearm.

Dassius was fascinated. "Mycelium," he whispered.

Baric's face vacated all expression as the white fungal threads burrowed into his skin and traveled even further up his arm and neck, visible like veins. With a jolt, his eyes glazed over. The tiny threads wove a labyrinth around his pupils, apparent in the whites of his eyes as subtle wriggling bulges. Then Baric blinked and the white threads traveled back down his arm and into the soil. He dumped what remained of the soil back into the jar. "Ah yes," he told them with a frown, "the story of the great fall."

His words triggered a memory. "Is this the story about the people who caused their own demise?" Dassius asked. "If so, Atmos already told us this story."

Baric just stared at Dassius for a moment. "Of course it's not," he retorted. "The great fall is the story of the fall of the trees." Baric looked displeased as he continued. "Your forest fell upon harsh times. It all began many years ago during an age when uncertainty was abundant. The planet was not performing its function in the conventional manner. Now this was no oversight on the behalf of nature by any means.

"The vegetation became sick. Trees were inflicted and became so diseased they did not adhere to their natural function. Some ceased to exist. Those remaining were unable to cycle the water from the soil back up into the atmosphere or release any oxygen. The soil also suffered. Drought occurred and desertification spread. More and more trees died off, creating a toxic atmosphere. Without oxygen, all life on this planet's surface began dying out."

"All life?" Dassius asked. "What about us Semions?"

Baric's gaze was stone cold.

"Sorry, please go on."

"The animals feeding off these plants starved to death. The animals feeding off the plant eaters, they died too. This deadly cycle broke many links to existence. Much of what you see around you was no more."

"What caused the planet to behave this way?" Dassius asked.

"You could equate it to an epidemic or perhaps an infection. It infiltrated through the evolutionary cycle. Once it took root, it spread rapidly. As is nature's way, it multiplied with great speed and severity, impairing everything. It made all you see around you susceptible to death. Soon the elements had no choice but to intercede."

"The war," Ceera spoke up. "Luma said the elements were fighting a war."

Baric's deep gravelly laugh shook the ground. "She would dramatize what happened to fit her needs. She has a lust for power."

"But how could our planet be so vulnerable?" Ceera asked.

"This planet is by no means vulnerable. The better term is adaptable. Fighting disease is the same as building immunity. It is the same as when one suffers from a sickness, overcoming it makes you stronger. It took thousands of years for the planet to mend itself."

"So allowing the devastation to spread was the only way to get rid of the problem?"

"Correct," Baric looked pleased. "Nature is infinite. Time, to her, doesn't exist. She revolves continuously and forever. If life at present must die for the betterment of the future then so be it."

"But our forest, we're told it still has some sort of defect," Dassius said.

"That is the intriguing aspect, isn't it? It cannot forget."

"Why can't it?" Dassius persisted.

"Your forest has a secret. It harbors this memory of its past."

"Does this memory have anything to do with what I am seeking? Is it one and the same?" Ceera asked.

"One beckons; the other conceals. It is up to you to decide whether they serve the same purpose or exist in dichotomy." Baric interlocked his fingers.

"When will we know?" she said.

"You will have to wait until the forest decides to acknowledge you. Only then can you get to the root of the issue," Baric said with finality. He sat still as a statue.

"I take it you are done with our questioning," Dassius said.

"You are correct. We are done."

Ceera and Dassius stood.

"Would you like my wolves to escort you back to where you came?"

Dassius exchanged a quick glance with Ceera. "We appreciate your hospitality but we can manage," he replied.

Baric raised an eyebrow at him.

"As long as you approve of us traveling back on our own."

"Yes, but you must promise to retrieve the items you carelessly left behind."

"My pack and knife," Dassius said. "I hope I can find them again."

"If you can't find them then my wolves will help you."

"I'll do just fine."

Baric extended his hand which held a glass vial shaped like a sphere. Various colored stones vibrated within the enclosure. The vial's lid was smaller than the rocks contained inside.

"Here is my essence I prepared for you." He ignored Dassius's outstretched arm and handed the vial to Ceera, who accepted with a puzzled expression.

"The stones are larger than the lid," she said.

"The stones will serve their purpose," Baric said, "as long as the vial remains in your care."

"I believe you and will gladly hold onto it." She smiled brightly at him.

Jealousy pricked Dassius's skin, and he sensed her gratitude stretched far beyond the gift of the vial. The Archaic handing it to her signified something, and Ceera caught on to this truth.

He nodded goodbye to the Archaic, who eyed him knowingly, placed his hand on Ceera's back, who shrugged it off, and walked toward the door.

Their crawl back through the tunnel was slow and tedious. The flashlight kept slipping out of place, leaving them in darkness until he readjusted. A few times, he even bumped into the side of the tunnel. Being the leader of such clumsy maneuvering gnawed at his confidence. Every move forward served as a harsh reminder of his lack of foresight.

When they reached the opening, he poked his head out, his eyes taking a moment to adjust to the shock of sunlight. No wolves lurked outside, and he gestured for Ceera to follow.

They had only walked a short distance when a loud

thud shook the ground behind them. A large rock now blocked the entryway to the cave. A bushy tail retreated from the hilltop, but the visual was brief. There was no clue there had once been an entrance.

As they hiked through the woods, Dassius couldn't help but feel terribly small. Although the pesky feeling would not wane, he attempted to at least act as if nothing was bothering him.

Ceera, of course, was elated and walked with a spring in her step. Her cheeks flushed pink and light radiated from her eyes. He suspected her jovial mood was because Baric confirmed her significance.

Dassius already knew Ceera was significant. The mystic he conjured had verified this, which now seemed to have happened so long ago. What grew on his mind was the possibility, and yes, he was certain, the probability that perhaps his own presence was unnecessary. The first mystic disappeared before parting with the answer to that particular question. He didn't even bother to ask the second mystic. He had already abandoned the idea and moved on to more pressing issues. The question now lingered in his mind.

His companion paused to peer at a cluster of violet colored flowers. He waited while she studied them. Why hadn't he been the one to tell her how important she was? Was his pride so fragile that it caused him to deny another their worth? Now her pleasure was a result of something the Archaic had told her, instead of something he could've just as easily disclosed. The realization stung on both counts.

A decision formed in the midst of his shame. He would never deny her anything again. Not even a truth he hid from himself. But he had to be gentle about it. Relay it when the time was right so she wouldn't get hurt.

By the time he recovered his pack and the knife he had been stripped of earlier in the day, her face conveyed an unwavering confidence. When he tried to walk close to her, she twisted away, always preferring to be a few steps to the side. Her reactions that day started to piece together in his mind. She was avoiding him for pulling away from her during their kiss, the kiss that had been the opposite of satisfying because his desire never waned. He craved to feel her lips against his again, her body pressed close.

Deciding it would be best to explain, he turned toward her, but she only forced a smile and sidestepped past. Anger came and went. How could he be mad when protecting her had become so satisfying? If anything happened to her inside the forest, he wouldn't be able to live with himself.

Chapter Twenty-Two

THE NIGHT HAD been uneventful. Leynin monitored what he could of the progress of Ceera and Dassius. They had changed locations. Dassius resent the transmit from the previous night, probably since High Service had not sent a transmit back.

"We tried," Leynin muttered under his breath. "We did try."

He assumed they were looking for the fourth Archaic, and perhaps had found him already. They had yet to send another transmit which meant they had not returned to the cylinder, although Leynin knew nothing for sure.

In the meantime, several experts of the field had attempted to figure out what was wrong with the AT system. Despite their efforts, no solutions were found.

So when the last light went out on the screen, Leynin thought it was just his own energy that had dwindled away to nothing. It was very late at night and the atmosphere in Semadon had become very anxiety ridden. His stress levels were higher than he had ever experienced. There was talk every official would be raised to the next sphere level if the present situation ever resolved. Those at the top may even be compelled to retire.

The thought was reassuring; however, Leynin came back to reality when he viewed the controls before him yet again, probably for the hundredth time that night alone. They were dim, which could only mean one thing. The entire system had shut down. Not only would High Service be unable to send messages, but Ceera and Dassius would no longer be able to successfully send a transmit. The officials would also have no way of monitoring them if they kept transporting between working cylinders.

Leynin's eyes widened as he acknowledged the danger. He leaned closer to the controls until they were only inches from his face. No matter how hard he willed them to shine, the controls remained unlit.

He slumped back in his chair and decided he wouldn't move again. What did eventually break him out of his stupor was the sound of his own breathing. His shallow breaths filled his head, filled the entire room. It was suddenly very hot.

High Service had been counting on the AT system to prevail for just a few more days, that it would somehow retain the capacity to bring Ceera and Dassius back to Semadon before a total collapse. Some were even confident it would be fixed beforehand. This hope had evidently been a terrible waste of thought.

Leynin pushed buttons on the control panel. He stood up and wiped the sweat off his brow. He closed his eyes and breathed slowly, attempting to prepare for how he would break the news to the other officials. The report would not be well received.

❧

Falken waited until close to midnight before stepping out

into the orbits. With the moon illuminating his figure, he resorted to taking more secretive routes to the CfNL's garden. Thus, he darted between dwellings and snuck in the shadows.

His weapon burned mildly in his pocket. He kept slipping his fingers inside, fueling his motivations with each slight touch.

When he reached the garden, he scanned the area for Semions before opening the gate. There was no one nearby. He listened carefully, not a sound. He crept inside and checked behind every tree.

Confident he was alone, he reached inside his pocket for his weapon. The heat was noticeable, but it would be bearable until he pressed the button on the side compartment. Even then, he could hold it by the rays; balanced in his palm he would feel no pain.

He aimed his weapon at a large tree battered with age and released the catch. The fire shot out like a laser and lit the tree. The flame spread rapidly through the crown.

Falken had only a moment to enjoy the splendor before he outstayed his welcome. He sprinted past the flaming tree, over the gate, and back through the complicated tangle of secret paths that would lead him to his dwelling and a realm of self-glorification.

⁓

"Nope, nothing," Dassius informed Ceera when he stepped out of the cylinder. "I sent the next transmit anyway."

"What could be holding them up?" she replied.

"At first, I thought they were just busy analyzing what the Archaics said to us or dealing with the AT installers."

He ran his fingers roughly through his hair. "Yet here we are, with nowhere else to go but the forest, and still not a word sent our way."

"Something's not right, I agree," she said wearily. "What should we do?"

"There's only one thing we can do. We'll go back to Semadon and see what's going on." Dassius looked at her as if to measure her reaction.

"I can't say I'm disappointed," she told him with a sigh. Talking to Baric had eased her mind at the time, but doubt had crept back in. The danger aspect coincided too closely with her recent dreams. If she searched for clarification within them, then death was always the answer. She wanted to find the relic, but would someone or something be seeking her out as well? Even worse, would coming face-to-face with what had driven her mother crazy destroy her too? Was that her fate? A feeling of dread had hovered in the back of her mind for days now. She was no longer sure of anything.

"Why?" He was incredulous.

"My latest dream scared me." She gave him a sheepish look.

"What dream? The one from three days ago?"

"I had another one last night," she admitted.

"I see," he replied with a frown. "What happened?"

For a moment she hesitated; then before she could stop herself, the details spilled from her lips.

Instead of looking sympathetic, his face turned red with anger. "So you have no desire to go with me into the forest anymore?"

"I don't know," she said, though it bothered her to say it.

Dassius stared grimly down at his feet. "You need to think this over. Really weigh your options, Ceera; you have to."

"I will," she said, confused by his reaction. It was enough to make her consider that she was making a rash decision.

"We should wait." The words fell from both of their lips at the same time. Their eyes locked together in surprise.

"I mean, I'm feeling conflicted right now but maybe it'll pass."

Dassius nodded, seeming to relax a bit. "We'll wait until morning then. This will give you time to decide what you want and them more time to respond."

"Fine," she said. "Morning it is."

"And while we're on the topic of you," he said, "what's been with you today?" He moved toward her, stopping only a few inches away, and looked at her so intently she took a step back.

"What do you mean?" she asked, avoiding his eyes.

He placed his hands on her arms.

She twisted away. Why was he so hands on?

"That's what I mean," he said. "Look, I made a mistake last night. Please forgive me."

She forced a laugh, using indifference to shield her hurt feelings. "Oh, that was my mistake too."

"Your mistake?" He glowered.

"I was overwhelmed from our visit with Luma. The kiss was just…a reaction to stress."

Dassius scowled at her, an odd reaction unless he wanted to be the one rejecting her, which seemed most likely. "You didn't like it?" he asked gruffly.

"No," she said without conviction because she was con-fused. "I don't like being kissed."

Dassius's annoyed expression softened into its own confused look.

"Or touched for that matter."

Dassius continued to stare at her in a way that made her feel exposed.

Her cheeks burned. "Honestly, I'd prefer it not happen again."

"Oh you would?"

"Yes," she said, though a traitorous ache in her body said otherwise.

His dark eyes searched her out, and a strange feeling washed over her.

She shivered. "Stop it," she accused. "Stop trying to read me."

"There's no trying; I can see it clear as day."

"See what?" She turned away to hide her face.

"You liked the kiss," he said.

She whirled around in anger. "Is your ego so important that you must embarrass me like this?"

His eyes were laughing at her. "I liked it too. Should I also be embarrassed?"

She opened her mouth for a nasty retort, but then the meaning of his words caught up with her. Blood drained from her face. Part of her wanted to embrace him despite his irritating smile, but the unfamiliarity of the situation won her reaction. So she did nothing.

His smile faded as he took a step toward her. "How could you think—"

"We shouldn't get involved with each other," she said.

"Why not?" He sounded angry again.

"It's not professional."

"Don't make me laugh. That's not why. Just say it."

"Say what?"

"You're choosing fear over desire."

"Fear of what? What is it you think I desire?"

"This is what you desire." He wrapped his arms around her gently, like she was on the verge of breaking.

She couldn't stop her arms from holding him back. "I shouldn't let you do that."

"Why not?" he whispered into her ear. "Because you fear you might like it?"

"No," she protested. "I barely know you."

"You don't? Really?" He let go of her.

Ceera shrugged, avoiding his gaze.

"We've spent days together, more time than if we'd been dating back in Semadon. It's something else." Dassius stared at her and frowned. "I know what it is. After everything we've been through, you don't trust me. You're afraid to trust me."

When she didn't respond but only looked back at him, he drew her close and kissed her. Every muscle in her body relaxed.

He pulled away. "Would I do that if you couldn't trust me?"

"Maybe," she whispered.

"If only you knew how much you can trust me," he told her sullenly.

He walked over to his pack and unclasped their tent. Ceera watched him struggle with assembling it. Usually he had it up in a matter of minutes, but it took him three tries before it stood correctly.

Maybe she was being unfair. He had kept her dreams a

secret after all. Not to mention, he had kept her safe. Perhaps it wasn't such a bad thing to let herself be close to him. A few kisses here and there couldn't hurt as long as she prepared for what might happen once they returned to Semadon. And for the moment, she really needed someone to rely on.

"Dassius," she said when the tent finally stood upright. "Let's just take it slow okay?"

"My thoughts exactly," he replied, grinning mischievously as he gestured her inside.

She rolled her eyes but smiled sweetly when she passed him into the tent. She couldn't wait to fall asleep.

⤎

Marvus was still spending sleepless nights slumped over the railing in the room of the statues. Desnia had given up trying to dissuade him, for she could only take so much, and had left for her dwelling to sleep. He saw no joy in sleeping, not when his council was in such jeopardy.

The CfA refused to take back their accusation about the CfNL's involvement. It was not surprising the CfA would remain stubborn, but it did cause him to consider their motive. If they were willing to go to such extreme measures to forsake the CfNL, what came next? Should they win favor of High Service and the public majority, they would be allowed to enact whatever blasphemous idea they desired, which would undoubtedly destroy the entire Semion culture.

Marvus knew that nature was imbalanced, that something very big had yet to occur. If he could foresee what this was, he could alert High Service and they could take precautions to stop it.

In despair, he checked whether the stone figments of his imagination had resurfaced, but they were nowhere to be seen. He had grown accustomed to them now that he lived on no sleep.

When he had told Desnia about his new friends, she had attempted to not look concerned. He had seen right through her. From now on, he needed to keep that sort of thing to himself. The last thing he wanted was for Desnia to declare him unfit as head of the council.

Although the child statues had not presented themselves tonight, he did happen to notice the expression on one of the Archaics, Luma to be exact, was different than usual.

He leaned over the railing to get a closer look. No longer did her face depict indifference. A look of smug contentment had overtaken her features, emphasized by an obvious smirk.

It was then Marvus sensed something important was happening in the garden. The answer to his dilemma could be waiting there, a sign to be seen. He went to the back door and opened it, only to be greeted by hot fumes. Coughing, he waved the smoke away and rubbed his eyes, staring at the hideous spectacle.

The garden, the precious garden was in flames! Marvus averted his desire to faint, and instead rushed to turn on the sprinkler system and the outdoor lights. He watched in horror as the water eventually put out the flames and left him a ravaged sight matching his emotions. Then with great effort, he clomped pathetically to the correspondence orb to notify High Service.

Chapter Twenty-Three

FALKEN DODGED AROUND the orbits, catching snippets of conversation along the way. Everyone was discussing the garden fire, and most were greatly troubled by it.

"What a relief the fire did not spread across Semadon. Thankfully, no one was hurt."

Falken heard similar comments as he kept walking. He waited for the statement he knew had to have crossed someone's mind, for surely not everyone lacked common sense.

"It's a sign," someone finally proclaimed. "Nature is not pleased with the CfNL."

When Falken overheard these words, he felt validated. It was only a matter of time before the same thought infected everyone else.

Falken entered the CfA office, feeling suspect for his actions. Casma studied him as he took a seat. Even Nimren had a dubious expression. Having anticipated this, he acted as if he didn't notice. He sat down before them exactly like he had the previous times.

"Ceera and Dassius sent their latest transmit. I received it last night."

"Very good," Nimren said, eyeing him in a way that would have made a lesser man crumble.

"There's no new information about the forest," Falken said. "These Archaics tend to dance around the subject an awful lot."

"As they should Falken," Nimren said. "Why they probably don't even know what could be there themselves."

"They received their last vial, plus Baric mentioned something about a relic inside the forest. It sounds like this object is important."

Nimren and Casma looked at him with interest, the fire momentarily forgotten.

"Do you have any idea what it is?" Nimren asked.

"No, but I think it could work against us."

"I see what you mean," Nimren said thoughtfully. "Whatever this item is could spell disaster for us."

Falken mentally vowed to prevent that disaster from happening.

"We hear the AT system completely broke down. Your doings we presume," Nimren said.

"Yes, I went ahead and disengaged everything last night. So now the transmits only come to me, and I have the system programmed to take Ceera and Dassius to the forest when they set foot inside a cylinder again. In fact, I cannot stay long. I need to monitor them."

Nimren and Casma continued to stare at him.

"I have also decided," Falken went on, "the vials are not our biggest concern. I think this secret item is. I'll intercept it, bring it back here, and we can analyze it. We can destroy it if it aligns with the CfNL."

"How do you propose to intercept this item?" Casma asked. "Dassius is trained in attack methods, and you never said how you planned on overtaking him."

Falken paused as he considered how to phrase his

response. "I have created a weapon for this very purpose. It is powerful; they will quickly see things my way."

Nimren and Casma exchanged glances.

"Has it been approved?" Casma asked.

"It's unknown. I had no choice."

"You must destroy it before you return to Semadon," Nimren stated firmly. "We cannot run the risk of you bringing it back here once you've used it in the forest."

Falken nodded in agreement, although he planned to do with it as he pleased.

"Which brings me to my next question, what if they figure out who you are?" Nimren said.

"Then there is only one action I can take to protect myself."

"Which is?"

Falken said nothing but his thoughts were not so covert.

Casma gasped softly and placed her hand on Nimren's arm. "Do you intend to kill them Falken?"

"I will do what I must, but no, I am not planning to do so. If destroying them must happen for me to accomplish my task, then that is beyond my control."

"Let's hope they hand over the item without incident then," Nimren said with no emotion in his voice.

"It would be for their own good," Falken agreed.

"Are you aware our council is under great scrutiny over what happened last night?" Casma said.

"By whom?" he asked. "On the way here, I heard no one accusing the CfA of the fire in the garden."

"High Service corresponded with us first thing this morning," Nimren said. "They asked a few questions about our whereabouts last night. It's not clear who is accusing us, High Service or the CfNL, but either way, you must take precautions to ensure you will not give them further reason to question us."

"You have my word," Falken said as he stood. "The next publicity we get will be for the success of our weather enhancement project."

While walking back to his dwelling, it occurred to Falken that he had not succeeded in annihilating their suspicions about him. It was no matter, once he brought them what was hidden in the forest, a chair on the council would be his.

What was once a lush and healthy garden now resembled a scorched wasteland. Charred plants left traces of themselves, pathetic remnants that lay lifeless in the dirt. The tree bearing the brunt of the attack was now leafless with a blackened trunk.

When Desnia saw what remained of the garden, her insides twisted into a withering agony. She clutched her belly in despair. Then she saw Marvus standing in the midst of the ghastly scene. The sight of him distracted her from wallowing in the torment. The gloom in his face was disheartening enough by itself. Desnia decided not to dwell on the fate of her garden. No, there was a much more serious issue at hand.

"I should have known something like this would happen," he told her.

Desnia was no longer in the mood to cater to Marvus's pitiful ramblings. "Why?" she demanded. "How could you have known?"

"Luma, her statue, it,"—he looked Desnia square in the eye—"you should have seen the look on her face." Marvus shook his head sadly as he gazed over the expanse of singed plant life.

Desnia fumed more vibrantly than the flames that had overwhelmed her surroundings. She waited a moment to see if her fury would die down before she said what was on the verge of escaping her lips. When it did not, she set the words free. "Marvus, I'm going to have to ask you to step down from your chair for the time being."

Marvus grabbed onto the tree emblem on his necklace and froze. His mouth opened and shut a few times, but no sound came out.

"Don't ask me to reconsider," Desnia continued. "I have made up my mind and it's final. To be fair, I will refrain from choosing a new head for the time being. If you're able to recover from your mental breakdown in a reasonable amount of time, I will allow for your return."

"My mental breakdown?" Marvus said in shock.

"Yes, your mental breakdown. You are so absorbed in worrying that you haven't slept in days. As a result, it appears you are hallucinating. At the onset of these delusions, I thought you at least realized what they were, but now it appears you believe in them."

"But what will you do, all by yourself in this state of turmoil? We don't even know why the garden burned."

"I will proceed as we should have been doing all along," she snapped. Hearing the wrath in her voice, she made an attempt to talk in a calmer manner. "Tomorrow I will appear on the global update. I will say the Council For Natural Law will be withdrawing from any further commentary regarding the village, due to the severity of what happened in our garden."

Marvus gasped. "You cannot," he sputtered. "Have you

not heard the village spin? Semions are saying it's a sign from nature, a direct response by her to us in accordance to the speech I gave. Your withdrawal, your failure to take decisive action, will be taken that we agree to this fallacy. You back away from this attack and we are doomed. Do you hear me? Our council will be blamed!"

"Marvus, you did not let me finish. After I say we are withdrawing from further commentary, I will proceed to explain why. The reason is because we, from the Council for Natural Law, have decided to put our trust in nature. Since we consider our outlook to be fair and accurate, that nature is reacting to the CfA's disrespect, we will allow for her to rectify the situation. We will show our devotion by repairing what is left of our garden."

Now that Desnia had released what she wanted to say even before Marvus gave his last speech, she took a deeply satisfying breath. Although she stood in the midst of a charred paradise, her gaze attached to the greener aspects of her surroundings.

"I suppose I shall spend time in my dwelling then," Marvus said in a subdued tone. He let go of his necklace in an act of defeat.

"I would appreciate it. Come back to me when your outlook doesn't mimic this garden."

∾

Outside the Aurora, crowds gathered to voice disapproval over what they called High Service's mismanagement of village affairs. Semions waved signs and chanted noisily, which caused High Service to assign Order Patrol outside to monitor the scene. It was during the crux of the event, when Semions were becoming especially unruly, that Hegliod approached.

He enjoyed his work as a street cleaner immensely. No more did life squeeze him dry. Deep thoughts no longer fogged up his reality. He was free to view the world around him with a clear mind.

The monotony of the job made it easy for him to vanquish all complicated thoughts. There was no pressure except to make a clean pathway to walk upon. He hummed brainless tunes he heard on the global update, which he now had time to watch religiously since he only partook in his daily operations for a set amount of time.

He spent no more late evenings staring at equations or even at nothing for that matter. Nothing: the fertile place where many of his ideas had been conceived. It had looked as if he were staring at nothing, when instead very much was going on inside his head. No more. He was now externalizing, as he liked to call it.

Cleaning the streets, however, did tire his muscles. First, he felt it in his shoulders. Then the ache moved down his arms and even up to his neck. His legs burned like fire at times. Still, he kept moving and humming, a permanent smile plastered on his face.

It was during this state of intellectual absence when something sprang into his mind. He did not invite the thought; it came on its own accord. Although it was a very telling notion, Hegliod was not in the proper state to recognize its significance. Instead, he paused and formed a picture of the thought.

He envisioned a low lying machine, on wheels even, which sucked the debris from the orbits with vigor. It did the job much quicker than Hegliod, and was even more efficient due to its size. When he imagined remotely programming its movements, being able to set it on automatic even, he stopped motionless in his tracks.

It wasn't until he stood still that some of the Semions congregating in the Auroras's lawn noticed him. Laughing, one of them tore the program they held into tiny bits and tossed them in the direction of Hegliod's stationary figure. The wind carried them over to him and the pieces floated majestically down, landing before and behind him, in his hair, and even on his broom.

When he didn't react, they soon forgot him, and the commotion in the adjoining lawn continued on. Despite all this, he stood there unmoving for a good part of the day, his mouth agape and his eyes lit up like the Aurora itself.

⤐

Desnia knew it was important to show her mettle, despite the sad image of the garden around her. She used the state of her surroundings to elevate her; the contrast could even work to her advantage. After all, she was firm in her beliefs despite their garden catching fire.

She stood stoically in her strapless gown. An assortment of blue and yellow flowers wreathed her head. "Semions, it's good to see so many of you in attendance," she said. "I am also confident many of you have tuned in at home. Due to recent events, I feel compelled to update you on the state of our council. Our head chairman, Marvus Crewn, took a leave of absence. As the remaining head chair, I will be managing the Council for Natural Law." Desnia paused for emphasis.

"First and foremost," she continued, "I have decided

it would be in the best interest of my council to withdraw from further commentary regarding village affairs. We do so with the utmost of trust in High Service. Since we have already proclaimed our stance on the matter, we won't dwell on the issue. Nature's motivation is our own, and we will allow for her to implement herself in whatever way she sees fit.

"We will instead take action by rejuvenating our garden. As you know, we suffered a misfortune recently when it went up in flames. Thus, until further notice, we will be expending our efforts on replanting and the cleanup of our grounds."

⊰

Nimren took Desnia's firm nod as the cue to turn off the global update. "Did you hear that?" he cried out once the screen was blank. "The old crow resigned himself to his dwelling. Tell me what you think Casma. Tell me what you know I dare to think myself!"

"I'm more interested that the council is backing away from involvement," Casma said. "I always knew Desnia was a coward, a poor companion for even the likes of Marvus Crewn."

"You know what this means don't you?" Nimren continued. "They're admitting fault by withdrawing. They have nothing more to say, so they step away, like no one will notice this admission of guilt."

"Too bad for them, if they think no one will notice."

"Don't be too confident." Nimren lowered his voice. "I keep thinking about Marvus. Don't you find the timing convenient?"

"True," Casma pondered. "Too bad we no longer have Falken to go snooping around in his orbit."

"You are missing the significance here," Nimren said. "Ceera and Dassius are about to go visit the forest, *the* forest. Remember, something awaits them, or maybe even someone."

"What do you mean? Falken?"

"Perhaps the plan was for Marvus to be there to enact their plot."

"How will he do that when the AT system no longer works?"

"You forget they have been planning this for quite some time. Who knows what they have up their sleeves. Maybe their plan will succeed. Either that or it will come head to head with Falken Grihne."

Chapter Twenty-Four

CEERA WOKE TO the sound of Dassius stuffing the last of his belongings into his pack. She propped herself up on her elbow and yawned. "Did we get any transmits yet?"

"No." Dassius rolled up the door flap, attached it above the opening and began tossing his bedding out. He stopped suddenly, his back straightening. "What did you decide?"

"I decided I'm going." Ceera sat up and stretched her arms overhead. She had slept well without a single nightmare. It was the sign she needed. And since she couldn't decide what was worse, going crazy or being an abandoned nothing, it was probably best to proceed as planned.

"What changed your mind?" Dassius asked.

"Well, I remembered I'd have you with me." She smiled.

"I was going to mention that but didn't want any trouble for it." He grinned back at her.

"And besides, now I can spend a few days back in Semadon gearing up for it." This also meant she had time to again change her mind, but she didn't say this out loud.

"As long as you don't get too comfortable," he joked, obviously pleased.

They finished packing and entered the cylinder. Dassius pressed some buttons. A few seconds passed before they faded into the transfer. When it was over, he opened the door a crack and peered out. With a look of confusion, he opened it a bit wider. Moments later, he swung the door entirely open and they stepped outside.

"I thought you programmed us to arrive in the cylinder near the Aurora," she said.

"I did."

"Well then where are we? Is this the forest outside of Semadon?" Ceera shielded her eyes from the sun. She took a few steps in the direction of the forest which was a good distance away.

"I'm not sure." Dassius stepped back into the cylinder and stared at the control panel. "Maybe I entered our destination wrong. Let me verify."

A strange feeling came over her, suggesting there were more pressing issues than the reliability of the AT system. Her eyes dropped down in contemplation. Tools lay in the grass on the other side of the cylinder. She stepped backward. More equipment was there, hidden from view upon initial exit. Very slowly, she turned back around to stare at the gigantic cluster of trees stretching wide in the foreground.

There was something unique about these trees, a complexity entwined within their union. The mass of bark and leaves contracted inward and outward as if it were breathing. She was captivated, and once this sensation gripped her, the rest of her surroundings faded into nothingness.

"Very strange," Dassius said from inside the cylinder. His words matched the ones inside her head.

If he continued speaking, Ceera did not wait to find out. She began doing the only natural thing. She walked away from the AT cylinder, away from Dassius and toward the forest. She needed to take a closer look at these trees.

The splintered ends of branches beckoned like fingers. Was her imagination playing tricks on her or did they move with the breeze? Except, she realized, there was no breeze for the air was still. So perhaps it was not her own will spurring her to venture toward it. The forest had decided this for her. There was nothing she could do to stop herself.

Her trance was disturbed when a loud pounding sound came up behind her. A hand roughly grabbed her shoulder.

"Where are you going?" Dassius said. "There's something wrong with the AT system. We don't have time for this."

"Dassius, I know where we are. This is the forest from my dreams." She interlaced her fingers with his, squeezing tightly.

He looked past her, his body deflating slightly as he viewed it in full scope. "Are you sure?" he stared deep into her eyes. When she didn't reply but only looked back at him earnestly, he answered for her. "Yes, you are."

"It's attracting me stronger than I can resist." She began walking toward it again. It did not take long for him to join her.

"This can't be good," he said, "going into the forest before checking in with High Service."

"You keep saying that, yet you betray your own insight by coming with me. Why?"

"I'm drawn as well. The pull is powerful. It caught me before I was prepared. I may be able to ward off the attraction, but that means I would have to leave you."

"Please don't."

"I wouldn't." He slipped his hand back into hers.

Ceera smiled, and though this smile was intended for Dassius, she did not look away from the woods.

"I wonder why the AT system transferred us here. Did you verify what you programmed into the panel?"

"Yes. Something overrode what I input."

"Do you think the forest decided we should be here?"

"I have no idea what to think," he replied.

"Did you see the AT installers' tools lying at the other side of the cylinder?" she asked.

"Yes," he mumbled. "I did notice something there."

"I wonder how far into the forest they traveled."

"We don't know what happened to them," he reminded her. "Are you sure you're okay with this? What happened to you needing a few days rest?"

"I'll manage," she responded. "What about you?"

"I'm specially trained and thus unbreakable."

"What about your senses? What are they telling you?"

"I might be right."

She shivered. "What is that supposed to mean?"

"Look at it this way. We did as the mystics suggested. We visited the Archaics and have the vials they provided. Now we just need to finish what we've begun."

Her reservations from the previous day were strangely repressed. She could not hold herself back, even though they could be walking toward imminent danger. The closer they got, the quicker her feet moved and Dassius's did the same.

When they reached the outskirts, the forest loomed before them as a vast collage of enchantment and greenery. A sliver of an opening between two trees lured them closer still. Ceera slipped sideways between the trunks and pulled Dassius inside with her.

A frantic knock sounded on the door of the sphere seven's advising room.

As sole adviser for the day, Zivan snapped to attention. "Enter and be heard," he ordered.

The door opened a crack and Risa's head peered in. The rest of her followed, and she shut the door behind her. "We have some troubling news Zivan."

"Proceed," was his stiff reply. A pale wrinkled hand drummed fingers upon the tabletop.

"The rioting has intensified. Order Patrol is working hard to calm the masses, but we fear they may have to resort to force if it doesn't subside soon. We've also failed to regain control of the AT system. We're still incapable of transmitting and are unable to use it for travel. Cafold was able to turn on the system momentarily which did give us some insight on which cylinder Dassius and Ceera most recently used. We believe they have"—Risa faltered—"they have just transported to the cylinder outlying the tainted forest."

His fingers froze. As Zivan leaned forward, the chair creaked to accommodate the moment of silence.

Suddenly, the door behind Risa flew open. Fresdin appeared, his face red and slick with sweat. "The Planetary Stability Monitor," he said between shallow breaths, "we have just received word the energy wave reading jumped significantly."

Zivan's bones ached as he slowly came to his feet. The gravity on his face spoke volumes.

"Call a meeting of our peers." His voice was unnaturally calm. "We have some things to discuss."

❧

Upon entering the forest, Ceera's lingering concerns quickly dissipated. Even though they were only a few steps inside, she was already overcome by its charm. The sensation was tantalizing, and although the opening was still behind them, going back through it did not seem like a viable scenario.

"I feel like I've been here before," she said.

"You have been here before," Dassius responded, "inside your head."

Trees lush with thick vines towered above them. Plant life wound its way up and around the hulking trunks. Smaller trees grew between the taller ones, splaying leaves in every direction. Everything looked as if it had been dipped in moss; it clung to the trunks and blanketed the ground.

"This is the same type of moss I was covered in after my vision," she said, scooping some up with her finger to study it.

Dassius almost fell backward as he gazed up at the massive trunks. "These trees," he said. "How did they grow so big? I would say they are at least a few thousand years old."

"That would make them far older than the old growth forests scientists from Semadon have studied," she said thoughtfully.

"Just think of what they could learn by coming here, if they are somehow as old as they look."

A sense of urgency gripped her. She had an obligation to fulfill. "Dassius," she said, stepping between him and the tree, "we have to find the relic, remember?"

"Okay," he said with a slight frown. He stared into the distance looking perplexed. He took a few steps in one direction then stopped. He walked a different way but this was also short-lived.

"What's the matter?"

"For the first time ever," he replied in a strained voice, "I'm not sure which way to go." He looked around and tapped his forehead a few times with his fingers. Then he shook his head in disgust. "I think maybe we should leave after all."

The thought of leaving repelled her, being in the forest felt as natural as breathing. Before she could respond, he began retracing their steps but stopped short yet again. The trees stretched farther into the distance than seemed possible. Acknowledging this, Dassius swiveled around, trying to pinpoint where they had entered.

"Incredible," he said.

"I don't think the forest wants us to leave."

"Yes, I can attest to that."

"Let me lead the way," she coaxed, linking her arm through his. "I'm capable of it."

"Look, we're already lost and this is just the beginning."

"Not lost," she said, "more like ensnared."

"Like that's any better. We're not lost you say; we're trapped." Dassius yanked away from her.

"We can still remain in control."

"What will you use to guide us? Memories from your dreams? How do you know which way to go?"

She didn't know the way, but Baric's words about asking the forest for help were at the forefront of her mind. "Something tells me the way will open up if I ask."

"If you *ask*?"

"The forest called me here," she reminded him. A quivering in the undergrowth drew her attention. "There," she said, pointing to where the narrow dirt path had formed. It twisted off into the distance.

Dassius stared at her. "How did you do that?" he demanded.

"I don't know," she said with a shrug. She couldn't explain it. What happened seemed natural in the frame of the moment. They needed to keep moving.

She motioned for him to follow. They walked in silence, stumbling past roots grazing the path's edge and climbing over toppled trees.

Ceera failed to notice that the path they followed only went in one direction. After their feet passed, the trail was overtaken by the undergrowth. The forest was swallowing them up with every step.

⁓

When Falken learned Ceera and Dassius had reached the forest, he activated the AT cylinder he planned to use and made his way to the village outskirts. Since his dwelling was in the outer orbit, it would take him five minutes to reach it. He had practiced this walk twice already, to ensure his timing would be accurate.

What he hadn't been expecting was the clutter serving as a barrier between him and his destination. He surveyed the area before him with distaste. Semions littered his immediate surroundings like pieces of trash in a recycle yard. With only seconds to spare, he would have to come up with a plan to sneak through unseen. Walking around the event would take far too much time.

He peeked around a building and scanned the crowd with careful consideration. His victim would have to be standing in the outer rim of the crowd. Within moments, he had her in focus.

She was a glowing, cheerful-looking innocent, about the age of ten, holding a basket of colorful glass balls that gleamed in the sun. She stood unprotected within a group of children, all of their eyes trained on the speaker of the event as they jumped and struggled to peer over those standing before them. The girl, of course, did not jump up and down with the rest, but had a vantage point allowing her the ability to see without straining. There was a small opening in front of her, and within this emptiness his opportunity waited.

Nothing could divert the public's attention like a distressed child, and Falken would take advantage of this trivial reality. He walked up to her, took one last look behind himself to make sure no one was watching, and gave her a quick, rough shove.

The child flew forward though the opening while the basket tumbled out of her grasp. Falken continued to walk swiftly past. He caught a view of her out of the corner of his eye landing on her hands and knees. The sound of glass breaking preceded a mournful wail.

Several of the children standing nearby shrieked loudly.

"My planets!" the girl cried out. She began to cry, and the event speaker fell quiet as Semions gathered around her.

"How did she fall?" someone exclaimed from the edge of the crowd.

"Did she trip?" a woman asked.

"I saw the boy push her," Falken whispered to them as he passed.

Those who heard him rushed over and pointed at the

young boy. He lifted his hands up and frantically shook his head as the girl's sobs resonated through the crowd.

Falken noticed the sign hanging in the distance. It read Planet Day, which was a holiday established by the Council for Natural Law. His measure to deceive was even more fitting.

He passed by some vacant dwellings and reached the rarely used cylinder within minutes. There were no event stragglers in sight. He opened the door and slid inside.

He waited exactly five more minutes and an extra thirty seconds, before pressing the buttons on the control panel. It was important to give Ceera and Dassius an adequate amount of time to distance themselves from the cylinder. He figured the ten minutes was a good approximation, and the thirty seconds was just for good measure. A comfort span really.

He spent the time readying his disguise. The black cloak he put on over his normal attire, but the mask he would save for when he confronted his foes. The mask's silver stretchy cloth fit over his entire head and featured three sheer ovals, one for each eye and another to breathe through. He tucked it away next to his weapon into the small bag that hung at his waist.

The brief transfer left him unfazed. When he resurfaced, he peered out the round window to see if he could catch a glimpse of the two of them. They were many yards away. Dassius's black coat flapped in the breeze behind him, and Ceera's hair caught a hint of the sun as they proceeded toward the monstrosity of trees in the foreground.

Falken paused for a moment as he took the image in, suddenly hesitant for no apparent reason. A mild rush flowed through his body, but he decided to pay it no heed. It was merely his own recognition that he would soon put an end to the Council for Natural Law's ridiculous allegations. Somehow he knew this forest was a sanction for redemption, and this redemption was obviously his.

Before he exited, he typed his newly created code into the control panel. The energy depleted as the power switched off. He stared out the window to make sure Dassius had not noticed. Sure enough, Dassius's head did not even turn; his exalted training was a joke. He and Ceera neared the edges now, about to be sucked into the body of the woods.

Falken crept out of the cylinder, still feeling as if he was eluding the attention of someone. He reassured himself Dassius was unaware of his arrival and walked briskly toward the spot where his two subjects had entered the forest. It was time for him to assert himself.

Falken was unprepared for the wild terrain he soon found himself traveling through. Ceera and Dassius were already out of sight, and he would have a hard finding them. This in itself did not deter him; however, a bout of uneasiness surfaced in his thoughts. For some reason, he couldn't shake the feeling he was being watched.

As Ceera led Dassius deeper into the wood, the brush grew denser around them. The effects of the forest grew stronger as well. Something knocked subtly on her brain, trying to infiltrate her thoughts. She pushed it away but the mental invader returned, causing her morale to dwindle. Was Dassius fighting the same battle or was her worst fear beginning to come true?

"Dassius"—she whirled around—"there's something I have to tell you."

"What?" He eyed her wearily. His demeanor no longer matched his powerful physique.

"I don't know what it is, but something has come over me. My brain feels tired, or maybe overwhelmed. I'm not sure."

"I know the feeling. I'm having a hard time warding it off myself."

"What should we do?" Her thoughts strayed to the vials.

"There is no conquering the forest on first arrivals. You will have to wait until the forest decides to acknowledge you. Only then can you get to the root of the issue." Dassius repeated what Baric said to them the day before.

"I feel acknowledged," she told him. She tried to take a step, but her foot was stuck within a patch of weeds.

Dassius pulled out his knife. He looked at it and shrugged, as if deciding its help was unnecessary. He stabbed it into a nearby tree and instead bent down to wrestle her free with his hands. "Too bad I didn't bring an axe," he said.

"You shouldn't say such things," she replied quickly. She yanked her foot fiercely away from its captor. Dassius watched with a look of amusement on his face.

A heavy thud sounded in the distance, accompanied by leaves rustling.

"What was that?" she hissed.

"A wild animal," he responded.

Something scurried past, a few yards away, hidden by the trees.

"Do you see it?" She grabbed onto Dassius's hand and pulled him along to gain a better view.

Footsteps pounded the ground. Twigs cracked and

leaves crunched. The scenery trembled from the movement of whatever scampered around them.

Dassius fumbled with the empty strap on his hip. He walked back to where Ceera's foot had gotten caught. He ran his fingers along the tree, outlining a gash in the bark with his pointer finger. "Where's my knife?"

A whispering sound erupted in the midst, thick and absent of words. It grew louder and reverberated throughout the woods, mimicking the frequency of crickets at dusk. Its powerful echo rang into Ceera's ears. She placed her hands over them, but the sound forced its way in, pounding with intensity.

Dassius wrapped an arm around her protectively. He jerked his head around as if trying to catch sight of whatever it was from every possible direction. The noise picked up momentum. He pulled her closer.

The sound's intensity was so overpowering that Ceera worried it would never end, and their purpose would soon be forgotten. Her surroundings faded as her sense of hearing dominated her perception.

The noise withered away without warning. She dropped her hands from her ears while Dassius let go of her. The wood turned peaceful again although a residual eeriness hung in the air around them.

Dassius drifted back to the tree with the gash mark. "Did you see what happened to my knife?" He bent down and searched the undergrowth.

"No." It being missing was strange, yet so was every moment since they had stepped foot inside the forest.

After several minutes, he stood and looked at her with bewilderment on his face. "No wonder the AT installers lost their minds," he said, chuckling in an odd tone that lacked true humor.

The thought gave Ceera pause, for with all the focus on her mother's issues, she had forgotten about that aspect of their plight. "I wonder how long they lasted," she said, her statement masking an even bigger question that needed to remain unspoken.

"However long, the truth is they were not welcome and were ousted. You and I, if we can stand it, are here to stay."

"What do you mean if we can stand it?" Her voice wavered.

"It's obvious something is trying to have its way with us, like it did them."

"Is it succeeding?"

"I don't know," he admitted. "Not to mention my knife disappeared."

"Maybe we just don't see it," she told him lamely. "All the trees look alike to a degree."

"They are all starting to look alike," Dassius said. "Your path is gone too. At this point, I have no idea which direction we should head, whether we are even coming or going anymore."

"The path is still here," she insisted. "It just went away when we weren't looking."

"Figure out where it went and let's get going. I'll start putting reflectors on the trees so we can find our way back. And I'm going to use my compass. Maybe between the two of them, things will make more sense."

Ceera allowed him a moment to gather the necessary items out of his pack. He pulled out several reflectors, his compass and a long skinny case containing a spare knife which he attached at his hip. She searched until the path divided the understory again, and they were on their way.

Chapter Twenty-Five

THE BANGING ON the Aurora's main door was startling to some, but others recognized the familiar beat. Its rhythm had been heard in the same manner one week ago, before all had turned chaotic in an otherwise orderly society.

An attendant answered the door and ushered the older gentleman into a small conference room. Asfin and Leynin joined him within minutes. The eager expression on their faces went unnoticed by Hegliod, who was focused on the words he came prepared to speak.

"Hegliod," Asfin said. "What a treat it is to have you back at the Aurora."

"Thank you," Hegliod replied.

"So, tell us why you have come to visit," Leynin said

"I've had a revelation and decided I should share before proceeding with it."

"Please go on," Asfin prodded.

"An unexpected notion struck me, while I was cleaning the orbits of Semadon the other day." Hegliod paused and frowned.

"Yes?" Leynin urged.

"Before I continue I must ask, have they been swept to your satisfaction?"

"Yes, we have seen your good work," Asfin said, scanning his face in desperation.

Hegliod smiled brightly. "I am thoroughly committed to it."

"Please continue, Hegliod," Leynin said.

"Well, you see, I pay close attention to every turn. When one positions the duster at a certain angle, it maneuvers most efficiently."

The High Service officials eyed each other with pained expressions.

"Didn't you say something about an unexpected notion, to use your exact phrasing?" Asfin asked.

"Ah yes. This notion came at a very odd time. Snuck in when I wasn't paying attention. Not the same idea I lost a few weeks back, but a very interesting one to say the least."

The officials dared not move a muscle so as to distract him.

"It involved a machine geared to cleaning orbits, although I appreciate your kind critiques of my work."

The officials deflated. Asfin's head even fell forward.

"Now, don't get all disappointed. I promise you this machine will work well. It will do a better job than even I am capable."

"That's very reassuring," Leynin choked forth.

"There is a problem though, or more like a setback to creating such a fine piece of machinery."

"Yes?" Asfin perked up.

"What I have envisioned will more than likely put me out of work. Then I will be out of a description once again."

The officials looked at him with renewed interest.

"Are you resigning your position as an orbit cleaner?" Leynin asked.

"I suppose I am. Once I get this machine up and running there is no reason for me to continue."

Leynin stared expectantly at him.

"And I suppose," Hegliod continued, "this revelation also suggests something else."

"Which is?" Asfin asked.

"It suggests"—Hegliod puffed up his chest—"I should resume my description as an inventor. It is only natural after all."

Asfin broke into a smile while Leynin let out a huge breath of air.

"Is that okay?"

"Yes," Asfin blurted out. "The AT system stopped working, and we need you to figure out the defect. We have no way to communicate with the Semions using it for travel. Your wish is granted right away."

"Immediately in fact," Leynin added.

"You have specific orders to place your orbit cleaner idea aside until we get this problem fixed. Are up for the task?"

"Yes," Hegliod said. "I shall go to the controls at once."

Desnia was pleased at how well the garden responded to her attempts to recover its beauty. Though she and the council members couldn't change the blackened color so much of the greenery had succumbed to, they did transplant healthy plants into the dirt to overshadow this dismal coloring. They also scattered seeds onto the ground, which they watered profusely, since it wasn't the rainy season and the sun shone down in such an unforgiving fashion.

The effects of such simple enhancements surprised her.

She decided it best not to trim or alter this natural process, thus allowing the plants to grow unhindered. When Desnia did call in the experts who would implement their craft of accelerating growth, she asked them to abide by her wishes. So they inspired the plants to grow even wilder.

Soon the blackness only tinged the green. The charred remains turned to dust and replenished the soil. Vines roped around the trunk of the fire-massacred tree, detracting from its dead looking state.

The recovery was phenomenal, and it didn't take long for the area to become resplendent with colors and designs yet again. The blackened garden had transformed back to a maze of lush greenery. The result took her breath away.

Desnia found it easy to relax in her position as head of the council whenever she stood within this realm of peace and beauty.

&

Someone was following him. Assuming it was Ceera and Dassius, Falken slipped on his mask in hopes of hiding his identity before they recognized him.

He kept walking, more carefully now, with a keen eye on his surroundings. Their sounds behind him were as consistent as his own small noises and kept pace with him a certain distance away.

He was troubled as time went by and they did not confront him. It was one thing for someone like himself to be out sneaking around, another for the likes of Ceera and Dassius, two Semions with perpetually good intentions. Was an animal stalking him perhaps?

Something ran past, stopped a short distance in front

of him, and scurried over to the side. He turned but nothing was there. Sweat dampened his mask and dripped down his neck. A whispering sound echoed around him, low but perceptibly wicked. He halted in terror. The sound entered his ears and rattled his insides. He knew then it was not Ceera or Dassius that he should be concerned about.

Falken broke into a run. He jumped over a few tree stumps and dived down to crawl through the brush. Whatever it was came up behind him, its pressure bearing down.

He got tangled in the canopy of a fallen tree with his foot wedged under a branch. As he struggled to free himself, he remembered his weapon.

Falken retrieved it from his bag and held it out, his hand shaking at the prospect of using it once again. It slipped casually between his fingers, unaware of its own importance. He watched it fall, seemingly in slow motion, toward the undergrowth greedily awaiting it.

No, he could not lose his weapon. He flung his other hand down to catch it before it vanished from sight. Success! He clasped onto it fiercely.

When he looked up, only the calm face of the forest looked back. There was no one and nothing nearby. Falken slipped the weapon back into his bag. For a moment he thought he heard the peculiar sound again, but it was so brief and faint, he figured he just imagined it.

⁓

Ceera led the way like she was walking in her dreams. Even when the dirt path would disappear momentarily within the tangled undergrowth, her subconscious would take over. There were places that drew her, and she would slip easily between the trees while Dassius tracked behind.

It didn't take long for her tranquil wanderings to come to an end. A low-pitched sound invaded the silence. From within its vibration, the faint whispering resounded again.

Dassius stood silent as if he, too, was listening. Droplets formed on Ceera's face as an unannounced heat accosted her. Feeling feverish, she placed her hand on her warm forehead.

The tone then deepened into a murmuring in which words could not break free. Their surroundings closed in on them, and suddenly the forest was very crowded. The trees took on shapes resembling twisted manlike figures. They poked and prodded her with their abrasive limbs. Ceera wrenched her body from one to the next.

As she bounced fitfully between them, her sight blurred. Her thoughts jumbled and dispersed into small fragments, each shard a word that she could not connect to the next. *Forest. Ancient. Lost. Relic. Dream.* The words taunted her and danced around inside her head until she felt dizzy.

She spun into a pair of hands. Fingers dug into her shoulders. She winced in pain and attempted to wrestle free, but the hands held strong. Indignation restored her vision and she realized she was facing someone. His eyes begged for recognition.

"Look at me," Dassius commanded, "and nothing else."

Ceera trembled and gasped for breath as she strained to focus on the intensity radiating from his eyes. For a moment the blue in his pupils dulled, like something lurked behind them, but they flashed back into color with vigor.

"Don't let your mind be prey," he coerced though his voice was not gentle. He cupped her face in his hands.

The trees infringing on her personal space shrank back into the surroundings, and it was only Dassius and his look of stark determination in the forefront of her mind. He was willing her back to reality. The confining vibrations lifted and faded away, allowing her thoughts to regain form. A breeze blew past and cooled her. Water rushed somewhere in the distance. She had been freed.

"Thank you," was all she could think to say.

Dassius let go of her, but he did not look pleased. He glared suspiciously past her. "This forest is evil. I can't imagine it wants you to find anything."

"The forest was leading us somewhere. I know it."

"It leads to something alright. All we've been told is now evident. This forest is tainted. It's almost as if the very nature of this forest, or shall I say the nature in this forest, is flawed."

"We should go back," she said as tears pricked the corners of her eyes.

"We can't go back. We tried, remember? Besides"—he turned away—"you made the right choice."

"What do you mean? How do you know?" His reaction from the previous evening surfaced in her mind. He had been unhappy when she mentioned wanting to go back to Semadon.

"Because you need to find the relic. Going back without it, or leaving before you find it, won't do you any favors."

A few snippets of conversation with High Service officials broke into her thoughts, things they'd said that rubbed her the wrong way. She'd brushed them aside at the time, but their meaning now became clear.

"Dassius"—her voice shook—"what's going to happen to me if I go back without it?"

"Look, I was never fully let in on it."

"Will my life as a scribe be over?" She had no other options if this came true. How would she take care of herself?

"There's more to it than that," he said grimly.

"Tell me," she whispered.

"All these dreams and visions you've been having, they're not normal. Not normal for a scribe. It just makes you seem a little, well, you know what I'm getting at."

Ceera's cheeks flared, and she could no longer fight back the tears. "Go ahead, say it."

"Crazy." Dassius spoke the word softly as if to lessen the weight of it.

"So they planned to commit me?" Questions swirled in her thoughts. Had High Service found out about her mother? Who told them? Her father's words played in her mind: *word always gets out eventually.*

"Only if you came home empty-handed. Ok, maybe I did overhear a little."

"And you weren't going to tell me?"

"I'm telling you now."

She covered her face. Dassius had been protecting her this entire time, not only during their travels but also from High Service.

"Why do you think you didn't have to fight me to keep the dreams from them?" Dassius placed his arms around her, lessening her despair.

"I don't know why," she replied honestly.

"Because I have a mind of my own," he said as he stroked the side of her face. "And I knew you were in a precarious position. Plus, I can read people. I may have asked the mystic about you in the beginning, but I wasn't looking at you with a clear head."

"What did the mystic say?"

"He said you were necessary." Dassius responded almost too quickly, and she wondered if he was just trying to make her feel better.

"Do you think I'm crazy?" Through her bleary eyes, she caught a rueful grin.

"Not in the way they're suggesting."

"But you tried to take us back as soon as we got here."

"Yeah, for different reasons than you not finding the relic. But now we're here and High Service knows we're here, and we've been here too long to back out."

"My mother went crazy," she mumbled before she could stop herself, "from the same type of dreams. Back when I was a child."

"What did you say?" His look was a cross between anger and shock.

"You heard me."

"Does High Service know? What happened to your mother?"

Ceera shrugged. "She's dead."

"Why didn't you tell me this before?" he demanded.

"I only found out a few days before we left, from my father who I hadn't seen in years."

Understanding dawned on Dassius's face, and she wondered whether she had revealed too much.

"Ceera, you are not crazy."

"Not yet. I'm doomed though. If I go back without it, High Service will think I am, and if I keep having these dreams then I might live up to that. And just being here in this creepy forest, well, that might make me crazy too."

"It's not going to happen okay?"

She nodded at him, for once relishing his confidence.

"We're going to figure this out. We're going to find the relic and get out of here."

"Find it how? Do you think we should open the vials?" she asked.

"No, we have to wait for the right time."

"What do you have in mind?"

"The river, can you hear it? Remember what Oc~ea said? 'The forest will not allow you to travel through it easily. However, if you find water, it will lead the way.'"

She gave him a weak smile.

"A temperate forest like this will have a massive body of water flowing through it," he continued. "We can follow it for the time being."

"What about my pathway?" she asked, though she no longer had the same confidence it would open up to her again and, if so, whether she wanted to follow.

"Following a river is a lot less deceiving than wandering through trees. We need to get away from these trees." Dassius gave them a scornful look.

They were proving themselves fickle, these trees, subject to the whims of what she did not know.

~

Hegliod was visibly dismayed with the state of his AT system. Cafold watched every move the older scientist made, with his pen poised on his notepad.

"Someone's been messing with the codes." Hegliod grumbled, eyeing Cafold suspiciously. "It could not have become this disordered by itself."

"Believe me, I did nothing of the sort," Cafold retorted.

"I know better than to mess with something I don't fully understand."

Hegliod pressed a button and a long list of symbols flashed on the screen. "Unbelievable," he groaned. He pressed more buttons and a map of the Aurora appeared. The system displayed the setup of various rooms. "Ah yes. There is a foreign object attached to my system in room 5R."

He turned and exited the room. Cafold and the two officials were close behind.

"What do you mean a foreign object?" Asfin asked.

"Something was added to my invention that I did not put there." Hegliod continued around the hall.

"Do you think removing it will solve the problem?" Leynin asked.

Hegliod stared up at the ceiling and shook his head. "No, but at least it could give us a clue to what's going on."

Hegliod stopped at room 5R. He entered and approached the correspondence controls. He tinkered with the dials and buttons, checking to make sure they were set correctly.

"We stopped receiving transmits prior to the machines not working," Leynin said.

"Yes, a two-part malfunction. Very suspicious." Hegliod opened the compartment below, releasing the high-pitched screeching sound from the silver orb within. He moved his hand around in the darkness. "I knew it!" he cried, pulling out his clenched fist. He loosened his grip to expose a small black oval object, which caused everyone in the room to gasp.

"It's an intervention bug!" Cafold exclaimed.

The officials were aghast.

"I thought we outlawed those," Asfin said.

"We did not realize someone was listening in," Leynin added.

Hegliod paced the room. "Do you know what this means?" He clasped the object between his thumb and fore-finger, shaking it in their direction. "Not only is someone playing with the codes, but this someone also tried to sabotage the entire system!"

Hegliod handed the oval object to Cafold, who took it begrudgingly, and stalked out of the room. Cafold held out the bug to Asfin and Leynin, but neither was ready to accept its existence just yet. They continued to stare in disbelief until Cafold grew weary of their hesitation. Not knowing what else to do, he sighed, stuffed it in his pocket and headed out the door to find Hegliod.

As they walked, Ceera's wits faded and resurfaced. She struggled to maintain their permanence, all the while evading the anxiety of what had already happened. The prospect someone or something lurked nearby was difficult to ignore. Or worse yet, the entire forest could be considered the enemy. Whatever it was remained unknown. The whispering rose and fell sporadically, an underlying threat that could overtake them at any moment.

She refused to think about High Service's intentions for her if she came home without the relic. That would be for another time, in a safer place. Finding it was all that mattered now. And if it made her crazy in the process, well, then they would get their way, and fate would thereafter be known to her as the great deceiver.

They walked without speaking. Branches snapped and

birds cackled strange rants. When the sound of rushing water grew louder, she felt on the verge of accomplishment. It managed to drown out the erratic whispering sound, a welcome development.

"Here we are," Dassius said.

A small stream flowed forcefully through a ravine filled with various sized rocks.

"Oc~ea was right," she said. "The water flows in the direction we need to go. I can feel it."

Dassius gave her a strange look. Only a few days ago it had been his senses leading them as she straggled hopefully behind. It was funny how their roles had reversed. Did he resent her for it?

"Let's follow it and see what happens," Dassius said.

He set up pace beside it and Ceera followed, admiring the glistening water as it flowed alongside the bank. As they walked, it was evident the forest did not like their strategy. The plant life near the banks grew more thick and gnarled with every step.

❧

While High Service attempted to trace where the intervention bug had come from, Hegliod was absorbed in figuring out what else ailed his machine.

Cafold observed him quietly, still taking notes. After Hegliod had uncovered the bug, Cafold did not dare utter a peep to distract him. He watched with reserved awe, wishing one day he, too, would have the power to alter the entire course of events in Semadon.

Back in the control room, Hegliod nudged dials and pushed buttons. Entire streams of codes appeared on the

305

screen. He skimmed through them, pausing every so often to scratch his head and stare up at the ceiling. Soon he went back to the panel to sift through numbers.

Cafold was surprised when Hegliod addressed him. "Cafold, how would you like to do me a favor?"

Cafold perked up at the thought of being more involved than he truly was. "Yes I would be honored." His note taking ceased and he hovered attentively.

"Very good." Hegliod cleared his throat. "Could you please drop in on the Caretaker of Ancient Affairs? He has a book I wrote about my machine. Its whereabouts could prove useful in my figuring out what's wrong."

Cafold was disappointed but nodded humbly. "I will go at once." He turned to exit the control room but then paused. "Er… Hegliod?"

"Yes, Cafold?'

"Do you think I could read this book? After you are done with it, I mean."

"Why, of course." Hegliod smiled. "That's a fantastic idea."

Cafold's feet moved quickly down the hall.

Although Falken thought he had shaken the odd feeling from earlier, he found it resurfacing in his thoughts. This time he wasn't being followed; he was being joined. Someone other than himself was now telling him what to do, guiding him this way and that, telling him what to think.

The strange sound returned in the form of sinister laughter which sporadically rang into his head. After awhile, Falken wasn't sure if the laughter came from his surroundings or if it was even his own. His mind became more muddled by the minute.

It wasn't long before he peeled off his mask to try and bring some clarity to the present. The laughter came strong then, whatever its source, and Falken grinned. Bothering with such a hindrance was quite silly; he could see that now.

With this enlightened outlook, he stuffed the mask inside his bag and continued to wander through the woods. Sooner or later he would run into Ceera and Dassius, and when he did, he would be ready. The smirk on his face became permanent and matched the swagger in his step.

Chapter Twenty-Six

WHEN THE BRUSH lining the river became too thick, they stepped inside the water in order to keep a steady pace. Once within the river, they walked as close to the bank as the plant life allowed. The water reached just over their knees and nudged them gently along.

The greenery alongside the river played tricks with Ceera's mind. Though she made every attempt to focus on the span of the water, she caught slivers of oddities out of the corner of her eyes. Bits of the scenery followed along with them, traces of green that drew her attention, though when she stopped and turned she was only greeted by what appeared to be a normal landscape. If it wasn't for the subtle rustling accompanying this diversion, she would have ignored it entirely.

Dassius walked ahead of her by only a few steps and kept pausing to glance at the river bank as well.

"Do you see it too?" she asked.

The flow of the water cascading through the rocks must have drowned out the sound of her voice, for he did not respond. He kept walking, his eyes trained ahead.

As the river gradually widened, the trees pushed her and Dassius farther toward the middle. These trees hung over the edge, taking advantage of the extra bit of sun the expanse of water provided overhead. Over time, the water deepened and reached past her waist. Her pace slowed as if she were floating instead of walking. The plant life framing her view added to the effect.

Dassius stopped and stared downstream, shielding his eyes from the sun peeking between the treetops. She followed his gaze. The river branched off in two different directions not more than a quarter mile away.

"Which way do you think we should go?" he asked.

"I'm not sure yet," she said.

"My senses are back. I think we need to get back on land."

"Why?"

"Change is forthcoming or necessary. I can't really tell."

A shift occurred in Ceera's brain as they neared. "We need to follow the waterway to the left," she asserted.

"I still contend we get back on land," Dassius replied, though he altered his direction slightly to coincide with her suggestion.

"No, I don't agree. We're making much more progress following the water than we were on land."

He was silent, apparently deep in thought.

"It must be difficult to follow my lead after being able to rely on your senses for most of our travels," she said.

He scowled. "Your lead has yet to be determined as valuable."

"Why say such a thing," she demanded crossly, "when it's obvious I have a connection with this forest?"

"Don't forget, earlier I rescued you from this forest. Now you want to continue following the water, and I think we should get back on land. We can still follow that branch of the river on land, you know."

Much to her annoyance, Dassius was right. An image of the tree on the left side of the island formed in her mind.

"Fine," she mumbled. "Just let me know when."

"Over there," he said, pointing to where the land divided the river. "We'll climb up there and continue on land."

The water flowed vigorously to the right. She questioned her earlier intuition, but it did not falter. She could still envision the tree they were seeking when she focused to the left. It was definitely only the will of the water that wished for them to proceed in the opposite direction.

Dassius seemed oblivious to all this and moved forward intently. He was nearing land, and she was only several steps behind.

A glistening in the water caught her attention. Something was floating alongside her not more than a few feet away. Underneath it was part of a log or a tangle of weeds. It drifted past and veered into the right hand passage of water, before getting caught near the river bank on the far side.

Ceera paused, curious as to what the shiny object could be. She glanced at Dassius, who was now crouched above her on land. He held out his hand.

"Wait," she said, walking away from his hand.

"You said that was the wrong way."

"There's something floating over there. I want to see what it is."

"Why does it matter?"

"It doesn't. I just want to know." She was unsure why her curiosity needed to be quenched so badly. Could this item be a clue as to what was going on in the forest? She glanced back at Dassius, who stood watching her with focused attention.

The water now reached her chest, so she lifted her feet and swam. The river was too deep for standing at the opposite bank, so she resorted to treading water while she stared at the shiny object. It was oblong, at least six inches long, and attached to a wooden handle. "It's your knife," she called out.

The plants tangled beneath held the knife in place, though it bobbed up and down with the mild waves. Her image rippled alongside the blade, but when she reached for the handle her reflection changed. Suddenly, she was staring at a blurred face with angular cheekbones and two black holes for eyes. Panic consumed her. The image sank into the water. Something grabbed onto her ankle. On the way down, she tilted her head back to take a quick breath before becoming submerged in a bluish eeriness.

Her feet touched down, but her efforts to propel herself back up were thwarted when a body pressed against her from behind. Powerful arms restrained her. Water fluttered strangely near the side of her head, and the familiar whispering slithered into her ears. The sound was emphatic this time, angry even.

One arm released her. A dirt-caked hand with long spindly fingers plunged the blade toward her chest. The cracking sound of her own bones breaking rattled through her. Except, where was the jab of its sharp point? Then she remembered the ammonite Waive had given her, tucked discreetly beneath her shirt, and though she had considered it a decoration, it now served as a shield to her heart.

The circular shell gouged into her chest, and she doubled over in pain. Through half closed eyes, she saw the blade falling through the water and resting near her feet. The wooden handle was quickly tossed aside.

She stumbled backward, crossing her arms over her chest to stifle the pain. Her attacker was swimming away. His crooked stature was more creature-like than Semion, with wrinkly skin and knobby elbows resembling tree knots. Her mind flashed to the twisted tree figures she had stumbled between earlier, and she wondered if they hadn't been a delusion after all. Clothes of a material she did not recognize hung off his body in tattered shreds. Scraggly wisps of hair streamed behind him in the water. His toes curved away from his feet like broken roots.

The creature swam into a cluster of algae that grew in long spiny strands. The plants wrapped around his body, engulfing him until he disappeared.

Something pricked at her feet and legs. Algae now slithered out of the dirt like snakes, the strands intertwining with each other. She quickly thrust her body upward and brought her head above water. Breath awaited her and she accepted it gratefully, though her chest still throbbed with pain. Dassius was swimming toward her.

"What happened?" he asked with alarm.

"Watch out," she called out to him.

The water now jerked calamitously as the underwater plants continued to grow. One wrapped around the bottom half of her leg and swiftly made its way up the rest of her body. It bound one of her arms tightly to her side. She struggled fiercely, but the plant was strong and pulled her underwater. Dassius was suffering the same fate. He looked shocked before his face hardened into the expression he made when danger was upon them.

Ceera kicked her leg in an attempt to loosen the grasp.

A rash of plant life had sprung within the last few moments. More grabbed onto her and enclosed her in a complicated web of vegetation. Her heart was beating rapidly as she continued trying to yank free.

The man-creature was nowhere to be seen. Would he be back? Her question was answered when the urgent whispering penetrated the water, and she closed her eyes tightly so it wouldn't get the best of her. As she strained from the imposed force, she began to lose her recently acquired breath. Her tears dispersed into the water as soon as they pricked her eyes.

Dassius was making a huge commotion somewhere nearby, his aggression washing her way. He would not be able to rescue them this time. In anger, she struggled violently and made every effort to salvage what remained of her breath. She twisted her arm and finagled it out of the grips of the plant.

Someone was calling her name; the muffled sound echoed in her ears and seized her will. She glanced briefly in the direction where Dassius continued to struggle. As she did, she caught something out of the corner of her eye. A vial floated past with an unmistakable sparkle. She snatched it up and pried open the lid with a flick of her thumb to release its potent captive.

The liquid trickled out and pushed the existing water aside. An image of Oc~ea filled the empty space, her body as transparent as the water. She gazed over Ceera's head with lifeless eyes and pulled the same seashell she used to call Serpa out from within the folds of her gown. She brought the shell to her lips and blew. The sound fluttering through the water was mystical and dreamlike. It traveled through Ceera and around her. She sensed vibrations and suddenly there were fish everywhere. They began zealously eating the algae.

Despair-ridden echoes undulated around her. The plants withered and fell onto the mud. She reached out to Oc~ea in thanks, but the Archaic melted into the water.

Dassius was now beside her. They made their way to the surface between the squirming fish and swam to land. Dirt had never felt so wonderful upon her fingers. They pulled themselves onto the bank and crawled a short distance before collapsing in a heap together, gasping for breath. The river was still in turmoil. An occasional fish emerged and soared through the air momentarily before diving back in.

"You opened the vial," Dassius spoke between gasps of breath. "You must have. I tried but it got knocked out of my hand."

Ceera nodded and took a huge gulp of air. "I saw it floating by. Right after you called my name."

He turned to stare at her, still breathing hard. "I didn't call your name. I had no breath to speak it."

He seemed in no condition to tease her. She lay back down beside him. As their breaths became normal, the disturbance in the river lessened. Then the water glistened and was still.

∾

Hegliod and two officials were conversing about the status of the AT system when Cafold burst into the control room.

"It's gone. The Caretaker does not know where the book is." Cafold wrung his hands, his notes from earlier having vanished from sight, and shifted his weight uneasily.

Hegliod glanced at the clock on the wall. "You've been gone an awfully long time."

"I know. When I got to the Caretaker's office, he admitted the book was lost in his office somewhere, or at least should have been."

Hegliod's forehead creased and he nodded impatiently.

"I told him it was important, that we needed to find it as soon as possible, so we spent the rest of the morning searching for it."

"And?" Hegliod asked as he surveyed him. Cafold's face was tinted gray and covered in dust. His fingertips were smudged with dirt. He made a mental note to berate the Caretaker for allowing his office to be so filthy.

"We looked everywhere. It's gone." Cafold shook his head sadly.

"You're sure it is gone?" Hegliod was not alarmed at the prospect.

"Yes, the Caretaker said he had never taken it from the room, would remember most certainly if he had, and had not allowed anyone to part with it."

"And were there inquiries about this book?" Hegliod asked.

"Yes," Cafold said with a proud smile. "I did think to ask such questions. The only inquiry according to the Caretaker was by Dassius Rucien. He asked prior to his and Ceera's departure from Semadon. But the Caretaker denied him since the book was lost."

"What about visitors other than Dassius Rucien? Has the Caretaker dealt with anyone else recently?"

"The only recent visit he was skeptical about was when Falken Grihne came to see him."

Hegliod scrunched up his face in disgust while the officials looked slightly taken aback.

"He is a member of the Council for Advancement correct?" Asfin said to Leynin.

"Yes, I believe he is."

"Why would a member of the Council for Advancement want to speak with the Caretaker?" Asfin asked.

"The Caretaker wondered that very same thing. Apparently, Falken asked him a very strange question and left. He said the experience was entirely unpleasant."

"Did he say what this question was?" Leyin said.

"Yes, something about whether another culture of people ever lived alongside the Semions. Shouldn't he know better?"

The two officials exchanged glances.

"Then my suspicions are confirmed." Hegliod turned to the officials. "Someone is in possession of my book, and this person is most likely the one who planted the intervention bug."

"We'll get Order Patrol out to visit Mr. Grihne," Leynin said. "He must be interrogated at once."

"And I shall continue to examine these controls. Sooner or later I will find the one that has been altered..." Hegliod's words trailed away as an incident came to mind he had almost forgotten. Since he was now facing the controls, no one saw his pained expression. "Where is the password to change the codes recorded?"

"Nowhere that I know of," Leynin replied. "Don't you have it?"

"I do. But I thought maybe you recorded it somewhere for safekeeping, in the event I did not return to science."

"No, we hoped you'd return."

The officials left the room.

"Thanks for your work with the Caretaker," Hegliod said as his fingers flew across the controls.

"Do you think it will take much longer to figure out the problem?"

"Yes," Hegliod replied grimly. "I have a feeling it will."

⚶

Falken couldn't believe his luck. Or maybe he just couldn't believe the ignorance level of his victims. They were affixing reflectors to trees, making their route easily traceable. It had taken him awhile to find the first one, but after that there was always another a few trees away.

When he reached the water's edge, he was disgusted to think he would have to start wading to keep up. There was no disputing they had taken this route because there was a reflector facing the river. He looked around for an alternative since getting wet was not a pastime he enjoyed. A few fallen trees lay nearby.

An idea came to light as Falken recalled some seemingly useless information taught to him in his youth. How to make a canoe was not something he ever believed he'd need to know, but this knowledge was about to come in handy, and his weapon was the perfect accompaniment.

Now he just had to find some conifers so he could extract their resin. This was a highly flammable substance after all and would aid in burning a spot for him to sit inside a trunk.

CHAPTER TWENTY-SEVEN

AS THEY RESTED along the bank, Ceera found it difficult to accept the water had regained peace. She could not believe the threat of the man-creature and his murderous plants had become obsolete, that the river contained no remnants of the previous danger.

"Did you catch a glimpse of the man in the water?" she said. "Or perhaps he was a creature, I'm not sure."

Dassius stiffened. "It wasn't what you think."

"What do you mean?"

"I'm sure you saw something, but we can't be sure it was real."

"Why?" She sat up and looked at him incredulously.

"Because things aren't always what they seem here. Haven't you figured that out yet?" He propped himself up on one arm and stared back at her.

She was silent for a moment as his skepticism infiltrated her sense of reality. She had seen the man-creature with her own eyes. He had tried to kill her.

"He attacked me with your knife, but the handle broke when it struck my ammonite." She pulled the fossil out from underneath her shirt to show him the indentation.

"Let me see it."

She removed it from around her neck and handed it to him.

He held it up and stared at the mark. "It was like that when you got it," he said, tossing it in her lap.

"That's not true," she snapped, "and you know it."

"Besides, my knife was skillfully crafted and wouldn't break on impact."

Ceera hung the ammonite back around her neck. "You're wrong."

"Prove otherwise."

"I can't, unless you wish to retrieve it from the water."

"Sounds like a fool's waste of time," he said. "Who knows where it's drifted."

"Well then how do you explain what happened with the plants?" she demanded. "I saw him disappear into a cluster of algae, right before they started growing like mad."

Dassius fell onto his back and stared up at the sky. He squinted and laid his hand on his forehead. "It was all a figment of our imagination," he said in a decisive voice. "A way for us to view what was happening in a manner we could comprehend."

"That's ridiculous Dassius! I saw it happen," she insisted, "and you did too."

"The eyes play tricks to appease the brain," he responded in a flat tone.

Ceera lay back down, confused. Dassius's stubborn resolution perplexed her. What she had seen in the water was strange, but that didn't mean it hadn't happened. A disturbing realization came over her. "You do think I'm crazy," she accused.

His features darkened. "Don't go there okay?"

Her desire to persuade him increased. "The man-creature, he grabbed onto me. He whispered strange sounds, the same ones we heard earlier when your knife went missing." She maneuvered onto her knees. "I heard the same whispers," she continued, leaning toward him, "when the plants restrained me."

"What happened earlier when I had to rescue you? What did you see then?"

"What does that have to do with it?" she asked.

"Do you think what you saw then was real too?"

"It was real at the time."

"Let me ask you this. If you saw a man, what did his face look like?"

Ceera frowned. All she had caught was a blur. Dassius looked at her expectantly, waiting for her to say what he already knew.

"I didn't see his face very clearly," she admitted.

"That's what I thought."

She eyed him shrewdly. "Why does it matter?"

"If you had, it would prove he was actually a man. Since you didn't, it just means the forest tricked us again."

"I don't follow you. I saw him swimming away. I heard him, felt him and almost died. What more proof do I need?"

"If he was real or part man, then where did he go?" Dassius stood up.

"Oc~ea," Ceera said. "She put an end to him."

"Really? Because dead men float." He shielded his eyes and scanned the area. "I see no one."

She stood to join him. "You know he was no ordinary man."

Dassius laughed though his expression lacked humor. "He was no ordinary man because he wasn't a man."

"Why are you arguing about this?"

"I argue because your delusions cannot be allowed to continue." He threw his arm out toward the river and their surroundings. "Show me," he challenged, "where this man is who is no ordinary man. Explain to me where he went."

Stunned by his sudden hostility, she shook her head at him. "I can't. I don't know where he went."

"That's right," he told her. "You can't."

"How can I explain—"

"You can't because he never existed in the first place." His spiteful smirk made her feel like she was standing next to a stranger.

She shrank away from his scrutiny. "You said you didn't think I was crazy."

Her reaction seemed to awaken him. He blinked and his mouth fell into a straight line. He roughly wiped the sweat from his brow. "I don't. This forest is getting to me."

"It's turning you against me." Her voice trembled.

"It's tainting my logic. My senses are coming and going. I didn't anticipate what happened to you in the water. I thought we needed to get out, but I let you wander away and that frustrates me. Our disagreement made it worse."

"We've disagreed before."

"You have to understand something. I'm not used to feeling that I'm not in control." Dassius turned away from her. His shoulders drooped as he brought a hand to his forehead.

She actually felt sorry for him. "Good thing you were able to get out the vial."

"Didn't I tell you our instincts would tell us when it was time to use the vials?"

"I still contend you called my name."

"Sorry, but I didn't."

Ceera frowned. There was no reason for him to lie.

"Here, take these." He pulled the remaining vials from his pack and held them out to her.

She stared in disbelief. "You want me to carry them?"

"Yes," he said. "Baric was right. Plus, you need something to protect yourself with in case we get separated."

She hesitated before taking them. Their powers vibrated within her palm. She slipped them into her pack. "I'm flattered you have that kind of faith in me."

"It's what needed to be done." He shrugged.

Overtaken by her emotions, she flung herself into Dassius's arms. He embraced her tightly. She laid her head on his chest and listened to his heart speed up then gradually slow to a steady beat. He rested his chin on her head.

"Don't turn against me again." She tilted her head so their faces were only inches apart.

"I won't." His lips brushed softly against hers. "It was a temporary defect."

Her lips parted slightly as she waited for Dassius to kiss her. He pressed his mouth firmly against hers, and while she expected satisfaction amidst the resulting warmth, instead her desire increased. She pulled him closer while his fingers slid into the hair at the nape of her neck. Their kiss deepened, igniting places on her body that before had seemed content.

"We could do this all day," he whispered in her ear between kisses, "but somehow I think we're not that reckless."

"You're right." She pulled away slightly, trying to ignore the still pulsing sensations. "What now?"

He smiled through his disappointment. "We need to figure out how we're going to cross back to that island."

They reluctantly pulled apart and stared out at the river.

"Do you think it's unsafe to walk through it?" she asked.

"I have no idea whether Oc~ea's power is permanent or temporary."

"I don't think I'm comfortable going back in." She didn't want to say it out loud, but what if the man-creature still lurked inside?

"I agree, and now we have nothing to combat it with." He looked over her head and muttered something beneath his breath.

"What did you say?" she asked.

"Follow the force of the wind and let it guide you," he repeated, pointing at the trees swaying gently with the breeze.

She recognized the sentence as one Atmos had uttered during their encounter with him.

"See the tree curving over the water?" He pointed. "Its branches meet with one on the other side. We could climb it and cross over."

"Okay," she agreed.

Dassius approached the trunk and crouched down to fumble in his pack. He pulled out a long, stretchy rope wrapped in a tight loop, along with a grapple. He unraveled the rope and attached the grapple to the end. "Maybe once we start climbing, we will prefer the trees to the ground."

He positioned himself beneath the tree and hurled the end of the rope with the grapple into the air. It arched and swung over a high branch, dangling over the side.

He pulled another rope out of his pack along with a differently shaped grapple. He attached the second grapple to the rope and tossed it upward. It took him several tries before the two grapples fastened onto each other.

When they were securely joined, he pulled the first rope

down and tied a sturdy knot. He attached a small contraption to keep the knot in place. He pulled while the contraption and the knot traveled upward until they met with the branch. "This way of traveling will make us less likely to get lost. Our vantage point will be better."

Ceera wanted to believe him.

Dassius picked up his pack and strapped it to his chest. "Climb on my back," he told her.

She put her arms around his neck and wrapped her legs around his waist. The position would have embarrassed her just last week. His stance barely wavered with her added weight. Impressed, she closed her eyes and hung on. The muscles in his shoulders tensed as he raised them above the ground.

He pulled them higher, his feet walking up the tree at times. It didn't take long to reach the branch holding them. "Get on the branch," he told her, "while I prep the rope again."

She obeyed. When he was ready, she hung on tightly and listened to his heart race from the exertion.

When they reached the next branch, he undid the rope. The branches, though slippery with moss, were much closer together so they switched to climbing. She was careful to get a good grip. As she had learned, it was best not to look down.

They came to a sturdy branch extending to a tree across the river.

"This one's wide enough," Dassius said.

They edged their way across, using a branch above them for support. Only the river flowed beneath them now. Ceera stubbornly averted her eyes.

Their branch soon overlapped with the other and

formed a bridge, which Dassius crossed onto. Once he was safely on the other branch, he held both branches steady for her. She crossed over on her hands and knees, continuing to crawl until she reached the trunk. She rested against it.

"Well, we made it to the island," he said. "Now how do we get down?"

About a hundred feet separated them from the ground. The branch beneath them was not within dropping distance. A breeze rustled the undergrowth near the tree's base.

"I think it may be easier to cross over to another tree instead of dropping down from this one." Dassius pointed to a nearby tree with branches spaced closer together.

He flung the end of the rope up and outward. The grapple lodged onto a sturdy branch extending from the opposing tree. He tugged on the rope to test how securely it was attached, then helped her stand. "When we get to the other branch, don't let go until I say."

She put her arms around him and clung tight. Just prior to them swinging outward, the tree branches behind her curved like arms to grab onto her. Their ends scraped against her back as Dassius cast the two of them away. *Not this again*, she thought as they swung through the air.

Dassius's feet met with their intended branch and they sat to examine their new surroundings. "The branches are still too far apart." He frowned.

The next branch was a good twenty feet beneath them.

"I guess I forfeit my rope for nothing." He let go of the rope. It swung back and forth before coming to a standstill between the two trees.

"What do we do now?" She did not like the idea of being stranded high up in a tree, especially after what she had seen moments ago.

"I have more rope," Dassius said. He jammed his hand into his pack and produced another few strands.

The breeze picked up some leaves resting on a mossy heap nearby. They rose in the air and circled the two of them. Dassius paused to watch with a rope in each hand.

A cold waft of air struck them, carrying with it the familiar whispering sound. Or perhaps the whispering carried the wind.

She crossed her arms and shivered. "It's getting chilly up here."

A huge gust whipped past and disrupted her sense of balance. She fell forward and clamped her legs around the branch to keep from falling. Dassius dropped the ropes in his lap so he could help her back to a seated position.

Another hefty breeze hurtled by. The ropes spun into the air and wrapped around Dassius's neck. His hands flew to his throat, and he quickly unwound the ropes.

"Atmos said to make sure we keep a close eye on the wind," he shouted out gruffly. "Apparently we missed our cue."

The wind blew more powerful by the second. The great tree shuddered and swayed. Other trees in the vicinity shook too, but were not as taken by the wind. Ceera's eyes widened as she clung to the branch. Dassius looked around frantically.

The tree groaned each time it tilted to the side. A loud cracking sound came from below.

"It's going to tip over!" she exclaimed. "This tree is going to fall!"

Fueled by her panic, Dassius fumbled with the end of the ropes. One of them dropped onto a branch below them. She cried out but he was unfazed. He tied the remaining rope around their branch. He secured it with a fat knot and tied the loose end to his pack, winding it through the straps.

"Get ready." His words barely sliced through the howling wind.

She watched helplessly while the tree rocked back and forth, creaking loudly as it swayed.

The final knot proved problematic. The rope slipped from Dassius's fingers and he tried again. Any second the tree would fall and they along with it. She pressed the length of her body against the branch.

At the same time Dassius secured the knot on his pack, the tree lost independence. Its roots broke with a loud ripping sound, and it joined with the force of the wind.

"It's falling!" she screamed.

Dassius quickly slid his arms through the straps on his pack. He leaned forward to grab onto her but instead teetered over the side.

"Dassius," she called out to him, but was unable to view his fate. The rope tensed and she laid her head on the limb, the bark scraping her face as she strained to hold on.

The tree collided with one of its own. The deafening sound and impact ricocheted throughout her entire body, rattling her bones and jostling her insides. Behind her closed eyes, the blackness erupted into an explosion of lights, and she waited for the effects to dwindle before daring to consider whether she was even still alive.

When she opened her eyes, specks of light floated. Tree parts tangled around her, lightly poking her body as if in warning. Her tree was propped against a much sturdier tree arching over the river. Luckily, it had not smashed her in the process.

The bits of light grew fainter. A brown face with craggy cheekbones materialized within the cluster of leaves and branches. Jagged ears poked out from a head of matted brown hair streaked with green. His nose protruded like a bulbous root before meeting back with his face. Ceera realized who she was staring at and she screamed.

Ignoring the pain in her body, she scrambled backward on the branch, but he grabbed onto her arm with his bristly hand.

"Why are you doing this to me?" She fought back tears.

He brought his face close. Grooves were embedded into his rough skin. His sunken eyes bore sheer darkness. Fear thrashed wildly within her.

His mouth opened, and he tilted his head back slightly before thrusting it forward. He went through the same motion again, as if he were trying to physically push something from his throat, before firmly clamping his lips shut and with a look of fierce determination spoke. "Because you"—he thrust his head forward yet again—"know the way."

The words were rough around the edges, as if they emerged from the depths of a forgotten pit overflowing with rock and debris. They confirmed this creature was both man and very real.

With his breath the wind picked up, and the man backed away. Unaffected as it blasted past, he climbed onto a nearby branch and blended back into the surroundings. His words echoed inside her head as she clung onto the branch.

The wind cajoled her. *Let go*, it seemed to be telling her. The urge was tempting. For letting go had crossed her mind. It would be much easier to let go, a release of the tension on her body and her mind. She could fall with the force of the wind, and all her struggles would end. The wind continued to coax her into releasing the branch and succumbing to the torrent of air.

Air. The deceitfully weightless word stuck in her brain as stubbornly as she attached herself to the branch. It was a meager word for portraying such a powerful entity. Ceera recalled Atmos's jovial explanation of the power of air. Now that she felt it in full force, it was time to unleash his tiny tempest.

She inched her way back and toward the fallen trunk. In the process, she crossed over the knot Dassius had tied and looked down to see if he still hung by his pack. Neither he nor his pack was in sight. Her heart skipped a beat, but she refused to wonder whether his final knot had worn thin.

The trunk faced downward at an angle. She braced herself against it. Her hand found the zipper on her pack. The wind continued to scream as she pulled the twisted vial out of the pocket.

It flew out of her fingers and wedged itself into a crack in a branch extending from the opposing tree. She fell forward onto her hands and stared helplessly. She would have to climb onto the other tree; there was no other option.

Very carefully, she moved forward on her hands and knees. The vial rested on a branch that met with hers halfway across. She would have to cross back over Dassius's rope. She didn't know if she could succeed without him. "Where are you?" she whispered.

She placed her hand onto the branch to test it. It would hold her. She brought her other arm and then both her legs. She crawled a few paces then extended her arm in the vial's direction. It was so close she could see the tiny tempest swirling inside; the vial vibrated in effect.

The branch shook, interrupting her concentration. The man slunk toward her from the other side. He reached for the vial.

"No!" she screamed.

He gave her an evil glare, bounded forward and landed on top of her, knocking her backward onto the branch. She screamed again, but he stifled the sound by wrapping a piece of Dassius's rope around her neck. Choking, she wriggled fiercely while her fingers dug under the rope to rescue a bit of breathing room. The man struggled to restrain her. She refused to look at him but instead focused on the vial, which still vibrated farther down the branch.

I have nothing to defend myself with, she thought desperately and recalled Atmos's lesson on the powers of nothing.

The air looks like nothing, she envisioned Atmos saying, *yet witness the power of the wind.*

The vial shook violently and uprooted itself from where it perched. It shot toward her, taking advantage of a strong gust, and she removed her hand from under the rope and caught it with an agility she didn't know she had. She gasped from the pressure now imposed on her neck, but this did not stop her from flicking open the lid.

The tiny tempest squeezed out of the opening, expanding into a large cloud shaped as a head. The face was both whimsical and weary. She eyed the image gratefully. As her attacker looked over his shoulder, he released the pressure from around her neck.

Atmos puffed out his cheeks, and the movement of the air changed quickly. He pursed his lips, expelling a high-pitched whistling sound as he blew in the direction of her adversary.

The man trembled uncontrollably while Atmos's breath moved past. The force ripped him from his position. He tumbled out of sight, lost within the torrent of breath and wind. Atmos's image followed behind.

She lifted herself up slowly. Trees in the distance rocked wildly back and forth. The air around her was still.

Someone spoke her name. A hand grabbed onto the branch near Dassius's knot, and her body tensed. Dassius dangled beneath, and she released all her anxiety with a deep sigh. He heaved himself onto the branch to join her.

"You're alive," she mumbled.

"Same to you."

"What happened to your neck?" he asked sharply, bringing his fingers to the reddened marks.

"It's from your rope," Ceera said though her words were barely audible.

He pulled her close, and she leaned against him for support. Together they witnessed the wind in the distance whip around.

"You used it didn't you? You used Atmos's vial?"

"I had no choice."

The wind spun faster now. Ceera thought she saw the man slip out of the torrent a good distance away and fall between the tree crowns.

"You need to follow me down."

"I don't know if I can." She closed her eyes and waited for the dizziness to stop.

Chapter Twenty-Eight

CEERA RELAXED INTO Dassius's embrace while he monitored their surroundings. Her eyelids drooped uncontrollably and her body ached.

"We need to get out of this tree," he said, sooner than she would have liked.

"I don't think I have the energy." She knew she would have to get down eventually. How she would undergo this task was too complicated to ponder.

"I can try to make it easy on you." He gently pushed her up and began picking at the knot around the branch. "If I can loosen this, I may be able to rig the rope so I can lower you down."

While he worked to undo the knot, she thought about the man who the wind had carried away. Words were difficult for him. Either he had not spoken for a very long time, or speech was unnatural for him to begin with.

"Aha, I think I figured something out. Come here."

"What's the hurry?"

"Our feet need to be on the ground. Plus, I want to show you something."

"What is it?"

"It would be better if you saw it with your own eyes."

He attached the recovered rope around her waist. "Hang onto the rope for extra support."

She dangled her legs over the side of the branch. Ignoring the ache in her arms, she maneuvered down until she hung by her hands. She grabbed onto the rope with one hand and then the other. Dassius lowered her until she was about three feet from the ground.

"Sorry that's the best I can do," he shouted. "Now I'm going to release the rope. Are you ready?"

"Yes." When her feet touched down, she stumbled over to the side and sank to her knees. She remained there while Dassius climbed down with what remained.

Much to her disappointment, this didn't take him long at all. Within moments he stood over her, demanding the rope still tied around her waist, and she undid the knot and handed it to him.

"Ready to see what I found?" He stuffed the rope into his pack and held out his hand.

She grabbed onto it and stood.

Dassius led her to the splintered remains of an enormous tree. He ducked his head and entered the hollow trunk, pulling her inside with him.

Soon they were surrounded by bark. Dassius ran his fingers over scratches in the trunk, scratches that were not part of the tree, but formed actual words.

"How did you find this?" she asked in amazement.

"I found it when our tree fell over, and I smashed into the trunk." He gestured to a large splintery hole above them. "Good thing it's hollow or you would be standing down here by yourself." His lips formed a tight smile.

"No I would still be up in the tree," she replied with a nervous chuckle.

"Anyway," he continued, "I took my chances dropping the rest of the way down."

"You must have good knees."

"I do knee strengthening exercises. Plus, I used my arms to slow the fall. I noticed the writing while I was catching my breath. I didn't stay long though because I had to figure out what happened to you."

Ceera examined the letters etched into the bark. The message was unmistakable. "The wood entraps me," she spoke the words out loud. "I cannot break free."

"What?"

"This is what it says. 'We are joined and grow united. By the wood's design I am no longer a man, but I remain.'" She turned to Dassius. "Who do you think—"

"The AT installers," he interrupted, "carved this in the tree."

Puzzled, Ceera turned back to the writing. "You think so?"

"It makes perfect sense. They had no defenses like we do. By the time they made it here, they'd lost their minds."

Perhaps Dassius was correct. An AT installer may have felt compelled to etch his thoughts into the bark, had he realized what the forest was doing to him.

"I need to rest for a bit," she told him. "Before I end up like them."

"Yes," he said, wiping a strand of hair out of her face, "you do."

❧

Falken was busy spreading the rosin he had made, with the help of a Douglas fir, onto a fallen tree. It was just the right size for turning into a canoe. He had spent several minutes breaking off the branches and roots extending from it. He applied the rosin generously into a gaping hole that showed signs of rot.

The wind howled above and his hair moved with it. "You stay up there," he muttered. He did not want it spreading his weapon's fire.

Something thumped a short distance away, probably the wind knocking down a branch. Earlier he had heard a much louder thud and surmised a tree had fallen somewhere far away.

He aimed his weapon at the smeared rosin and pressed the button. The rosin lit up quickly, and he feared he would not be able to contain the resulting fire. Sparks already darted onto the forest floor. Not to mention there was now a disquieting feeling in the air that escalated as the flames ensued.

He needed to act quickly. It would do him no good if the entire log burned through. He shoved it into the nearby waterway. The resulting sizzle delighted him, and he stared dreamily at the puffs of smoke emanating from the log. He certainly was clever; he had to hand it to himself.

Smelling a plant burning, he stomped the near vicinity to kill any escaped sparks. He lugged his log, which already floated like a canoe, albeit upside down, back onto the bank. Using a stone, he began to scrape away the charred bark. The trunk was still very hot and he snatched his hand back, irritated with himself for overlooking the obvious.

At least a solution was close by. He had brought flame resistant gloves, not knowing to what extent he would have to use his weapon. It could get quite hot after a few applications. He thrust his hands into the gloves and scraped. Sweat dripped from his forehead. Something was still not right. The feeling he was being watched resurfaced. He jerked his head up and looked around. His surroundings were fuzzy, perhaps due to the physical labor. He was not used to it, usually only working on a miniature scale.

He sat back against an upright trunk and took slow, deep breaths. The sounds of nature blended into his dizzied state. He lifted his hand and was startled to see it inside the silver glove. He had already forgotten he put it on.

Something nudged his shoulder. Thinking it was just a leaf or twig, he wiggled his arm to loosen the debris. He felt it again; this time it slid past his shoulder and around his chest.

Falken surged forward. What had begun to wrap around him broke with a loud crack. He rolled onto his hands and knees. A strangler root was moving down the trunk and engulfing the tree, looking as if it did not want to stop there. He scrambled to his feet and backed away, falling into the opening in his canoe. It was less hot but the bark stabbed his skin.

He scrambled to get out. The end of the strangler root reached the ground and slithered stiffly toward him. It wrapped around a short appendage extending from his canoe and dragged it farther from the water.

Falken yanked his canoe away and heaved it onto his chest. He half ran, half stumbled, over to the water's edge and plunged into it, landing on his stomach over the hole. The canoe rocked but stayed afloat. Ignoring the discomfort, he grabbed a thick branch floating nearby and used it as leverage to distance himself from the bank.

Seclusion was usually his friend; however, this forest had wormed beneath his skin like an infected parasite. He took one last look. The area appeared normal, at least the strangler root had stopped moving, but something else drew his attention: the rough outline of a man, standing beside the tree. On second glance the figure was gone.

At first he was afraid, but then a realization struck him and his blood boiled. Nimren had suggested that someone from the CfNL would come to the forest to enact their plan. Of course they would use their ability to manipulate nature to scare him. The council pretended to use their talent for good, but now it was apparent what they experimented with behind closed doors. If someone from the CfNL was messing with his mind, they would suffer the consequence. He'd make sure of it.

Falken drifted down the river, watchful along the banks for any clue as to the location of Ceera and Dassius.

✑

Dassius erected the tent for Ceera near the hollowed out tree.

"Are you sure this is okay?" She gave him a backward glance.

When Dassius nodded, she wasted no time going into the tent and zipping it back up behind her. No, he was not sure, but what else could they do?

He sat on the ground. His only option was to use this time to his advantage. Meditate, try to mentally merge with his surroundings so he could sense what lay in store. He closed his eyes and instead of blackness, saw a replica of the forest. Intricately woven leaves hung between rows of tall trees; this pattern embedded so deeply in his brain, he could not force it away.

He decided to take advantage of the visual, so in his mind he stood up. He began walking in this forest he imagined. Perhaps if he explored it using his senses, he could figure out where they needed to go. That way when Ceera woke up, he could guide them efficiently instead of resorting to all this dreadful wandering. Dassius was not a follower. It killed him certain aspects of his training had escaped him once they entered the wood. This was his chance to regroup, and be the leader he was supposed to be.

His senses led him, and there was a confidence in his step that had been missing for some time. He mapped the route inside his brain. A few paces here, around this tree, take a slight left. The directions came clearly. He moved toward the destination with assurance. Then an inkling of uncertainty rose up, and he paused to analyze this new development.

The intrusion was at first light. His senses prevailed during the onset, still directing him, though his pace slowed. Then the pressure intensified and his senses subsided. Someone was coming up behind him, but had already managed to preside inside his thoughts as well. Dassius moved faster as if this could thwart the invader's progress.

The pressure expanded from his brain and resounded throughout his body. Soon he was charging through the labyrinth of trees in escape mode, his senses no longer helping him. What followed grew closer and overshadowed his ability to reason. He was no longer in control of himself at all, which is why when he felt a hand on his shoulder, he ripped away from it.

"Dassius, wake up." Ceera's voice brought him back to reality.

His eyes opened. "I wasn't sleeping."

"Okay," she said, looking at him strangely. "Then what were you doing?"

"I was meditating."

"Isn't that supposed to be relaxing?"

"Things went awry." He let his forehead drop down on his palms.

"I just had a weird dream. I think we need to get going." Her voice shook, betraying that she was rattled as well.

"I'll take down the tent."

"No Dassius, I'm serious. We can get it later."

"Then let's go." He started walking where his senses had directed him during his meditation.

"One second, now I have to show you something." She grabbed onto his hand and led him a few paces away to the hollowed tree trunk. "I dreamed we missed something in the writing of the tree."

She ducked and pulled him in the rest of the way. They stood facing the markings as she ran her fingers over them. "We are attached and grow united," she read out loud. "By the wood's design I am no longer a man, but I remain. I remain," she repeated and rubbed the space after.

"What are you doing?"

"Rebial," she said.

"What?"

"I remain Rebial." She pointed to the end of the sentence.

"What is Rebial?"

"I don't know," she replied. "I uncovered it during my dream."

"What does it mean? What happened next?"

An abrupt sound in the distance shook the ground beneath their feet.

"That did," Ceera responded, "and then I woke up."

~

Once Hegliod accepted that Falken had indeed changed the password, and his only option in recovering it was to guess the number, he thought about the propensity of this feat.

Given the number had to be five digits, there was thousands upon thousands of possibilities. Which meant the code would take an enormous amount of time to figure out. He was not one who could withstand this routine of testing a number and keeping a record of each attempt, although he was sure Cafold would be willing to help him with this task.

The alternative was to create a way to bypass the code requirement entirely. The average scientist would be intimidated, but since Hegliod had no less invented the machine he attempted to outwit, this did not deter him.

He began devising a plan for a mechanism he could implement within the controls to accomplish this feat. Perhaps to an observer this would seem an unlikely solution; however, Hegliod had spent the last few weeks in mental remission. To say he was refreshed was an understatement. What he set out to create drew a picture of itself inside his head, and before long he was forming this picture into reality.

Chapter Twenty-Nine

"YOU HAVE TO stop denying it Dassius," Ceera said. "I don't know what Rebial means or what it meant to the AT installers, but someone is after us. The same man I've used the vials on twice already."

They hurried past the tent and into the trees. No one led anyone. Dassius followed what he had mapped out in his brain during his meditation, and she walked alongside him as if in agreement.

"I didn't tell you this before, but I had a confrontation with him in the tree. He said he was after me because I knew the way. He tried to get me to fall and used the rope you left behind to choke me. Somehow I was able to open the vial. Atmos appeared and used the wind to carry him away, but he is on his way back to us." Ceera's voice rose. "He will not let himself be defeated."

She was telling the truth. The presence during his meditation confirmed it. He was not sure whether out-chasing this man was even possible, but they only had two vials left. The more progress they made the better.

"He's no longer sneaking around. He no longer cares if we know he is coming." She spoke almost frantically now.

The man's pursuit caused a vibration on the ground

much like what Dassius had experienced during his meditation. It ominously foretold what was to come.

"He should care," Dassius said. "We have two vials left."

"But Dassius, I've already used two of them! And he is still following us! What will happen when they are used up?"

"Maybe we won't have to use them all." He didn't even believe his own words.

"Yeah right," she scoffed.

"So get one out and have it ready."

Their pace matched the intensity of their discussion.

"You mean have it out in the open so he can see? He has to be catching on by now of their powers."

The ground trembled beneath them. Together they whirled around. The trees were leaning away from each other, their huge trunks groaning terribly as they parted. The widening path revealed a figure in the distance; his hands separated the trees remotely with a slow steady motion.

"It's him," she whispered in terror.

The trees continued to lean farther away. Roots ripped and the ground broke open. The opening grew larger, and soon the dirt cracked near their feet.

They turned to run. After a few long strides, Dassius realized she was no longer beside him. He turned but there was only the gaping chasm. She must have fallen in. Her cries for help assured him that at least she wasn't dead. He mentally berated himself for not grabbing onto her hand.

The strange looking man crept toward him. He was a mixture of man ingrained with forest, a contradiction of evil melded with nature's intrinsic goodness. His eyes hid within deep crevices on his gnarled face, yet still managed to emit such hatred Dassius felt inclined to take a step back.

Knowing his retreat sent a message of who was dominant, he regained his stature and stood still but ready. He didn't like that this man reintroduced him to fear. It was time to act brave, if only superficially. He pulled his knife out and readied his stance to fight.

The man smirked, an expression that seemed strangely definite. He lifted one hand and twisted it. Something grazed Dassius's ankle and he fell backward, cracking his head on a large rock bulging from the ground. Inside the resulting blackness, he focused on the lone speck of light pulsating determinedly. This tiny beacon was his only hope; it would either dim or guide him slowly back to consciousness.

§

Ceera balanced precariously on a branch extending from the ravine, her hands gripping a rock that protruded from the dirt. Her knees shook and her breath was quick and shallow. The hole deepened and loomed darkly beneath her.

The man walked down the opposing side of the ravine which receded gradually, his long, narrow toes wedging into the soil. He glared at her, his eyes black and penetrating, and though she longed for Dassius's rescue, she did not dare avert her gaze. Her free hand inched back to grab a vial from her pack.

"You seek"—the words struggled to emerge—"what's mine." His voice was scratchy and strained though more audible than before.

"No," she contested as fright seized her. "I was called here. What's yours begs to be found."

He did not like this answer and scowled. "She left it

for me. So it would"—he paused and looked around as if in desperation to find the right words—"bring me to her."

"Who is she?" Ceera asked, her mind reverting to the woman who had appeared in both her vision and dreams.

The wildness in his eyes faded ever so slightly, but it was short-lived. "You do not belong here."

"That may be," she countered back, "but you are the one who taints this wood." Her hand reached the zipper.

"I protect this forest," he said in a menacing tone. "It is mine."

"Who says it's yours?" Very slowly, she dragged the zipper open.

"The forest decided."

"Perhaps only you decided."

"No," he snarled. "The wood attached itself to me."

Her hand reached the vial. She paused as a realization struck her. "By the wood's design you are no longer a man," she whispered, "but you remain, Rebial."

He glared at her calculatingly as if deciding whether to acknowledge her insinuation. She could see it in his eyes. He did not like that she had spoken his name.

She brought her arm around to release the vial's catch, but his knotted hand grabbed onto hers. He squeezed tightly, attempting to loosen her grip. Her hand turned red as the pressure increased. He would break her bones and kill her after all.

Tears were already streaming down her face when the vial shattered. Glass pierced her palm and fingers. Accompanying the pain was a strange green light which emanated off their clenched hands. Rebial drew his quickly away. Ceera opened her palm to reveal the glittering stones amidst the shards of glass. Blood spurted from the cuts. Rebial grabbed her wrist, allowing the stones and glass to fall from her hand, and stared at the birthmark on her thumb.

She watched in despair as the contents of the vial fell into the abyss and out of sight. Her heart beat quickly as she expected him to toss her in next. Instead, he leaned in so close all she could see was the hollows of his eyes. His breath smelled like musty dirt.

"Is it you?" Rebial asked in his raspy voice. He raised his free hand and brushed her cheek very lightly, but its roughness scratched her face.

She winced and his grip on her arm loosened. The effects of his words lasted longer. He had noticed her birthmark: the mark that she had never thought twice about, the mark that no one had ever mentioned except for Dassius in the garden…and now Rebial.

A rumbling sound came from the depths of the chasm. A growing mass of jagged stone emerged out of the blackness. It was composed of knuckles and fingers tightened into a fist. As it neared, the fist loosened. Large stone fingers raked the dirt at Rebial's feet, crumbling the ground beneath him. Baric's speckled brown face peeked out from the abyss to ensure his aim was accurate.

Rebial looked surprised as he fell, but managed to grab onto a root much farther down that looped out of the chasm wall. He swung and hit the side, while Baric's fist broke apart and dropped back into the chasm. Rebial hung with one arm as his other hand grasped the air for something to hold on to. "The forest," he howled in a tortured voice. "I saved it. It won't let go."

Time stood still as she pondered his words. He saved it, from what? And was he talking to her or the person she reminded him of? Before she could ask such questions, the root broke and Rebial tumbled into the darkness.

Something like disappointment impinged on her left-over thoughts, unexplained yet strangely warranted. Rebial was more than just a monster. He had seen the mark on her thumb and refrained from hurting her. But why? Had she just killed someone who knew secrets about herself? Who was the real enemy here? So many questions would remain unanswered.

"Where is he?" The words came from above.

Ceera pointed, not yet ready to compose her thoughts with words. She stifled the urge to cry, though she did not understand the totality of her emotions. Curiosity mingled with relief that she was still alive.

"Good," Dassius said, oblivious to her conflicted emotions. "Grab my hand."

She lifted her free hand, the one smeared in blood. Looking concerned, Dassius knelt down. He grabbed her wrist, tucked his other hand under her arm and helped her out.

"I'm sorry I let you fall in," he told her, pulling her close.

"Couldn't be helped." The words tumbled out her mouth as she buried her face in his neck.

"I was knocked unconscious or I would have helped you sooner." Dassius pulled away and turned to show her the bloody gash on his head. "What happened to your hand?"

"Baric's vial broke open." The scrapes stung and she clenched her hand in an attempt to bear the pain.

"Do you want to wash it?" Dassius asked, nodding in the direction of the river.

The pull she felt came from the opposite direction. "No, there's a clearing up ahead. We must hurry."

"You think he might be back?"

Ceera let out a shaky sigh. "Let's not take any chances." She grabbed onto Dassius's hand with her usable one and led him away.

She sensed Luma's vial burning mildly inside her pack, waiting patiently to be opened.

We may not need you after all, she told it silently, though its intensity would not wane.

❦

When the river divided, the rope hanging from the tree had tipped Falken off to which waterway he should take. As he floated alongside the strip of land, he heard strange sounds that were impossible to decipher.

He wanted to get out of his canoe to investigate, but did not want to subject himself to any danger. Perhaps it would be best to watch from afar until the right time. He would wait until Ceera and Dassius were in possession of what they intended to find, before making himself known.

Small bits of color flashed through the trees. He studied the movement. Two figures ran away from him and deeper into the woods.

Falken maneuvered over to the bank and stepped out. He pulled the canoe onto land so it wouldn't drift away during his absence, and began jogging toward the fleeing figures. When he reached the chasm, the unnaturalness of it gave him pause. Then he found a spot narrow enough to leap across and continued on, not noticing a small crack branched off and followed.

❦

As soon as they entered the clearing, the large tree in the foreground commanded her attention. The enormous trunk minimized the trees nearby. Its base spawned rambling roots that snaked in and out of the ground with clever intricacy, and its branches spread to such great lengths they broke through the canopies of the surrounding trees. The ground dropped to a cliff a short ways behind it. The spectacular view oversaw miles of trees below. Despite the scenery, the tree dominated the area surrounding it with doubtless clarity, an alluring feature in what was already an extraordinary landscape.

"That's it," she said. "That's the tree."

"Are you sure?"

"I'm sure," she responded. Out of respect, she walked toward the tree slowly. She sensed it was sizing her up, deciding whether she was worthy of its presence. The tree had something to tell her, this much was certain, and if it could talk, it would have even more stories to tell. Whatever it concealed would be as old as the tree itself.

Just like in her dreams, the roots were parted at its base. She dropped to her knees and uncertainty came over her, for this was when her dreams turned into nightmares. This was when someone came up behind. She looked over her shoulder. Only Dassius stood at the edge of the clearing.

Reassured, she crawled into the opening at the base. Light peeked in through the cracks in the tree bark, the tiny imperfections not visible from the exterior. A narrow tunnel dropped through the dirt. She lowered herself down and into an area encased in roots. Some roots jutted out farther than the rest. Her hand slid across them. Something hid behind the bulge. She carefully moved them aside.

The ancient manuscript was nestled within the roots. She picked it up gently, feeling a subtle energy pulsating from it. Thin woven rope bound the book closed. The spiral symbol adorning the cover glittered as it had in her vision, though it was partially obscured by dust and dirt. She hoped the pages were still readable.

A sensation came over her that was all consuming, like she had just fulfilled a deeper purpose she had yet to understand. Not only that, but bringing the relic back to Semadon would secure her future. No matter the fate of her mother, she was not crazy; the relic's existence would prove that to High Service. Being in possession of it should kill the nightmares. Fate had not dealt her a bad hand after all.

She frowned, remembering Rebial said it had been left for him. The thought made her uneasy, and she had the pressing urge to hurry. She maneuvered first the relic, then herself, back up to the tree's base. Clutching it to her chest with one hand, she crawled out, using her other hand for support.

Dassius helped her to her feet.

"I have it," she said, holding up the relic.

He surveyed her find curiously but refrained from touching. "That looks very old. You better be careful with it."

"Of course I will be."

"Well, put it somewhere safe. We need to figure a way out of this forest and back to Semadon." He looked troubled.

"What's wrong?" she asked.

"Something just doesn't feel right."

A swishing sound cut through the air. She was appalled

to see an object, a rope shaped like a cross with grapples on its four ends, whirling past. It wrapped around Dassius's body and attached him efficiently to the tree. He struggled to release himself but was clearly stuck.

Ceera was confused as to why a weapon used in Semadon now restrained her companion. The practice was familiar; Order Patrol used the ropes to capture the occasional deviant Semion. But it was strange to see the weapon outside of its normal capacity.

She placed the relic on a pile of leaves and tried to loosen the rope, tugging at it in hopes the grapples would release.

"Don't bother." A familiar voice interrupted her efforts. "Even if you free him, you won't get far."

Chapter Thirty

FALKEN STAGGERED INTO the clearing, exuding a recklessness accentuated by his unruly hair and sleeves that hung in tatters. His eyes darted wildly between Ceera and Dassius. He extended a rigid arm, his gloved hand clasped onto something hidden behind his fingers.

"Falken Grihne," Dassius said with disgust. "At least you're consistent about something, even if it's only being up to no good. Let me go; Ceera and I are busy."

"I'm the one who is busy." Falken self-consciously lowered his arm down to his side.

"Falken," Ceera said. "What are you doing here? High Service made no indication you'd be joining us."

"Really? Is High Service not keeping up with their messaging?"

Ceera glanced at Dassius, who scowled knowingly. "What have you done?" she demanded. "Why are you here?"

"I am here for redemption." Falken looked around. "What a place for redemption."

A chill invaded the air. The trees stiffened, their bountiful limbs now seeming farther away and devoid of greenery. It grew very quiet as if all the animals and bugs, even the plants, were listening. Dusk gave their surroundings a shadowy and sinister glow. The ground rumbled beneath them, and she turned to Dassius to tug on the rope that bound him.

"You best help Ceera release me," Dassius said. "It won't be long before we have company. Then you may need my help"

"I don't need your help. I'm the one in control."

"In control of what?" she asked. Despite her efforts, the rope stayed tightly wound.

"In control of acquiring what you came for."

Ceera picked up the relic and pressed it to her chest. "You can't have it."

Falken took a step forward but a crack formed on the ground between his feet. It traveled away from him and beyond the clearing.

He feigned surprise and stepped to one side of the crack. "This forest is full of tricks," he said, looking her directly in the eye, "but I refuse to be deceived any longer."

The oncoming crack created a boundary between Falken and the tree Dassius was attached to.

"You have no idea what's going on," she said. "You're making this too easy for him."

"Don't try to distract me with your nonsense. I already have everything figured out. That silly council member does not scare me."

"What council member?" Dassius squirmed aggressively.

"The one hired by the Council for Natural Law." Falken smirked. "I saw him when I was floating on my canoe."

"There are other council members here too?" Dassius did not sound convinced.

"Never mind, you need only concern yourselves with handing that over."

"There's no way I will give you the relic." Her voice was firm.

"Your protector is confined," he reminded her. "You have no choice."

"I won't be for long." Dassius scraped something against the bark. "Then you will regret you came."

"Give me the relic," Falken demanded, taking a step toward her.

"No, you have no business with this old book," Ceera said, hoping to deter him.

"Old book? You've just confirmed what I suspected all along. I'm sure what it says will demean my council and elevate our foe."

"What are you talking about now Falken?" Dassius asked impatiently.

The crack deepened, causing the ground to shift. Falken stumbled back while Ceera steadied herself against the tree.

"That relic is a fake," Falken said as he regained his footing.

The ground rumbled violently and, with an ominous ripping sound, the crack widened. Ceera screamed, clutching onto Dassius and the enormous tree as it held on with its strong roots to the stable piece of ground.

Trees tipped over slowly, allowing Falken to dodge a falling trunk with a quick sideways run. One fell across the resulting rift, which had grown to several feet wide, and formed a bridge connecting the two sides.

Falken crouched on one side, while Ceera huddled against Dassius on the other. The ground finished shifting, and the noise died down soon after. The crack in the ground spewed out dust, though she wished the particles were more magical than plain dirt.

Falken broke the silence. "Looks like I chose the wrong tree to attach you to."

"You chose the wrong forest to hike through as well," Dassius said as he stared into the dark opening near his feet.

They now had two choices for escape. One involved climbing down the cliff behind them into the maze of trees below, not particularly feasible but possible. The other was easier though more dangerous; they would have to cross over the fallen trunk and meet Falken on the other side, who was sure to have the advantage being the one on higher ground.

Although their surroundings had stabilized, an unsettling presence remained that could not yet be accounted for. It was in the air, beneath her feet even. Dassius, too, looked around as if he was searching for something. Even Falken whipped his head about in anticipation.

"Can't you see what's happening?" she screamed. "We don't have time for your games. He's coming!"

Falken's eyes grew large. "Is he?" he asked condescendingly. Then his voice became matter-of-fact. "I am the one you should fear, and for the sake of my council what you have needs to be destroyed. Please allow me the privilege." He crept toward her.

The dust finished settling. Her only solace was that the rift had not weakened the position of the large tree beside her. Its roots wound down the side and went deep into the ground, keeping it from plummeting downward.

"No, it's not possible." She would protect it at all costs, just like Rebial.

"Don't bother with your riddles of possibilities and probabilities you learned from your friend the science project." Falken neared the rift. "Do as I ask and I'll allow your return to Semadon."

"What does our return have to do with you?" Dassius retorted.

Falken edged toward the fallen trunk bridging the chasm. "The AT system is not working. Only I have the code to reinstate it."

"Only you? What of the man who invented it," Dassius sneered. "You're telling us you know more about his machine than he does?"

"The man who invented it? Ah yes, Hegliod Avatus: very talented, yet fickle to his description. Too bad he is out of commission, sweeping orbits as we speak."

"Sweeping orbits? Why?" Ceera asked.

"Because he retired his description as an inventor, gave up, decided he was finished. And to think he made this decision because of you."

"Me? I had nothing to do with it!" she protested.

"You started the chain reaction. I'm expecting more to follow your lead. We'll have Semions changing from this to that now. All the training done in their youth will be wasted."

"Ignore him," Dassius told her. "He's only trying to rile you." He turned back to their adversary. "We're too strong to fall prey to your threats. The AT system is not the only way home. We'll find our way back, it may take weeks but my skills are more than capable of—"

"Your skills," Falken scoffed, "aren't even able to free you from that tree, much less, guide you back to Semadon."

"I'm not afraid of you, Falken. I will break free and when I do—"

"You may not fear me, but you will fear this." Falken opened his palm. Streaks of light came down from the sky, and the circular contraption he held pulsed accordingly. Tiny beacons of light emanated between his fingers.

"What is it?" Ceera stepped closer to Dassius.

"It's something that can destroy both you and your precious relic."

Dassius laughed a broken sound, and she could not help but allow a hopeless sensation to waft over her.

"It gets its power from the sun." Dassius's tone was bitter. "High Service would never allow the use of heat-cores as a weapon, which means it's unauthorized, forbidden. Falken doesn't have permission to be in possession of that thing."

"Permission?" Falken's eyes glowed. "Why would I need permission? I invented it."

"He's broken the doctrine," Dassius said, "forsaken High Service. He's discarded the Semion way of life for his own twisted agendas. He's exactly what we all knew was true since his beginning."

"You know nothing of what I'm capable."

"You're a villain," Dassius said, "a traitor. And there's nothing more I need to know."

"You'll give me the respect I deserve," Falken said. "But first, you'll give me the relic."

"You'll have to come get it yourself." Ceera's arms remained crossed over the ancient manuscript.

Falken hesitated. "If you put it on the fallen trunk about halfway down, I'll let you live. Once I take it and depart, you must wait until morning before making your way back to the AT cylinder. I'll arrange for it to work only then."

"You expect us to believe you?" Dassius groaned. "Spare us your pathetic ramblings."

Falken shoved his hand into his pocket and pulled out a silver mask. "You see this? This is what I'll use to shield my eyes from the luster of my weapon." He pulled the mask over his head. It fit snugly, and he adjusted it so the sheer circles aligned with his eyes. The thin mask was so transparent that his facial expression showed through its covering. He pulled his hood up and around his shiny reflective new skin.

"You do know that old book you're protecting was planted here right? By the Council for Natural Law? You're pawns in their game to destroy my council."

Out of the corner of her eye, Ceera noticed Dassius had finagled his knife off his belt and was working the blade against the rope.

"This whole thing, your venture was a scam. Just like the mystics, those Archaics you visited; they aren't what you think they are. The Council for Natural Law put them up to it, telling you their lies, it was a set up." Falken paced, taking a moment to gaze up at the surrounding trees. "This forest isn't special—"

"Yes," she countered, "it is."

"The Council for Natural Law has been planning this for quite some time," Falken said derisively. "This trickery is just to distract you from the treasons they've committed. They manipulated the records. They even changed the maps."

"We always knew you were different, Falken," Dassius said. "But we hoped you weren't the raving madman you've just proven yourself to be."

"Don't confuse madness with genius," Falken shouted.

"A genius wouldn't allow himself to be the fool of a council," Dassius said. Having finally freed himself, he flung the rope and grapples back and over the cliff.

"You're the fools for believing in their game of make

believe! Pawns!" Falken aimed his weapon at them. It emitted a faint buzzing sound as it geared up for the attack.

Before they could react, a sound rustled out of the rift. A gnarled hand appeared and grabbed onto a root sticking out near the edge. A head of thick matted hair came next. Then Rebial gingerly pulled himself up and over the side. Falken's hand dropped and he took a step back. Rebial was on all fours panting like a wild animal. He slowly stood.

"Rebial," Ceera whispered, and Dassius looked at her in amazement.

Falken seemed less amused. "You," he accused. "Who do you think you are bothering me again?"

Rebial's chest heaved as he took large breaths. He looked around calculatingly but seemed disoriented. He was now more manlike than creature, the color of his skin closer to flesh than bark, his face not as disfigured looking. His demeanor was less threatening and more conflicted, almost as if he were fighting something within himself. He took an uneven step toward Falken and stopped to regain his balance.

Falken aimed his weapon at Rebial, and a beam of light shot out. It created a circular black outline on Rebial's stomach, which he looked down at curiously. Then it erupted into flames, causing him to writhe forward in pain. When he lifted his head, his face glowed like one that had seen many evils. He somehow remained standing as the fire ravaged his body.

"That's what you get for meddling in my business."

Rebial took a stiff step toward him. Falken aimed his weapon yet again. Another ray of light struck Rebial. He flinched and stumbled to the side, nearly falling over.

"Falken, stop!" Ceera cried out.

Rebial lifted his head and gazed over to where Ceera and Dassius stood. His scowl deepened when he saw her holding the relic. He took an unsteady step in their direction, though the rift separated them, and fell to his knees. His hand reached toward her.

"Don't bother with them," Falken said. "They're next."

The relic began vibrating with an urgent energy as its symbol glittered more intensely through the dust. Ceera's grasp faltered. A jolt of energy thrust her backward and knocked Dassius into the nearby tree. She fell onto her elbows, dangerously close to the cliff, and watched as the ancient manuscript tumbled to the ground. Roots rumbled and latched it securely into the dirt.

Dassius helped her back to a standing position. He started to reach for the relic.

"Leave it," she snapped. No matter her dreams, the relic belonged to Rebial. She would no longer fight him.

Dassius gave her a confused look, but her attention shifted back to Rebial. He picked himself up from the ground. His eyes had sunk back into his head, and his skin was again mossy and grooved. The fire swarming him crackled one last time as the flames desisted. His smoking body emitted curling wisps that hid the damage Falken had inflicted.

"Your special effects are impressive," Falken said, "but your allegiance to the CfNL is a disgrace. Did they not tell you death was your reward?"

Falken's weapon shot more rays toward Rebial, but this time they did not enliven flames. Instead, larger clouds of smoke billowed around him. Rebial stood taller, stronger, and the corners of his mouth lifted into a wicked smile.

Falken seemed to realize he'd miscalculated what he was

up against. His face became stricken with fear while his skin turned a ghostly white. He closed his palm and his weapon ceased emitting light. Rebial stepped toward him, leaving puffs of smoke behind.

"You're not a member of the council?"

Rebial laughed maniacally. Falken cowered and backed away.

"Trespasser," Rebial said in a raspy voice that cracked with every syllable.

"I didn't realize." Falken fitfully shook his head. "I had a reason. I only seek redemption."

"You found mine." Rebial's words were interlaced with menace. He took slow, even steps toward Falken like a cat stalking its prey.

Falken hunched over and shrank inward. One hand snaked inside his cloak. "Likewise," he replied, hurling a grappled weapon at Rebial, the same type he'd used against Dassius.

It whirled through the air and wrapped around Rebial's head. He fell amidst a garbled choking sound, twisting and yanking on the rope covering his face.

Falken held a crazed expression as he stared at Rebial, in apparent disbelief his weapon restrained him. "I'll leave when I'm ready," he said to Rebial's contorting figure. He lifted his shaking hand and aimed his weapon at Ceera and Dassius. "I tried to play fair"—his eyes darted between them and Rebial—"but you refused to cooperate."

With a vicious snap, Rebial ripped the rope from around his face. He jumped back to his feet and landed with such force the ground trembled. He stooped down, grabbed a fallen limb and whipped it in Falken's direction.

When the branch collided with his chest, Falken flew

backward. His body slammed against a tree. He scrambled to his feet and placed one hand on the trunk, attempting to gain back his breath. Roots wrapped up and around his legs, which he jerked back and forth.

Rebial bounded forward, but Falken succeeded in ripping free and dodged him. The sound of Rebial's fist hitting the bark ricocheted throughout the wood. The tree tipped over; its branches landed on Falken's fleeing figure and knocked him to his knees.

Falken struggled to break free from the tree's crown. The branches dragged across his face and neck, cutting into his mask and skin. He managed to escape, but his movements were erratic as though his own brain was incapable of leading him away.

Rebial sent a gust of wind toward the fumbling madman with an abrupt flick of his wrist. It knocked him to the ground a third time. Falken grabbed onto a nearby stone and threw it at his opponent. Undeterred, Rebial stepped out of the way, and Falken half crawled in a frenzied manner until he was back on his feet running again.

He attempted to leap through a gnarled skeleton of hollowed tree trunks, but Rebial sabotaged his efforts. His long spindly fingers jerked into a fist, causing the trunks to contort inward and bind Falken within the splintered bark. He screamed and wrenched away, staggering out of the shattered wood. Rebial tackled him, inflicting Falken with the heat still smoking on his body. Falken uttered tortured cries of pain.

Rebial pushed Falken away and sprang to his feet. Falken rolled over onto all fours and stood, his wobbly legs barely sustaining him. His shredded clothes exposed burned chunks of skin. He looked down at himself, howled a miserable broken sound, and threw his arms out in despair.

Rebial reached inside his own smoldering body, then pulled his clenched fist back out. Smoky wisps curled around it. He used this hand to grip onto Falken's face.

Falken's mask went up in flames and he screamed. Rebial raised him into the air.

"I still have the power," Falken choked forth, "to destroy these woods." He held his weapon out and pressed the button, but nothing happened. He tried again; it did not respond. In an act of defeat, he threw the weapon and it rolled toward the edge of the rift. He began scratching Rebial's face.

Rebial responded by slamming him ruthlessly against a tree. Falken's skull bore the impact with a sick cracking sound. The tree leaned crookedly away.

Falken's face was now a mixture of shock and agony. His body twitched. He coughed up blood and garbled an unintelligible utterance. Then he wheezed his last breath. His body dangled lifelessly from Rebial's outstretched grip.

Rebial threw Falken onto the ground and stood over him, his fists still clenched and his body tense with anger. "Be gone," he growled in a monstrous tone. "Be gone now."

Suddenly there was movement all around them. The ground quivered, and soon Falken's body fluttered with beetles and slugs. Large flying insects swarmed him. Small animals hurried over, burying their faces in his already dwindling heap of skin and bones before scurrying away with mouthfuls of dripping flesh.

Falken's remains shrunk away as the forest dwellers worked quickly. Rebial remained fixated on their work with a menacing expression. Ceera closed her eyes and buried her face in Dassius's chest. He allowed her only a moment to collect herself.

"Grab the relic and let's go," he whispered, clearly shaken. "If you lose me do your best to keep running!"

Ceera could not bring herself to obey Dassius's command. She looked back to where Rebial stood. Falken was now just an outline in the dirt.

Rebial kicked the ground where Falken had once lain, and a cloud of dust obscured what was left of him. He walked toward the rift, not yet meeting their wide and watchful eyes with his own. He stared with a mournful expression down into the gaping hole. At a glance, he blended into the scenery with artful precision.

Feeling their eyes on him, he looked up and glared momentarily at Dassius before turning to Ceera. "Take it," he spat out. "My time here's done."

"What are you?" she demanded.

"Ceera, what is going on?" Dassius muttered beneath his breath.

"I'm what you see around you," Rebial said with a passion so fierce it sent shivers up her spine. He dangled one leg over the chasm, dropped down and grabbed a root.

"But what are you really?" she asked. "Where are you going?"

"To face the end." His dismal tone was absolute.

Ceera's heart stopped and her breath fell short. Rebial ventured down, blending back into his surroundings before he was even truly out of sight. She fell to her knees and watched him vanish into the darkness. The relic lay nearby, no longer bound by roots. Dassius crouched beside her and pushed her head roughly to the ground.

"Stay down," he commanded. "Cover your eyes."

CHAPTER THIRTY-ONE

CEERA HEARD A familiar buzzing sound as she placed her hands over her eyes. It grew in intensity and culminated in an earsplitting eruption followed by a blinding flash of light. An intense wave of heat moved in, and she instantly broke into a sweat. When the brightness dulled, Dassius pulled her to her feet.

"It's safe now," he said grimly. "At least it's safe to look. Falken's weapon exploded."

Fire blazed all around them. The area across the tree bridge was now impassable. Flames had also soared over the cliff and were consuming the trees down below. The only nearby vicinity that had escaped immediate danger was the pathway around the tree by which they stood.

"What should we do?"

"Give me the last vial," Dassius said.

Luma's essence burned hot as she pulled it from her pack. She handed it to him, stooped down and picked up the relic.

Dassius flipped open the lid. The smoke contained inside coiled seductively near the vial's throat. A sound escaped, resembling the tickling laughter of a female, but one with dangerous intentions. The smoke followed and floated above them, swirling into an image of Luma that perked up the surrounding flames.

She stepped onto the ground between them, extended a finger and held it to her pursed lips. "Shhh." The fire obeyed, died down, and flickered less intensely. The flames parted and exposed a pathway. She smiled with smug approval. "You got your way."

Dassius grabbed Ceera's hand. She allowed herself to be pulled across the log and through the opening. The flames danced dangerously close but did not cross onto their path. When they reached the fire's boundary, she wrestled from his grip and turned. Luma was still visible through the path of dancing flames.

"Please," Ceera pleaded, "don't burn down the forest."

Luma looked back at her distastefully. "Fire is impatient. It does not stand still." She turned her back, tossed her hair over her shoulder and sauntered away. Sparks flew off the ends of her hair and excited the once inactive flames.

"Run," Dassius commanded, "before it's too late."

Flames scorched the grass beneath their feet as they departed.

"This way," Dassius said, "to the river."

"Why?" she cried out. All logic had fled her thoughts.

"Because Falken said he had a canoe. Let's find it."

They ran quickly through the brush. Luma's fire chased behind. When they reached the river, Dassius ran along the side until he found the battered canoe. "Come on," he called over to her.

"That's a canoe?"

"Get in," Dassius ordered.

Ceera climbed in quickly. The bark scratched her skin. Her right hand still throbbed in pain.

He shoved the canoe into the river and jumped in. The canoe got off to a shaky start, and she wondered whether the pathetic thing would even float. When it finally steadied, she rested against the side and watched as the fire raged alongside the river. Luma's laughter could be heard within the crackle. She imagined the Archaic dancing amongst the flames, enthralled her precious fire wreaked such destruction.

The forest fire grew with immense speed, and the quality of air deteriorated with it. Dassius grabbed a floating limb and thrust the canoe through the water. Would they make it out alive? She cradled the relic in her arms and closed her eyes, but instead of blackness she saw red and orange flames curling in the same patterns again and again until she thought she might get sick.

⁕

Hegliod installed his override device into the main controls and flipped the switch. Every AT cylinder on the screen lit up and vibrated with the same intensity they possessed prior to the shut down.

Hegliod grinned wider than he had in a long time.

"You did it," Cafold exclaimed. "You have it working again."

The clatter in the distance was the sound of many footsteps coming their way. High Service officials surrounded the man with the silly grin, clapped their hands together and patted him on the back.

"You haven't lost a fraction of your skills," Leynin told him.

"Quite an impressive feat," Asfin agreed.

"I'm honored to have been at your side," Cafold said.

Hegliod was too pleased with himself to know what to do. He was locked in the glory of the situation; the prospect of victory ran rampant in his mind.

"Well, what do you have to say for yourself?" asked Karnen.

He tried to think of something to say that would epitomize what he felt. Finally he spoke. "My genius is repaired."

His words caused an eruption of applause, and in the ensuing merriment, no one took the time to wonder what exactly Hegliod referred to as his genius. Was it the AT system or the brain inside his head? Only Hegliod knew for sure, and he was drained of all words.

Dassius noticed one of his reflectors stuck to the tree facing the river and steered them to the bank. They got out of the canoe and he led the way. His senses were no longer obstructed and allowed him to navigate easily through the darkness with the aid of his flashlight.

When they burst free from the wood they fell to the ground, shocked to be in empty space. Dassius pointed at the AT cylinder in the distance, and they sprinted toward it.

Barging inside, Dassius hurriedly set the controls to take them back to Semadon. "Let's hope Falken was wrong."

There was a brief moment before they began to fade. Then only a rhythmic throbbing prevailed.

When Dassius came to, he was sprawled haphazardly across the floor of the cylinder. Ceera faced the wall on her knees, bent over and hiding the relic from view.

The AT cylinder's door was wide open, for everyone in

the vicinity wanted to see who had made the first successful travel since the machines had been put back in working order. It being the two of them made the spectacle that much more interesting to the bystanders. High Service officials shooed the spectators away, while Dassius watched Ceera drift back to consciousness.

⁓

"Nimren," said the voice over the correspondence orb, "High Service requests you and Casma come to the Aurora at once for questioning."

Nimren played the message again, terrified by what the words could be spelling out for them. Casma paced the room.

Ceera and Dassius had returned unharmed according to a fellow council member who had witnessed them emerge from the main AT cylinder. Nimren and Casma still held hope that Falken had carried out his plan. They waited for him to contact them, and assumed it was he who called on the correspondence orb.

Nimren had not answered by accident. He had tripped on his way over, and before he could right himself the messaging had begun. When a High Service official's voice came through, he had stiffened. Wisps of hair on the back of Casma's neck stood on end. It wasn't until Nimren replayed the message for the third time that Casma begged him to stop.

"Nimren, please! No matter how many times you play it, the words will be the same!"

"But what do you think this means? Where's Falken!" Nimren muttered harsh sounds beneath his breath.

"He failed." Casma shook her head. "There is no other reason for their asking us to go."

"But where is he?" Nimren asked again.

"Do you think he revealed our involvement?"

"To who? Where *is* he?"

"In hiding," Casma said. "There's no other explanation."

"Maybe High Service is merely asking whether we know where he is. Perhaps he is in hiding like you said. There's no reason to overreact."

"But for questioning Nimren? They want us to go to the Aurora for questioning. They're not calling us up to ask a single question. They're calling us because they have many."

"Yes, that does imply a heavier involvement than just knowing where he is."

"Shall we go? What other choice do we have?" Casma placed her hand across her chest.

"There are choices," Nimren stated gravely. "As for now, I say we wait. Let's see how long we can hold out. Not answering the correspondence orb will buy us some time. Had I answered, we would be stuck abiding to their demands. Now we have time to wait and see if Falken calls."

"And what will we do if he doesn't?"

"Flee," Nimren responded. "I refuse to live a life in detainment. We could possibly join a settlement. Or start our own."

An abrupt pounding sounded down the hall from Nimren's office. The two of them froze in horror.

"Is it Falken?" Casma whispered.

Nimren pressed some buttons. An image of Order Patrol in front of the main doorway appeared on the screen. "Looks like our fate has been decided for us."

"They've barely given us time to respond." Casma's voice was frantic.

"Which could only mean one thing," Nimren said as he grabbed Casma's hand. "We'll take the back way."

⁂

Nimren and Casma were grateful dusk was forming, and they could slip out the back door without feeling too exposed. Neither of them was very adept at sneaking around, although they shielded their faces in hooded cloaks and walked in a manner that was brisk but not desperate.

Since their sense of security had been stripped of them within a matter of minutes, their anguish was intoxicating. As they advanced through the orbits, a barrage of emotions muddled their minds. Their newfound fear was so preoccupying that when they quickly reached the outskirts of the village and found themselves within the realm of the outlying forest, they did not question the speed of their progress.

The forest had not been tended to in quite some time. Their pace was challenged upon entrance. To avoid getting tangled, they took care in the maneuvering of their passing. Even this became difficult. The forest was restricting them, would not release them from its clutches. Though their advancement ceased, they refrained from calling out for help, for there was no one they trusted to oblige.

Chapter Thirty-Two

HEGLIOD WAS FINISHING his design for an orbit sweeper when something grazed past his awareness. He dropped his pencil and it rolled onto the floor. His eyes snapped shut.

The feeling was vaguely familiar. He gently prodded the idea to surface. When it arrived without too much resistance, Hegliod was elated. He dropped to his knees, found his pencil and wrote furiously for the better part of the day.

❧

Upon hearing of Ceera and Dassius's return, Marvus decided he could no longer remain at his dwelling. He confronted Desnia the very next morning, telling her he was well rested and ready to resume his position.

She looked at him wearily, took a few long, deep breaths and stared upward at the sky. It wasn't until he insisted on remaining an inactive partner for a time to redeem himself and thus allow her full reign on all decision making, that she dutifully accepted his request.

He was quite thankful and gushed to her how beautiful the garden had grown since she was in charge of it, for he had gotten a good view of it on his way inside. Both its bulk and height rivaled the building itself.

With her permission, he decided to go for a walk in the splendor. He quickly passed through the room of the statues, though not before noticing Baric's statue giving him a sideways look as he passed. Refusing to acknowledge this unwanted visual, he burst through the back door and into the fresh air.

He marveled at the wildness the garden now possessed. He strolled about until he reached a massive tangle of plant life near the center. What he saw within the midst of it made him gasp and he nearly choked. The bodies were apart by only a few feet, wedged beneath thick clusters of plants.

Marvus raised his hand to his forehead and rolled his eyes to view the fragments of the sky visible between the thick branches overhead. He was glad Desnia approached him moments later, for he was sure she would prefer to see the bodies with her own eyes instead of hear about them from Marvus's mouth.

One of the first things Ceera and Dassius did upon returning to Semadon was alert High Service about Falken's conspiring with the Council for Advancement. Nimren and Casma were called to the Aurora, but neither of them complied. When it became obvious they weren't going to show, Order Patrol marched straight to their dwellings and then to the council building to apprehend them but found each deserted.

Messages aired on the global update to alert of their

disappearance while Order Patrol made every attempt to follow their tracks.

Both were found within the newly refurbished garden outside the building of the Council for Natural Law. How they had gotten the area confused with the forest outlying Semadon was peculiar in itself. The fact plants foreign to the area restrained them was also an odd circumstance, considering Desnia did not recall planting them in her rejuvenation attempt.

Nimren and Casma were interrogated and imprisoned. The Council for Advancement held a meeting to reinstate new leaders. They began reorganizing themselves and laid low for many weeks to come.

Ceera and Dassius spent days conversing with High Service. After analyzing the findings, the officials determined it safe to release the information obtained from the Archaics to the public.

The Caretaker of Ancient Affairs was the first to be updated since he was required to be the expert of the new yet ancient information. The matter of Rebial and the relic, however, remained classified since his existence was still much of a mystery.

At first resistant to the truth, some Semions suggested the information had been hiding in their subconscious, waiting to be loosened from the grips of time. Others swarmed the library to consult with the Caretaker. They reread the history books, declaring there were clues hidden in the words that before seemed so plainly stated. They now viewed some of their stories as precursors to the present day.

For their travels, Ceera and Dassius found themselves at the height of interest. Neither could go anywhere without being the center of attention. They received invitations to speak about their experiences at a series of meetings.

The AT installers woke up shortly before Ceera and Dassius returned. They had no remembrance of what had happened to them after they had built their last AT cylinder. Even Darmyn recounted nothing, having no recollection of the strange words he had uttered days before. They were hailed as heroes for their feat in installing so many AT cylinders, and also for surviving such misfortune.

Breaking news on the global update relayed that the Planetary Stability Monitor had stabilized. All energy readings now read normal. This was a relief to everyone.

Drusilla fawned over Ceera upon her return, even though she was temporarily relieved of her scribe duties. Litha called right away and Ceera relayed what she could. Her father even left a message on the communication orb, and when she finally spoke to him, he promised he would visit again soon.

While Dassius underwent testing to determine the effectiveness of his training, Ceera tended to the ancient manuscript. It had to be cleaned before she could even begin the translation. The cleaning took her several weeks, for it was a slow and grueling process.

Next, she transmitted images of its pages onto a PID. The original relic was kept at the library, preserved inside a case not viewable to the public.

The interpretation task was the most daunting. Though the language was similar to the Semion tongue, the problem was interpreting what seemed written to deliberately confuse. The ambiguous wording prompted her to consult with the Caretaker of Ancient Affairs as needed. She met daily with High Service to discuss her progress, and they continued to interrogate her with various questions about Rebial. They had no idea what to make of him, and Ceera was purposely scant with information because she felt protective of him. For reasons she could not explain, she kept his recognition of her birthmark a secret.

High Service made no mention of what her fate would have been had she come home empty-handed, though it stayed at the forefront of her mind. She knew they continued to analyze her along with everything else, so she was careful to remain guarded.

Still amazed by the turn of events in her life, she daydreamed incessantly when she wasn't working. She often pondered the bits and pieces of conversation she had with Rebial in the short time she spoke with him. She found herself reliving the moment when he mistook her for the woman who had hid the relic. This woman also had something to do with her birthmark, the one she shared with her mother. She wished she knew more.

She was musing about this at present, sitting outside the library on a bench near some trees, when someone walked up behind her.

"I thought I'd find you here," he said.

"Dassius." She stood and gave him a hug. "It's good to see you."

"You as well." He kissed her. "How's the translating going?"

She smiled at his show of affection, knowing they were in plain view of anyone who happened to be watching. "It's coming along slowly. I want to make sure I get it right."

"Any new developments?" He sat on the bench and pulled her down to sit beside him.

She bit her lip. "I'm not supposed to say. I have orders

from High Service not to divulge anything. The writing does imply things that strike me as odd. I have to remind myself not to overanalyze anything at this point."

"You can't even tell me, huh?"

"I don't even know if I have it right yet." She shrugged. "Plus it's difficult because every day High Service tends to make me question my translations."

"Yes, their analysis never ends," Dassius said. "They've been interrogating me daily as well."

Ceera waited to see whether Dassius would reveal how he felt about this, but he refrained. "Do they ever ask you about Rebial?"

"Every time. I don't know how many different ways I can tell them I don't know much."

Ceera stared into the distance.

"I still don't understand why he decided to protect us in the end. Do you?"

"Not exactly," she replied.

"Come on, you must know something. It was after your last encounter that his behavior changed toward us."

She remained silent.

"You still think about him, don't you?"

"Yes," she admitted, "I do."

"What do you think about?" His question hung in the air between them.

"Does it matter?" She dug her shoe into the dirt.

He squeezed her hand. "It might. Just tell me."

"I wonder if he's still alive or whether he died in the fire. Or is he somehow still trapped in the wood?"

"Based on what he said before he went into the ravine, he is surely dead," Dassius replied.

"Yes, but how do we know for sure? Until recently we

thought we had the past all figured out. Now I wonder if there is more out there to know than we thought. What do you think?"

"I think you could go crazy asking yourself those questions."

"You're probably right."

"May I ask"—Dassius cleared his throat—"why you're so interested in what happened to him?"

"I don't know."

"You don't know?" He raised an eyebrow at her.

"Okay I do, but you have to promise this will stay between us. I'm not ready to talk about it publicly."

"I can keep a secret. You should know that about me."

Ceera took a deep breath. "Even though I know I should be scared of him, I consider him sort of a hero."

Dismay crossed Dassius's handsome face. "Why?"

"Don't take offense." She stroked his palm. "I'm talking in regards to the forest. He said he saved it. I assume from the poisons the Archaics mentioned."

Dassius slung an arm around her and pulled her close. She laid her head on his shoulder.

"A noble act," he agreed, "yet still inexplicable."

"It was when he saw my birthmark that he changed."

"Let me see it again." He grabbed her wrist and studied her thumb. "Glad your hand is almost healed."

"He asked if I was her," she said softly.

"Who is her? Your mother?"

"No, the female that left the ancient manuscript in the forest. He said she left the relic so it would bring him to her." She sat back and cradled her hand.

"Then the relic must contain some sort of map. Directions maybe?"

"Yes, there's a map."

"A map to where?"

"I cannot say," Ceera mumbled.

"You can't or won't?"

"I shouldn't; however, it seems it leads to a place where no one can exist."

"Sounds dangerous. Want me to accompany you?" His playful smile betrayed his unending confidence.

Ceera couldn't resist smiling back. "We can't. High Service says it's improbable the route still exists."

Dassius just looked at her with renewed interest. The light in his eyes gave away what he was thinking. Improbabilities were his specialty.

Acknowledgments

I'd like to thank my family and friends for support during the writing of this book. To my husband, for suffering through the first drafts and inspiring me to do better. To my mother, whose encouragement helped me through my many moments of doubt. To Jolivia Porter, for giving me helpful thoughts and opinions on one of the latest drafts. And to Stephanie Vallez, for her valuable insights on multiple drafts and help with editing. She has a special talent for finding all my misused words and knowing which ones I meant to use instead, which funny enough, sometimes end up rhyming. Any remaining mistakes are my own.